PASSION'S FIRE

Sam lifted Lucy in his arms, cumbersome bustle and all, and carried her into her bedroom. He set her down in the center of the room and proceeded to slowly, deliberately disrobe her before the lacy curtain that hid the lights of Blessing from their view.

Lucy sighed as his large fingers worked with surprising confidence down the tiny row of buttons that held her bodice together. Her insides began a fierce trembling, heating into a steady flame.

Sam allowed his palms a leisurely summation of her gentle curves until they met with cold metal. "What the—?"

He rucked up her petticoats and pursed his lips at the sight of the sidearm sported on one shapely hip. "You think you were going to need that at dinner? You're one lethal little lady. I'd better pat you down for my own peace."

An intriguing thought. One that made her shiver . . .

CAPTURE THE GLOW
OF ZEBRA'S HEARTFIRES

AUTUMN ECSTASY   (3133, $4.25)
by Pamela K. Forrest

Philadelphia beauty Linsey McAdams had eluded her kidnappers but was now at the mercy of the ruggedly handsome frontiersman who owned the remote cabin where she had taken refuge. The two were snowbound until spring, and handsome Luc LeClerc soon fancied the green-eyed temptress would keep him warm through the long winter months. He said he would take her home at winter's end, but she knew that with one embrace, she might never want to leave!

BELOVED SAVAGE   (3134, $4.25)
by Sandra Bishop

Susannah Jacobs would do anything to survive—even submit to the bronze-skinned warrior who held her captive. But the beautiful maiden vowed not to let the handsome Tonnewa capture her heart as well. Soon, though, she found herself longing for the scorching kisses and tender caresses of her raven-haired BELOVED SAVAGE.

CANADIAN KISS   (3135, $4.25)
by Christine Carson

Golden-haired Sara Oliver was sent from London to Vancouver to marry a stranger three times her age—only to have her husband-to-be murdered on their wedding day. Sara vowed to track the murderer down, but he ambushed her and left her for dead. When she awoke, wounded and frightened, she was staring into the eyes of the handsome loner Tom Russel. As the rugged stranger nursed her to health, the flames of passion erupted, and their CANADIAN KISS threatened never to end!

DANA RANSOM
WILD WYOMING LOVE

ZEBRA BOOKS
KENSINGTON PUBLISHING CORP.

For
My Dad
Who was always John Wayne to me
as I was growing up.

And for Obie,
Happy Birthday!

ZEBRA BOOKS

are published by

Kensington Publishing Corp.
475 Park Avenue South
New York, NY 10016

First printing: June, 1991

Printed in the United States of America

Prologue

Liberty, Missouri
February 1866

It was a cold afternoon. The streets of Liberty were deserted. While its population gathered in the Justice Court to savor the details of a trial, a dozen men rode into the quiet town. They were muffled in long soldiers' overcoats. Some wore their six-shooters on the outside. Three riders dismounted and separated, each going to a different point in the hard-packed square where they would have an unrestricted view up and down the empty sidewalks. None spoke. Two men strode into the small bank while the others waited and watched.

Inside the Clay County Savings Association, two men were at their desks, busy with their accounts behind the high wooden counter. The cashier, Greenup Bird, glanced up to see the strangers warming themselves at the stove. It was bitter and he didn't begrudge anyone the chance to thaw a spell. Beside him, the clerk, his son, William, continued his scribbling, looking up when one of the men slid ten dollars across the polished surface.

"I'd like a bill changed."

5

As William reached for it, he found himself staring into the black bore of a revolver and the initial request was amended.

"I'd like all the money in the bank."

William backed away in disbelief. A robbery, in broad daylight? He'd never heard of such a thing. But the two men vaulting the counter verified it was so.

The second man leveled his revolver at Greenup and stated, as if the two weren't already convinced of the seriousness of the situation, "Make a noise and we'll shoot you down."

Abruptly, William reeled, struck by his assailant's gun. The young man staggered as he was pushed toward the vault with the threatening growl of, "Damn you, be quick." Hands shaking from the excitement and the unexpected blow, William began to gather the gold and silver from the vault's shelves, pouring it into a grain sack the robber produced from under his coat.

The man at Greenup's desk asked gruffly for the paper money.

"In the box," the elder cashier mumbled. He tried to pull his mesmerized eyes from the steady steel of the robber's gun to ascertain his son's well-being. He could hear the sound of coins funneling into the bag behind him.

With his six-shooter in one hand, the robber opened the large container resting on the table and began to stack its contents: paper currency, bonds, bank notes, and sheets of revenue stamps. That legal tender was efficiently added to the sizable weight of coin in the other's sack.

Father and son waited in mounting terror. Would they be shot dead for their cooperation? Contrarily, and much to their relief, the elder Bird was urged at gunpoint to join the other inside the vault. As the heavy door was being shut, one of their assailant's remarked in jovial humor, "You know all Birds should be caged!"

The two men stood stunned in the stifling darkness. The robbers knew them by name. After agonizing seconds slipped by, father and son waited, then pushed against the door. It moved. The lock had failed to catch.

Through the front window, they saw several riders gallop past, whooping loudly and shooting into the air. As Greenup threw open the window to shout an alarm, the Birds were witness to a senseless act of savagery.

Liberty's streets were empty of all but one young man. George Wymore, a nineteen-year-old student at Liberty's William Jewell College, was walking briskly to class, his books tucked under his arm. At the sound of shots, he gave the horsemen one startled look then started to run for cover. While the Birds watched helplessly from the bank, young Wymore fell to the frozen ground, struck dead as one of the riders fired purposefully on him. Any one of the four rounds that hit him would have been fatal.

The Clay County Savings Association was a small bank but the robbers had netted a big take. Between five to fifteen thousand dollars in gold and silver and fifty-seven thousand dollars in bonds and currency was stolen but it was the cruel loss of an innocent's life that galvanized the town into action. Scraps of bank paper were found at a county church where the afternoon's profits had been split. The enraged posse of townsmen followed the trail to a Missouri River ferry crossing but a sudden blizzard forced them to turn back. As soon as weather permitted, the pursuit continued, pressing westward into Kansas, sweeping right by a little dilapidated farm at Kearney, Missouri, a railroad stop north of Liberty. It was the farm of Mrs. Zerelda Samuel. Her two sons were recently home from Confederate service. The younger, Jesse, was recovering from a nearly fatal war wound and his older brother, Frank, was rumored to be more interested in book-reading than in doing chores. Not for four more years, until after their sixth holdup, would the sons of the Widow James be linked to the doings in Liberty.

Chapter One

Only a half-dozen dark, wheeling shapes broke the endless cruel blue of the Wyoming sky. Buzzards. They moved in great, lazy arcs, in no hurry. As if sure their prey was going nowhere.

Sam Zachary lowered his squinted eyes to the harsher glare of sunbaked earth. At first, he could only see the scrubby growth of clumped grass and pockmarkings of cacti, yucca, and greasewood. What could the damned scavengers be after? Some luckless prairie dweller? Wondering whether it be of the two or four-legged variety made him pause. He nudged the lathered flanks of his horse, steering it in the direction of the big birds' interest. Soon, just as one of the predatory creatures began its descending circle in anticipation of a meal, he saw a figure sprawled on the dusty ground. The figure of a man.

Two of the greedy birds were already perched and feeding. Sam grimaced as he reined in his nearly blown mount. A shot sent the vultures skyward in the unfurling fervor of black wings. He dismounted and approached the unfortunate with a reluctant distaste. Thankfully, the birds hadn't garnered much of a dinner. Nor had the lifeless figure suffered in the brutality of the midday heat. He'd been sent straight to

9

glory by a pistol ball from someone who meant business. The body was untouched by whomever had done the deed, still sporting a pair of fancy-stitched boots. He hadn't been killed for his belongings. That left his beliefs.

Sam lifted one side then the other of the dead man's coat. The sun glinted off a piece of tin pinned to the ventilated shirt. A deputy marshal's badge. That answered a lot, right then and there. Even a lawman was entitled to have his family notified of his passing, though Sam, himself, felt no loss. He gave a quick search of the man's pockets, yielding two gold eagles and an official-looking sealed letter. It was addressed to the mayor of Blessing. He felt no compunction in breaking the wax. The bearer wouldn't mind.

The words were neatly penned and to the point, a recommendation of Deputy Marshal Wade to the post of local marshal in Blessing. It described Wade as a man of good moral fiber, of solid service and with no family ties. There were a few lines of a personal nature as one acquaintance to another, then Sam studied the name scrawled at the bottom, long and hard.

Grant Tolliver.

Poor Wade stretched out before his boots was a stranger. Not so, Grant Tolliver. Sam felt a bone-crunching tension seize his features. Tolliver. The man had been a Pinkerton and had made life a living hell for him and his family back in Missouri. He could picture the big, raw-boned face with fat cigar squarely planted. Tolliver with his tireless men and unnerving cunning. He *was* law and order. Ole Wade here must have been one fine lawman to earn a recommendation from the likes of the legendary Pinkerton. And the town of Blessing would sleep snug in its beds knowing their marshal made that elite cut, confident that Tolliver had sent the best man for the job.

Smiling grimly, Sam folded the letter and pressed his thumb over the warm wax to reseal it. He tucked it into his own shirt pocket then reached down to relieve Wade of his badge. Then, not out of any particular religious motivation but rather because he couldn't bear the thought of those hideous birds making a meal off any man's bones, he began to dig. It was hot work, sweaty work with dust filtering up in the searing air to choke him, but soon Wade was in his final resting place, hands folded over his punctured breast with a layer of prairie dirt and shale to see it wasn't violated. Sam took a moment to stand over the unmarked mound. He didn't know the right kind of words to say so he merely doffed his hat for a silent second then used his sodden kerchief to wipe his brow before restoring the Stetson to his head. The wind would soon erase any sign of disturbed ground and Wade's grave would be unnoticeable.

Sam swung up onto his winded horse. He was just as tired, bone tired, from the long ride and the unexpected toil. But no longer was he drifting. Now, he had a destination.

Blessing.

Lucille Blessing made the brisk walk between her fine home and the main street every morning. Usually, it was her favorite time of day. There was a sense of freshness as pastels washed the horizon, a lingering of the night chill that woke the mind as well as the body. It gave her a cherished moment to organize her thoughts and plans for the day, a chance to savor the freedom of her existence. And it was quiet. No rattle of harness tracings, no murmur of conversations, no hoorawing from excited cowboys come to town. It was peaceful. Her town looked its very best in early morning before dust and townfolk stirred, and always she felt a swelling sense of satisfaction, a touch of what their Maker must have felt upon seeing what he'd created.

She was smiling to herself as she rounded the side of Murphy's Feed and Grain and from habit began to step up onto that smooth wooden sidewalk. It was then her bonnet suffered a damaging collision and her heart a few seconds of utter paralysis. A man's body dangled from the porch post, as stiff as a pair of long underwear left hanging outside to dry in December.

Lucy stumbled back a few steps, hands clutched over her bosom as if to arrest the agitated beat within. A cry of dismayed surprise silently strangled in her throat. After the initial fright subsided, she was able to draw a decent breath to the limit of her stiffly boned bodice. She was a woman of the West. The sight of a man brought to Judge Lynch's justice was no more uncommon than a fresh scalp would be to her founding sisterhood of the East two centuries prior. Frontier means were harsh and ugly. It did no good to hide one's eyes and pretend it was otherwise. That was just the way things were. And she hoped the coming of the new marshal would change them.

Features screwed up in determined distaste, Lucy stepped around the suspended figure and forced herself to take a closer look. The man was a ghastly sight; blue, swollen face, tongue and eyes protruding in a horrible manner, his head cocked at an unnatural angle and fists clenched in a last convulsive struggle. The distorted features were known to her and she shook her head in distress. Lute Johnson, a dirt-poor farmer scratching in a small spread east of town. She knew him as a loner, as a loudmouth and a heavy drinker who tended toward trouble. And she knew he had an outstanding mortgage of two hundred dol-

12

lars—two hundred dollars she would undoubtedly never see.

With an angry sigh at being cheated by Lute Johnson's premature end, Lucy continued her walk but the pleasure was gone from it. There was no more time for quiet thoughts. She had business to attend. She would have to act quickly to salvage what she could. Perhaps she could gain back some of her investment. She'd known he'd turn out to be a poor risk and her instincts hadn't failed her. Lucille Blessing knew people. She could spot their failings, their weaknesses, their tendencies to do the easy instead of the fair. That's why she was so successful. That's why she was hesitant to lend to men like Lute Johnson; poor risks with nothing to keep them to their bargain should things take a bad turn. Well, things had taken one last bad turn for Lute and she would suffer for it.

With a key taken from the hanging pocket on her dark-colored taffeta skirt, Lucy unlocked the door to the bank. It was an imposing building, located like a sturdy fortress in the center of the block. Unlike the other structures that lined the broad street, it was constructed solidly of newly made Laramie brick. Behind the large plate-glass window emblazoned with the proud words, BLESSING SAVINGS ASSOCIATION, were metal bars set deep and secure. Her husband had seen that the town's first and only bank was as impenetrable as the jailhouse. Oliver Blessing hadn't believed in half measures.

As she withdrew her key and turned to close the door behind her, Lucy cast a displeased glance across the street. Even at this early, pristine hour, sounds of illicit merrymaking escaped the batwings of the Nightingale, the town's most prominent saloon and gaming establishment. Its wheels and dealers worked around the clock to accommodate the odd hours of cowboys and miners looking for a little fun. There was always a game and a girl to be had at Nightingale's. Or so she had heard. Sin set no standard hours, either winding down or starting up. At the Nightingale, it was always in full swing.

" 'Morning, Miz Blessing."

The wiry figure of Cecil Potter slipped beneath her raised arm and, like a shadow, through the narrow space as she closed the door. Her clerk was a small, fragile-looking man who always appeared to look at things in perpetual surprise from behind his thick spectacle lens. Lucy wasn't misled by his rather dainty stature. Cecil had a buxom wife at home and six robust children to attest to his manhood. He was also a wizard with numbers.

"Good morning, Cecil," she responded as she flipped the sign on the door from "Closed" to "Open." "I need you to pull Lute Johnson's paperwork. His loan's defaulted."

As he'd come in from the other side of town, the little man didn't catch the significance of her words. He merely murmured an efficient, "Yes, ma'am," and secured his hat and box lunch within his desk before scurrying to the files.

After tugging off her gloves and unpinning her hat, Lucy stoked the fire in the bank's big potbellied stove. Mornings were still cool enough to require a flame to cut the chill and she liked a cup of fresh-brewed tea while she sorted through her ledgers. Another of the civilized touches she'd learned from Oliver Blessing. He was a man who appreciated them and insisted upon their keeping even in the untamed frontier town where culture fell before crude necessity. As the fragrant scent of steeping tea rose from her steaming cup, Lucy Blessing looked up to the large portrait of her husband which hung in a place of honor next to

14

the bank's impressive vault. A smile touched her lips as if she were wishing him a silent good morning. That, too, was a morning ritual.

With Lute Johnson's thin file in one hand and her teacup in the other, Lucy moved to her own desk where it sat shielded by the massive mahogany counter Oliver had shipped all the way from St. Louis; another touch of civilization. As she began to sink in a bunching of crunchy taffeta to the comfort of her chair, she paused, leaving the movement incomplete, her attention arrested by the figure of a man. He was lingering on the walk outside. She could see him plainly through the expensively clear window glass and warning signals tingled through her. She set her cup down and instinctively felt for the security of the Remington Over-and-Under two-shot .41 she wore strapped to her thigh beneath the feminine folderol of her puffy skirts. She had each one of her stylish dresses altered, adding a concealed slit through which she could reach for her pocket pistol unseen. Caution and self-preservation warranted the modification of her wardrobe. And so did the business she was in.

There was nothing particularly threatening in the manner of the man who stood outside on the walk. He appeared to be casually compiling the makings of a cigarette. But he wasn't looking down at his hands. Even beneath the shaded tilt of his hat brim, Lucy could see he was studying the inside of her bank. There was nothing in his manner of dress to suggest he was any different from the drifters who wandered through the streets of Blessing on their way to range work or the hope of the gold fields. He wore nondescript attire for the West: a dusty oilcloth slicker, its yellow dulled by travel, yoke-shouldered blue shirt collared by the ample folds of a black bandanna, open vest, denims tucked out of his boots in the way of a cowboy rather than a farmer or miner. She'd learned to read where a man hailed from by the shape and attitude of his hat. His didn't have the "Jackdeuce" angle of a Lone Star Texan. This man was from one of the Border states, most likely Missouri. None of those factors deserved attention. But the brace of pistols riding casually beneath the open drape of his slicker did. It was a fast-draw rig, the kind she'd seen sported on the lean hips of countless gunfighters. Twin staghorn-handled Colt Peacemakers rested butt forward. The fact that he carried them easily, not blatantly in the open to make an impressive statement claimed he was a professional. And that boded ill for a raw town without a marshal.

Just then, he caught her staring. A languid hand lifted to tip the brim of his dusty hat. She could see the faint sketch of a smile on his unshaven face before he ambled along the walk.

"Cecil."

The little clerk looked up in alarm at her terse tone.

"See that man? If you spot him again, let me know."

Cecil squinted through the thick glasses, following the lanky figure until the man moved out of sight. Then he took off his spectacles and gave them a nervous polishing. Lucy Blessing was a young woman, only twenty-three, which was half the age of her late husband and younger than her manner would convey, but Cecil trusted her implicitly when it came to matters of business or intuition. "Trouble, you think?"

"I don't know."

But she did know. Men like that were always trouble to somebody. She just didn't want him to become her trouble.

Her trouble arrived in a different shape and form;

16

the kind that was daily and the most difficult.

John Mercer had come up from drought-ridden Kansas with his wife and children to start over — in his case, going from bad to worse. He had no talent for farming. It wasn't that he didn't work hard. He was plain unlucky. It was evident from the way he wrung his flat crowned hat between his hands that some new plague had befallen him. Lucy felt a heavy sadness crowd her breast. Another failure. She'd hoped, when he'd come to her the last time, that he could make a go of it. She'd gone beyond business with the last extension of his loan, crossing the dangerous line into the personally involved because she'd wanted him to have a good place to raise his family. She wanted them all to succeed, each and every one of them that came through her doors. But she couldn't let that want get in the way of what she knew was best — for them as well as the bank. Oliver had taught her that, that sometimes the greatest kindness came in denial. She watched surreptitiously as his conversation with Cecil grew more and more heated. Finally, she rose.

"I can handle this, Cecil. Why don't you come on back, Mister Mercer."

The farmer calmed only in the slightest degree when confronted by a lady. He mumbled a civil how-do and took the seat Lucy offered, perching precariously upon its edge.

"I come to see about getting an extension on my note," he blurted out.

Lucy gave no hint of response. Her smile was mild, courteous. Completely void of any emotion she might feel. "Cecil, could you get me Mister Mercer's papers, please."

The farmer grew more noticeably fidgety as Lucy took her time in scanning the documents. He mopped the dappling of sweat from his brow with a worn

17

handkerchief, his eyes darting between the papers and the woman reading them. Finally, Lucy set them down on the desk before her and regarded the agitated farmer with a professional distance. Her words were cool, remote.

"It says here you've already advanced on your initial credit twice. First to replace your windmill when it fell in high winds, then to replace the stock you lost last winter during the freeze."

Mercer swallowed hard, hope rapidly fading in his washed-out eyes.

"It also states that you're behind two quarters in your payments."

The movement of Mercer's hands became convulsive, distorting any shape his old hat ever had. "Miz Blessing, I needs that money. I had me a fire in my barn last night. It done burnt up all my seed. I won't have nothing to plant. Nothing to feed my animals. Nothing to feed my family. If I don't get my grain in, I won't have no way to pay on my loan."

"I can understand, Mister Mercer." It was difficult, but she kept her feelings from intruding into her necessarily blunt words. "I'm sorry and I sympathize with your troubles but this is a bank, a lending institution, a business. There's a limit to what I can do. I already hold the title to your property and a chattel mortgage on your animals and all your belongings. If I were to give you more credit, I'd be allowing you to dig yourself into a hole you'll never climb out of. You don't want that, do you, Mister Mercer? Perhaps you should think of recovering what you can."

"Meaning?" There was a hard, unfriendly edge to his question, as if Lucy Blessing had just turned from possible supporter to threat.

"Perhaps you should sell out while you can still get enough to pay off your debt. Then you could salvage

18

enough to begin again. Someplace else." That last was offered gently.

Mercer didn't take to her calmly leveled suggestion. His eyes got all squinty and his face took on a ruddy stain of anger. "I already done started over. You ain't going to run me off my place."

"No one's trying to run you off your farm, Mister Mercer," she stated firmly, attempting to placate his temper while it was still negotiable. "I just want you to think of what's best for your family."

"My family? What the hell do you care about my family?" There was a loud scraping of thrust-back chair legs as he stood, abruptly, menacingly.

Lucy didn't rise. She didn't let on that she was in any way alarmed by his sudden hostile behavior. But her hand fell to her lap, close to the hidden rent in her skirt. "I do care. I care about everyone in Blessing."

Her sentiment was wasted on the desolate Mercer. He didn't want to see reason. He couldn't see beyond another failure and it was more than his masculine pride could stand. He glared down at the banker, irrational plays of helpless rage darkening his pleasant features.

"You only care about how much you can make offen them. And I guess you sees me as a dried-up well. Thanks for nothing, lady."

Lucy sighed as the irate farmer stormed around the counter and out the door. The plate glass shivered with the force of his anger as the door slammed shut. She'd done the right thing but it left an emptiness behind. Lucy stood, arranging the impotent papers back into Mercer's file, wishing things didn't have to be so final. The farmer would come to his senses and see she offered the only practical solution. In time. It was a hard country. Only the strongest and most determined eked a living from its near barren ground.

19

However, she underestimated John Mercer's determination. He didn't come to his senses. He figured he'd been pushed about as far as a man could be pushed. It rankled him something fierce that the wealthy banker-lady who'd never had to struggle could coldly pull his dreams out from under him. He wasn't thinking clearly, his brain all inflamed with fury and unfairness. He stalked to the wagon he'd brought to town in hopes that he'd be using it to carry replacement seed back to his farm. From under the plank seat, he withdrew a double-barreled scattergun he used for chasing off varmints and hunting small game. Feeling the power of the buckshot packed into its 28-inch barrel, he marched back inside the bank.

Both Lucy Blessing and her four-eyed clerk rose up from behind their desks in surprise. They didn't look so cocksure of themselves now. A crazy confidence swelled within him, blanking his mind to the futility of what he was doing. He knew only that the surge of control felt wildly exhilarating.

Lucy fought to contain her panic as a similar scene flashed painfully before her. Her knees shook within the restriction of her backswept skirts. For a moment, she was completely numb. Whether it was Cecil Potter's urgent, silent plea for guidance or the knowledge that her husband looked down on them from the wall behind her, the terror was stemmed and a cool composure settled in its place.

"Mister Mercer, please put that down. Violence won't change anything and I know you don't want to hurt anybody here."

"Don't I?"

The walls and her eardrums reverberated as one of the chambers discharged. A hole the size of a dinner plate was torn through the wire mesh that caged the teller's window, slowing the pellets just enough to make a harmless peppering upon the wood paneling in the back. A small whimpering sound escaped from the cowering clerk. The still lethal barrel made a continual arcing motion between Lucy and Cecil.

"What I want is my money and a little respect, Miz High-Falutin'. I'm plumb tired of being treated like I was dirt by the likes of you. I want what's coming to me."

With all the attention focused on the unstable figure of John Mercer, none had heard the door slip open. So when a strange voice sounded, all jumped in surprise.

"Unless you want to get what's coming to you point-blank, I reckon you'd best put down your piece."

The no-nonsense sound of a hammer being cocked strengthened the request. Feeling a cold circle of metal pressing to the nape of his neck, the farmer had no recourse lest he wanted nothing but air to remain above his shoulders. The shotgun angled down to bead harmlessly on the floorboards until it was efficiently removed from his dangling hands.

Once the shock of the situation eased, Lucy recognized her rescuer as the stranger she'd seen hanging around the front of the bank that morning. And now, he was inside. With gun drawn. Her relief suffered a tug of reservation. Had the moment been saved or merely turned from inept handling to that of a master?

Close up like they were, she could see his features plainly and the sense of foreboding intensified. The man probably would have been handsome if wind and worry hadn't worn the softer edges of his face away, leaving only harsh planes. He reminded her of the savage, inhospitable land. The hair that brushed his collar was the color of sunbaked sand. His lean, angular features looked shaped by the elements, as sharp and craggy as the outcroppings of desert rock, his skin brown and weathered as saddle leather. Both nose and mouth were thin and straight, severe. Creases fanned at the sides of eyes that were as bleached and faded as a gray winter sky. And just as cold. His stature wasn't overly impressive. He was average tall with a long, sinewy build, like one of the tough, rangy longhorns. He didn't need size or the brace of Colts to give him stature. There was a lethal tension in his loose stance, a kind of dangerous ease that made the looker uncomfortably aware of him as a potential threat. And as a man. Lucy regarded the stranger with all the calm she could muster.

"I guess I owe you my thanks, mister."

He smiled crookedly. It wasn't a particularly reassuring gesture. "I guess you do at that, ma'am." His soft syllables were quietly accented, not by a deep South drawl but by a gentle Missouri laziness as she had at first supposed. He saw her hesitation, her suspicion, and grinned wider to show he did and to bring a faint blush of color to her cheeks. Apprehension or annoyance?

"Quite a stroke of luck that you just happened by." Her words were mild but their meaning was laced with cautious innuendo. She put the slightest emphasis upon the word "happened."

"Not at all, ma'am. I saw this feller fixing for mischief and figured I might be needed. You might say it's all part of the job."

Lucy began to frown, an unwelcomed bit of foresight starting to build. Then, he stated it plain.

"I'm Blessing's new marshal."

Chapter Two

"Marshal?"

There was an element of dismay in Lucy Blessing's voice as she repeated the title. *This* man was their new town marshal? She began to shake her head. He wasn't at all what she'd expected, what she'd hoped for. The request she urged the mayor to pen had been for a man beyond reproach, one of sterling references, of incorruptible quality. She'd hoped for a dapper figure, for someone smoothly competent and urbanely sophisticated. Someone who could deal with the problems of Blessing with a cool head and calm capability. This man wore his references on his hip. He would deal with problems with a 230-grain bullet and 28-grain powder charge. And nothing would change. Someone faster, someone more clever would come along and they'd be out a lawman again. Violence bred the like. She was mightily disappointed in the man Captain Tolliver had sent them.

"Sam Wade, ma'am. Could you tell me where I can store this feller? I figure he'll have a whole new frame of thinking happen he has time to cool down a mite."

"The jail is at the end of the street," Cecil piped in happily. He seemed to have no qualms in accepting the authority of their new marshal. "Across from the livery."

"Now that was some shrewd thinking. A man figuring on breaking jail won't have far to run for a fast horse."

The maligning observation stuck Lucy like a careless hat pin. She winced. Her features tightened. In town half the morning and already critical of what he saw. She didn't like the kind of man Sam Wade represented. And she began to conclude she didn't much like Sam Wade, either.

"If the marshal's doing his job, Mister Wade, it shouldn't matter if the horses were kept inside the jail, now should it?"

Sam Wade's narrow lips quirked then lifted on one side. There was no answering amusement in his steady stare. "No, ma'am, it shouldn't." That stare was assessing and faintly contemptuous. Like his half smile. "Will you be wanting me to hold him till the circuit judge comes through or will an overnight and a stiff fine do the trick?"

Lucy sighed, the starch leaving her as she looked at John Mercer. He was a sad, broken man who'd given way to the foolish passions of the moment. She didn't think she had anything to fear from him. He already looked repentant, his features as droopy as a whipped pup. "Just see he leaves town without any more trouble. He has a family waiting. I wouldn't want them to worry over him."

Mercer regarded her with a sullen gratitude and murmured his thanks for the sake of his wife. He regretted what he'd done but the simmering resentment lingered. He didn't want to be beholden to Lucille Blessing's charity.

"Come on, hard case. Let's get you to your wagon. Be expecting a bill for repairs and be right prompt in paying them, hear?"

24

The marshal steered the slouching farmer from the bank and only then did Lucy sink into her chair on boneless legs. Glazed eyes surveyed the damage to the room, seeing not the sprinkling of a light load of buckshot that ruined nothing more than a bit of mesh and paneling, but the aftermath of a full-charge double-barrel blast that had taken her husband's life in a ruthless instant. A nerveless shaking got hold of her and tactfully Cecil busied himself with cleaning up the mess, making no comment to embarrass her or call her to her weakness. He'd cleaned up after Oliver, as well, silently, efficiently while she went quietly to pieces that time, too. He was a good man, Cecil Potter.

Finally, the trembling subsided. Lucy brushed the trails of wetness from pale cheeks and reached for her cold tea, wishing for once that it was something of the stronger variety like they served at the Nightingale across the street. Something that would ease her memories and warm the cold that settled deep inside.

Life was full of little ironies. Sam Zachary never expected to be putting in time on this side of the cell bars. It was a sturdy jail, built of batten board and brick. The office end was sizable, housing a big desk scarred by spurred boot heels and careless cigars, a bench beneath the barred windows that looked out on the street and a bunk against the opposing wall, where the marshal was meant to spend his nights when the cells were occupied. There was a small stove to provide homey comforts and a large rectangular board to provide for business. It was already a patchwork of dodgers offering up descriptions and rewards for the desperadoes of the day. Of the cells, themselves, there were four, each with its own iron door, two on either side of a walk wide enough for the jailor's safety. He should have felt uncomfortable—considering. For now, he was too amused.

Sam pulled the chair from beneath the desk. It moved on smooth rollers. Once situated upon it, he gave the desk a cursory look. The drawers seemed to serve no organized purpose other than to conceal a number of whiskey bottles in various stages of depletion. Was that the fate of his predecessor? A lawman needed a clear head not a gutful of brave maker if he was to collect a respectable number of years and the hope of retirement. The same for any man who toted a gun.

The shoosh of stiff broom bristles across the boards outside came to an abrupt halt. Sam glanced up to see a young man gawking in at him through the open door. He was a big fellow with head of lanky brown hair and large shoulders that seemed to bend his body under their weight, dressed in sod buster overalls. He was probably pushing manhood in age but retained a sort of guilelessness to his expression, a mildness in his eyes that made him appear much younger. He hugged to the broom handle, appearing to debate on whether to speak up or not. Finally, curiosity got the better of his hesitancy.

"Is you the new marshal?"

"Sam Wade. And you are?"

The boy brightened, encouraged by the man's interest. He lost that hound-dog-expecting-a-quick-boot-in-the-rump look and advanced into the jailhouse. Sam noted immediately that there was something not right about him. He moved slowly, awkwardly, his left foot turned out and seeming to drag with each halting step. His attention didn't linger on the deformity but instead moved back up to the boy's face. He could see a fear flicker there, an anxiety that he would be met with jeering or rejection.

"I'm Newt Redman, Marshal Wade."

Sam stuck out his hand. "Right pleased to meet you, Newt. What can I do for you?"

Again, there was the hang-back reluctance as he took the strong hand offered, the anticipation of contempt. Then he allowed a deep breath and squared those big shoulders. "I used to clean up and do odd jobs for Ole Tom. I was wondering if I might do the same for you?"

"Ole Tom? Was he the former marshal?"

"Yessir. He was."

"What kind of lawman was he?" Sam continued his search of the desk, opening one of the drawers to send a bottle of McBryan rolling from front to back to front again.

"Tom, he was a good sort. Always had a cheery word to spare a body."

"But was he a good lawman?"

Newt gave a shy smile, surprised and pleased to have his opinion solicited. He murmured, truthfully, "Not much of one. I don't like to speak bad of the dead but he did like his liquor and his ladies a bit more than he did his job."

"Killed in the line of it, was he?"

Newt Redman gave a strange giggly laugh. "Ole Tom, he stayed out of trouble when he could. He got hisself a case of lead poisoning at the Nightingale over some bawdy gal. Not much of a marshal but I liked him well enough." That was added solemnly, with a touch of sadness. Sam guessed that the big, lamed Newt Redman didn't have too many friends.

The mild blue eyes lit with animation when Sam hefted a dog-eared manual to the desk top and raised a brow in question.

"That's the marshal's law book. It's got all the territorial codes and statutes listed in simple words that's meant to be understood. None of that Latin gibble-gabble. And there's samples of warrants and writs and attachments and stuff you might need." A slow flush of color crept up to his cheeks when he read the marshal's look of surprise. By way of explanation, he muttered, "Tom used to let me read in it. I'd help him fill out forms and the like when his eyesight was none too good."

"You interested in the law, Newt?"

The boy practically glowed. "Oh, yes, sir, Marshal Wade. Like I said, Ole Tom used to let me help with the paperwork and mind the prisoners for a long bit every week."

Darn cheap labor. Sam repressed his scowl, imagining how the old reeling sot would take advantage of the eager boy to do his job for him. Newt Redman was the kind who would snap up scraps and not complain. Kind of like a hound who'd known a cruel hand responding to a friendly pat.

"You were making a long bit a week?"

Newt studied his scuffed boots. "If that be too much—"

"I was thinking of something a little different, is all."

Newt waited, breath held in suspended hope. This new marshal wasn't like most of the town folk. He didn't get a particular light in his eye when he looked at the twisted foot. He didn't talk to him as if because of the game leg, he wasn't all there every place else. Even Ole Tom, as good a soul as he was, hadn't been above a good laugh at his unintentioned clumsiness. There was a cruel humor in that laughter, the kind that prodded a man to make fun of another to make himself feel bigger. Newt didn't think Marshal Wade would need to puff himself up at anyone's expense.

He seemed to have a good firm handle on his own self-worth. His handshake had been strong, man to man, as if Newt was an equal, not the town cripple who was the butt of ribald teasing and often heartless pranks. A man like Marshal Wade would make an honored friend. Heck, he'd work for him for nothing and was about to say so.

"Newt, seeing as how you know the town and you got a passing respect for the law, seems to me, a man couldn't do better when he was looking for a body to serve as deputy."

Newt stared. Slowly, his jaw began to loosen and sag. *Deputy.* Only in his wildest dreams had he ever considered such a thing as possible. Deputy. A position of authority and respect. That would show them. Even his paw would have to take notice then. He could even carry a gun. The younger boys would look up to him instead of pitching things too foul to imagine at him before running off, laughing with hurtful glee. Others would look at him with interest instead of amused contempt. Why maybe even a certain pretty lady . . .

Suddenly, the boy's bright eyes became shadowed and suspicious. It was a joke; one crueller than any he'd endured because it struck so close to his personal longings. The marshal was funning him—just like all the others, teasing then delivering the swift kick. He tensed for the laughter.

But the marshal wasn't laughing. He was looking Newt up and down with an appraising eye. "You look to be man enough for the job, maybe a mite young. If you don't think you're up to it—"

"I know I am," Newt was quick to claim. Hope flared once more, firing his insides with a delicious warmth. "You serious, Marshal?"

"About who I have working for me? You bet."

And he did look serious. There was no hint of mirth in his cool steel gaze. It was sober. Newt was too flustered to look further or he might have seen something else in that stare; something deeper, darker. A look of cold speculation.

"Then I'm your man."

Sam Zachary smiled, a chill half smile that never reached his contemplative eyes.

". . . carbine worn on the right of his saddle. A cavalry man, I'm betting."

"For the damn Rebs."

"Who better than one of their own to tangle with them Texas boys when they ride in to tree the town?"

"Me, I don't care much where he hails from so long as he gets the job done. Never had no use for Ole Tom. Only thing he were good for was sopping up whiskey and lining his pockets with bribes."

"You think this 'un will be any better?"

"With that cross-draw rig of his? Has the look of a gun-slick, iffen you ask me. I don't want no part of no lawman who'll be bait for every grown-up kid fed on dime novels coming in to test their mettle and their draw."

Lucy could hear the gossip bantered back and forth the moment she opened the door to Davis's Goods Emporium. She didn't spare a glance to the group of a half-dozen men. It seemed they spent the better part of their day gathered in crude chairs around the stove and cracker barrel sipping from the tin cup tied to the whiskey barrel Jeremiah Davis kept in back for his steady customers, talking politics, weather or just plain gossiping like a flock of old hens. Their topic this morning was the new marshal. It didn't take them long to have all formed an opinion, whether they'd gotten a look at the man in question or not. It was something new to chew on while their womenfolk purchased necessities.

"Morning, Lucille."

Lucy nodded to the two old ladies seated on the bench by the door. Separate from the men, it was where the women took a respite from shopping and daydreamed about what they couldn't afford.

At the sound of her name, the murmuring at the cracker barrel immediately shifted to talk about the ruckus in the bank and how the new marshal had stepped in. Lucy skirted around the kegs of sugar, vinegar, flour and molasses, trying to hold to her composure as the conversation slipped to a discussion of her late husband's demise. A couple of the men were a tad hard of hearing so voices weren't lowered out of respect for her presence. She'd heard it all, of course, the endless replays of Oliver's last minutes, the speculation and gruesome details. It still brought a roiling of emotion in the pit of her belly and a burning behind her eyes. Damn the old hens, anyway, she thought. She'd give them no further food for comment. With head held high, she moved to the dry goods counter and took a minute to breathe deep, letting the comforting scents of tobacco plugs, boot leather, fresh-ground coffee and musty fabric on the bolt waft through her like a calming balsam.

"Morning, Miz Blessing," wheezed Jeremiah Davis as he eased his near three hundred pounds of fleshy bulk from his high proprietor's stool and sidled behind the counter. "Quite some doings this morning."

"Yes," she answered brusquely then moved on to discourage further discussion. "Alice said my package had arrived."

"Lemme see here." Jeremiah wriggled himself around and poked through the crates he'd stacked behind the counter to serve as letter slots. Having established the first mercantile in Blessing, he'd also become its postmaster, shrewdly bringing in an even greater clientele when he hoisted Old Glory to announce the arrival of the mail. "Here it be. All the way from New York City." He withdrew the large envelope and peered at it, reluctant to relinquish the intriguing package until he'd learned its contents. He weighed it expertly and wagered a professional guess. "A new mail-order catalog?"

Lucy removed the temptation of the unopened parcel from his beefy hand. "Fashion plates from Worth," she corrected distractedly.

"Ain't he that Frenchy what makes ladies' dresses?"

"His salon is the finest in Paris."

"Do tell. Mind if Alice has a look see when you're through? She's getting mighty handy with those new Butterick paper patterns."

Lucy smiled politely. "Not at all." She couldn't picture Alice Davis, who matched her husband nearly ounce for ounce, squeezed into snugly wrapped skirts and a bustle. They'd have to rid themselves of half their inventory to allow her room to turn around within the store.

Jeremiah leaned forward on conspiratorial elbows and pitched his voice low. "Say, what do you think of our new marshal?"

Lucy was instantly aware that the chatter around the cracker barrel dropped to an expectant silence. Even the two ladies at the door paused in their discussion of the benefits of Dr. Kilmer's Female Remedy to hang upon her answer.

"I've only just met the man," she began but Jeremiah and the others prompted her with their continued attention. She was not unaware of the considerable weight of her judgment. What could she tell them? Certainly not her true opinion. That she thought their new town marshal was most likely up to no good, a quick-draw drifter who blew in on one ill wind and would tumble out on the same. That she didn't trust his lazy smile and cold stare. That she felt he was mocking her beneath his genteel manners. Or worse. She settled for a mild reproof that would convey the tone of her sentiments if not the depth. "He does not dress well. And he's not at all what I'd expected as a referral from Captain Tolliver. He makes me wonder if he's not standing on the wrong side of the bars."

There was the soft clearing of a throat and the jingle of Davis's front door as it quietly closed behind the man she'd just condemned. Marshal Sam Wade couldn't *not* have heard her but he gave no sign as he tipped his dusty Stetson first to the ladies on the bench then to Lucy where she stood growing rapidly crimson at the counter. Then his steely eyes met hers and held, betraying his amusement at her embarrassed circumstance. The high color in her cheeks grew rosier in anger. Lucy added arrogant and insufferably rude to her list of complaints.

"Morning, ladies, gents," he drawled, supplying a congenial smile. "Ma'am." He let his attention linger on her just a second beyond politeness then went to join the men's intimate circle, leaving her to fume in silent mortification. After nodding through the introductions, he put one well made but dirty boot up on a chair seat and leaned upon his knee. He got down to business in a roundabout manner, as if the topic was as bland as the weather.

"Say now, I couldn't help but notice as I rode in that one of the local citizens has been jerked to Jesus down at the end of the street. That's a mite strong statement to be making to visitors to our town. Think

33

a couple of you boys could cut him down and take him over to the coroner? My guess is death by strangulation but it should be done all proper like before the burying."

As two of the men went to comply, Sam accepted a tin of Davis's refresher then asked after the victim in a mildly curious manner.

"Lute Johnson. A dirt-poor farmer from just outside of town" was offered up.

"Any idea of who might have done the deed?"

The marshal sipped from the goodwill tin and looked from face to face, seeing expressions freeze into a sudden paralysis. He kept his inquiry casual, as nonthreatening as his easy posture. "None at all?"

Only Lucy caught the thread of steel behind the languid question and for a moment was encouraged. Then when the men shuffled and lowered their eyes to exchange quick, darting glances, she grew impatient. Old hens.

"It was vigilantes, Marshal, hooded cowards who've been taking the law into their own bloodthirsty hands. I can't imagine them having a reason to lynch poor Lute for other than his surly nature. It was murder, plain and simple." Having said her piece, she waited for him to follow up, to pursue the matter of Lute Johnson's death and see his killers punished.

Sam Wade took his time. He drained the last fire-laced drop from the cup then regarded Lucy with his full attention. And she fought not to squirm beneath it, for there was no trace of the lethargy of his attitude in his intense gaze. His stare burned like a cheap cut of whiskey. His narrowed eyes roved slowly from crown to toe and back again, measuring, appreciating. Insulting. He displayed more interest in the long line of her boned bodice than in the stretched neck of Lute Johnson. And Lucille Blessing grew slowly furious.

"Could be, ma'am. No man goes willing to his own end. There's no need for the good citizens of Blessing to take matters in their own hands anymore, not now that the law is here."

"Good citizens?" Lucy made no effort to curb her temper. Her eyes blazed. Her fine nostrils flared. Her fine bosom expanded with a breath of pure indignation. Sam Wade's lazy stare enjoyed the display. "They're nothing more than midnight assassins. They murdered that man without benefit of trial or justice. What are you going to do about it, Marshal?"

Every pair of eyes in Davis's Goods Emporium arced between the two figures, one rigid with wrath, the other indifferently indolent. Not a one of them would come up against Lucy Blessing when she had that hot fire in her eyes but their new marshal seemed immune to the scorching heat. And each came to their own conclusion that they'd found the perfect man for the job.

"Do, ma'am?" he drawled, dragging each sound out with a patronizing clarity. "Don't rightly know that there's anything I can do. Restoring Mister Johnson is out of my jurisdiction."

A smattering of laughter was quickly muffled as Lucy grew pale. A dangerous sign that Marshal Wade ignored. Either bravely or foolishly.

"And besides, ma'am, unless you know the name of at least one man on Mister Johnson's jury, it don't seem like I have much to go on. Do you have that name?"

Lucy glared at the languid marshal, hating him for the controlling way he made her look ridiculous. Compared to his easy logic, her demands sounded petulant and impractical. And the matter of Lute Johnson was neatly swept under Jeremiah Davis's

35

braided rug to be forgotten and unanswered. She knew in that moment the exact nature of the new marshal of Blessing. He was going to do no more against the lawlessness that plagued them than old drunken Tom.

Helpless and, for the moment, beaten, she drew up every scrap of her dignity and marched by the men, feeling Sam Wade's mocking gaze track her all the way to the door. She let it close behind her with unnecessary force.

Sam allowed a genuine smile to play about his mouth. He sensed the relief in the other men and the warmth of renewed respect. Somehow, besting this prickly female had earned both.

"A feisty little thing," he remarked easily but instead of joining him in his amusement the others looked a tad uncomfortable. A watered-down bunch to be cowed by one pretty woman, a woman who wasn't the wife to any of them. "She work at the bank? Don't recollect I know of any lady tellers."

Jeremiah Davis cleared his throat. "Marshal Wade, Miz Lucille Blessing *is* the bank. In fact, since her husband got hisself killed, you might say she's the whole damn town."

Sam Zachary stared at the door. It still shivered in its frame. Mrs. Lucille Blessing. Female banker. Now that made things right interesting.

Chapter Three

Blessing's banker stood at the barred window of her institution and watched the town's new marshal saunter from Davis's. Her dark eyes narrowed as they followed him along the boards. Even his stride conveyed an arrogant confidence: not with a strut but an easy glide. Everything about him appeared deceivingly easy: his walk, his manner of dress, his speech, his attitude. But Lucy wasn't fooled. She knew people. The marshal wasn't what he seemed. There was nothing easy about him. Sam Wade didn't need aggressive affectation to telegraph his message. He didn't need to strut and crow. Beneath his lazy quiet, he was razor sharp and about as stable as the nitroglycerin used to cut through the mountains of the Wyoming Territory. He was explosive, a potentially dangerous disturbance to the well-being of the town. And to herself. She realized that the moment she found her stare gauging his walk. Her mind termed it provokingly male. Comfortably controlled, latently powerful. Suggestively masculine.

Lucy jerked back from the window, startled by the sultry turn of her study. She was barely out of mourning and ogling the first pair of snugly stretched Levi's to come along the walk. No, that wasn't true. And that made her all the angrier. That a man like Sam Wade should be the first to stir the female in her was as infuriating as it was impossible.

The marshal's destination helped her get her discomposed emotions under a tight rein once more. Batwing doors pendulumed at his passing. The Nightingale enfolded him in her garish embrace. She wondered what lure would hold him: the games, the liquor or the women. Or all three. And the wondering had her inexplicably annoyed. So much so that she was unaware that she was no longer alone.

"Howdy, Miz Lucille."

She gave a nervous and frustratingly guilty jump then turned toward the speaker.

"Oh, good morning, Newt. I didn't hear you come in." Did she sound as breathless as she felt? She prayed not. She managed a warm smile and consciously struggled to slow the agitated pounding of her heart.

"Sorry if I put you in a fright, Miz Lucille," the boy mumbled. He always had a difficult time finding his voice when around the attractive Widow Blessing. It had a want to shift up into a shaky adolescent pitch. He thought Lucille Blessing was the best-looking, best-hearted lady he'd ever known and her very presence made him jittery.

"You're late this morning, Newt. Everything all right at home?"

Newt colored uncomfortably, lowering his gaze. Only Lucy would think to ask with such gentle concern. "No, ma'am, nothing like that. It's just that I won't be coming by no more."

Her aggravation was distracted from the new marshal to focus on Luke Redman. The man was a mean-spirited bully whose brutality deprived his only son of every joy. He'd agreed to let Newt work odd jobs in town to keep himself in whiskey. She couldn't believe he'd be so ornery as to forbid Newt his meager chance of independence. She *could* believe it, but she wouldn't allow it.

"You see I gots me another job."

Lucy held her tongue, nearly biting it in her surprise. She knew how desperately Newt had sought employment and how devastated he'd been at each curt rejection. The people of Blessing weren't broadminded enough to see the goodness of the man inside the imperfection of the form. So, who had hired him?

His gaze canted up. Lucy saw an excitement shining there, a happiness that made his blue eyes blaze with pride. "Marshal Wade made me his deputy," he blurted out, unable to retain the news any longer. He studied Lucy's face, eager for her response, for her to share in his joy. When her reaction was slow in coming, he began to frown. "You don't think I can do it?" His features fell.

"Oh, no, Newt," she was quick to assure him. "I know you'll do just fine. Just fine. I know how much you helped Tom. At least now you'll get paid a decent wage."

While Newt went on to expound on Sam Wade's virtues, Lucy stayed silent and seethed. Why would he do it? Why would Wade choose a boy like Newt to do a rigorous man's job? Newt was bright enough and enthusiastic enough but his physical limitations were obvious. How could the marshal think him capable? For too long, Newt had been the receptacle of the town's merciless taunts. To place him so abruptly into a position of authority was asking for trouble, and heartache for Newt. How they would laugh at him. Marshal Wade's careless act would crush the boy's spirit. What could he have to gain for it? A chance to ridicule a stranger? To cruelly misuse a vulnerable boy's trust? Why? To share the laugh with the towns-folk?

As Newt went on and on about the hopes he held for his new position, Lucy felt her temper ferment into a nearly uncontrollable outrage. She was tempted to storm across the street right into that dim den of sin to confront the thoughtless snake with his unforgivable deed. She wanted to seize him up by the throat until his face swelled purple and his mocking eyes bulged nigh to popping just like Lute Johnson's. Never had any one act angered her quite so completely. Or did that have to do with the man behind it? Sam Wade had crossed her path just this morning and had already knocked the stable footing of her emotions out from under her. And she had the feeling he enjoyed doing it.

There had to be some means of turning the balance. This was her town. She wasn't about to let some two-bit gunslick mock her in public and undermine the respect she held. And she wouldn't let him make a joke of this boy's hopes. She wondered if Sam Wade knew he was in for one hell of a fight.

Sam paused, letting the batwings brush his backside as he sized up Nightingale's. He could tell in a glance that it was no cheap rotgut parlor. There were red plush curtains, fancy chandeliers to throw a dim dusky light even in midday, rich brass spitoons every few yards to discourage carelessness. Everything he saw gleamed with style, but it would take closer examination to tell what else it was.

Despite the early hour, there was a respectable crowd, mostly gathered around the buffet table, which offered free salty fare with the purchase of a five-cent beer. It was an ample spread of sausages, bologna, corn beef, smoked, pickled and kippered fish, various cheeses, five types of bread, pickles, radishes and little green onions. A generous gesture meant to increase consumption at the bar. Sam ignored the food and went straight to that long, elegant length of carved cherrywood, his footsteps muffled in the clean sprinkling of sawdust which had yet to absorb its quota of drips and foam.

It was one of the finest bars he'd ever seen in a day when making them was a pridefully significant craft. Running the full length of the wall, there was plenty of room for several bartenders but only one was at work, running a chamois over the gleaming wood. He was a white-aproned dandy with oil-slicked hair and a quick white smile.

"What can I get you, Marshal?"

News traveled fast. "Beer. And have one for yourself."

As he settled at the bar, Sam watched the tender select from the high altar of glassware pyramided on the central section of the backbar which was flanked by a bung starter, a plate of lemons and bottles of muscatel, port, catawba and rock and rye. Nobody ever selected one of those fancy decanters but they gave an air of undeniable elegance. The dandy poured then withdrew his own glass from behind the counter. It was an old bartender's trick. If pushed by a congenial customer, he would join in a "snit" of beer in that private glass, which was no bigger than an eyecup and carefully filled with foam. That way, he could play amiable host all night and still charge each buyer the cost of a full glass.

"Nice place," Sam remarked as he leisurely enjoyed the wet refreshment. "The manager around?"

"I can get him if you want."

"Do that."

While he waited, Sam observed and appreciated. Whoever had set up this establishment knew his business. Pure class yet comfortable enough to invite a man to sit a spell just to gaze upon the life-size canvases. Nude and nubile females shaped like dray horses reposed in soft oils set temptingly at eye level. Interspersing the Saturday Night paintings were pictorial ads supplied by distillers and rectifying houses sporting patriotic and pugilistic themes. The massive mirror hung above the backbar was decorated with mottos to make the reader smile: "If you spit on the floor at home, spit on the floor here — We want you to feel right at home" and "Don't Shoot the Piano Player — He's Doing His Darndest." Then there was the more practical sign: "Don't Ask For Credit."

In that polished mirror, Sam surveyed the room. There was a stage set for nightly entertainment with a sizable dance floor in front. That was dark and empty as the main focus of the day was at the tables of chance. The Nightingale offered a good variety. He counted four faro banks, a Hieronymous bowl, roulette wheel, two crap tables, two for stud poker and two for draw, one for short faro and one for vingt-et-un. He guessed keno games were held in the back rooms along with the other type of nightly entertainment. As of yet, there were no ladies present. Most likely, they were catching up on their sleep to be ready for the dusk-to-dawn shift. Women were still enough of a scarcity to make a man ride hell-bent for leather thirty miles just to gander at one.

The bartender returned and after a nod to the marshal, busied himself at sweeping the walking board behind the bar. Sam's attention was pulled immediately to the man who emerged from a sturdy door at the end of the counter. He was dapperly dressed in a new suit with a heavy gold chain stretched across his vest. A cluster-diamond pin glittered in the center of his tie. His smile was just as dazzling but possibly not as genuine.

"Marshal Wade, I'm Henry Knight, part owner of the Nightingale."

Knight was a misnomer. The owner of Nightingale's was as golden as a July afternoon. He was tall and athletically built, his neatly trimmed blond hair gleaming from a touch of Madagascar oil. Though his profession called for dim artificial lights, he still managed to maintain warmly tanned skin against which his teeth flashed a brilliant white. He exuded charm and congeniality as long as one didn't look too deeply into his eyes. They were as black as the coal brought out of the Wyoming hills and just as soulless. Sam pegged him at once: smooth, hard and dangerous. When the two men shook hands, the bar owner's grip tightened just enough for an impressive show of strength. Not a man to cross.

"You just stop in to say howdy or have you got something else on your mind?" Right to the point. The smile stayed fixed and welcoming but the black eyes chilled.

Henry Knight had seen his share of lawmen and considered himself a good judge. In a single meeting, he could tell if a man could be bought and would know his price. And would meet it. Old Tom he'd figured in less than a minute, the time it took for his red-rimmed eyes to caress the whiskey glasses on the bar. This man was not that easy. He played it close to the vest like the best gambler. His expression was inscrutable. His eyes revealed only what he wanted to be seen. There was an intelligence there that went beyond brute authority, a man who would use his brain as well as his revolver. Knight deemed him to be either a potential benefit or a grave threat. But which? That required a test.

"Partly that," the marshal drawled. "Partly because I wanted to see what kind of house you run, seeing as how it's the finest in Blessing."

"Why thank you, Marshal. We pride ourselves on supplying our customers with the best—of everything. Can I have Jeff pour you another?"

Wade nodded and he was pleased to see the marshal accept a second beer. At least he wasn't a temperate man. A man who didn't like his drink made him uneasy. Now, he needed to find out the limit of what the new lawman would take from him.

"We provide our visitors with a good cigar, a good game, a hearty laugh and fine variety theater. We have a billiard parlor in the back and a collection of the prettiest girls this side of the Mississippi. Jeff and my other five bartenders consider it a matter of professional pride to be able to run up a hundred and fifty different cocktails, rickeys, fizzes, cobblers, punches and cups, though most prefer their beer and red liquor. We serve a nickel beer, a bit shot and two-bits for anything fancy."

When he saw the marshal's attention had drifted to the tables, Knight began to grow more confident. Even if the man couldn't be bought, he could be had and owned at the gaming tables. He led his guest toward them, expounding as he did upon the quality of play he housed. Covertly, responding to a silent question from his dealers, he shook his head. He'd let things run as they usually did, making no attempt to cover anything up. He would as soon know now how much he could get by with.

"Our dealers here come from the finest boats along the Mississippi, from New Orleans and Chicago. We hold to a two-dollar limit in poker. The bets in faro and monte run from two-bits to a dollar. The chips are a short bit at roulette and the dice are five cents a throw. The house holds the right to accept larger bets depending on the ability to collect."

They came to a halt to watch a hand of vingt-et-un. Star-backed cards flipped expertly from the dealer's well-manicured hand. Even at this early hour, the gambler was dressed to suit the finest Eastern theater in a dark frock coat, narrow trousers, frilled shirt with a hand-knotted tie wound about its stiff collar and a fancy embroidered single-breasted five-button vest. Jewels winked on his fingers to distract the player from the origin of the card and from the tiny needle set in one of the rings used to mark fresh decks during play. Excitement over a hand of twenty dimmed to despair when the dealer turned up a face card to pair with the queen and ace showing.

"Seems luck is running against you, Herb," Henry Knight sympathized with a sad shake of his golden head. He fished into his coat to produce a brass check which he handed to the loser. "Here. This is good for your drinks through the evening. Wouldn't want a poor run of luck to ruin your relaxation."

The big loser accepted the token with a murmur of thanks and watched the professional dealer rake in the benefit of the past week's toil. His expression was morose. It would take some mighty fancy explaining as to why there was no supply money but that lie would come easier after a bottle of Nightingale's best. He pushed back from the table and slouched up to the bar to begin collecting off Knight's charity.

The marshal reached down to pick up one of the discarded deck. His expression remained immobile as his thumb ran along the sides and back of the cards. He was aware of Knight's black stare upon him. He gave the card a toss. As the dealer reached to retrieve it, he caught the man's arm. The gambler flashed a quick look up at his boss then sat rigid in his chair as the marshal exposed the small pocket cut into his coat sleeve at its seam. It was empty, the face card it had held now laying on the table to complete the winning hand. He shook out his arm and rearranged the folds of his jacket the moment he was released.

Knight watched and waited. Instead of confronting him with the obvious trickery, Sam Wade moved to the next table and felt beneath it. His roving fingers snagged the bag clip used to hold cards until play warranted their use. Slate-colored eyes lifted to the ornate ceiling, locating several well-placed holes drilled through the wood to spy upon the hands of the unknowing. In a few short minutes, he had discovered not all, but enough of Henry Knight's secrets. Now it remained what he would do with the knowledge.

"Are you against a little free enterprise, Marshal?" the saloonkeeper asked smoothly.

Sam shrugged. "I figure every man who isn't a professional gambler is bound to get up a loser. It's not my job to educate the ignorant."

It was too soon to relax. Wade was holding something back and Knight waited to hear his terms.

"A sweet little piece of business. When I come to collect your licensing fee every month, if there should be a little something extra, say a percentage of the tables and from the dust you let fall on the carpet when you weigh out the gold on your scales, I'd be obliged to let it continue. Don't see no reason why we both can't profit from the overhead you're skimming."

Knight offered a narrow smile. He still wasn't certain about Wade. He proved to have few scruples but he was also a smart man. And a greedy man. Old Tom had been willing to turn a blind eye for the price of drinks and favors, up until the end, at least. Wade was more of a businessman, and his business looked to take a sharp bite out of the Nightingale's business.

"You drive a hard bargain, Marshal."

"I like everything up front. Things tend to run smoother that way. Now you wouldn't want a bunch of hoorawing cowpokes to come in and blast up your pretty pictures and bust up your fancy blacklegs."

It was a lazily drawled threat but far from subtle. Things would go much better with Marshal Wade's cooperation. Knight wasn't used to being manipulated with so casual an ease. He liked making terms, not agreeing to them.

"I'll have to talk things over with my partner," he said coolly. "Marshal, Ruby Gale."

Sam turned then looked from the woman before him to one of the voluptuous oils. The one that caught his eye was of a well-endowed red-haired Venus emerging *au naturel* from a pink-tipped shell.

"I was a few years younger then," Ruby confessed with a husky laugh.

"They've been mighty kind years, ma'am," Sam replied. His appreciative gaze lingered over curves that had ripened but not shifted in the passage of time. Even clothed in subdued silk with her titian hair caught in a modest chignon, Ruby Gale fairly oozed sensuality. Her mouth was wide and infinitely kissable, her kohl-colored eyes sultry with promise. Age hadn't dampened her allure. She simmered with it when the marshal lifted her hand for a gallant kiss.

"How kind of you to say so, Marshal. I like a man who has a good eye for art."

Sam suspected she just plain liked men. She held to his hand, her fingers stroking within his palm.

"Ruby runs the parlor-house next door," Knight explained and that explained everything about their business partnership. "Wade's cutting himself in for a

47

little taste of the profits."

Ruby pursed her lips. "Nothing wrong with that, Henry. A man's got to look out for himself. Why don't you come with me, Marshal, and I'll see you're introduced properlike to the girls."

With her arms wound serpentine around one of his, Ruby led him through the door that connected both establishments. Knight watched them go, a pensive look upon his face. It would be pushing luck to dispose of one lawman so soon after another. But then, if Sam Wade proved a problem, the risk would be worth taking.

Chapter Four

Lucille Blessing's fine home was built on a slight knoll, rising just high enough to look down upon the town with a proprietary fondness. It was two stories high, crowned with a cupola. Its battens were of a warm yellow that matched the pool of sunlight gathering behind it. A carpet of green grass grew within the whitewashed picket fence surrounding the yard to keep livestock out, making it a lush oasis. Maturing lilac bushes flowered determinedly along the narrow veranda. The air was touched with their scent and cooled by the shade of several tall cottonwoods.

As the doors were opened into a dimly lit hall by an impassive Chinese woman, Sam could hear the voices of Blessing's town council murmuring within the parlor on the right. He had a glimpse of etched-glass globes set in polished brass and a tapestried runner climbing a flight of stairs up to a second floor before he was shown in with the others. Conversation ebbed as he stood, hat in hand, on the threshold of elegance.

It was like nothing he'd seen before. The room was a bastion of Eastern wealth and extravagance in the heart of a rugged frontier. Potted palms as tall as a man graced the corners with an exotic air. Their broad fronds shadowed an upright piano, grander than he'd

49

seen in any saloon. In a bowed niche of windows, a half-dozen bright yellow canaries fluttered and chirped within a large gilded cage. Elaborately carved pieces of furniture were covered with a dark crimson damask in the same shade as the heavy drapery and looked much too frail for a man to take his ease upon. It was a room designed for show, not comfort, making Sam feel misplaced and inferior in the presence of such opulence. A feeling strengthened by Lucy Blessing's cool reproving stare.

She was one fine-looking female, as tall, straight and graceful as one of her treasured cottonwoods. A man might prefer a shape rounded into more obvious contours but there was a pleasing symmetry in her sleek lines. No artificial coaxing was needed to shape her waist into tiny perfection, just the right size for the span of a man's fingers. Glossy black satin hugged to a bosom that promised no more than a handful—but what a promise. It was enough to have a man's palms itching.

For all her slender proportions, there was nothing fragile about Lucille Blessing. Her proper carriage impressed an image of supple strength, like the cottonwoods that would bend and hold firm against any harsh wind. For all the dainty femininity suggested by the flounced and fringed silhouette of her gown, her gaze had a get-to-the-point directness more suited to the male gender. That dark, shrewdly intelligent stare almost made a man forget the soft curve of her cheeks, the rosy blush of her full lips, the haughty sweep of her brows, the long white column of throat brushed by a cascade of chestnut curls. Almost. It did, however, make him have second thoughts. A good-looking woman was a rarity in the West, enough to make any man gape in appreciation and entertain foolish thoughts. The cold cut of her stare was as protective as a bristle of barbed wire, saying bluntly, look but don't think of touching. But a man couldn't help the thinking.

"Evenin'," he said to the company gathered in the grand but not gracious surroundings.

Lucy appraised him from bared head to dusty toe and addressed him with admonishing civility. "Good evening, Marshal. We would have been happy to wait should you have wished to change into more proper attire."

"That's right kind but I saw no need to inconvenience you-all." His smile was crooked, that wry bend telling her he was amused rather than chastened by her subtle censure. He drew a parcel from his coat and extended it, explaining when she stared at it incomprehensibly. "Your package from this morning. You forgot it." His grin widened, suggesting he'd been the reason for her memory lapse. She nearly snatched the envelope from him and that brusque movement confirmed it.

Chafing beneath his knowing smugness, Lucy let the package drop upon a table. Her mobile lips tightened into a disapproving line as she, again, regarded the prairie-soiled clothes he'd worn since his arrival and found another point of contention. "You can leave your armaments with Li."

"No, thank you, ma'am. I'd as soon go naked."

The image she entertained in that brief moment, of Sam Wade standing in her parlor in a state of virile undress, brought a hue to her cheeks that was only slightly less dusky than that of her drapes. She fought those transgressing thoughts with a curt rejoinder.

"I assure you, no one will give you reason to draw down on us."

His thin, unyielding mouth took a slow, upward curve as if he knew the intimate track her imaginings had taken and was arrogantly pleased. "Just the same, ma' am, I mean to keep my hardware. Being marshal makes it part of my formal dress."

Lucy's lips clamped together. She had asked politely. To restate the request would be argumentative and he'd already made his refusal clear. Not wanting to launch into a full-scale battle of wills, she conceded to the presence of his guns with a cool reluctance. In doing so, she vowed to lose no further footing.

"Shall we get started? This is Blessing's mayor, Edgar Mayhew."

Sam shook hands with the short, rotund man, his palm coming away damp. He wiped it unconsciously upon his pant leg as he nodded to the other members of the town council, surprised to note that Henry Knight was among them. All the men were dressed in their Sunday best but Knight far outshone them in his understated elegance. He looked more the part of an Eastern senator than the procurer of a thirst parlor and sporting house. Appearances could be deceiving unless one was willing to look hard and beyond the obvious. He wondered tangentially if Lucy Blessing knew what kind of man the owner of the Nightingale was. Or did she merely prefer the man's smooth veneer over his own trail-worn roughness? He felt a curl of annoyance. He could be just as slick and courtly as the dapper Mister Knight.

"It was mighty generous of you to offer your fine home up for this meeting, Miz Blessing," he began with an easy smile. Instead of responding with an answering warmth, she stiffened. He continued doggedly toward his own downfall. "Don't feel you have to entertain us. I can imagine our business must be taxing to a refined lady like yourself."

Lucy finally returned his smile. It was as sharp as the blade of a well-honed Green River knife. "I appreciate your concern, Marshal, but as head of the town council, I feel my place is here."

He blinked and she enjoyed his moment of confusion before explaining, "Wyoming is an enlightened territory. It's given women the right to vote and to hold public office, a notion I'm certain the other states will take to in time when their female population grows tired of playing hostess and being dismissed whenever something serious needs be discussed."

"My apologies, ma'am," he murmured with appropriate contrition. She found that faint humility was sweetly potent. When she'd savored her gloating, Lucy returned to the purpose of the evening.

"I believe you have some papers for us, Mister Wade."

Mister not marshal, he noted, realizing she'd intentionally stripped him of his title until she and her council could officially bestow it. A little game of power. He gave a wry smile and produced the letter from Grant Tolliver. Lucy read it over, glancing from the glowing reference to the man before her, trying to juxtapose the two. Then, scowling slightly, she passed the missive to the mayor.

"Everything seems in order here," Edgar Mayhew pronounced. "Pay's one hundred dollars a month and four bits for every unlicensed dog shot within city limits. You'll be expected to collect town taxes and license fees, serve subpoenas, keep the local lockup, records of arrest and prisoner's property, give evidence at trials, supervise elections, keep hogs out of the streets and serve as health, fire and sanitation inspector."

"As you can see," Lucy inserted silkily, "we expect more than just a fast gun."

"Yes, ma'am. And I aim to see you get exactly what

53

you deserve."

While she mulled over the subtle innuendo of his words, Mayhew continued.

"You've the right to appoint two deputies. Pay's twenty-five dollars a month apiece or thirty-five dollars if you think you can handle the job with one."

"One will do."

Lucy chose that moment to speak up. "I think you'd better advise the council of your choice, Marshal Wade."

"Newt Redman."

"Newt — ?" the mayor sputtered.

Henry Knight gave a muted chuckle.

Her tone laced with contempt, Lucy said, "Surely you must realize how totally unsuited he is for the position."

Sam regarded her with an indolent gaze. "The boy's smart, eager and strong and from what I can tell, he's been running the office. And I believe the choice is mine. But, if you object, ma'am, feel free to tell him he's fired." Then he waited and watched the plays of frustration upon her lovely face.

When she had nothing more to say, the council seemed willing to accept his rather unconventional appointment of deputy and the swearing in commenced, making Sam Wade the official marshal of Blessing, Wyoming Territory.

After the ceremony was finished, Lucy's Chinese manservant issued in a tray of coffee and dainty little tea cakes frosted in pale pastels. Lucy stood to the side, watching the new marshal ingratiate himself to the other councilmen. Apparently, they didn't mind the insult of him appearing in filthy trail clothes, crudely sporting a shooting iron on either hip as if he was expecting a brawl to break out at any minute in her stately parlor. Apparently, they had no objection

54

to his rudeness, to his lazy mocking ease, to the outrageous appointment of Newt Redman as the town's deputy.

But she did.

She objected to everything about Sam Wade, especially the way he cozied up to Henry Knight. If the new lawman wasn't already in the saloonkeeper's pocket, he was safely in his palm. And that meant no justice in the town of Blessing. After all her fighting and finagling, nothing would change. Knight would go on running his crooked games. The hooded henchmen would continue to terrorize the innocent, she suspected, at his beck and call. And no one would be safe to conduct their businesses or walk the streets while their marshal languished in the saloon, turning a whiskey-glazed blind eye to all but what Henry Knight wanted him to see.

Feeling an emotional dampness well in her eyes, she turned away from the company on the pretext of checking something in the kitchen. As Chu's domain was always beyond reproach, there was no reason to linger there. Instead of going back into the parlor, which now rang with the husky murmur of man-talk and probably stank from liquor fumes after Mayor Mayhew doctored the innocent cups of coffee in her absence, she stepped silently out onto her veranda to drink in her favorite sight below.

The fate of Blessing meant everything to Lucy. In lieu of children, she cosseted and fawned over the growing town that spread below. Scant years ago, there were no welcoming home lights winking amid darkness, only unclaimed prairie lands. There had been no broad main street, no booming businesses. She and her husband had nurtured them from a crude tent row to territorial prominence. Oliver had negotiated for a Union Pacific spur, bringing with it the wealth of the coal mines and range lands which depended upon the railroad. He courted the pillars of a fledgling community, advertising in the East for professionals to stock his town; for a competent doctor, for a schoolteacher to service the growth of young people, for an editor to supply the trappings of civilization, for the craftsmen needed to hew a town out of a raw prairie. A fine hotel sprang up where guests had once paid five dollars a week to sleep on a blanket upon the floor. He lured a qualified blacksmith and livery tender by providing them with the land on which to build free of charge. Jeremiah Davis had come to establish his general store, offering bottled liquor, sugar, salt, molasses and meat along with gunpowder and ammunition, crockery and coal oil, all the necessities for subsistence. There was a continual chorus of building, dinning, deafening on all sides. A few pleasant whitewashed warehouses and residences began to spring up next to unpainted shanties. Eager settlers dwelt under heaven's canopy or in snowy tents while busy workmen plied ax, hammer and saw. Their first town paper was published on a hand press set up beneath a tree.

The initial efforts were ugly: old board, packing boxes and building paper the basic construction materials with flattened tin cans for roofing. Slowly, a sense of permanence began to develop and those early shelters were replaced by more substantial walls. Cottonwoods and evergreens were transplanted — Lucy had overseen each one and nursed them like sickly babes — but not enough survived at first to shade the sagebrush, greasewood and prickly pear.

She had watched the trees and the town grow while at her husband's side. She shared his pride, his sense of accomplishment as the town of Blessing achieved a touch of elegance with its brave false-fronted structures springing up along the broad streets he'd laid out. The batten boards held up massive cornices and housed phony windows, an impressive billboard from which the proprietor could blazon his business title and advertise his wares. The effect was substantial and imposing, the look of a prosperous community backed by slabs of sod. Oliver used the bank to foster those emerging businesses, treating each like a new branch of the family. She remembered his paternal joy with each new arrival: butcher, bootmaker, barber, gunsmith. But with the establishment of every decent, solid business aimed toward prosperity and growth, came another kind of enterprise that grew with the virulence of a prairie plague: the saloons.

Professional gamblers, prostitutes and desperadoes swelled the census figures and there seemed to be no stopping them. They brought with them the symptoms of the disease: noise, violence, sin and shootings. Henry Knight was one of the original pioneers, he and his partner Eliot Gale, bringing their fine, hand-carved bar and string of fancy girls. He didn't start out the way the others did, with a hastily thrown-up building in which the cuspidors were the only shiny object. His place was never a dirty, smelling blend of tobacco, liquor, straw, horse, kerosene and the sizzle of tobacco juice on a hot stove in winter. He came with a grand vision and the Nightingale rose, a splendid structure, rivaling the bank as a mainstay of the community. And Henry Knight, with his golden looks and affable smile, became one of Blessing's leading citizens. Oliver had liked him but Lucy felt from the first that something unpleasant crawled beneath his amiable façade.

Her husband knew business like no other; however, he was blind when it came to human nature. He never saw Knight's corrupting influence as he sat upon the council board, lobbying for his own interests. He never knew the smiling Henry Knight was a dangerous competitor for the control of the town. Nor did he heed Lucy's warnings to be careful, dismissing them right up to the day he died.

The night had grown chill, or was it the cold turn memory had taken? Lucy shivered and almost immediately was draped in warmth. She grasped the edges of the shawl as it settled about her shoulders then stood rigid as a more substantial weight rested there as well. Later, she would wonder why she hadn't struck off his hands at that first improper touch but for the moment she was too startled, too mesmerized by sensations of heat and strength as his long fingers lightly kneaded tense muscle.

"I wanted to thank you for your hospitality. I'll be saying good night now."

She hadn't been aware that he stood so close. When his words whispered low and soft next to her ear, so close she could feel the warmth of his breath, she experienced a jolt of surprise. And something else. Something so subtle, so unexpected, so unseemly that it rooted her to the porch boards when she should have stepped irately away. She could almost feel his lips brushing past her soft curls as he straightened. The chill was gone. If anything, she was too uncomfortably hot. The evening had grown sultry in an instant, with a damp, enveloping heat. The contrast woke gooseflesh along her arms and a resistant pucker to the tips of her small breasts. As if drawn by that reflexive tightening, his big hands slipped from the caps of her shoulders, dipping down until his fingertips reached the tempting foothills of her satin-covered bosom. Then, before she had ample time to summon reaction or response, his hands were gone.

Hugging the lacy shawl about her in an insulating

cocoon, Lucy watched the marshal saunter toward the lights of Blessing. Her wide eyes followed the taut shift of denim, the sensuous roll of the six-shooters resting on either side of his lean hips. That daze of trancelike fascination lasted until darkness surrounded the figure of Sam Wade. Then came the horror of what she'd let happen. She'd allowed him to freely fondle her person while she stood paralyzed like some green young virgin. Her lack of resistance implied consent. Furiously, she pulled the shawl tight but that only served to intensify her awareness of the tingling warmth swelling within her breasts. As angry as she was at the marshal for his crude liberties, she felt a greater rage directed inward. Because she had liked the feel of his strong hands. Because, while she stood unresisting, she'd been wishing they'd move lower. Her husband had been in the ground for six months. Only the week before had she discarded her weeds of mourning and already she'd suffered a stirring of desire for another man. Disgusted by her weakness and horrified by its cause, she returned to play hostess in the parlor, trying to forget the way her body had come alive for one brief moment at the coaxing of Sam Wade's caress.

She almost succeeded. It was easy to lose herself in talk of the town. However, when the last of her guests filed out and silence filled her fine house, she had nothing to distract her thoughts from what had transpired on her porch. Determinedly, she picked up the package the marshal delivered and carried it with her upstairs. She would submerge herself in the latest styles while preparing for bed. That almost succeeded. Until, as she was leafing through the Paris fashion plates, she came across a page with the corner bent down. The engraving was of a fine white linen sleep dress. Embellishments of lace made it softly feminine. Insets of lace made it blatantly provocative, for there was nothing save a web of peek-a-boo Brussels point from shoulder to waist. A gown fashioned for seduction, a gown someone would see draped upon her willowy form.

Sam Wade.

At once, she was infuriated by the violation of her privacy and, contrarily, excited by a perverse thrill. She looked at the etching, imaging hungry slate-colored eyes devouring the sight of her thusly garbed. So, the marshal would see her clad in wisps of lace. Well, she would see him in hell first. She flipped the catalog shut and flung it to the far corner of her bedchamber where it lay in disgrace while she pulled on her own demure linen bed gown. Climbing up into her big bed, she jerked up the covers and lay rigid upon the solitary sheets. She closed her eyes, trying to empty her mind of all but sleep but restless images kept intruding upon her peace. Finally, with a wrapper tied about her slender figure, she trod quietly below to pour herself a glass of Oliver's favorite brandy. Glass in hand, she moved once more out onto the cool of the porch to gaze down upon Blessing. This time, unconsciously, her gaze beheld not an overview but focused upon one distant point. The jailhouse.

What made him, of all men, different? She despised him, both for his arrogant personality and his loathsome profession. Yet there was something about him that called to a hidden recess of her soul. In the months since Oliver's death, she'd felt comfortably embraced by his memory within the rooms of the home they'd built and shared together. Those fond recollections had kept the grief at bay and made it possible for her to go on, applying her energies at the bank, busying her thoughts with the problems of the town. But on this night, something had changed.

There was no solace in the silence of her house. It felt empty, hollow. For the first time, she felt the desolation of being alone. Sam Wade's touch had kindled that knowledge and she found she resented him for it. There had been a safe serenity in the detached business of her days, a calming reverie in the reminiscing nights. That muffling dream had shattered, forcing her to face the intense reality of life without Oliver Blessing. And the loneliness was an insurmountable ache.

It was time to think of herself and leave the ghosts behind. That was what the evening told her. It wasn't Sam Wade. He was just the catalyst that brought her back from limbo. It wasn't the scruffy gunman, it was the future calling her from the deadened past. Marshal Wade had quickened her emotions, triggering sensations that flooded back into her being, restoring her, reviving her. Perhaps she did owe him something but certainly not the reward he sought. He'd made her feel like a woman after long existence in the shadow of a domineering man. It was independence she savored now, not submission to yet another controlling male. She refused to let Sam Wade have his way with her imagination. Nor would he have his way with anything else. She would weather his disturbance as if he was an unpredictable summer storm. The turmoil would blow over in a matter of time. She had only to wait and to hold tight to her resolve.

She found herself rubbing her shoulders, not to instill warmth but to recreate the tempting friction of Sam Wade's caress. She forced her hands to fall to her sides and purposefully returned to the house. With the door bolted and lights extinguished, she went up to bed, determined to shut him from her mind. And almost succeeded. Until her dreams began.

* * *

61

Sam Zachary tipped back in his office chair and savored the remainder of his predecessor's best whiskey. The badge pinned to his vest glimmered in the light from his oil lamp. What a sweet situation. Blessing's bounty was at his feet. And it was ripe for the picking. A town fat with prospects: taxes to be collected, fines to be levied, licenses to update. It wouldn't take long to amass a respectable sum. The slick saloonkeeper wasn't the only one who knew how to fleece a pocket while its wearer stood thanking him. He toasted his own cleverness. Who'd suspect the man sworn to protect? The man whose reputation was backed by the recommendation of Grant Tolliver.

His humor faltered then, becoming something not nearly as pleasant. He'd waited long for evens against Tolliver. Only the knowledge of those who depended upon him kept him from exacting a violent settling years ago. He'd had to fight for control, for patience, weighing those who remained against those he'd already buried. He couldn't bring back the dead so he had to put the needs of the living foremost. But he'd never stopped seeking that means of retribution. He'd never forgotten Tolliver. And now he realized that a quick killing was no fit vengeance. That would be a swift, merciful end. He wanted Tolliver to hurt and nothing wounded deeper than a cut to a prideful man's honor. Discredit and disgrace would mete a more satisfying justice: lingering, irrevocable shame. What a delicious revenge upon that infallible individual. He'd sown the seeds of his success carefully, courting Henry Knight's trust, choosing a deputy who'd be no threat. Only one barrier remained, one he looked forward to breaching.

Boot heels coming to rest on the edge of his desk, Sam lifted a toast to the town's other bountiful Blessing. He'd felt victory as she trembled beneath his touch. A victory that would be almost as satisfying as claiming the money in her vault. He wondered which she would guard more zealously. Either way, he meant to enjoy the challenge.

Chapter Five

He dreamed of Lucy Blessing's kisses. Even at the edge of slumber, he could feel her lips move wetly upon his face, her tongue touch impatiently upon his mouth. He reached out to catch hold of that tantalizing fancy, caressing, stroking the softness of her . . . fur?

Sam's eyes flashed open to the sight of a large black nose with dark, flaring nostrils. A snuffling of air blew upon him. Then that great pink tongue lolled out to plant another soggy bussing on his cheek. What the . . . He surged up into a sitting position, hands diving instinctively for his gun.

"Don't shoot him, Marshal. He don't mean no harm, less you fear a good washing will kill you."

Newt grabbed a handful of slack skin and hauled the big yellow hound backward by the scruff of his neck. It was the largest, ugliest animal Sam had ever seen but he could see he was in no danger. The beast sat on his scrawny haunches, grinning at him. He rubbed the back of his hand over his mouth, thinking he'd much prefer kisses from the prickly woman in his dream than the affectionate hound.

"Boy, whatcha doing with that homely bag of hide and bones?"

"Cornelius'll grow on you, Marshal. He just started follering me one day and we sorta stuck. He's smart, too. I taught him to do all kinda tricks."

"Cornelius?" He cocked one brow. An elegant name for such a poor excuse for dog-kind.

"Miz Lucille named him. She said he reminded her of one of her husband's friends. Some bigwig with the railroad."

Bringing Lucy to mind reminded him of his dream, stirring up an odd restlessness. He was disinclined to welcome Cornelius with more than a surly scowl. "Do you make good coffee, Newt?"

"Yes, sir."

"Start it brewing."

While the boy set to boiling water, Sam pulled on his boots and hitched his lean frame from the bed. An insistent itch beneath his ribs provoked the notion of how long it had been since his clothes had stood a wash. He glared at the grinning dog as he reached to scratch another spot, wondering if they'd shared more than a kiss this morning. Stepping around the lanky hound, he went to drop into his desk chair. When he saw Newt's canted glance slide unhappily to the empty bottle whose contents had inspired such lusty dreams about Miz Lucille, he deposited it with a stir of guilt in the bottom drawer. A gleam of tin caught his eye and he reached for it as a chance to make amends.

"Here you go, Newt. All official."

The boy looked at the badge Sam slapped down on the desk top, his eyes all round and glassy. Then he reached for it with a hesitant hand, as if he feared it would be withdrawn. In fact, until this moment, he hadn't been sure. He'd mentioned his new job to no one but Lucy. If the new marshal had meant the offer as a jest, only she would not deride him mercilessly for being gullible. He weighed the meaningful scrap of metal in his palm. It felt much heavier than its actual ounces. That was the weight of responsibility that came in tandem.

"How'd things go at the council meeting, Marshal?" he asked as he caressed the embossed lettering with his thumb.

"All sworn and sealed."

"How 'bout me?"

"Raise your right hand. Do you solemnly swear to uphold the laws of the Territory of Wyoming to the best of your ability?" At the whisper of "I do," Sam concluded, "There you go. Pin it on." Fearing the boy would draw blood with his shaking hands, Sam took the badge from him and affixed it to his shirt. He gave it a pat then his jovial humor fled when Newt's damp eyes rose in an expression of gratitude. He found he couldn't face that look of naked emotion. That surprised him. He'd thought himself hardened beyond the reach of conscience. To shake himself from it, he muttered, "For your first official duty, fetch me some of that coffee."

"Right away, Marshal."

Somehow, Newt's eager exuberance made the knot within his chest twist tighter.

The coffee was good, strong, dark, just what he needed to clear the fluff of sentimentality from his mind. "You just keep a pot of this handy every morning and you won't have any trouble keeping your job."

"What's my job going to be?"

"Well, now, just what you've been doing, I reckon." When he saw the youthful face begin to fall, he added, "I'm going to need a man I can trust here in the office. Any darned fool can strap a gun to his hip but it takes a certain kind of man to tangle with paperwork." Newt nodded but looked no happier. "And then there's evening rounds." The boy's features brightened and he felt absurdly pleased. "Just jiggling doorknobs and the like, you understand, but the folks like to know they got a lawman on hand."

Newt liked the sound of that, the townspeople looking to him for protection. Then that image caught a snag. His shoulders slumped.

"Not enough work for you, boy?"

"Not that, Marshal. It's just that I don't . . . I don't own no gun."

Sam stood and clasped his hand down on one dejected shoulder. "Well, that's easy enough to remedy."

The town's gunsmith had a sighting alley out behind his shop where a man could test-fire his weapon before its purchase. Newt handled the sawed-off American Arms 12-gauge shotgun like a new father handed his firstborn. Nervously.

"Newt," Sam began easily. "What you're carrying there is the most useful argument in any crisis." When he saw the boy's gaze slide hopefully to his cross-draw rig, he waved off his disappointment. "You're no gunslick, Newt, and these here folks are going to know that. You strap a brace of shooting irons around your waist and there's going to be somebody who wants to see how fast you can pull them. Speed is fine but accuracy is final. You just remember this, there's always burying with buckshot. Now you just settle the butt nice and cozy into your shoulder and squeeze off a shot real gentle like."

The first blast sent up a puff of dirt and Newt reeling backward. When he'd regained his balance, he frowned down at the target circle which remained untouched.

"Don't you go getting discouraged, boy. You got to practice. You want to be good at something, you work at it. And when you know you're good, folks can sense you're confident. Right now you'd more than likely shoot off your own foot than somebody sneaking out of a back window with a money bag."

Newt pouted his lips and squinted down at the circle. "I don't see how anybody can be expected to hit that."

Almost before the words left his mouth, he was aware of a blur of motion at his side. Both Colts cleared leather faster than he could comprehend the move. Ten shots rang out, alternating five from each gun, coming so close together it seemed like one loud roar.

Lucy paid no mind to the occasional shooting at the range, though the hour was considerably younger than she'd expect to hear it. She was used to the sound of intermittent shots and continued her walk toward the bank. But when that rapid-fire staccato echoed in the morning air, she was drawn by a curious expectation to the alley overlooking the range. She came up short at the sight of Sam Wade calmly ejecting shells and reloading all but the last chamber. Beside him, Newt Redman stood gawking and pop-eyed. She followed his stare to the small target circle and counted out ten deadly holes, all close enough to be touching. With a nerveless shiver, she withdrew but nothing could shake the image of that tidy pattern from her mind. His marksmanship hadn't impressed her as it had Newt. It terrified her.

As the two men emerged onto the covered sidewalk, Newt cradling his new shotgun like a swaddled child, they found a pretty young girl waiting. She was a tiny blonde with huge doe eyes and a dimpling smile. Sam guessed she hadn't been long out of short skirts.

"Marshal Wade, I'm Nell Mayhew." Her voice was light and breathy, like the shiver of wind through cottonwoods. "My paw wanted me to personally give you an invite to the barn raising out at the Thompsons' this afternoon. It'll be a fine affair with dancing after. I hope I can tell him you'll be there. It'll be a fine opportunity for you to meet the rest of the townsfolk."

With a tip of his gray Stetson, Sam offered a dazzling smile. "Why, Miss Nell, however could I say no to such a charming invitation?"

She colored prettily, an effect he was sure she'd practiced to perfection. "I'll be counting on you for a dance." With that breezy vow, she whirled in a rustle of taffeta and hurried down the walk.

He found Newt scowling. "What's eating you?"

"I ain't much for dancing," he growled. He also had noticed that neither the invitation nor Miss Nell Mayhew's attention had included him.

"I don't expect you to be dancing. I'll be doing the socializing. I expect you to be doing the enforcing. Things can get out of hand blamed easy at these doings. Think you can handle that critter well enough to see to the peace?"

Newt beamed. "You bet, Marshal."

"Then let's get breakfast."

The Thompsons had a modest spread just south of Blessing. Their crops and herd of sinewy beef had increased steadily, calling for the presence of a new barn to replace a scattering of dilapidated sheds. The yard was filled with every kind of conveyance, from saddle horse, to buggy to freight wagon. Several hundred people from the streets of Blessings and its outlying acres swarmed the property. Children chased and laughed with barking dogs on their heels. Beneath a stand of scraggly cottonwoods, the women gathered to prepare lunch while the men wielded broad axes, saws, draw knives, mauls and hammers around the area roped off for the barn. Thompson had the timber shipped in by rail and the lumber was rapidly pieced and fitted into the network of grooves and pegs that would form the building's framework.

From under the scant shade of the trees, Lucy was spreading a cloth over makeshift tables when her gaze happened on Sam Wade. He was working like the others with shirt stripped off in the heat. The sleeves of his long underwear were shoved up over powerful forearms. They glistened and bulged with each swing of his ax. The front was unbuttoned nearly to the navel with only his bandanna to cover the slick contours of his chest. Even as he toiled, his fancy six-guns hung at ready. She stared longer than she should have, long enough to have several of the ladies smirking and murmuring betwixt themselves. Had she heard them, she would have put a quick end to their nonsense. Having her name linked with the likes of the trigger-fast marshal would have shamed her to the quick.

Once all the ropes, pulleys and braces were in place, the barn's skeleton formed in a matter of minutes. The preassembled sides were hoisted into place and quickly secured. Then crosspieces were hammered to give strength and support and the rib cage of rafters spanned end to end. With the shell in place, hungry men lined up to have their meal dished up to them. It was hearty fare befitting hard labor: boiled potatoes, pickled pork, roasted game, baking powder biscuits, fresh bread and hot pie. Lucy was turning out wedges of sweet potato pie, her smiled fixed, her móvements efficient. Until she heard the drawl of his voice.

"Howdy, Miz Blessing. Who's minding the bank?"

Her gaze darted up. The wedge of pie slid from her server and would have fallen to disaster had he not been quick to get his plate under it. She flushed in annoyance at her clumsiness and at the fluttering of nerves brought on by his proximity. "And who's minding the lawless, Marshal?"

He laughed. It was a husky sound, soft, beckoning, like creek water gurgling over a rough rock bed. Soothing and at the same time inciting. Disturbing, like the man. She crossed her arms over her breasts in an unintentional posture of defense, to repel the memory of his touch. The movement only drew his attention to that which she would deny him. And he grinned at her confusion.

"If you're meaning to stay until later, I'd be obliged if you would honor me with a dance."

A dance. Lucy nearly shriveled away in dread. How could she bear the feel of his arms holding her close when she failed to compose herself against a memory? He might well have asked her to strip naked and roll with him upon the Thompsons' lawn.

"I think not, Marshal," she replied tartly, voice pitched cool to cover her distress. "I don't believe yesterday's clothing could coax me close enough to share a waltz."

One end of his smile fell, leaving a lopsided curve that was more grimace than grin. His eyes narrowed, registering the insult more cruelly than she'd intended. His drawled response was thickly laced with sarcasm. "Since these are the only duds I own and there's not sufficient time to have them laundered, you may consider yourself safe from my advances for this evening. It's not my want to offend your delicate sensibilities. Good day, ma'am."

She watched, aghast, as he strode away and was about to hurry after him to beg his pardon—after all, her embarrassment was no call to cut him with her rudeness. Then she saw his destination and her purpose hardened. He sauntered over to where Henry Knight sat perched on the rear gate of a wagon and joined him there. Turning back to the man who held his plate out to her, Lucy smiled thinly and levered beneath another slice of pie.

"A fine blood you have there," Knight commented, nodding toward Sam's bay stallion. "Bet he can run."

Henry Knight was an intriguing man. He'd managed to put in a good morning's work without losing the crispness of his white shirt. Nothing there to offend the particular Mrs. Blessing, Sam begrudged as he followed the man's gaze toward his horse. His mood lifted a notch.

"Fastest in the Border States" was his casual remark. It had saved Sam's hide more than once with its powerful, ground-eating strides. While the man might go without, the horse was always treated to the best. "Good enough" shoes tacked on cold from out of the barrel were never adequate. Even in his biggest hurry, Sam took the time to have a proper shoe fitted, not out of new iron but out of the well-worked and longer-lasting "old stuff" forged from used shoes. He chose a blacksmith and livery with more care than he selected his own eateries and lodgings. He could make do but a good, strong horse was worth the fuss. Even now, while he wore his worn, single set of clothes, the bay was sporting a smart new saddle: a Cheyenne roll rig, designed with a long leather flange over the rear of the cantle board for extra stability. No sir, he never scrimped on horsewear or hardware, not when his life depended on the both of them.

"Mind if I take a look?" Knight asked as he set aside his empty plate.

After forking in the last bite of pie, Sam ambled over to the string of horseflesh. The bay gave a welcoming nicker and he murmured affectionately to the big animal as Knight ran an expert hand over withers and hocks.

72

"Damned fine," he pronounced.

"Know your horseflesh, do you?"

Knight grinned. "Almost as well as I know my women. That's my mount over there."

Sam surveyed the leggy sorrel with appreciative interest. Its deep chest spoke of good wind but it was Knight's choice of tack that caused his gaze to linger. The animal's bridle, like the expensively stitched saddle, was of glossy black leather and shiny silver conchos. Wedged into the horse's mouth was a Spanish bit. Unless a man was riding a pack mule, Sam considered anything more severe than a modified curb bit too harsh on the tender flesh. The Spanish style was a twist of torture left over from the Inquisition days, to his thinking. And he reassessed what he'd said about Knight knowing horseflesh. No man who claimed knowledge of horses would need cruelty to control his mount.

"You a wagering man, Marshal?"

"Only when there's a fair chance of me winning." Which left out games of "chance" at the Nightingale.

"I'd like to see this here stud matched up against mine. I've got quite a reputation from here to Laramie."

"That right." Knight was nothing if not subtle. He was hinting at more than a contest between horseflesh. It was a challenge for the respect and control of the people of Blessing.

"What say we treat the folks to a friendly little race? I'll let you name the bet." That proved to him right there that the wager wasn't the important end of winning.

Sam appeared thoughtful for a moment then his gaze shifted to the table where Lucy Blessing was still dishing up pie. Slowly, one side of his mouth lifted. "You've got yourself a race and I know just what the

73

stakes'll be."

Life in a frontier town was harsh and mostly devoid of amusements beyond the lure of the saloon. When a chance for socializing and entertainments arose, folk flocked from miles around to partake and enjoy the distraction. With all the serious work done on the barn; it being weatherproofed with a roof—the men were ready for some serious fun. The prospect of the race was greeted with more excitement than the dance to come and gentlemen crowded to get down bets held by the Honorable Mayor Mayhew. With currency in short supply, wagers were covered with anything from pocket watches to pigs, while the womenfolk stood ignored and irritated. Knowing they had the dance to look forward to made them more tolerant of the proceedings, and, secretly, most of them were anxious to see the match-up between the town's two most eligible bachelors. Some even indulged in their own circumspect wagers, the odds slightly favoring the sinewy marshal over the smooth saloonkeeper.

The course was charted out and the riders readied. Using his old '51 Navy revolver, Mayor Mayhew stood between the restless horses and sent up the shot that had both animals surging forward. There was an immediate race for saddle horse and buggy by spectators too impatient to wait for the outcome at the finish marked out between Mrs. Thompson's vegetable garden and her wash line. The dust set up by the two galloping horses was rapidly compounded by the crush of vehicles all jockeying for position on the road to Blessing.

Standing with the women who were trying their best to look disapproving rather than excited, Lucy cast a surreptitious look down the road. She justified the degree of interest by telling herself it wasn't as much her desire to see the marshal win as it was her want to see the pompous Henry Knight lose. Two more swell-headed, overproud, immodest, vainglorious ne'er-do-wells she could not image. And here their prideful competition was picking the pockets of the poor just to feed their arrogance. She couldn't bear the thought of the posturing and boastfulness to come regardless of the winner. Men and their games to earn consequence. No better than children and a frightfully sad example. Yet, when the first shout rang out that riders were coming, she did her share of pushing to guarantee a clear view of the finish.

It was neck and neck. The horses were too similar in color and the riders too gray with dust to tell them apart at any distance. Lucy strained forward, realizing she risked an ungainly topple should someone bump her cumbersome bustle with her balance so overextended. But it was a risk worth taking for a glimpse of lathered horseflesh and the rush of suspense. One of the laboring mounts began to pull ahead, its rider's hand rising and falling just once while the other man flailed away mercilessly with his crop. She nearly cried out his name as she recognized the shape of Sam Wade's Stetson but forced herself to remain silent as others around her took up the call. And when the marshal flashed across the finish line two full lengths ahead, she denied the swelling satisfaction and refused to allow herself the luxury of a smile. She eased out of the crowd that surged forward to surround the winner, unaware that the victor's gaze swung about until finding her retreating figure. She missed seeing his wry smile.

Sam slid down off his blown stallion to accept the congratulatory slaps on the back and vigorous hand pumping. The clump of well-wishers parted to let the loser through. Henry Knight offered his hand and a smile of no hard feelings. There was little else he could do and retain his congenial reputation. His smile was as bright as a newly minted silver dollar but his eyes were flat black and cold as he gauged the marshal's mounting popularity.

"Now to collect part of my bet," Sam announced. He strode to Knight's winded sorrel and unbuckled the bridle, easing the harsh piece of steel out of a mouth sawed raw. His own lips thinned at the evidence of blood in the froth around the horse's muzzle. Angrily, he tossed it to the saloonkeeper. "Get rid of this lessen you want to wear it."

Knight caught the costly headgear, maintaining his tolerant smile. Inside, he was seething under the humiliation of the moment.

"Shall we go get the rest of my winnings?"

The moment might belong to Sam Wade but the owner of the Nightingale made a silent vow to see he was never bested again in public.

It was one thing to ignore a man and quite another for him not to be on hand to appreciate it. Though her intent was to snub Sam Wade, when he didn't reappear after the race, Lucy began to subconsciously watch for him. Noting Henry Knight's absence, she concluded with a touch of annoyance that they were most likely at the Nightingale, having found the fare too tame among decent folk. The bawdy girls not allowed to mingle with the proper females of Blessing were probably more to their inclination. Good riddance, she thought as she kept an eye on the road from town.

With dusk settling, the trappings of toil were put aside in favor of a well-earned celebration. Men and women took turns changing into their presentables in the Thompsons' sod house. The barn would be christened in proper frontier fashion, with music and dancing. The dirt floor was wet to keep the dust

76

down. Bales and barrels lined the perimeter to provide a spot to rest weary feet and lanterns were pegged above. A refreshment table was spread with punch and cake and during the course of the evening, the former was certain to take on an alcoholic nature, though none would admit the deed. There was much laughter as neighbors who'd had no opportunity to seek each other out enjoyed one another's company: the men to talk crops, politics and horseflesh and the women, babies, fashions from the latest catalogs and the lack of a proper church. The children ran circles around the tall windmill, worried the livestock and finally fell into exhausted slumber in the back of their family's wagons.

Then, as darkness fell and the cool of the evening sifted in through the open framework of the barn, couples began to form and turn to the sound of a pair of fiddles and a squeeze box. Every female from eight to eighty had a full card for the night, as men far outnumbered the ladies of Blessing. Most looked overwhelmingly lovely, having shaken out their wedding dresses as the only gowns fit for a festive occasion, as they were passed from gent to gent to the strains of "Little Brown Jug," "Buffalo Girls," "Old Dan Tucker" and the sentimental tunes reminiscent of the war between the states.

Lucy stood behind the refreshment table ladling up punch but there was a world of difference between her and the other ladies who served. They were the old and gouty and she by far the most lovely woman in the room. She wore a plain white apron pinned like her housemaid's over the front of her stylish gown and served up each cup with a smile while her foot tapped unseen to the beat of the music. Had she come from behind the table, she would have been besieged by requests for a turn about the floor but the townspeople respected her wistful gloom and want for exclusion even though she'd officially put aside the vestiges of mourning. Each one of them owed too much to Oliver Blessing and now his wife to wish her uncomfortable when among them. And so they made merry and left her to her solitary choice, thinking she preferred it that way.

It was not at all what Lucy preferred. The music was enticing, beckoning to her like an old beau she'd set aside. The tempo flowed through her in a bittersweet caress, hinting at joys long repressed. Once, she'd loved to dance, to sing, to celebrate in abandon. Until those delights grew tainted and defiled by circumstance. Now, she thought it easier to deny herself than to suffer the loss of innocent pleasures. However, that did not stop her from following the twirling couples with a light of longing in her eyes.

"Can't enjoy yourself from back there with all the old biddies."

Lucy slid Henry Knight a disparaging glance and a cool, "I'm fine, thank you."

The owner of the Nightingale leaned upon the table, blocking the way to the punch bowl. He made certain Lucy couldn't ignore him in favor of any other. Flashing his most charming, female-melting smile, he crooned, "Just consider the pleasure you'd bring to all us lonely males, deprived of your fair company."

"Mister Knight, I am not here to provide the entertainment."

"Now that, Miz Blessing, has not always been the case."

While she stared at him, speechless, a dull flush of fury and shame seeping upward to stain her cheeks, he continued in that same smooth tone. How could he not know the torment his words caused her? But then, of course he did, which was exactly why he spoke them. Thinking he'd taken some of the starch from her manner with that humbling reminder, he grew more bold.

"Now then, Lucille, what possible reason can you have for not wanting to dance this waltz with me?"

"She's already promised it to me."

Chapter Six

Lucy never expected to look upon Sam Wade as salvation, yet the intrusion of his voice made her feel faint with relief. Henry Knight looked upon it as something else altogether. His black-eyed glare swiveled to the marshal and for a moment he made no effort to conceal the equal blackness of his mood. Then, the smile bloomed like some pleasant desert flower atop a nettled cactus.

"It would seem I'm forever in your shadow today, Marshal Wade. I must admit, I regret the loss of this occasion every bit as much as the other." He inclined his golden head toward Lucy. "Another time, Miz Blessing." The purr of his words held more threat than hope and an equal thread of promise as he nodded to Sam. "Marshal."

As Lucy watched the tall man stride away, her relief was tempered with reluctance; something about making an incautious leap from the skillet into the flames. She would have stepped out with the Devil himself to escape that dreadful moment with the silky, sinister Mister Knight. That he would dare throw the ugliness of the past into her face left her shaken and vulnerable to another's soft suggestion.

"I believe this is our dance, Miz Lucy."

Her fingers trembled slightly as they unpinned her serving apron. She was committed by her own words. How bad could one short dance be? And then she looked up at him as he waited to take her hand in escort and she saw Lucifer himself, waiting to lead her into the fires of temptation.

Sam didn't feel the frailty of the hand she tucked into the bend of his arm. He was too taken by her appearance to notice much of anything. On most females, he thought the bustle-rumped getups looked ridiculous. The unnatural pouf of bows and swags and geegaws gave the silhouette of a ruffled pigeon eager for mating and could be downright upsetting if the lady had a mind to make a sudden turn. However, on Lucille Blessing's long, lithe form, that backward sweep of drapery seemed elegant, spilling into a cool waterfall of pale green satin and frothy white lace. Tiny puff sleeves left a creamy expanse of slender arms and gracefully sloped shoulders enticingly bare. A low neck and tight-fitted waist created an attractive display of nicely rounded femininity. Her thick hair was swept up and away so as not to distract from the loveliness of her features and was left to cascade down her back to repeat the rippled design of her skirt.

With her hand held possessively upon his arm, with her large dark eyes gazing up into his in an expression of quizzical confusion and for once, without the remote guard of hostility, he felt an odd turning within his chest. A pleasant panic all wrought up with pride. Confidence fled and for a moment, he floundered, searching for stable ground.

"You look right handsome this evening, ma'am," he managed. It was a rough, rumbling compliment but it brought the softening of a smile to her stiffly held features.

"So do you, Marshal."

And he did, Lucy realized. He was wearing a black frock coat cut in the style Henry Knight favored. The stark white of his shirtfront with its tight stand-up collar made a healthy contrast to his sun-darkened skin. Instead of a tie, a black bandanna rested in loose folds upon his chest. His silver-gray Stetson had been groomed and his Levi's dusted. It was then, Lucy remembered his claim to owning no formal clothing. It was then she deduced the nature of his bet with Henry Knight. The coat and shirt were not just in the saloonkeeper's style—they were Henry Knight's.

"I trust you find me a mite more presentable this evening."

She had the good grace to blush as he led her out onto the well-trampled barn floor. Though she didn't admit as much—her pride wouldn't allow her that degree of humbling—she found herself quite taken by the figure he presented. And it went beyond the tidiness of his dress. Between afternoon and nightfall, he'd obviously paid a visit to Ned Pomeroy's Barber Parlor for a ten-cent shave, a two-bit haircut and a hot bath in back. All trimmed and smooth and smelling cleanly of soap and bay rum, Sam Wade was something to look at. Scraped of the untidy stubble, his cheeks lost their look of shadowed gauntness, leaving lean, strongly cut contours. A face that coaxed the charting of her palm the way the rugged mountains called to the explorers of the plains. In this cheery company, the thin line of his lips relaxed into sensuously chiseled curves that encouraged the inquiring touch of her own. Would his kiss be as hard and unyielding as the length of his body or as searching and pliant as the caress of his sweeping gaze? She allowed herself to wonder these things as the magic of the music surrounded her, as the potent power of his nearness overtook her. And she forgot all reservations as he moved her about the floor.

There was an achingly poignant joy in being carried along on the melancholy strains of "Lorena" and a disturbing contentment in being guided by strong male arms. In the months since Oliver's death, Lucy had convinced herself that she needed no one to steer her destiny. And she hadn't. She managed her business affairs quite nicely. But until now, she hadn't reckoned with a more basic need, that of simple companionship. No ledgers, no cold currency could provide it or lessen the emptiness of her days. Until she was awakened by the shocking warmth of Sam Wade's hands, she hadn't realized how much she missed the closeness of another. The walls of restraint she'd built to hold back grief crumbled, leaving her exposed to the misery of her own company. She longed for the deeper registers of a man's voice, for the security of a figure lying next to her in the dark, for the comfort of belonging and the warmth of sharing. Those desires came to a keen focus as the scent of barbershop bay rum made her senses swim.

The feel of engulfing masculine fingers clasped about her own and, resting masterfully at her trim waist, stirred a delightful weakness when she'd prided herself on remaining strong. She vowed never again to depend upon any man and here she was, willing to be led by the most unsuitable of them all. Sam Wade wasn't going to supply her with comfortable companionship. What he offered was ruggedly displayed in the rack of broad shoulders, in the swell of proud chest, in the power of lean hips which even now sported the tools of his profession. He was dangerous. He was virile. He repelled and frightened her. Yet, in the madness of the moment, while the moon shone with silver magic through the open weave of timbers, as the evening breeze slipped silkily over bared skin to leave it hot and tingling, she didn't care. She wanted what he could give her, if only for the duration of the dance. She wanted to feel gloriously, sensuously alive, to revel in the frailty of being female, to admit to her attraction for him as a man and delight in his awareness of her as a woman.

He seemed to sense her complex yearnings for his embrace tightened, drawing her closer to the abyss of no return. She could feel the alternating shift of his thighs against her skirts and her mind was taken wickedly by thoughts of a more basic rhythm. During her years of marriage, it had been Oliver's learned conversation she enjoyed more than the elements of quiet, controlled intimacy. With Sam Wade, it was not a mental stimulation she craved; it was his raw, threatening sexuality. She was bewildered by the reckless fascination. He was not the sort of man to dally with. He was unstable, unreliable, untrustworthy—a hazardous risk. Or maybe he was exactly the right man, someone who wouldn't demand more than she wished to give, who would insist upon no ties, no deeper meaning than the fulfillment of the flesh.

With her thoughts lost in a sensual haze, with her senses intoxicated by the potency of his presence, Lucy moved by instinct through each step of the waltz, just as she'd move with him through the rituals of pleasure. Her hand had slipped beneath the bartered coat to rest upon the satin back of his vest. Would his bare skin feel as hot, as sleek? Would lying with him—just once—relieve the itchy restlessness plaguing her since he'd disappeared into darkness the night before, abandoning her to the frustration of empty dreams? Would he show her kindness or the rapid-fire savagery she'd sensed in him that morning upon the shooting range? Would it matter?

Then the music stopped and her wildly explicit fantasies shattered in an instant to harsh reality. She became aware of her neighbors, her customers all crowded close beneath the warm lantern light. Of her hand tucked inside the marshal's coat, stroking, sampling the taut curve of his satin-clad ribs. Of her own desire-flushed features as she came close to languishing against him. Had anyone seen? Had anyone watched her cozy up to the town marshal like an overheated member of the horizontally employed? She stepped away and darted a stricken glance to those around her. The couples were politely applauding the musicians. No one seemed to pay any mind to a lonely widow who let a sweet tune and a firm embrace wreak havoc upon her sensibilities. No pairs of eyes observed her fall from respectability. None but a pair as deep and steely blue-gray as a smooth metal bore coated with Colt's Best Citizen's Finish.

Though her transgressing hand had dropped away from his middle, Lucy's other was still caught in Sam's grasp. Slowly, purposefully, he lifted those captured fingers, bringing them up to meet his lips. The damp heat of his mouth incited a furious trembling in hand, in arm, rippling all the way down to settle into a fluttering palpitation about her heart. He turned her hand within his to brush a kiss across her fingertips and then, as if he'd read her wayward thoughts, guided those unsteady fingers along the freshly shaved plane of one cheek, down the clean bold angle of his jaw to the disturbingly strong pulse of his tanned throat.

"Thank you for the dance, Miz Blessing. Perhaps we'll share more. Later."

She recoiled from his suggestion. Not that it was crudely offered. Not that he mocked what he must have seen and felt when she was malleable in his arms.

She was distressed by the sheer force of his statement, by the intense certainty of it. And by her own thrill of anticipation. She let her hand fall bonelessly when released.

"And while I might not think much of Mister Knight's opinion, happens I agree with one. It's a powerful shame to keep yourself shackled behind that table. Leave it to the ones who've done their share of dancing." With that bit of well-intentioned philosophy, he tipped his silver Stetson and ambled off through the crowd.

Lucy stared after him for a long, dazed moment. Her blood was churning, as if they'd just finished a lively reel instead of a stately waltz. Like an undisciplined child, she wanted, irrationally, greedily, desperately, those feelings enkindled within his arms to continue. Yet, as a woman she knew the danger of such thoughts. For some reason she could not claim to understand, Sam Wade sparked a note of purely primitive, pleasure-bent need within her. Her sensibilities screamed in outrage and warning. Acting upon such a base attraction could only lead to ruin. She knew that. It was foolishness. It was folly.

Later.

Newt Redman lingered on the fringe of the merry-making. It was the first time he'd ever witnessed such jollification and the festive spirit held him captive with the delight of the long excluded. There had been town dances before but he'd shied away from them. What would a cripple do at a dance? The anticipation of jeering taunts kept him away but had never quenched his curiosity. It was every bit as wonderful as he'd assumed it would be.

He was careful not to get too caught up in the gaiety. He was, after all, on duty. He glanced to where his personal ideal leaned negligently against an exposed beam and consciously aped that slouching posture. With his shotgun resting easy in the crook of his arm, he hoped he achieved that same look of confident languor. His badge gleamed in the lantern-light and his chest swelled beneath it. Not one snigger had he heard all evening. The town toughs who usually bullied him on the streets regarded him with bewilderment. The men murmured polite greetings and when one lady actually said, "Why good evening, Deputy Redman," he'd felt an invincible ten-feet tall. With his daddy safely seeking entertainment at Nightingale's, he was certain nothing could spoil this perfect moment.

Wrought up in his self-importance, Newt didn't realize that it was Marshal Wade's presence that freed him from merciless derision. There was snickering aplenty behind turned backs and discreetly tipped whiskey bottles. Particularly amused was a group of young cowboys from the Lazy J. Lack of money had pulled them temporarily from their usual occupation—loafing around any town that would put up with them and terrorizing any citizen who failed to show courage in their presence. Though they wore the duds to claim they were cowhands, a discriminating eye could tell they lacked the tanned faces of one long exposed to the elements of outdoor work.

The leader of the ne'er-do-well band was Jimmy Jarret. His father had built the Lazy J, shipping longhorns by rail to stock his range, going so far as to travel back East to purchase a carload of purebred shorthorn bulls to upgrade his stock. It took forty acres of Wyoming scrubland to supply for a single cow and Jarret's herd stretched out across free government land as far as the eye could see. While the people of Blessing, especially those hoping to settle on a good homestead to farm, resented Jarret for grabbing up huge tracts of public domain to support his growing empire, they needed the trade he provided. The demand for beef was high, with the army buying mass quantities to feed its soldiers as well as the reservation Indians they policed, and as a rail spur Blessing profited nicely as a shipping point.

The bane of any town was the rush of newly paid cowhands bent on shooting up the place. Add liquor to the average high-spirited cowpoke and he became ornery, cross-grained and mean as hell, just like the stringy beef he drove. Citizens would tolerate a degree of harmless funning but now that Blessing had itself a marshal, they were less inclined toward leniency.

The rowdy bunch gathered in Thompsons' new barn wasn't intimidated by the presence of the law, especially when its choice of enforcers had the cut of Newt Redman. Jimmy Jarret had nothing but mean contempt for anyone or anything weaker. All fired up with his father's prominence, he was spoiling for a good time at the expense of another. His right-hand pard was a rangy young Texan named Coffee who was itching to earn himself a reputation as a gunman so he could put aside honest toil to live off his nefarious name. The two of them surveyed the too-tame goings-on in search of a reason for deviltry. Coffee had his eye on the new marshal and decided in his own liquor-soaked brain that taking him on would be a good start upon the road to infamy. He was confident that his 1860 Army Colt snug in its low cavalry-twist draw holster could match the butt forward pair the marshal wore so indolently. In his inexperience, he confused a professional easiness with a cocky bravado and wrongly assumed since Marshal Wade adopted a lazy posture that he was inattentive. He should have marked the razor-sharp cut of the man's steely eyes as they followed the increasing noisy antics of the cowboys from beneath the low-tipped Stetson. He should have seen purpose in the casual gesture that brushed coattails away from holster leather. But he was young and blind to all but his own image. And fatally unaware that he'd get no older or clearer sighted should he tangle with Sam Wade.

"Why, Newt, you look right handsome in that deputy's star."

Newt could imagine no higher praise than such words issued from the cherry-ripe lips of Nell Mayhew. He'd suffered from an unrequited hankering for the pretty Nell since she'd put down her skirt and up her hair upon entering young womanhood. She was, to his thinking, everything sweet and desirable about female kind. To earn even her fleeting attention was a lifelong goal but a compliment — a compliment was a ticket to heaven.

"Thank you kindly, Miss Nell," he mumbled, unashamedly lost in her big brown eyes.

"I'm plumb wore out from all the whirling and stomping. Might I impose on you to share a glass of punch with me?" As she spoke the sugary words, her gaze canted over to see if Jimmy Jarret was paying her mild flirtation any notice. Coffee dug his elbow into his friend's ribs and directed his attention her way with a nod. Nell immediately returned her interest to the awkward deputy.

"Why, ma'am, I'd be most happy to but I'm here on official business, not to socialize." He took an incredible risk in rejecting her treasured offer, hoping that she'd be duly impressed with the nature and responsibility of his job. He wanted more than anything to appear the stalwart man in Nell Mayhew's gentle eyes.

Nell pulled a pretty pout meant to melt the sternest

opposition. "Why, Newt Redman, are you so important now that you can't share so much as a glass of punch with a friend?" He blushed deeply, as she'd intended, and stammered a quick apology. Instantly, she was wound about his arm, half dragging him toward the refreshment table. Even as she kept up a steady line of frivolous chatter, her determined stare was gauging the degree of Jimmy Jarret's devotion.

The cattleman's son had been looking for a means to mischief and Nell Mayhew's transparent ploy to wring a jealous response provided the perfect foil. Hitching up his tooled gunbelt designed for the speedy withdrawal of his pearl-handled Navy Colt, he strode toward the mismatched couple, shouldering dancers from his path. Coffee nudged his companions and followed, but his attention was on the lounging marshal.

Newt and his engaging escort had reached the punch bowl. He exchanged a shy smile with Lucy as she supplied him with two cups. It was her sudden frown over his shoulders that gave him warning.

"Whatcha doing with my girl, limpy? You thinking of spinning her around the dance floor in the next quadrille?" He glanced behind him so he and his friends could share in their ugly laughter.

Newt stiffened. Slowly he turned to face his defamer but Jimmy Jarret showed no trepidation at either badge or shotgun. In fact, their presence seemed to increase the ridiculing sneer upon his handsome face.

"My, my, boys, I reckon I've done tangled with a dangerous man."

Young Jarret's snide observation froze Newt solid. His shotgun barrels were still pointed at the ground and while he wished for the nerve to swing them up to blast away that scornful expression, he was afraid to move.

Nell hung on to the paralyzed deputy's arm. "You just leave him be, Jimmy Jarret," she riled up at him. If anything could have worsened matters, it was the cowman's almost steady girl snubbing him before the entire town in favor of a hulking cripple. The insult could not be borne.

"Step away from there, Nellie," he growled, bristling upon like a territorial hound dog.

"Who are you to order me around?" she sniffed disdainfully. "I go where I please with whom I please."

That display of independence was too much. Jimmy reached out to snatch her arm and wrench her forward. Just then, a large hand clamped down over his wrist with bone-crunching sincerity.

"Let the lady go."

None but Coffee had seen the marshal slide on up and into the thick of things. His drawl was easy but the press of his fingers brooked no further nonsense. Jimmy opened his hand and Nell lunged back, looking flushed and vengeful.

"Now, I don't cotton to the manhandling of womenfolk, yours or anyone else's. The lady asked to be let alone. You boys go on about your business before I make it mine."

"She got no call to be flipping her skirts like some highstrung filly," Jimmy argued. He could see Coffee's smirk provoking him to stand ground. And then there was the sight of sweet Nell on Newt's arm. "Girl, I said come here where you belong!" Red-faced, he glared as she planted her feet and refused to budge.

"Looks like you got no claim here," Sam concluded.

Desperate to save face before Nell and his friends, Jimmy drew himself up into an impressive display of indignant, manly rage. "Are you calling me a liar?"

Those who hadn't been following the tableau now stopped to give it their full attention. No words were made to bring about the flinging of lead like a questioning of one's integrity. Sam sighed to himself. There would be no backing down, no graceful way to exit on either side now that the challenge had been hurled. Quietly, without taking his eyes off the young cowman, he ordered, "Newt, you take Miss Nell home. Right now, hear?"

"Yessir, Marshal."

From behind the table where she stood tense and horrified, perhaps Lucy was the only one to see the gloating pleasure on Nell Mayhew's pretty face as she was led away.

Sam sized up the competition. He knew Jimmy Jarret's type. Silver conchas glittered on the band of his white Stetson. A pure silk bandana trailed down the front of his expensive shirt, almost to the band of his Levi's. Had he been able to examine the boy's hands, he knew he would find them soft, without a day of hard toil to toughen them. A wealthy bully and braggart, but no gunman. He glanced behind him to gauge the threat of those in his company.

He recognized Coffee's kind, too, that hell-bent-for-trouble arrogance but Sam dismissed him as well. Coffee stood with legs braced apart, knees slightly bent, his fingers spread over the butt of his Colt. His stance telegraphed his intentions. No trained gunfighter would ever give himself away with such a blatant warning. He could tell by the excited glaze in the boy's black eyes that he had never pulled down on another man. Maybe he was fast. Maybe he was the fastest damn draw in all the Wyoming Territory but plugging a few cans on a fence post was not slapping leather against an armed opponent. Fast didn't mean squat if a man couldn't back his play with the determination to end a life.

The others in the group sported truculent expressions but it was clear they meant to let their boss and his right-hand man handle their own gunplay. That left only the two to concern himself with. The Jarret boy was pride-prodded for evens with an ungovernable temper that made him reckless. Coffee was steady, anxious to claim his first kill. That made him the more dangerous but it was Jimmy who made the initial stab for his gun.

Coffee had studied his adversary carefully and decided a man who responded to trouble with a relaxed and lazy manner would be easy to surprise with his fast draw ability. But the shock was his. Sam Wade was not only aware of the imminent danger but more than ready to answer with the smooth cross-draw pull of his .45s. Since few men who wore a double rig, mostly because the frequency of misfires called for another ready piece, were actually ambidextrous, the hopeful gun slick put little weight on the marshal's chance of outreaching him with his left hand. But not only were both pistols gripped with equal surety, they both cleared leather and leveled before he could register the incredible speed of the move.

Because Jarret was the closer of the two and had made the first move, Sam dealt with him immediately. Up, across and out licked his right-handed Colt, its barrel colliding with Jimmy's handsome face to make a messy pulp of his nose. The boy went down with a yelp, losing all interest in continuing the confrontation.

Seeing the marshal momentarily diverted by his harsh dealings with his friend, Coffee mimicked the fast draw, closing his thumb around the hammer to draw it back as soon as the butt filled his palm. The move was meant to speed the discharge of a single action weapon but was safe only if full cock was reached after the barrel cleared holster leather. The pump of adrenaline made him hasty, causing him to pull back on the trigger at the same time. But it was the sight of the full dark bore of death beaded right between his eyes that made him commit the final folly. He released the hammer in surprise. It snapped down on the copper head of the waiting percussion cap. The report was deafening. Flame spurted out. The bullet ripped through the bottom of his holster and tore, in a streak of pure agony, down his thigh.

Paying no mind to the two would-be hard cases writhing and howling on the ground, Sam covered the group of startled cowboys with both revolvers, making a somber arc that had each man sweating.

"Any of you mean to have a piece of this?" he asked softly and to a man they paled. "Pick up your pards and see them to the doc. I'd run you in but I'm fixing to have another dance."

As the Lazy J men scooped up their moaning compatriots, Sam twirled the twin revolvers on forefingers and they slid effortlessly back into their contoured holsters. He made an impatient gesture to the musicians. The squeezebox player, a Louisianan, launched into a peppery Cajun tune, vocalizing in a muddied French as the fiddles wheezed and raced. Sam stretched a commanding hand across the serving table. For a moment, Lucy simply stared at him. Her face was white, her eyes huge haunted circles. Thinking she'd been frightened by the near gunplay, he offered a small coaxing smile. The flash of straight white teeth against his browned features had a galvanizing affect. Her hand came forward. He wasn't sure she was even aware of it, for she looked surprised when his large fingers closed about it. Still, for a moment, he wondered if she would resist. Her expression

94

was strange and stiff. Not exactly reluctant. Closer to dazed.

"Lu?"

His soft voice altered her odd mood and she came around the table with a wary narrowing of her eyes. That look of haughty warning relieved him. That was the Lucille Blessing he'd come to know, the woman he enjoyed sparring with, toying with. He held no compunction about bedeviling a female with a fair amount of wildcat in her blood. And Miz Lucy was far from the tame society dame she would pretend. He'd seen her anger flash and watched her struggle between temper and decorum. Now, it was time to shake out her stiff skirts a little.

He moved her out onto the makeshift dance floor and whirled her immediately into a series of quick turns. He gave her no chance to protest how tightly he held her by refusing to let her catch her breath. The music was boisterous and bouncy, inspiring high steps, perilous dips and twirling moves. Lucy was surprisingly light on her feet, despite the restriction of her wrapped skirts and wide-swinging bustle and managed to backpedal in mirrored time to his quick forward two-step. The unexpected dips forced her to hold tight to him and he enjoyed the feel of her pressed close. He enjoyed, just as much, the sight of her features lifted to his, rosy with high color, her eyes sparkling with rare pleasure. She seemed to forget herself: the staid and proper Widow Blessing falling away before a woman who was yet young and filled with life. As he spun her rapidly through a number of reverse circles, her laughter lilted up, a surprisingly carefree sound.

Right then, he should have let her go. At that moment, he should have realized that she was more of a danger to him than he, with his six-guns and deadly past, was to her. As a splendid buoyancy rose within his chest, he grinned down in delight to see her overcome by such animated zest. Her response had his head spinning just as crazily as the turns of the dance.

Then the music slowed and ambled into the sentimental strains of a waltz. They stood, Lucy still in his arms, her face flushed with a feverish heat, her bosom racing with a breathless anticipation. When his hand slipped up the curve of her back to rest at the nape of her neck, she gave no struggle, letting him guide her head to the pillow of his broad shoulder. The movements were languid, dreamy, interwoven. Lucy closed her eyes and absorbed the feeling. Her heart was still hammering, partly from the rigors of the dance and partly because of the lingering terror she'd felt when she'd thought he was in danger. He could have been killed. It was an integral part of his job, dealing with threat and danger. She'd vowed never to suffer through the agony of losing someone at the hand of senseless violence. Yet, here she was courting that same disaster.

The shaky sensations ebbed, clearing the way for rational thought. Sam Wade was dangerous. If she allowed herself the madness of becoming involved on any level, she would surely pay the price in pain. How much pain could she stand in one lifetime? How many could she see buried? Already he held a powerful thrall over her emotions. Though it was physical alone for the moment, who was to say when that might change? And if she came to care for the marshal of Blessing, how could she survive his parting either through desertion or death? That was the only end in store when it came to a man like Sam Wade. How could she accept that kind of punishment willingly?

Sam felt the difference. She was all molten availability one minute and as cold as Wind River rock the next. She levered away from the comfortable plane of his chest. While fighting an honest battle to resist his nearness, she failed to reinforce the confrontation with her gaze. Her eyes remained canted downward in an all-absorbing study of his vest buttons. And when the final note trembled on the cool evening air, she broke away from him with a quickly murmured good night.

He walked to the open framework and leaned against the clean smelling lumber to watch her hurry to her buggy. She paused once, just before climbing aboard, and looked back at him. She seemed to hesitate. Then, she scrambled into the seat and applied determined force to whip up her horse. He lingered there, a partial smile playing about his lips, until the last distant whorls of dust settled into calm darkness.

Chapter Seven

Sam woke to a tease of coffee and the sight of a sullen Newt polishing his worn boots. Wordlessly, the boy handed him the footgear and fetched him his first of the morning cup off the burner.

"Looking mighty long in the jowls there, Newt."

The boy said nothing as he picked up a broom and began to give the cells a thorough sweeping. Sam watched the brusque, determined movements for a long moment as his coffee cooled then got right to what was eating his young deputy.

"You said you knew the law, Newt." The boy paused and gave him a glance. "Then you know no self-respecting lawman goes around putting holes in every big-mouth jasper that doubts his right to wear a badge."

"Maybe they was right, Marshal," Newt mumbled glumly. His expression was as mournful as his old yellow dog's. "Maybe I got no right to this here badge. I was powerful scared. I didn't know what to do."

"You did right." Sam's words were soothing to a fragile soul, with the needed amount of firm reassurance. "When a man gets scared, a lot of times he makes a stupid mistake trying to prove something to himself. You didn't make any wrong moves. You wouldn't have wanted the little lady to get caught in the middle of something ugly, now would you?"

"Of course not."

"There you go." Sam dismissed the matter from mind but Newt would dwell long upon his words. "Are you meaning to wear out that floor or are you going to tip a cup with me?"

By the time Newt had poured himself a cup and had settled on the bench with the hound dog stretched across his feet, Sam was feeling pretty good about meeting the crisis. He knew about fear under pressure. The boy had choked and was feeling about as lowly as a man could feel. Why, he could tell young Newt tales that would chill his milk but it came right down to fear having nothing to do with being a man. He could have told the boy that he still felt that trickle of sweat whenever he drew down on a man. Yet he didn't. He couldn't quite bring himself to tarnish the adulation in the young man's eyes.

At that moment, the jailhouse door swung open to emit Lucy's bespectacled clerk. Without taking his boot heels off his desk top, Sam hailed him on in.

"Marshal Wade, I'm Cecil Potter from the bank." He sounded tentative and gave a nervous glance behind him as he closed the door.

"Do something for you, Cecil?" The furtive movements had not gone unnoted.

"Miz Lucy would have my hide and most likely my job if she knew I was here."

Sam was beginning to get interested. He eased his feet down and prompted the wiry little man with a sympathetic nod.

"She's fixing to ride on out to the Mercer place this morning. He's that gent with the shotgun you met your first morning in town."

Sam understood his worry without further explanation. The fool female was courting trouble. With her leaving town for the morning, it would have been the perfect time to mosey on over to the bank but something surprising stopped him. As much as he didn't want to offer to play nursemaid to the stubborn banker, an annoying protectiveness had risen. He wasn't responsible for Lucy Blessing but he knew with a certainty in that minute that he couldn't let her ride out to meet the sullen farmer alone.

With lazy effort to mask his true concern, he drawled, "And I suppose you're wanting me to go along to see she doesn't get her bustled tail peppered."

Cecil smiled weakly. "I'd be beholding to you."

They emerged from the jail just as Lucy reached the livery. Her stern gaze sent Cecil scurrying back up the street toward the bank then she waited for the marshal to saunter over. Her features offered no welcome and her manner was as rigid as the steel springs supporting the bunch and bows of her overskirt.

"Morning, ma'am," he called with a tip of his hat brim. "I hear you're fixing to go a'-calling and thought I might ride along to pay my respects."

"Is that what you thought?" The cool of the morning had nothing on the frost-laden words. "No matter what Cecil told you, I have no need for a hired gun."

Sam smiled, not in the least discouraged. "You've a mite unfriendly way of putting things."

"I'm tending business this morning, Marshal, not a social call. So if you'll excuse me."

He let her walk away from him so he could admire the way her anger set the fringe of her bustled skirts in motion. In three long strides, he was at her elbow then in her way.

"Let's just say I aim to pay a business call, too, and it seems a shame that we should both make the trip separate when we could enjoy each other's company."

With her dark eyes flashing and her bustle all tipped and bristling, Lucy Blessing looked like a she-cat with its back up. When her effort to stare him down earned a mildly mocking smile, she gave up in reluctant exasperation.

"Suit yourself, Marshal," she snapped and strode inside the livery. It took only a few minutes for the proprietor to harness up one of the horses to a shiny rig in the buggy shed and to lead it out onto the street where Sam lounged next to the large sliding doors.

"Morning, Marshal Wade," the burly man called out. "That bay of yours is some bale burner."

"He enjoys his pleasures when he can get them," Sam replied with a slow grin. He glanced toward Lucy to appreciate the way she colored up in fury.

"Saddle him up for you?"

"Not today. I'm going a-calling with Miz Blessing." He stepped up to settle himself on the left side of the buggy seat, leaving the man to aid Lucy and draw his own conclusions. "I'll let you drive, ma' am. I'm just along for the ride."

As she angrily arranged her skirts, the big yellow dog ambled down the walk and helped himself up into the buggy boot. She snatch the whip from its socket and sent it popping over the horse's back with such vigor that the animal surged forward in surprise, nearly unseating man and dog. Sam leaned back and put a steadying hand on the hound's bony head.

"Feller, looks like you and me picked the wrong day to take a pleasure ride."

The moment the buggy whirred out beyond the break of buildings, the wind whipped up with unpleasant grittiness and the surroundings lost all evidence of hospitality. Thinking of the farmlands in Missouri, Sam couldn't help wondering why anyone would choose such desolate digs. It seemed only the bunch grass and sage could set down decent roots. Most of the farmers would end up like the wandering tumbleweeds. Like Mercer.

He let his attention drift to the woman at the reins. She was dressed like a socialite going to tea in the beige moiré with its tease of dark blue fringe and white ruffled blouse filling the bosom opening of her jacket. The jaunty little hat with its feathers and narrow ribbons set at a forward tilt upon her low chignon did next to nothing in the way of warding off the elements. Only her durable gloves made any sense. What was such a stylish bit of womankind doing in the wilds of Wyoming when she should be sipping lemonade in some parlor back East?

"Mind me asking what keeps you here now that your husband's gone? I mean, from the look of it, he must have left you well-enough off to go just about any place that took your fancy."

Lucy responded to the casual attempt at conversation with a curt "I mind."

To her thinking, it was bad enough to be wedged on the seat with Sam Wade without him prying into her personal life. Perhaps he could sit there, slouching indolently, hat tipped to shade his face, and pretend nothing had happened in Thompson's barn the night before but she was having one heck of a time at it. With every mile they traveled, she became more acutely aware of how alone they were together. And she didn't know whether to be relieved or insulted at his lack of courtly interest. He had to have sensed her response to him; she'd practically dissolved in his arms. And then there was the sultry promise of "later." She glanced sidelong at him. He was dressed in the clothes he'd worn when he rode into town though now they were freshly laundered and unobjectionable. Was he smarting over her insult? Was he

102

making her suffer for the wound she'd afflicted upon his pride?

And as the silent miles sped onward, Lucy's tumbled thoughts shifted from an anxiety as to when he would try to make a move upon her to an annoyance of why he was not.

"Mercer owe the bank a lot, does he?"

Sam's question jolted her back to the business at hand and shamed her for hosting such improper thoughts. Her frustration at not being able to control her wayward interest made her answer terse. "Everything he owns belongs to the bank. I heard whispers last night that he and his family were getting ready to default by leaving the territory."

"Would that be so bad? I mean, you can always resell the property to get your money back."

"It's not just the land, it's everything he has: his livestock, his furniture, his wagon, all of it. He signed it all over to the bank and now he's trying to take it with him. That's stealing, isn't it, Marshal? Perhaps it's a good thing you're on hand, after all."

"You going to have me arrest the whole family for trying to take their belongings?"

She stiffened at his tone, that long drawn-out drawl of contempt. "Not their belongings, Marshal, the bank's."

"I see. And that makes Mercer a hardened criminal. What does that make the bank?" When she shot him a frowning look, he continued his wry observations. "You see a man like Mercer, down on his luck, struggling to provide for his family. He wants to borrow money from your fine bank to put down a grubstake, roots for his wife and children. You say, 'Sure, happy to oblige you' and sign him up for one of those twelve-ten loans. He asks for three hundred dollars, you give him two hundred and seventy and he pays twelve percent on the full amount for the next five years. First bit of trouble and you're right there to lend a helping hand, only this time, he's signing over all he owns. If you could take his soul and his firstborn, you'd probably do that, too, wouldn't you? But now, poor old Mercer, dirt farmer that he is, can't make your twelve percent so the bank just sidles on in and pulls his livelihood out from under him to sell it all to some other poor dumb farmer. Now I ask you, Miz Blessing, who's the criminal here?"

"I didn't set up the system, Marshal Wade," she returned in her own defense, thinking it odd that she would want to explain away her own culpability. She was not ashamed of her business.

"That's right. No one's going to blame you, Miz Blessing. After all, what have you got to do with the damned Republicans coming in with their Yankee-Protestant greed to strangle good folks with their greenbacks and bank notes." His lazy pose was gone. In its place was a hard-edged anger smoldering just beneath the surface.

"And I suppose you think the Jacksonian Democrats had all the right answers." Debating politics with a gunman? Perhaps there was more depth to Sam Wade than she'd imagined. She enjoyed a good tangle of words over a heated cause. Nothing like a difference of opinion to set the blood pumping and the mind turning. It was exhilarating. Almost as stimulating as the feel of the marshal's arms around her. But infinitely safer.

"They surely did. A man's got a right to live without interference from the government. Banks should be local, not part of some political machine that chews up and spits out everything in its way, using their useless paper instead of hard money to run roughshod over folks."

She'd heard his views before, voiced in anger from the citizens of the South who felt the banks were controlled by Northern monopolists. She'd heard Oliver argue eloquently on the subject and tried to restate his words. "The country needed a safe, uniform currency. At the start of the war, every bank in every county thought it had the right to issue its own notes until over seven thousand different kinds of paper currency flooded the market. My husband ran a free bank in Ohio under Senator Chase. He lobbied for a national banking system to reform the disaster of debt the war left us in. He had the foresight to see a free banking system was necessary nationwide to provide credit to those in need, to insure the safety of bill holders, to promote equality and opportunity."

"In need? Don't you mean in greed?" His words were harsh, raw with angry emotion, making her own sound as empty as the sentiments in a political pamphlet. A cold fire burned behind the steel gray of his eyes, an anger that would not be quieted by reason or resolve. And Lucy was stunned to see him manipulated by the desperate, dangerous passions of a cause lost. "Banks aren't there for those in need. Where were the banks when farmers cried out for loans to restore what the war had torn from them? Where were your fine notions of equality and opportunity when widows were turned away for lack of good collateral? Collateral! Hell, everything damn thing we had was burned around us and you high-and-mighty bankers sit there on your pile of greenbacks asking for collateral, killing us with your high interest rates. Robbers, robbers in fancy clothes with the government behind them, that's bankers. I'll bet that's the way Mercer sees it. Men like your husband should be behind bars, not the farmers who believe in their lies." With that, he clamped his lips into a thin, pale line and stared stonily ahead.

Lucy jerked up on the reins. The debate had suddenly become uncomfortably personal. It was one thing to take up opposite sides in an issue and quite another to hone an attack on a man's character.

"Don't you speak of my husband in that manner," she warned but he refused to favor her with a glance or an attentive ear. "You've no right to judge. You never met him. Just ask anyone living in Blessing what Oliver did for the town. He took a barren stretch of land and made it into a place people are proud to live."

Sam didn't turn to express his cynical conclusion. "And made a tidy profit on it, too. Somewhere between fifty and one thousand dollars a lot. And what did he offer the railroad to bring it into town? Some shady windfall deal? One-third of the town company's land, a decade of no taxation, bonds to help pay for construction?"

Lucy remained silent, trying to gather her objections. But he was well informed, taking the facts and twisting them so that her husband's shrewd business moves sounded sinister and self-interest motivated. His argument was so intense, it had her wondering over Oliver's intentions — just for a moment.

"And was he a part of the railroad's Credit Mobilier? Was he one of the insiders of the Union Pacific who made their millions by giving themselves the railroad construction contracts? Was he smart enough to sell his interests out early and walk away before the government got wise and investigated the scandal?"

Still, Lucy said nothing. Oliver hadn't been one of the UP directors but he'd been an active supporter of the Credit Mobilier and deeply involved in the financing of the UP. Sam's words implied he was no better than a thief and that wasn't true. No matter what he'd done, no matter what he'd involved himself in, he'd done it for the good of Blessing, to see his town grow and prosper. And no outsider was going to tell her different.

"You didn't know him," she stated firmly.

"I don't need to. He was a banker." He spat that out distastefully, as if the title described every aspect of the man. And when he happened to glance at her where she sat stiff beside him on the seat, she could see in the cold, clear light of his eyes that he shoved her into that same loathsome mold. Lucy fought not to recoil from the hatred in that gaze but she was shaken when he looked away. This wasn't the same indolent, teasing man who'd whirled her about the Thompsons' barn, or even the cool pistoleer who reached for a gun as easily as some would a word. What she saw in the man beside her was a flame of fury, the kind of anger that took to burning in hearts — as the Border States smoldered in ruin.

What must he have seen and suffered to contain such unrequited bitterness? What made him hate the bank system so much that he would despise her link to it? She hadn't misread his look of animosity nor was she fooled when he turned back to her with an offer of his impassive smile.

"Sorry to go on like that. I'm still Southern enough to get riled at certain things. I didn't mean nothing by it."

Lucy didn't buy into that for a second. What she had witnessed in that brief impassioned exchange was the raw essence of the man behind the laconic grin and narrow, guarded gaze. A truth that was more powerful and frightening than the myth he garnered to surround himself. What lay close to his heart were matters of family, of the earth, not of the gun as she'd supposed. Whatever else Sam Wade might be, he was

107

not without conscience. She had seen its torment burn bright in that telling instant. And she was more confused by him than ever.

It was with relief that she looked ahead to see the low sod house and burned-out shell of Mercer's barn. As the buggy grew near, it was plain her suspicions were founded. The house and sheds were empty. The Mercers had fled with all they could carry leaving her with little more than paper and dust.

"They couldn't have gotten far that heavily laden."

Sam glanced at her in reproving surprise. "You mean to take out after them?"

"Of course, I do. All the way to Laramie if I have to. They have my property."

My property. The significance wasn't missed. It was a personal thing with Lucy Blessing, a need to punish a misbehaved child to serve as an example to others. She didn't need the goods the Mercers took, not like they did. It was pure principle that drove her onward. Stubborn, greedy principle. And Sam couldn't like that about her. Yet it made things a whole heap easier. He sat grim and silent in the seat as she headed the horse after the deeply scored wagon tracks. He'd come to protect her against Mercer. Who would protect the luckless farmer from her?

Lucy was nothing if not determined. She followed the track like a chicken rancher on the trail of a coyote. With every dusty mile, he grew more disenchanted with the female in question and less inclined toward the reason for pursuit. Especially when he saw the Mercers' wagon up ahead.

As if he expected opposition, John Mercer was driving the team of horses hard. They strained in the tracings to pull the Mercer household, stacked and lashed into the wagon bed. Furniture, clothing chests, a crate of chickens, plow and egg crocks—all the means for existence. A pair of sturdy mules were led at the rear. The farmer and his wife sat on the seat. Behind it crouched four children. A fifth was swaddled in Mrs. Mercer's arms. Mercer turned at the sound of the rapidly approaching buggy. There was no malice in his expression; just a weary inevitability. He made no move to reach for his shotgun as he hauled back on the reins when Lucy circled around in front to cut off further escape. The big yellow hound hopped down from the buggy boot and began to circle the wagon with a far from menacing lope.

From her buggy seat, Lucy stared somberly at the farmer. He returned the gaze sullenly, somewhat repentantly, as if he knew he was in the wrong but couldn't be faulted for trying.

"Mister Mercer," she called out in a clear, final voice, "I have here the terms of your chattel mortgage and the marshal from Blessing. Please don't make this any more difficult for any of us. What you have does not belong to you, as well you know."

The children set up a chorus of sniveling from the shade of the bench seat and Mrs. Mercer herself, was subject to dampness of the eyes. John Mercer sighed, his big shoulders rising and falling to echo the turn of his fate.

"If you'll just accompany us back to Blessing, we'll hold a public auction of the belongings. If there's an excess over what's owed the bank, it can be used to stake you somewhere else."

The faded eyes of Joanna Mercer flashed to the pile of memories and hopes in the wagon bed, tearing at the sight of her wedding bedstead, at her husband's front porch rocker, even at the box of sad irons she used to neatly press her children's clothes. She clutched the babe at her breast more tightly and something inside Sam Zachary broke.

. "Boy," he called out, gesturing to the eldest of the Mercer brood, "you go on back there and untie those mules."

When the youngster scrambled to do as told, Sam felt Lucy's puzzled gaze upon him. He didn't favor her with a look, fearing she'd read too much in his emotion-taut face.

"Tie 'em to the back of the buggy," he instructed.

That done and the boy back in his family's wagon, Sam waved his hand toward the miles that stretched out into desolate plains. When he spoke to the puzzled farmer, his words were rough, almost hoarse.

"Go on with you. Make your new start." He slapped his hand down on the seat back and the dog bounded up and settled into a bony ball.

Understanding hit Lucy with the stunning force of a scatter gun loaded with rock salt. It stung and provoked a violent reaction.

"What?" She stared at Sam through wide, disbelieving eyes. "What do you mean go on? They're not going anywhere except back to Blessing to pay their debt."

Sam's reply was soft but very unconditional. "You've got the property and this brace of fine mules. Consider it payment in full."

She sputtered and steamed like a kettle left too long to boil. Anger spouted, hot and hissing. "You can't do this. That comes nowhere near reclaiming what the bank has invested. They knew what they risked when they signed away their property."

"You're not talking property, Miz Blessing. We're talking life."

Lucy panted in rage, looking from the dazed Mercer family to Sam Wade's set features. "But you're the law—"

"And the law states I have to step in to prevent a

murder. You'd be killing those folks if you sent them out with nothing and you know it. I won't see a family stripped bare of what they need to survive. I won't," he echoed more softly. Then to John Mercer, he shouted, "Go on. Git."

"God bless you, Marshal," Mrs. Mercer cried out as her husband slapped down the reins. Unlike his wife, he wasn't much of a believer in divine intervention and meant to put as many miles between them and the bank of Blessing as he could lest Lucy Blessing have her way.

Lucy settled back upon the buggy seat. Her dark eyes followed the retreating wagon with an impotent frustration. That flamed to rage when she regarded the marshal.

"Have you any idea what you've just done?" she seethed through clenched teeth.

He looked at her long and insolently then that mocking half smile curved his lips. "Yes, ma'am, I surely do."

"You had no right."

"Maybe not legal but I sure as hell had moral grounds."

She took a deep, sizzling breath and promised, "You're going to pay dear for this."

"It won't be the first time, Miz Blessing." Then he tipped the Stetson down to shade his eyes, dismissing her anger and her threat.

"Damn you," she concluded helplessly and turned the buggy toward Blessing.

Chapter Eight

The ride to Blessing was fraught with tension.

Lucy stewed. She simmered. She seethed. The anger she felt for her companion was boundless, as was her vexation with herself. She'd lost control of the situation and that rested poorly with her pride. The pistol she wore strapped to her thigh had proved useless. What could she have done? Shot the marshal down? Threatened Mercer in front of his wife and children? It had been an impossible impasse. Worse were her own conflicting sentiments.

It went against her grain to pull security out from under a needy family. Yet, she could argue their problem hadn't been of her making. The bank had given them every chance and they'd run rather than make honorable restitution. And Marshal Wade had shown them the open road. She'd fought long and hard after Oliver's death to build the kind of respect in others that it took to manage a successful business. The people of Blessing trusted her. They knew her for her fairness, her generosity, her willingness to extend — to overextend — a helping hand. But she'd also had to make it clear that she was a woman of business and that meant doing many things that sat bitter in her belly. Regulations and rules were meant to be followed. A word, a bond, was everything. A debt had to be repaid. It was a matter of personal honor that went beyond legal responsibility.

She wouldn't have been helping John Mercer by letting him escape that, by allowing him to build his future in the shadow of disgrace and failure. Success was something you worked for, honestly, something you struggled for, individually. And if you were beholden to another, you saw them repaid before enjoying the fruits you reaped. Plain and simple, it was her philosophy. She wouldn't have pushed them out of Blessing without the means to survive. Once their obligation to the bank was satisfied, she would have rallied the people of Blessing: Mercer's friends and neighbors. They would have seen his family lacked for nothing. It was every man's duty to supply the needs of another—not the bank's. But Sam Wade had given her no opportunity to display her charitable intentions. He'd cut the legs from under her and condemned her with his glare. He wanted to believe the worst of her. It was the loss of his respect that hurt more than the few dollars the Mercers would cost the bank.

The entire affair had ended badly. The bank lost its investment. The Mercers lost their home. She'd lost her self-respect. Because of his unconscionable act, Sam Wade would lose his job. She'd have no recourse but to demand the retraction of his badge. He had to have known that when he stepped between her and the law. Yet he'd done so without hesitation, without regret. And he left her feeling as though she was the one in the wrong.

She felt a slow, smoldering fury toward Sam Wade. He'd done nothing but complicate her life since coming to Blessing. He'd caused her to question the memory of her husband's goodness, he'd interfered in the conducting of her business and he'd sent her emotions into one dandy of a spin. All in the course of a few days. She'd pegged him as trouble and rightly so. However, when they returned to Blessing, his threat would end. There'd be no reason for him to remain in town once the council had stripped him of his office. And that husky promise issued amid the moonlight and sweet scents of hay and fresh-cut lumber would go unexplored. All for the best, she tried to tell herself. How empty that satisfaction felt.

Lucy pulled into the livery yard and descended on her own before the marshal could offer his assistance. Or refuse to give it. When the proprietor approached, she instructed him to place the mules in the civic pound then began to stride purposefully toward the bank. Though she didn't look at him, she was very aware of Sam Wade at her side. The nerve of him, she thought furiously. He should have slunk off to cower from her retribution yet he remained defiantly in her company. Almost as though he'd done nothing amiss. Arrogant, interfering, disturbing length of man!

Her thoughts were arrested by the sight of Mayor Mayhew hurrying in their direction. She should have felt a vindicating pleasure in meting out Sam Wade's fate but she was strangely reluctant to speak of his misdeed. As it was, she hadn't the chance.

"Marshal! Marshal Wade, something awful's happened." Edgar Mayhew's features were more ruddy and damp than usual. His small eyes were round with distress.

Lucy noted Sam's instinctive move to clear his holsters of his coattails as he calmed the breathless mayor and asked to hear the cause of his agitation.

"It's my daughter, Nell, Marshal. She's gone."

"Gone?" He urged more information with a cant of one brow.

"After the dance at Thompson's, she was seen arguing with that Jarret boy. She didn't come home. I just know he's done something awful to her." The anxious gaze began to seep.

"Now, Mayor, you don't know any such a thing," Sam

argued easily. "Why don't you just go on home and let me poke around a little. I'm sure I can turn up your little gal without so much as a chip to her fingernails." He smiled broadly, confidently and the distraught father reflected on his words. "Go on, now. I'll let you know as soon as I've found her. She's probably hiding out with some female friend hoping to punish the world for Jarret's foolishness."

Mayhew managed a nervous nod and headed for his modest home located at the street's end.

Lucy had forgotten her discord with the marshal. Nell Mayhew was only sixteen, a pretty, impetuous thing. "Do you really think she's safe with a girlfriend?" she asked of the taut figure.

"No" was his curt reply.

The sun smeared a vivid crimson across the distant mountains as Sam leaned down from his saddle to search the hard-packed ground. There, he found the faintest trace of what he was looking for; the imprint of a notched shoe. The blacksmith hadn't had time to replace it on Jimmy Jarret's horse before the boy came to claim it late the night before when he'd left town in a hurry with the other riders from the Lazy J.

In questioning an anxious Newt and the owner of the livery, he'd discovered that though she'd been seen safely to the door of her home by his deputy, Nell Mayhew hadn't remained there. She'd taken a horse and had ridden back toward the Thompsons' where, according to what witnesses told him, she'd come across the limping riders from the Lazy J. An argument ensued between Jimmy and Nell. And that was the last anyone had seen of them.

He'd tracked the cowboys after they'd left town, having no way to know if Nell Mayhew was riding with them.

115

Then the group separated, with the main batch of riders heading toward the Lazy J and three horses splintering off to the east. It was the trio Sam followed as one of their horses had a notable notch in one shoe.

They reached high country by nightfall. He reckoned they couldn't be more than an hour or two ahead. He'd been pushing hard and they had no reason to think he was following, at least that was what their trail told him. As it was senseless to go crashing about in the dark, he made a cold camp for himself. After first seeing to the bay — a nightly ritual of checking his condition and examining his shoes — he allowed the horse a good roll and ample feed before seeing to his own limited comfort. Finishing the cold and far from satisfying trail food, he bedded down against his saddle and stared up at the stars as if they could provide the answer to what plagued him.

What in tarnation was he doing tracking a silly girl and her cowboy lover? He could have been back at the Nightingale enjoying a cold beer and a warm woman. It wasn't as though he was really the marshal of Blessing. Its citizens weren't his concern. So what was he doing tangling with an ornery female banker and playing nursemaid to a wayward child? If he had half a brain, he'd be circling back to town to get on with his business while they least suspected. The longer he stayed, the greater the chance of a snag in his perfect plan. He'd no want to be a resident of Blessing's jail rather than its keeper. So why was he delaying?

A rustle in the brush distracted him from finding a resolution. He came up slowly, guns filling his palms. Tension gripped in his belly then relaxed at the sight of a great lumbering hound.

"Cornelius," he scolded as the animal came over to sniff around his fire for scraps. "You big, stupid, bag of brittle bones. I almost had me dog for breakfast but then it don't look like I'd be getting much in the way of a meal off your stringy hide. Sit."

Cornelius cast a baleful look in his direction then let out his tongue in a lolling grin. Sam scowled. Tricks, Newt had told him. The animal hadn't the sense to know when he wasn't welcomed let alone the brain to obey an order. Like his own mind when it came to entertaining thoughts of a certain banker.

When Sam settled back onto his saddle, the dog came to plop beside him, groaning as it rolled onto its side. Against his better judgment, he gave the dusty coat a quick pat and closed his eyes for sleep.

Crouching low in the scrub brush covering, Sam observed the camp coming to life below. Nell Mayhew, looking no worse for wear, was making breakfast for Jimmy Jarret and his friend, Coffee. Scrutiny revealed bedrolls still spread out, one on one side of the small fire and the other two, close together on the other. He had no time to consider the importance of that setting as Cornelius chose the moment to get acquainted with whoever was making biscuits.

The appearance of the big, rawboned hound brought the two cowboys up in alarm. His surprise ruined, Sam shouted down, "Give it up, fellers," and was answered almost at once by the flat, angry "splat" of a close-passing bullet. Ducking behind the negotiable cover, he saw Jarret make a grab for Nell, holding her, not in front as a shield the way he supposed, but behind him, away from danger. His fancy piece was out, arcing for a target. Coffee had disappeared from the fireside. Apparently, his leg wound didn't hinder his agility.

With Nell tucked behind him, young Jarret was frantically trying to saddle up their horses. The gunplay and the boy's jerky movements made them dance and shy away, leaving him exposed to Sam's guns. But he didn't shoot. Something wasn't right. Nell Mayhew didn't look to be in peril from the rancher's son.

There was a warning snap behind him. Sam whirled and lunged to the side all in one moment. This time, his reflexes weren't quick enough to spare him the vengeful lead of Coffee's revolver. Pain streaked along his ribs, causing him to lose his hold on the Colt in his left hand as his elbow squeezed tight against the wound. He was stunned and slow to respond to the danger that remained. The young Texan grinned as he threw down a bead upon the fallen man. The sight of the star gleaming on Sam's vest meant nothing compared to evens for his battered pride. The New Model Army Colt made a final sounding click as the hammer was pulled back to bring a fresh cartridge into play. From his awkward prone position, all Sam could do was glare his defiance and wait to die.

There was a crashing disturbance as teeth and bone, launched with the fury of a locomotive, collided with Coffee. It took only a second for the cowboy to shake off his surprise and the big dog but it was long enough for Sam's Peacemaker to gain a steady purchase. Before Coffee could realign his aim, the Colt spat out eternity with a single shot.

Sam staggered up to his feet, placing himself unwittingly in full view of the two below. Nell Mayhew gave a pitiful cry and broke away from Jimmy Jarret.

"Marshal Wade. Thank God you're here!"

She ran to him and flung herself upon him nearly causing him his precarious balance. Seeing the tide go against him, young Jarret put up his hands.

It was going on midafternoon when the four horses shuffled wearily into Blessing. One bore the body of the cowboy known as Coffee wrapped up in his slicker.

Jimmy Jarret was lashed to the horn of the next. The bedraggled figure of Nell Mayhew rode on the other side of Marshal Wade. She let out a forlorn sob when she caught sight of her father and nearly swooned from the saddle into his readied arms.

"Oh, Paw," she wailed. "It was awful. If Marshal Wade hadn't come along . . . I just don't know what would have happened!" She then collapsed into meaningful tears that had her father staring murderously at the young cowboy.

Sam viewed the scene curiously. Something about it, like the one at the camp, was askew, only he couldn't name what it was. He watched Newt approach and was relieved, for he was feeling decidedly strange.

"Newt, take this here jasper to the jailhouse and the other — well, he's not going anywhere."

Elated by the chance to perform his duties before a growing crowd, Newt raised his shotgun to catch the foregrip in his left hand. "You heard the marshal," he growled. And this time, Jimmy Jarret didn't mock him. He came along all quietlike to the jail, casting a bewildered look back at the sobbing Nell Mayhew. The crowd parted, some following the prisoner, some gathering around Nell, some morbidly prodding the dead man. Only Lucy Blessing watched the marshal. She saw him sway in the saddle and his legs nearly give way when he swung down to the ground. He looked done for it and she was moved by a surge of compassion.

The town undertaker approached Sam with well-intentioned seriousness. "You want me to set him up in front of Davis's so you can be having your picture taken with him?"

Sam stared at him with blank dislike. The idea of posing with the dead man as a warning to others, whether it be for personal glory or memento, chilled Sam's blood. "No," he growled. Furthermore, he didn't cotton to having his picture posted anywhere.

Lucy witnessed his disgust and felt a moment of satisfaction as he resisted the well-accepted barbarity of posing with the kill as if a man could be compared to a trophy buck. It made her well enough disposed to offer hospitality as a reward.

"Marshal, would you like a drink of something cool? I can't offer anything potent but it will refresh you some."

He looked at her rather vaguely and she was alarmed by the oddly intense unfocused quality of his gaze. "Thank you, ma'am. That sounds right nice."

She instructed one of the youngsters gaping at the body to tend the marshal's horse then walked with him to her home less than a half block away. He seemed winded by the short jaunt and when he stumbled slightly on her front step, she reached out quickly to grasp his arm. Had he ridden all night? She felt a tug of guilt. She hadn't thought him that dedicated to his job.

The house was shaded and cool but it wasn't the heat outside that troubled Sam. He was chilled to the bone and shivering. Even the slicker he'd put on to warm him had become inadequate. His strength seemed to drain away as he moved in a near stagger into the parlor. Dropping down onto one of the delicate chairs, his awareness waxed and waned, coming into focus on Lucy Blessing's worried features. He attempted a smile but even that small effort was too much.

"Marshal?" Lucy bent closer. There was something beyond weariness wrong with him. His eyes were huge, black and glazed as they roved restlessly about the room. He was panting lightly. Cautiously, she reached out a hand, touching it to his brow. She'd expected heat but his skin was ominously cold.

"Sam?"

His eyelids fluttered and he looked to her with a fierce concentration. After wetting his lips, he mumbled, "I

120

could use that liquid and a towel. I seem to be leaking mine all over your fine chair."

To clear the puzzlement from her face, he slowly drew back his slicker.

The sight of so much blood brought Lucy's rushing from her head. It was a nightmare returned. She reeled back, catching hold of one of her spindly knickknack tables. Some sound expressing her horror must have escaped, for her two Chinese servants were instantly on hand. Chu had come from the kitchen and wielded a wicked-looking chopping knife to fend off possible danger. Seeing it and their panicked faces brought reason and control back.

Using her trembling hands to pinch color back into her white cheeks, Lucy drew a firm breath and ordered, "Chu, bring me some of Mister Oliver's bourbon. Li, I'll need towels and something to use as a compress."

When the two silent servants went to fulfill her commands, Lucy looked back to the marshal, every bit as pale and shaky as he himself was. On the periphery of her frantically spinning thoughts, she saw a vital dark pattern begin to form on the parlor rug.

Having witnessed her fright and dismay, Sam made a futile move to stand. "I best be getting myself to the doctor."

Her hands were quick to still him. "He's not here. He's gone to deliver Mrs. Caldwell's second child and won't be back until tomorrow. What can I do to keep you alive until then?"

"Why, Miz Blessing, I didn't know you cared. I'm truly touched."

"Well, I can't have you bleeding all over everything, now can I. Do you think you could make it upstairs if I helped?"

"Ma'am, I hardly think this is the time."

She glowered at his feeble crudity and was mightily

tempted to let him await the doctor on her porch. Then she realized how much she was shaking. He was smiling crookedly, trying to take her mind off her distress with the weak attempts at humor. Finally, she, too, smiled to reassure that she would not fail him.

"The sofa will do fine for what we have planned. Now, I'll need to take a look."

Sam recoiled. It wasn't a modest gesture. He didn't want her swooning at his feet. "That's all right. It's a scratch. Just bring me the towels and I'll tend it myself."

"Don't be ridiculous," she snapped. Then, in a low, meaningful voice, she added, "I've seen worse."

She was careful, easing off first the slicker then his vest and shirt before finally peeling his long underwear down from the wide spread of his shoulders to the waistband of his denims. She knew she was hurting him. She could tell by the violent pulls of muscle. But he made no outcry. It was far from a scratch. The wound was ugly, a long furrow plowed through flesh but missing anything vital by scant inches. She had no fear that he wouldn't survive it, providing she could stem the blood loss and keep him quiet until the doctor arrived to do his fancy needlework. With the clean white towels, she blotted up the horrible wetness, trying not to give too much thought to the red stains that rapidly discolored them.

Sam accepted the glass of whiskey and gulped it down, holding the glass out for more. Lucy nodded to Chu. Then, when the marshal had finished, she took the emptied glass and had a drink for herself. The fiery strength of it restored her color and steadied the roil of her stomach for what she had to do next. She tipped the bottle up to pour the amber liquid onto a fresh towel, soaking it liberally. She found the narrowed gray eyes studying her movements and he tensed, guessing her intent. She waited, expression apologetic as he readied himself for the agony to come. His breathing deepened, his jaw tightened and then he nodded, eyes closing.

Even though she'd prepared herself for it, the sound of his pain, the hoarse suck of air, the telling staccato of his boot heels on her floor, she felt her courage flag as she pressed the towel over his raw wound. Her eyes stung and her throat thickened as she forced herself to keep the whiskey-soaked cloth against him for one, two, three long seconds. When she drew it away, they both sagged in relief. She allowed Li to move her gently to one side and watched through hazy eyes as the Chinese woman snugly wrapped the injured man's side.

"He should lie down now with feet up so blood that's left can reach his head," Li instructed softly and Lucy didn't argue. Between them, they managed to lift him off the fragile chair and shift his unresponsive weight to the tufted-back sofa. While Li arranged his long legs so that they were propped up on one rolled arms, his eyes fluttered open then were instantly aware.

"My horse," he blurted out.

"Taken care of," Lucy soothed, coming down on one knee beside him.

"Newt, someone should be with Newt." He was panting again. His words were rambling, anxious. Lucy stilled the tossing of his head with her palm, pressing it to one clammy cheek.

"Lie easy, Sam. Everything's fine."

"Lu?"

"I'm here."

His bloodied hand came up to cover the one she'd laid against his face. His fingers curled convulsively. "I'm sorry. Can't change the way things are."

Thinking he referred to their dissension of the previous day, she smiled slightly. The obstruction in her throat continued to swell until it was all she could do to swallow. In his fog of hurt, he was trying to mend the difference between them. "It's all right, Sam."

123

He continued to move restlessly for a moment as his eyes blinked rapidly and lost their focus. Finally, he let the weakness overcome him and he was still.

"Sam?"

His fingers fell away from hers to thump limply atop her silk-covered thigh. Lucy lifted it and arranged the slack hand over his bare chest. She was surprised to find tears cascading down her cheeks.

"He be okay, Missus," Li intoned quietly. "He strong. Wound not bad. Not like Mister Oliver."

No, not like Oliver.

"I go bring quilt to cover him."

Lucy nodded but stayed kneeling beside the unconscious figure. No, Sam Wade was nothing like her husband. He wasn't a man used to a sedentary life, closing on fifty. It would take more than a bullet graze through taut sinew and hard muscle to end his life. A life he had risked for a member of Blessing. That knowledge whispered through her. She forgot about the incident with John Mercer. It no longer mattered. The bank would survive the loss. He had rescued one of her town family and that more than made amends. And for that, she owed him.

In the late afternoon peace of her parlor, Lucy allowed herself the liberty to study the half-clad figure of Sam Wade. When he'd held her during their dance, she'd only a hint of his strength. With his upper body laid bare, she had irrefutable proof. He was lean, tough, without a spare inch of flesh not hewn into hard, virile contour. He was the only man she'd ever seen in a state of near undress other than her husband, and mostly Oliver had kept himself modestly covered. There was nothing soft or modest about the marshal. She let her palm move in a tentative exploration up the swell of his forearm. So firm, so capable of the violence she abhorred. Of tenderness, too? She wondered.

Li bent down beside her to spread a quilt over his recumbent frame. Without being told, she quietly withdrew, shutting the parlor doors behind her.

Lucy straightened the quilt, bringing it up beneath Sam's stubbly chin. That rough texture intrigued her hand into making a leisurely survey of his still features. He was handsome, she'd decided, rough cut and harsh like the land but no less beautiful because of it. Then, realizing what she was doing, she moved away to the impartial distance of an opposite chair to continue her appreciative scan. So handsome. So male. So threatening to the purpose she would claim for herself. He wasn't the sort of man a woman considered seriously. Not a woman who savored her independence, who was proud of her own opinions. She wanted no close-minded, quick-drawing man of Southern ideals intruding into her life. She bit her lip in agitation. Seeing him stretched out beneath the quilt evoked another image; of Oliver laid out in his expensive coffin in much the same spot.

What in heaven's name was she going to do about the problem of Sam Wade?

Chapter Nine

A flurry of pounding on her front door woke Lucy. She straightened into a moment of confusion. It was dark. She was seated in the parlor, fully dressed. A long figure lay in shadow upon her sofa. Then, she remembered.

Scrubbing the sleep from her eyes, she gained the front door steps before Li, anxious to keep the sound from disturbing the wounded man inside. She didn't know the young woman who stood in agitation upon her porch but she knew what she was. She wore the mark of Nightingale's; snug crimson satin, black lace, starched petticoats that revealed an indecent amount of stockinged limb.

"I'm sorry to be a-bothering you, Miz Blessing, but I was told the marshal was here."

Lucy went as red as the saloon girl's gawdy gown. It was late. She stood with her chignon in wispy disarray and her fashionable dress suspiciously creased. Inside, Sam Wade lay on her sofa, half naked. And the whole town of Blessing knew he was there, with her, the two of them alone. She eased the door so it began to close, seeking a way to discourage the girl as much to protect the wounded marshal's health as to salvage her reputation. Sam ruined it the moment he appeared behind her, rumpled, unshaven, with his slicker pulled on over his long underwear and Levi's. At first, she was too stunned at seeing him up and around to protest. Where had he found the strength? More fretful of his weakened state than of her shame, she sought to deny him access to the door but he brushed her purposefully, if gently, aside.

"Evening, Billie," he said easily, as if it was the natural order of things for him to be lounging in the Widow Blessing's house after hours. "What can I do for you?"

Billie. He knew her by name. That knowledge provoked Lucy to the extreme. She looked long and hard at the girl. A passably pretty young thing with glossy black hair and soulful dark eyes. The prettiness wouldn't last long in her profession but there was enough of it in evidence now to make Lucy grit her teeth. And she'd be darned if the marshal was going to meet with his sporting girl upon her veranda after he'd stained her carpet and her reputation.

However, it wasn't an interest in the flesh that brought Billie McCafferty to the home of the town banker-lady. It was the matter of saving a man's hide. "Marshal Wade, I heard 'em talking at Nightingale's, stirring up trouble something fierce."

"What about, Billie?"

"About that rancher boy you got in jail. And how he'd look dangling from a porch post. I thought you ought to know."

"Thank you, Billie. You best get back before you're missed. I'll take care of things."

She gave him a grateful, trusting look and hurried back toward town in a rustle of stiff petticoat netting.

Lucy forgot her suspicions about the saloon girl as Sam wobbled beside her. She was quick to supply support, her arm going carefully about his middle and her shoulder dipping to come up beneath his arm. He leaned upon her for a long moment, drawing air hoarsely, shakily.

"Sam, come back inside. You're in no condition for this."

Contrarily, he began to straighten, easing away from her in cautious degrees until he held his own. His teeth flashed white and brilliant as the stars above. "Why, Miz Blessing, you telling me that you want to let those midnight assassins run roughshod over your town after that silky scolding to the contrary you gave me in front of half the town?"

She stiffened at his mocking tone but the look of concern lingered in her steady gaze. "You're hurt, Sam. You should wait until the doctor—"

"Lucy, there's a boy down at the jail holding a shotgun and he's more liable to shoot himself by accident than any one of those jurors of Judge Lynch. If that bunch is getting all liquored up at the Nightingale, they're not going to wait until I get a clean bill of health from the doc."

Terror shot through Lucy. She envisioned him standing off an angry mob, weak, wounded. He stood no chance and her harsh words goaded him. A helpless moisture gathered in her eyes. How she wished she could take back the words, to keep him here, safe, in her parlor while the mob below had its way. But she knew that wouldn't happen. He was already garnering his strength, readying for the confrontation. And there was a gleam in his gray eyes, a cold gleam of sharpened steel, unsheathed and whetted and anxious to be tested. Good Lord, he was willing, even eager to meet his fate.

"Sam—" Her voice trembled and failed her. Her

hand reached out to grasp his forearm without a hope of stopping him. She knew, irrationally, she knew, she couldn't lose him, too.

Sam hesitated but only for an instant. Only long enough to seize her chin in the vee of his hand, anchoring her to meet the whirlwind of his kiss. She was too startled to struggle, too stunned to respond as his lips moved over hers in a moment of hard mastery. Then, he was gone, moving toward the main street of Blessing at an awkward lope.

Lucy's legs suffered from a watery instability. She sank down in a pool of skirts upon her dusty front step as her wide, insensible stare followed his retreating figure. Trembling fingers rose to touch the damp curve of her mouth where it yet throbbed from the pressure of his upon it. Her breath shivered out against them. Oliver had never possessed her soul so completely with a single kiss. He'd never left her bereft of thought, of movement, of anything beyond exquisite feeling. Yet, she sat dazed and bedazzled by a near-brutal exchange with a dangerous stranger. It made no sense. And she didn't care if it did.

"Be careful, Sam," she whispered into the night.

Through the slatted shutters, Newt could see them coming. They formed outside Nightingale's, milling, angry, shouting to bolster their convictions. And now they approached the jail house, swelling with menace, surging with meaning. Torchlight glinted off rifle barrels and made a halo around the coiled judgment of Manila rope.

Behind him, Jimmy Jarret strained against the bars to get a look outside. He didn't need to see the mob to know they were coming. He could hear their frightful clamor. A clamoring for his neck.

"Deputy. Deputy, you gotta let me out of here!"

Newt was too distressed to enjoy the irony of being called deputy instead of limpy. The crowd of thirty, maybe more, were getting closer by the minute. He hugged his shotgun to his chest. He didn't care if they hanged the loudmouthed cowboy. He deserved it for his treatment of the sweet Miss Nell. Had things been different, he might have been proud to tote the rope. But he was a deputy marshal of Blessing, sworn to uphold the law, be it to his liking or not. Sam Wade had placed his trust in him. And he would not fail him. Even if he had to step out alone with only the double barrels of his shotgun to fend off a small, determined army. He stood for the law, now and it had to be an unwavering stance. If only his knees would stop jiggling like a newly born calf's.

There was a quiet clicking behind him as Cornelius padded to the door and began to whine. Newt scowled.

"You deserting me, dog? Well, go on with you."

He opened the door to let the yellow hound out but the dog began to wag his thin tail and seemed content to sit on his bony haunches. As Newt puzzled over his behavior, the door was pushed inward and Sam slipped inside. Newt was hard-pressed not to gush his relief.

"Jarret still locked up tight?" Sam asked as he strode to the gun cabinet and selected a pair of Remington 10-gauges with twin twenty-eight-inch barrels. He broke them expertly and fed in shot shells. There was no sign of strength-sapping weakness in his exacting moves.

"Yessir, Marshal," Newt answered proudly. "What we fixing to do?" That was said with a tad less confidence. His faith in Sam Wade was of epic proportion but there was a sizable mob outside.

"Marshal," Jarret cried out from the cell. "You can't let them hang me. I didn't do nothing."

Sam swiveled a look in his direction. "Some folk would say running off with a young girl against her will is something."

"But it wasn't against her will! It was her idea. Marshal, listen to me!"

"No time for that now, boy. Duck your head and commence your praying."

The surly gathering spread out in the street along the front porch of the jail house. They set up a murmuring roar, calling for Jarret, for justice. In the glare of torchlight, their faces held a maniacal gleam, twisting features that during daylight hours could be recognized as those of the blacksmith, the livery owner, the butcher and even the mayor. It was the esteemed later that called out loudly.

"We want Jarret. Bring him out."

Sam glanced to the ashen-faced boy and said softly, "You stay inside, hear? Keep watch over the prisoner."

Newt surprised him. His big shoulders squared. His shotgun angled up in an offensive pose. "Jarret ain't going anywhere, Marshal. I mean to step out with you."

Sam said nothing. He gauged the boy, now a man and nodded. Then, he jerked the door open and strode out onto the covered porch, a Remington braced on either lean hip. He could feel Newt at his back and the brush of the hound against his leg. And a warm trickle of blood beneath his bandaged side. A right threatening defense against an angry town.

"Visiting hours is over, folks. You-all come back tomorrow."

131

"You know why we're here, Marshal," Mayor Mayhew yelled out. "We mean to see that boy hangs for what he did to my daughter."

"We don't know for sure that he did anything to your daughter," Sam replied. An ugly muttering rose up at that. "That's for the circuit judge to decide, not your liquored-up sense of what's right. If the boy's to hang, I'll see he's not late stepping up on the gallows. Till then, you-all go on home."

"Can't do it, Marshal."

Sam looked in some surprise to the source of that calm claim. Henry Knight lounging against the hitching rail. He was dapperly dressed and empty-handed. It seemed his weapon was dangerously effective — his silken oration.

"See, we here in Blessing got standards. We don't want any trail-happy cowboys coming into our town making off with our decent womenfolk." There was a rumble of assent and Knight continued smoothly. "We've got a right to protect our property and our families. You taking a stand to say we don't?"

Sam answered him softly, so the rough muttering of the crowd had to still in order to make out his words. They rang in the silence, full of quiet authority, full of power.

"I'm taking a stand behind this badge you, yourself, and the mayor pinned on me. I'm taking a stand against the things you folks said you'd had enough of. Things like taking the law into the hands of a few. You think that applies only if you're not one of the few involved? It applies every time. If you say different, you come on up here and take this badge off me. Then I'll step aside and you can do whatever you want with the man in there." Men exchanged hesitant glances. Seeing them weaken, Sam sealed his argument. "And tomorrow, when somebody comes to your door thinking they got enough of a grievance to stretch your neck, who you going to come to?"

Henry Knight drew a long drag on his cigar and peered at Sam Wade through the blue smoke. He was shrewd enough to read a crowd, to know when sentiment was turning. And it was turning in Wade's favor. He prided himself for being on the winning side whenever possible. "Could be he's got a point, folks."

Sam leveled a look at the saloon owner, gauging his self-interested motive. Whatever Knight's reasoning, he wasn't about to refuse the support. Not when he felt the steady ooze beneath his slicker. Not when a cold sweat chilled his skin and threatened to bring on the fierce tremors of fast-approaching faintness. He breathed hard to fend off the swooning sensations and made his voice firm.

"The point being, if you want law in your town, you stand behind the man you elect to uphold it. You don't want me up here, fine by me. For now, I got a job to do and any of you thinking to have a little necktie party with my prisoner best be thinking again."

The sound of the Remingtons' hammers locking back was a mighty strong argument against storming the jail. They began to mill and murmur and slowly seep away into the darkness until only a handful remained to stand with the mayor. Mayhew was flushed and frustrated by what he saw as interference in his fatherly right to avenge his daughter. His was armed with the old Navy Colt he'd used to start the race at Thompson's and was weighing it alongside the balance of justice in one beefy hand.

Sam let his shotgun barrels dip down but he was far from relaxed in his posture. He spoke quietly, with a man-to-man confidence. "Mayor, I don't blame you. If it was my gal, I'd be hell-bent to find the nearest tree and stretch hemp. But you're a man of position in this town. You brought me here to serve Blessing. These here folks look up to you and feel you did right by making me their marshal. You gotta back that decision now, even though it tears at your gut to do it. You got my word that Jarret will get what's coming to him."

Mayhew's fleshy cheeks quivered then his pistol dangled limply at his side. His response was heavy, laden with a responsibility that denied him his lust for revenge. "I'll take you at your word, Marshal. You saved my girl and I'm beholden." With that, he shuffled away and the situation defused.

Only when the door closed behind him did Sam give way to the waves of woozy weakness. He handed the disengaged shotguns to a surprised Newt then spun downward into a dizzy darkness.

Feeling sore but pleasantly pampered, Sam wolfed down the platter-sized breakfast sent over from the hotel. Newt had been shuttling about, granting his every wish all morning, ever since the doc had stitched up the five-inch gash in his side. The querulous old man had come straight from the midnight delivery of a six-pound baby girl and was drawn with weariness. However, he'd responded to Lucy's summons and his needlework was neat and precise. While Lucy hadn't come to see him for herself, she'd sent her Chinese servant with a discreet parcel he'd assumed to be the rest of his clothing. He was somewhat bemused to discover it contained a brand new drop-shouldered shirt of fine blue muslin and a vest of soft brown deerskin.

A shame, he reflected wryly, that he hadn't thought to leave his long underwear behind as well. They were in sad need of replacement.

With his belly distended to the point of misery and Cornelius gobbling up the remains of his meal, Sam nursed his cup of coffee while he studied Jimmy Jarret. The young cowboy caught his scrutiny and returned it with a sullen defiance.

"I guess you figure now I owe you something," the young cow nurse grumbled. "What difference does it make if they hang me now or later?"

"You don't owe me nothing, boy. Most likely I should have let them string you up and saved myself the trouble of feeding you."

Jarret got up to pace restlessly. "Why didn't you? We got nothing but bad blood between us." His handsome face was still swollen and bruised from the fracture of his nose.

"Can't say as I know for sure. Something funny about the whole thing. Can't quite figure it."

"What's to figure? I made a fool of myself over a woman and she turned on me like a bad steer."

Newt came close to the bars and rapped his broom handle against them. "You hush your mouth. Don't go a-talking about Miss Nell that way."

"Ho, boy, she sure got you hornswoggled. Just like me. You'd best be careful you don't pay for it, too."

Sam sipped his coffee and tried to find a focus for his objection. Then, it came to him. The bed rolls. Lying all cozy like, one next to the other. "Tell me, hard case, where were you fixing to go?"

"Cheyenne. Nellie had family there and said they'd grubstake us so we could take the Concord coach to Deadwood and hit the gold fields."

"Why go on horseback? Why not just hop the UP?

Lot faster and easier on a pretty little thing."

" 'Cause we couldn't let our fathers know we was going. Nell'd been after me to marry up with her. Her pa wouldn't have no part of it, nor mine. Hers said she was too young, mine said she was too flighty."

"Should have listened to them."

"Do tell." He sat heavily on his bunk, head in hands.

"So you were eloping. That about the gist of it?"

He nodded.

"That's no cause for hanging. A good whupping, maybe."

"You saw Nell, Marshal, the way she carried on. She's scared of her pa. She'll make it sound like it was all my doing, like she didn't want no part of it. No judge and jury are going listen to me when she turns on the tears."

Sam had to agree there. Nell Mayhew was a competent little actress and, he was beginning to think, calculating enough to send a man to the gallows to save her own hide. He had no great faith in justice. Jimmy Jarret would probably hang. But that wasn't his concern. He'd be long gone by then. He'd leave the conscience of Blessing to another.

There was a rumble of commotion outside the jail causing Cornelius to stir from his position across Sam's feet to pad to the door.

"What's going on, Newt?"

"You'd best come see this, Marshal," the boy replied with a grin.

Sam rose, groaning and wheezing like the big rawboned hound as he hobbled to the open door. He paused there to take stock of the situation, bewilderment etching his features.

It was reminiscent of the night before. The street

136

before the jailhouse was crowded with the people of Blessing, this time with women and children included in their number. The doctor had spread the news of his heroic injury and some stood shamefaced. In the forefront was Mayor Mayhew with the other members of the council board. Lucy was there, her gaze riveted to the ground at her feet. And Henry Knight, chewing rather than drawing on a cigar. The mayor climbed up onto the sidewalk to stand at his side, addressing the smiling crowd as much as Sam.

"Marshal Wade, we the people of Blessing would like to present you with a token of our appreciation. We consider it a privilege to place our town in your hands. As a show of our gratitude, it's my honor to personally thank you and give you this."

A shiny new rifle was pressed into his hands. Sam stared down at it, dumbfounded. It was a Winchester .44-.40 '73 model with an extra rear sight for greater accuracy and a seventeen round magazine; four more than his lighter, shorter barreled and less powerful carbine. It was a sleek, beautiful piece. His hands couldn't help caressing it. On the stock of the elegant, gold-mounted rifle were the engraved words: "For valuable services rendered the Citizens of Blessing."

It was then Lucy looked up at him and the warmth shining in her eyes was more blinding than sunlight off the extravagant trim. And he knew a moment of pure, simple, paralyzing panic.

It was late. A trip to Nightingale's had proven useless. His mind was still turning over thoughts he had no business entertaining. It was their fault, the people of Blessing, for embracing him with trust, for smothering him with unwanted responsibility, for making him believe again in fables — that there was such a thing as honor, as home, as happiness. And resentment simmered for the fools of Blessing because he knew it was a lie.

The Winchester was cradled in his lap. He'd been methodically, almost tenderly, polishing it. It was a fine weapon. He would attach no more to it than that. As soon as Blessing lay behind him, he would have the engraving filed off. He wasn't quite ruthless enough to view it as a joke. Maybe when he'd ridden in, but not now. Something awful and powerfully worrisome had happened to him since coming to Blessing. He was losing his edge. He was becoming caught up in their folly. Why should he nurture the confidence of an awkward cripple? What was it to him if an innocent man fell prey to the foolish nature of a female? And how did one look from an opinionated widow choke him up like a fierce dust storm? He was blinded. He couldn't breathe. He couldn't find the path he'd sworn to take. What was it about her, about this place that had him lost and at the same time held safe in the haven of home?

Home. That was a ridiculous notion. One he hadn't known or held for a lot of lonely years. It had gone up in flames nearly fifteen years ago and had been burning inside him ever since. Blessing had opened its arms to welcome someone named Wade, not Sam Zachary, a man who was their worst nightmare. He hadn't come to keep the peace and earn the respect of its citizens. He'd come to steal them blind and laugh as he rode away. He was about as far from a man of the law as a man could get. What irony that he should be set to guard a boy ready to hang for some harmless hoorahing.

The law. He had nothing but disdain for it. Lawmen were more interested in politics than people. Judges were unschooled and unprincipled. And often, it was the innocent who suffered because the true villains were too clever to be caught. Villains like Sam Zachary. It was a cruel sort of joke that he be tempted by a life behind a badge. The sort of joke that would make Grant Tolliver turn apoplectic. What kind of work was it for a man? He'd looked at the arrest ledgers of Blessing. For the last three years, its record was singularly dull: twelve drunk and disorderlies, ten disturbing the peace, six involving threats of violence, three assaults, one resisting an officer of the law and the rest a sad assortment of petty theft and reckless buggy driving. He had it figured that most of the serious crimes in Blessing were dealt with by hooded figures in the night. And perhaps they handled it best. Why would he be interested in spending his remaining years herding livestock off the street and chasing down desperadoes who were late in paying their mercantile bills? Tame stuff after the life he'd led. They didn't need a professional shootist of his caliber, they needed an ambitious street sweeper.

And why, he wondered, would he be thinking of settling someplace run by a damn prickly female who would accept his kiss but not his court? Lucy Blessing was at the heart of his frustration. He was crazy to even think of her as anything beyond a potential victim. She owned the bank. She went around callously foreclosing on the luckless and the weak. She treated the town as if it was her private little garden to be tended at her pleasure, with all the undesirable weeds plucked out. What would she consider him? Her opinion was low enough knowing nothing. If she knew the truth, she'd be the first to call out the hooded raiders to dispose of Blessing's most undesirable element. He'd thought it amusing to provoke her, at first. Now the jest had taken a wry twist.

He didn't want to believe that Blessing or its mentor had anything to offer him. He'd stayed too long, that was all. He'd been missing family. He'd been tired of the traveling, the running, the killing. Blessing was proving to be a dangerous place to rest.

His hands stroked over the Winchester. A token of their gratitude, their trust. He was so far gone, he couldn't force a cynical smile. A lump of emotion actually thickened in his throat.

Angrily, Sam pushed back his chair and stalked across the jail to where Jimmy Jarret lay sleeping in his cell. The boy came up in alarm at the sound of the key in the lock. His wide eyes flashed from the rifle in his hand up to his cold gaze, sure he was seeing his own death there.

Sam flung open the door and growled, "Go on. Git. You run far and fast."

The young cowboy didn't move.

"Reckon you didn't hear me. I said get gone. Lessen you want to hang. You won't get no fair trial here."

Jimmy edged slowly toward the door and the stony-featured marshal. He was beginning to think—to hope—it wasn't some trick to lure him out just so the lawman could shoot him in the back. "Why you doing this, Marshal?"

"Just say I believe in justice more than I believe in the law." As the boy started to slip past him, Sam gripped his shirt-front and twisted tight. "You ease on out of town real quietlike. You take a horse, you make sure you pay for it. You run across a citizen, you tip your hat. You make any trouble for me and this town again, and I'll hang you myself right from these here bars. Got that?"

"Yessir."

Sam's fingers opened and the cowboy went running. He stood for long minutes, listening for a cry of discovery, for the sound of shots but the streets of Blessing were silent. After a time, he returned to his desk and eased down into the chair and into a bottle of Ole Tom's favorite. His face was grimly set, his stare hard. The fancy rifle lay on the desk top and he refused to pay it notice. He didn't need any fancy shooting stick from the good folks of Blessing. He didn't need any nice new clothes from the lady banker. He didn't need the worshipping respect of Newt Redman. He didn't even need a damned bony hound for company. It wasn't his dog. This wasn't his town and Lucy Blessing sure as hell wasn't going to be his woman.

He took a long draw from the bottle of solace and made his plans. Tomorrow. Tomorrow he would start picking Blessing clean.

Chapter Ten

There, surrounded by games of chance and looked down upon by lusty nudes, heads were bowed in prayer.

There was no church in Blessing. Four saloons, three sporting houses but not one church. For humanitarian reasons and public opinion, Henry Knight allowed those who would worship the use of his saloon as a gathering place. He closed the games so they could cluster around the tables to hear the word of the Lord spoken by a circuit preacher. But the bar remained open. Humanitarian, maybe, but all businessman.

Lucy was pleased by the attendance. Every time they held a call to worship, more and more appeared. With creature comforts established, they began to tend to the direction of their souls. The more reserved ladies of Blessing, who were at first shocked and reluctant to come into the din of Satan to hear the teaching of God, were now stoic about their surroundings, even fired by them. They began to drag their menfolk with them, a handful at first, then a goodly number. Lucy greeted each and every one, trying to make them feel comfortable serving two very opposing needs under the same gaudy roof. At the end of the opening prayer, she counted heads. Three more had joined their number. She frowned only slightly to see that one was the saloon girl, Billie, who'd come to her home for Marshal Wade.

Made confident by that steady growth, she vowed to approach the town council at their next meeting with the plan to build her church. She had all the figures ready and the inspiring illustrations from Lyman Bridges' Ready Made Houses catalog. She, herself, would donate half the five thousand dollars needed to purchase the structure. When the rest was raised, they could place the order and the precut materials would come by rail from Chicago. She hadn't chosen a small room-size building but a big thirty-two by fifty-six-foot design complete with arched windows and a bell tower. It would take a long time to fill the two hundred-seat church but they would, pew by pew, growing as the need in Blessing grew. And when the materials arrived, they would have a church raising. If the townsmen could put up a barn, they could darned well build her a church. A church with its own preacher, a man of the cloth who would be a permanent member of their community. A dream come true for Lucy Blessing. A long-ago prayer, realized.

When her head lifted from giving thanks, Lucy was surprised to see Sam Wade enter the bat wing doors. For a moment, she held to a fragile hope. It soon faded as he tipped his hat toward their gathering and headed straight for the bar to order up a beer from Jeff, the slicked-up drink mixer who glowered at them while he polished glasses. Beer in hand, the marshal leaned one elbow upon the carved bar, the other still pressed to his injured side, and observed the doings with mild interest.

Lucy tried to keep her attention on the service but it

143

was fractured at best. The memory of Sam Wade's kiss kept intruding. While Reverend Longford spoke on temptations of the flesh, she was burning proof. She struggled not to chance a wayward glance. Her cheeks felt hot, almost feverish. Was he thinking of their embrace as well? Was he restless to sample more? Or was she, alone, left sleepless with longing? She'd had no opportunity to speak with him since that fateful kiss and, with uncharacteristic shyness, she hadn't sought a meeting. She was embarrassed—not because it happened but because she wanted so desperately for it to happen again. Her pride would not allow him to recognize how vulnerable she'd become. The female in her insisted she wait until he made another overture. She would not chase after him, wantonly, shamelessly, though her every fiber would urge it of her. Nothing indecent or improper could pass between them. After all, she was Blessing's leading lady and he its marshal.

However, when she would hazard a glimpse of him lounging back against the bar, clad in the shirt and vest she'd bought him, her thoughts toward Sam Wade were far from proper.

"Good people of Blessing," Reverend Longford was saying. "Might I introduce you to our newest member. Sister Billie is a follower of the town's fallen but it is her most fervent wish to restore herself upon the path of righteousness. Her request has evoked in my heart and I hope yours, a need within our community, one long overlooked by our Christian members. What are the Christian men and women of Blessing doing to aid the poor fallen women of their town? These unfortunate females are not a plague upon you but a mission, a test to your faith. They, like Sister Billie, come from humble roots, from the farms and Middle

Border states. It is not the wish of all of them to squander their souls in sin. Some are driven by personal misfortune or financial need. Some would gladly surrender the ways of evil were the road to righteousness shown them. It is our solemn duty to show them the way."

"There ain't nothing you can show them girls, Preacher."

That loud claim from one of the men lingering at the bar brought a shout of laughter to the other dozen or so early-hour patrons who resented their peaceable drinking being disrupted.

Reverend Longford continued without bestowing notice upon the sniggering cowboys. "We must consider ways to reclaim the prostitute."

"Two bits will do it, Reverend," sang out another raucous interruption.

The ladies began to blush and the gentlemen with them struggled to retain their smiles. Lucy glared at the disrespectful gathering of men at drink then let her gaze linger on Marshal Wade, calling to him silently to do something. He returned her stare unblinkingly, his long frame never moving to make a protest.

Looking a bit more harried but no less determined, Reverend Longford said firmly, "I call upon each of our Christian women to give counsel to the fallen. Show them the virtue of a moral existence and the joys of being cleansed by the Holy Spirit. Lead them away from a degrading life."

"Take away our 'erring sisters' and we'll be forced to turn to the good ladies of Blessing for our entertainment."

That sneering claim brought gasps to the gathering of females and their husbands were no longer smiling. Slowly, Sam drained his beer and withdrew one of his

Colt revolvers, placing it conspicuously on the bar. He spoke up easily, casually, but none would be misled by the soft tone.

"You've had your funning, gents. Now, have a little respect. In fact, let's show the good reverend that your hearts if not your souls are in the right place." He took off his Stetson and flipped a gold eagle inside. He then set the inverted hat upon the bar, next to his pistol. "I think we need to take up a collection. Don't let greed overcome conscience, now. Dig deep and give cheerfully."

Slowly, begrudgingly, they came, each and every one of them to deposit a piece of coin into the silver Stetson. When it was heavy with the weight of their prodded humility, Sam strode across the room to tip the contents on the baize table before the preacher. It was an admirable sum and Reverend Longford regarded him as somewhat of a miracle.

"Thank you, Marshal. Won't you join us?"

Sam saw the hope glow in Lucy's eyes and felt an uncomfortable twist take hold of his belly. He made his words wry but not arrogant. "No, thanks, Reverend. I got nothing against God but I don't think he has much use for me." He picked up his hat and settled it atop his sand-colored hair. "Put in a good word for me, if you've a mind."

As he walked back to the bar, he heard a prayer offered up and a sudden chill overcame him.

"Lord, we raise our voices to you in thanks for providing us with your bounty through Marshal Wade."

He walked faster, trying to shut out the words, trying to close tight his heart. He called for another beer and drank it down with a vengeance, his back to those who would praise him.

Lucy was saying her own prayers: one for the fate

of Blessing, one for the first time, concerned with her own happiness, and both linked to Sam Wade. More and more, she was convinced he was good for the town. What he'd just done was a beginning. He could be a powerful force in the direction of the community. She'd been wrong about him. He wasn't an indifferent drifter. He cared about Blessing and its people. And she wanted him to care about her.

She'd married once out of necessity. It had been a good marriage, one of kindness and respect. Never had she felt elements missing until now. Until Sam Wade. He set her emotions tumbling like a prairie whirlwind. He was exciting. He was aggravating. He had the depth and mystery of a shadowed well and she wanted to cast down pebbles to listen for the intriguing echoes. And she was attracted to him. She may have been the leading female figure in Blessing, concerned with reputation and respect, but she was also a woman, and Sam acted on that simple fact with a stunning force. He wasn't impressed by her achievements. He wasn't intimidated by her title. He wasn't covetous of her wealth. He responded to her, man to woman, and there was no other thrill like it.

Lucy was not one to wait passively for anything to happen. She'd been steering her fate for a lot of years and was used to being in control. Having decided she would have Sam Wade, or at least the pleasure of exploring the possibilities, she cast off her plan to primly sit back and pine for his attention. That was a foolish waste of time and energy. The direct course was always best. Eager to begin hewing the marshal from rough-cut timber into a support beam for the town of Blessing, a staunch pillar that would stand beside her, Lucy approached him as soon as the final amen was uttered.

147

"Marshal?"

When his gaze slanted at her, Lucy knew an instant of wondrous confusion. For a moment, she was completely, unprecedentedly witless. Her flustered stare fell from the cool gray of his eyes to his narrowed lips. They hadn't felt thin or inhospitable when crushed against her own. They'd held the promise of indescribable bliss. The tip of her tongue nervously wet her own.

"Miz Blessing?" he prompted in a distant tone.

That remoteness triggered her senses. She shook off her woolgathering attentions and got right to the point. "Marshal, I'd like to invite you to dine with me on Friday evening, if you've no other plans."

He was unresponsive for a long moment, as if he had to give the matter careful thought. She felt a warning flush of temper creep into her cheeks. It was an easy thing to say yes or no. He needn't mull it over quite so thoroughly. Quite so insultingly. When at last he answered, it was with a slow, languid drawl that spoke of no anticipation.

"Happen I'm free that night. Is there an occasion? Or can I show dressed as is?"

She gave his wardrobe a cursory glance and said curtly, "You look fine."

"Just you and me? All cozylike?"

She didn't like the lazy way his eyes wandered down the front of her gown. Slowly, with unmistakable insinuation. She felt her lips tighten and her words ground out between them. "It's dinner, Marshal. Do you or do you not wish to come?"

One corner of his mouth lifted. "Why, ma'am, I'd like nothing more."

Her features were stiff when she replied, "Fine. I'll see you at seven."

Lucy stalked away, feeling angry and elated. Now that she'd engaged him for the evening, she was half tempted to turn and jerk the offer back. The insufferable, arrogant man. What he implied she had planned behind the invite to dinner made her burn with furious indignation. And with half-realized longing. Maybe she had hoped that the evening would develop into something beyond the limits of the meal. Did that give him call to mock her and rub her face in her tentative expectations? Or to make her feel cheapened by the asking?

Outside the batwing doors, she paused, taking hold of her seething emotions. Something wasn't right. For all the crude suggestion blandished in his words, there had been no answering heat in his stare, no lurid light to accompany his smirking smile. It was the same way he'd regarded her upon their first meeting: mocking, contemptuous, as if no kiss had ever been shared between them. No promise of "later." Why did she feel as if his attitude had nothing to do with what he was feeling? Marshal Wade was a perplexing man. It was as if he wanted, intentionally, to rile her. Why, unless he didn't want to accept her invitation? A simple "no thanks" would have been less trying. So why had he said yes?

Newt looked forward to most Sundays; the ones that had his father home sleeping off the effects of Saturday night. He liked listening to the circuit preacher. It gave him a warm, positive feeling inside, a strength that went beyond the weakness of his body. Miz Lucille had encouraged him to attend and he'd never regretted it, especially once he spied the dainty figure of Billie McCafferty.

He'd never associated with the town's sullied females. The way several of them had coaxed him on then mocked him when he was little more than a boy, still scarred his memory. He saw himself as someone no lady, respectable or no, would ever show an interest in. That was why he experienced such a shock to find Billie gazing at him with a shy smile upon her face. She was dressed sedately, more like a shop girl than the sinnee she appeared to be when garbed in spangles and black stockings. He'd been taught by a mother he barely remembered to always be polite to a lady, so he doffed his hat and returned the smile.

She wasn't as pretty as Nell Mayhew, nor did she have that same fragile quality about her. Billie McCafferty looked old beyond her years. Alone and sad. That sadness touched a common chord in Newt Redman. He knew well what it was like to be alone. He couldn't understand her feeling that way. From what he knew of crib and parlor girls, they were an outgoing bunch who never lacked for company. Not that he held any hard feelings toward the way they made their living. Folks did what they had to to get by. That didn't stop him from thinking on her big dark eyes as he ambled to the jail house. Nor did it linger in his thoughts when he discovered the prisoner was gone.

"Have one on me, Marshal."

Sam tipped his hat to Ruby Gale as she sidled up beside him at the bar. She made a motion to Jeff and a tall glass was foaming before him.

"Where's your partner this morning?"

"Late night. He was still recovering when I saw him last." There was nothing subtle about that piece of fact. Ruby chuckled. It was a deep, throaty sound.

150

"Good thing. He wouldn't have cared much for this morning's sermon."

"I have the feeling that things Mister Knight doesn't care for have a way of rectifying themselves right quick."

Ruby answered his mild observation with an equally cagey smile. "You might say that. Henry's not a man who likes — shall we say, obstructions. You might want to remember that, Marshal." Her fingertips stroked over the back of his hand.

"I got no call to get in his way long as he stands by our bargain. You might be reminding him that his license fee is due tomorrow. He can send it round the office or I can stop in for it later."

"I'll be sure to tell him."

"And that goes for your establishment, too, Miz Ruby."

"Wouldn't want to go breaking no laws," she purred. "You can come up to collect tomorrow night, say after ten."

"Sure that won't be an obstruction?"

Ruby laughed. "Henry and I are in business together. In every aspect."

"Well, now I find that hard to believe." His gaze swept over her in appreciation and she fairly wriggled with delight. "Just in case, why don't you send it to my office."

When she began to frown, he pinched her chin between thumb and forefinger. She dipped her head to catch his thumb in her teeth, worrying and lapping at it for a moment before letting it go. "If that's what you want, Marshal."

"Just business, ma'am. For now." His potent male grin was enough to placate her. For the moment.

Sam was halfway to his office when he was set upon

151

by the mayor, his reticent daughter, Lucy Blessing and a dozen of the town's most prominent. He had a good suspicion of what had them het up.

"Marshal Wade, where's the prisoner?" the mayor demanded. "Has he escaped?"

"No, sir," Sam said easily. "I let him go last night."

Mayhew's florid face went alarmingly purple. "You what?"

"Mister Mayor, folks, I know I promised to see justice done and I haven't let you down. Ain't that right, Miss Mayhew?"

Nell Mayhew stood rigid as all eyes turned toward her. Her face was as pale as her father's was red. Her soft lips quivered and emitted a squeak of a response.

"I don't know what you mean, Marshal."

"No? Shall I tell them, then?"

"Marshal Wade," the mayor began. His voice held a warning rumble.

Lucy put a hand on his shoulder. "Let him continue, Edgar." She was remembering the gloating look upon Nell's face as she waltzed away from Jimmy Jarret on Newt Redman's arm. She noted the fear that replaced it now. Then she looked to Sam Wade and waited.

"Miss Nell?" he prompted. "Better from you than me," he added softly.

She bit her trembling lips in a moment of indecision, eyes trapped, panic rising.

"Do you want to see young Jarret hang?"

That suggestion finally broke her. "I ran off with him, Paw. It wasn't Jimmy's fault. We were running off to get married and everything happened fast and so wrong." She cast a resentful glance at the marshal then was all vulnerable, repentant tears when looking up at her father. And what father could resist them?

152

Lucy stared long after Sam's retreating figure. He'd known and he'd saved Jimmy Jarret from hanging. Justice was served but not within the perimeter of the law. Just like with Mercer. What kind of lawman was he? One who took it upon himself to play judge and jury. He was like no sworn officer she'd every seen. She'd never met Grant Tolliver but she knew of his reputation for sticking to the letter of the law. Was this the kind of man who'd earn his recommendation? A maverick? A vigilante with a badge? She thought not but she would know for sure just what kind of man Tolliver had sent them. Determinedly, she went to the telegraph office within the UP terminal.

"Bart, I'd like to send a wire to Cheyenne. To U.S. Marshal Grant Tolliver."

It was a once-in-a-lifetime opportunity. Sam realized that the minute Cecil Potter let him look inside the vault at the Blessing Savings Association. When he'd added the ample sums collected from the citizens of the community, the total swelled to tantalizing proportions. Upon voicing his concern for the safety of the deposit, Cecil obliged by taking him on a detailed tour of the bank's every security precaution, right down to where they kept their firearms, save one exception. Modesty prevented the clerk from mentioning the piece his employer wore on her hip. The time lock would be no problem. There was nothing to stop him from walking in during business hours. Nothing at all.

Over a cup of strong coffee, Cecil relaxed with the authoritative figure of the marshal and was convinced to confide in him.

"Yessir, Miz Lucille runs one solid bank. She's got

a good head for business, even better than the late Mister Blessing, God rest his soul."

"That him?"

Cecil looked respectfully up at the portrait. "Yep."

"Kinda old, for Miz Lucy, I mean." His narrowed gaze studied the aged yet commanding visage of Blessing's founder. Oliver Blessing had to have been twice Lucy's years. His hair was silver both on thinning top and in long trailing mustache. His expression was strong but not severe and there was a warmth the artist captured in his benign gaze. Sam could picture him as a community leader but not as the husband to Lucy. He thought of the way she'd responded within his arms. Had this old gent kindled the same reaction? He tried to place them together, Oliver and Lucy, in the house on the overlook, sitting together at the table, conversing on the parlor sofa, together upstairs. At that, his mind rebelled. It wasn't right. In fact, it was downright disturbing. Lucy was young, vital, a flashflood of passions. What could she have seen in the withered banker? Other than a bankroll?

"Not so you'd notice it, the age difference, that is," Cecil commented. "They were a pair, building the town up from dust with this bank to anchor it. Mister Blessing, he tied into the money from the mines and the ranches but it was Miz Lucille who got the army payroll to route itself through here. Did she mention it to you?"

"No."

"Got a shipment coming in at month's end. Miz Lucille might deny it, but we'd both feel a heap better if you'd give the bank a little extra attention until the paymasters come for it."

"My pleasure, Cecil. I'll give it my personal attention."

Sam smiled easily and Cecil responded in kind. The marshal inspired confidence. The nervous little clerk was able to put all his worries behind him. He had no notion what went on behind the cool steel of Sam Zachary's gaze as it swiveled back toward the vault.

Army payroll. Union army payroll. It was too good, too sweet to ignore. When his intuition told him to get and get now, he'd decided to make his move on Saturday, choosing the day after his dinner with Lucy. Even common sense couldn't provoke him into surrendering up that pleasure. He'd tried his best to get her to rescind the offer; he didn't have the kind of character it took to refuse it. But she'd insisted and he'd be there. And gone with everything the following morning.

But the payroll. Now, that was worth waiting for. A target that would serve both pocket and pride. All he had to do was continue the charade for a little while longer, to play marshal for the people of Blessing. It was easy. Surprisingly easy. They trusted him, which made it both simple and complex. All he had to do was harden his heart, to keep the inner fires burning. That scorching hatred would cauterize any attachments the town might make upon him. And he'd be able to ride away without a trace of conscience.

He hoped.

Sam finished his coffee and took another gander at Oliver Blessing. In mild curiosity, he asked, "How'd he die, Cecil?" He expected to hear of illness associated with old age but surely not what he was told.

"He was blown to eternity right on the spot you're standing." His face grew long and sad in the remembering. "A couple of drifters came in for the money. Miz Lucy managed to shut the vault so they couldn't

155

get past the time lock. Made 'em mighty mad. Mister Oliver took a shotgun blast to the middle. Nearly cut him clean in two."

Sam felt ill. "Right in front of her?"

"Ugly business. She killed them both, calm as you please. The town was right proud of her that day. Mister Oliver would have been, too."

Sam took a conscious step to one side, out of the martyred pool of Oliver Blessing's blood. *She killed them both, calm as you please.* He swallowed, hard. He could picture her with a smoking gun, thinking to save the town's money while bits of her husband were scattered all over her feet. What the hell kind of female was Lucy Blessing?

Chapter Eleven

The circuit preacher stirred up an unprecedented amount of Christian sentiment in the town of Blessing. Led by Lucy Blessing, the ladies undertook it as their mission to convert the soiled doves into respectable females. They began frequent visits to the girls of ill-repute at the tiny cribs where they conducted business. These visits were a shock to the moral fiber of any decent woman. They couldn't understand how a female could exist in the dingy little rooms which smelt of disinfectant, hair oil and cheap perfume. There, the only furnishings were a corner bed, an inefficient stove, a small dresser and washbasin. The only touches of humanity were in the pastoral prints upon the walls and photographs of family or other girls upon the dresser tops. They were a horror, an abomination and, to add to the insult, the girls had to pay to live in them.

During the visitations, they heard stories that brought tears and anger. They were pitiful tales of becoming destitute, of being seduced and abandoned, of falling before the perils of drink, of ill-treatment by parents or husbands. It was a shadowy life of fear. Looking back, there was nothing. Looking ahead there was the frightening future of walking the street as an aged, flat-footed, hard-working *nymph du pavé*, a fate that often lead to the morphine route of suicide. Some had been lured by the promise of an easy life and big money but few lived long enough to settle into a comfortable retirement. From the comfort of the parlor house it was a short fast walk to a dingy crib. Many tried to tell themselves they could save their money and get out but rarely did that dream come to pass. It was a simple way to earn a living. A girl had only to be friendly and willing. A pleasing shape and pretty face weren't necessary. The approach was a direct way to a man's heart and pocket. A sultry, "Hello, Sweetheart," a short dalliance at the bar, a few below-the-belt jokes, then the arm-in-arm promenade upstairs or to the tiny crib. A simple, desperate existence.

The ladies of Blessing came to offer compassion, prayer and hope to the "frail but fair." However, at Miss Ruby's, they found no fallen angels. They found businesswomen, not lost lambs. The brightly lit parlor house was a dramatic contrast to the dingy crib. There were glittering chandeliers, costly mirrors, an inviting array of decanters, carved woods, fine oils of titillating subject, strains of music and girls in fancy frills. Here, the dream of a better life still existed and the working ladies were unreceptive to those who came to pray for them. Some listened and said a pretty thanks but no thanks, others were rude and crudely jeered. Ruby's was a bastion of degradation and Lucy determined it her mission to bring the velvet-draped walls crashing down.

Little had ever moved Lucy to heartrending emotion like the plight of Blessing's unfortunate females. She had wept unashamedly to hear of their circumstance and hated the helplessness she felt each night while she lay in her pristine bed, knowing they were in the town below plying their miserable trade. She wanted to do more than offer empty commiseration. She wanted to *do* something to improve their situation. She started small, convincing local shopkeepers to open new positions to employ the most desperate of the lot. Many of the crib girls were eager to escape the treadmill of despair. She exerted the pressure of her position in the community, influencing the wife of one of the saloon keepers to have her husband close down his offer of horizontal pleasures and provide just dancing partners and company.

Surprisingly, it was the girl, Billie, who gave her the greatest encouragement. Her story was typical and tragic. She truly seemed eager to embrace a new life and in the time the two women spent together over tea in Lucy's parlor, Lucy was aware of a kindred warmth. Most of the women in Blessing respected her but there were none she could claim for a friend. Billie had the unlikely makings of a stalwart companion. Perhaps, because they shared more than the younger woman could guess.

Each success, large and small, was a celebrated personal victory. Little did Lucy anticipate the consequence of her week-long crusade upon the lusts of Blessing.

Billie McCafferty was making her way along the main street walk when she heard a low, undulating moan issuing up from a side alley. She paused. It was early and she was tired, having just finished up at Nightingale's. When the sound didn't repeat itself, she started to move on. Some dog or some drunk looking to sleep off his stupor. She was anxious to return to her tiny place to read through some more of the book

159

the Reverend Longford had lent her. She wanted to have it done by Sunday so she could return it and talk to him and to Lucy about the things swirling in her head. Possibilities had opened up in her once shuttered life. She was afraid but she was also willing to try just about anything to move from the line to a decent house. Her thinking had started in that direction again when she heard the groan a second time. It was no dog.

Cautiously, she peered into the alley. It was dim and scented with refuge. Not a pleasant place to go poking around. She saw only a shadow at first. A few more wary steps brought her close enough to see all. With a startled cry, she fled the alley, running to the nearest source of aid—the bank.

Lucy Blessing looked up from her ledger to the panting, wide-eyed Billie. "Miz Blessing, can you come quick."

The real fright in the girl's voice prompted her to respond. She followed the glittery spangle of the low-cut dress to the alleyway, then hung back, her hand readied to reach for her pistol. Then she saw the slumped figure and the reason for Billie's dismay.

"Oh, dear God. Stay with him. Can you stay with him?"

The dark, plumed head nodded jerkily.

Lucy wasted no time. She ran down the vacant sidewalk with one destination in mind. By the time she burst through the door, she was breathless and in a flushed disarray. Her words wheezed out from labored lungs.

"Sam, you've got to help me."

He was out of his bed in an instant. She didn't take in the fact that he only wore his long underwear; not at first. Large, firm hands caught her forearms, providing support, prompting a response.

"Lu? What is it? What's happened? Are you all right?" The words shot out as direct and rapid-fire as the way he emptied his revolver. A terrible dread gripped his belly and froze about his heart. His gaze raced over her, finding nothing amiss, to his great relief. She hadn't suffered any apparent hurt. His anxiety went down a notch. Still, the look on her taut face fostered a raw panic. "Talk to me, Lu."

Lucy struggled to catch her breath. She held to him by the shoulders, letting her head lean briefly against the breadth of his chest as she gasped and gulped for air. "Oh, Sam, he's hurt so bad. That animal. That vicious animal!"

"Who? Lucy, who do you mean?" He held her away, forcing her with the sheer intensity of his gaze to focus on what he'd asked.

"Newt."

Sam uttered one tearing curse and reached for his pants. His gunbelt was buckled on even before he donned his boots. He didn't bother with any more than that. "Where?" he demanded.

They could hear Billie's soft sobs of fear as they neared the alley. She was sitting in the filthy surroundings with Newt's bloodied head on her sparkled dress. The color he leaked blended with its vivid hue. Sam drew up short and made a soft incredulous sound deep in the back of his throat. Lucy had never heard the evidence of such agonizing grief. She started to reach out to him but he wheeled away, moving in a tight, distracted circle, his eyes squeezed shut, his voice a low lament. "Aw, Jesus — sweet Jesus." His features were etched with devastation.

"Sam?"

He blinked once, twice and was recalled to himself but she couldn't dismiss the incredible torment she'd seen in him. For Newt? Or was it something more?

161

Whatever its cause, he had control of it as he went to kneel down beside the boy. Gently, oh, so very gently, he scooped up the limp figure and carried him down to the jail house after ordering Billie for the doctor. Lucy trotted beside him, as upset by his strangeness as she was by Newt's appearance.

The doctor spent nearly an hour stitching and prodding. His verdict was cracked ribs and a possible concussion but that by no means entailed the savagery inflicted upon Newt Redman. He'd been beaten, cruelly, mercilessly, near to death and left to crawl away to seek assistance. His forehead was split, his features torn and bruised. One eye couldn't open through all the swelling. When asked what had done the damage, he muttered through bloodied lips it had been a whiskey bottle and his father's fists.

Lucy was shaken by a helpless rage. She stood at the window, staring blindly out over the street so Newt wouldn't see her hot tears of frustration. She felt Sam beside her.

"His father beats him?"

Lucy nodded in answer to that soft, throbbing question. "Since his mother ran off when he was a child. Luke Redman crawled into a bottle and hasn't come out yet. It's never been this bad before." Her words choked up and she took a shaky breath to ease them. "He can't go back there."

"He won't have to. He can stay here with me. I can put him up in one of the cells. It ain't much but—"

She put a hand upon his arm. The muscles were tight and quivering beneath her touch. Again, she sensed the immeasurable anguish and was puzzled by it. When she twisted to look up at him, it was as if his features were carved from native stone, as harsh as the alkali plains.

"It'll be enough, Sam."

162

"No." He said that with monosyllabic menace. "No, it isn't."

"What more can you do?" she asked softly.

"I'm going to kill that son of a bitch."

By the week's end, Newt was up and gingerly around. His features were a ghastly array of black and blue but his mood was high. The knowledge that he wouldn't have to return to his abusive father overset what he suffered in body. He didn't mind sleeping in an empty jail cell. Not one little bit. And his money earned would go toward his future, not into Nightingale's cheapest cut of whiskey. He vowed to mend and never make Marshal Wade regret that he'd taken him in.

In three days' time, his life changed radically. Gone was the lingering threat of violence. In its place came a thread of hope and happiness in the person of Billie McCafferty. She'd come by every evening on her way to Nightingale's to ask after his health and they'd talk. Sam, indulgently, made himself scarce and the two young people got on with the awkward business of getting acquainted.

Lucy's influence made that both easier and more complicated. Billie was taken with the other woman's authoritative elegance and began to question her own lot in life more somberly. Newt vowed he took no exception to her working at the Nightingale, if she had to, providing it was serving drinks and expending dances instead of pressing sheets. She didn't tell him how much pressure she was under to go from bar to bagnio. She was pretty. The men liked her. Ruby said she could triple her money. It was tempting but, Lucy had made her see, it was also a trap. She was confused by her choices. She respected Lucy. She thought the world of the shy deputy. But she was afraid of Ruby and Henry Knight and what they would do if she refused them.

At first, Henry Knight viewed the reforming effort as an annoyance then as an increasing threat. Girls were slipping away from the cribs he provided. In one week's time, the loss of income was marked. Ruby complained incessantly about the discontent among her workers. While none had yet to abandon the profession to clerk at selling yard goods, the whisper was in the wind and it blew ill. Having The Silver Eagle close down its joy parlors was an ease in competition but also an undermining of the business. If Lucy Blessing was allowed to meddle once, he was sure she'd followed through with a vengeance. She had the righteous females of the town in a lather and even the girls who weren't listening to their pap were thinking of using it as leverage for a bigger cut of pay. The sporting life in Blessing was becoming a powder keg of tension. All that was needed was a spark to send it all sky high. And Knight knew he didn't want to be seated on it when it blew.

"You see the problem, don't you, Marshal?" Henry poured another glass of his best rye. It was late Friday afternoon. The evening crowd had yet to gather.

"I see your problem," Sam conceded, "but why should that make it mine?"

Knight studied the marshal. He still wasn't sure about him and he wanted to be. It was time to test where his loyalties lay. "The ever-zealous Miz Blessing is no longer content to give the harlots religion. Now, she plans to strike a blow at the heart of a man's enjoyment." He tapped the half-emptied whiskey bottle beside them for emphasis. "A holy whore is bad enough but how many men do you think will come in to gamble if we're serving lemonade?"

"Not to mention how a clear head cuts into your profits," Sam drawled.

"Your profits, too, Marshal. I'm not going to have a bunch of foaming reformers axing my whiskey barrels and dragging out their wayward husbands. Damned bad for business."

Sam shrugged. True enough. "No man will put up with that for long. I don't see that a few harping old biddies will do any harm."

"No?" Knight drew a decanter from under the bar. It was filled with a repulsive black liquid. At Sam's curious gaze, he explained, "A barrel of my finest bourbon. Someone drove nails into it. Whiskey can't tolerate iron and here you see the result. I took that as a warning. Now I don't mean to lose any more of my inventory or my customers. What do you plan to do about it, Marshal?"

"You want me to run the lot of 'em in? How long do you think those customers are going to put up with no clean shirts or hot meals while their womenfolk cool their heels in jail?"

"Strike at the top, Sam. A group will crumble without a leader."

Sam's eyes grew all flinty and narrow. "You want me to beat up on Miz Blessing? Or are you fixing to send out some of your night riders to take care of it?"

Knight stiffened. The marshal was guessing, of course. There was no way he could know that for sure. He forced a smile. "No. Nothing like that. Maybe you can dissuade her. You know, man to woman."

Sam knew and he was tempted to fling the contents of his glass into Henry Knight's smug face. "I'll apprise Miz Blessing of the situation."

That wasn't good enough. The situation was growing critical. Someone had to take the matter in hand

and Henry could see the marshal wasn't his man. Somehow, he'd gone sweet on the sour Miz Lucille Blessing and a man like that couldn't be trusted. Ole Tom would have dealt a female a few good blows in a darkened alley. He knew how to do as he was told. Perhaps it was time Blessing had that kind of marshal again. Sam Wade was proving to be too independent-minded.

A disturbance at one of the poker tables reached them at the bar. A tall, obviously drunken man reeled up out of his chair. He was unshaven, unclean and unmindful of either. Something was vaguely familiar about him and prompted Sam to ask, "Who is that? He puts me in mind of somebody but I can't fix my mind to it."

"That's Luke Redman," Knight acknowledged and that was all Sam had to hear.

Luke never heard the approach of the man who nearly snapped his neck. One instant, he was scooping up his remaining coins to purchase a bottle to see him through the night, and the next, he was gripped by the soiled collar and jerked around to face a hard-eyed, gun-hung stranger. He stared in slack-jawed surprise.

"You scum-sucking, whiskey-sotted bastard. I ought to kill you where you stand. Give me a reason. Please."

Luke Redman was mean and mealymouthed but he preyed on the weak and this man didn't look to take abuse off anyone. "Who are you, mister? And what you got agin me?" Luke whimpered.

"You beat the hell out of my deputy and I take that mighty personal. Right now, I got about as much use for you as an udder on a bull. If you're smart, and I have my doubts, you'll get the hell out of my sight and stay away. I see you and I see something that needs

166

squashing bad. You might give some serious thought to living somewheres else. If you want to go on living."

Luke was slow when sober. When drunk, he was downright dense as a rock. "This about Newt? What lies that boy been telling? I been a good daddy to him. That sniveling, lame—"

Sam didn't let him finish. He dealt the man a fierce backhand, then when he didn't fall, returned with a closed fist. Luke Redman went down like a felled tree. A hot rage had settled inside Sam, a part of that which simmered in constant agitation just looking for a chance to fire up. It spilt out all over Luke Redman in senseless, savage waves. He struck the man, over and over, until his hand was numbed, until he was pulled off by four worried citizens afraid he was going to put an end to the man right then. Not that they'd consider it a great loss to Blessing. Still, they figured the marshal would want to be stopped before committing murder in a roomful of witnesses.

Restrained but by no means subdued, Sam snarled down at the barely conscious man, "You stay out of town, hear? You come round bothering your boy for whiskey money and I'll hear about it. And I'll finish this. You hear?"

Henry Knight heard. And he understood how he could rid himself of a troublesome marshal.

Lucy paced the parlor, checking out the front window for the umpteenth time and scowling down at the empty street. It was 7:30. Marshal Wade was late. If he was coming at all. They'd exchanged not so much as a how-do since Newt was sewn up in the jail house. She'd been busy with her reform work and he'd been out collecting tax money.

167

She'd been looking forward to this evening. All week. She'd tried on every gown in her closet at least three times trying to get the impassive Li to judge one superior to the rest. In the end, she settled for copper-colored taffeta that brought a burnished richness to her coiled tresses and a warmth to cheeks that tended toward pallor when she was overanxious. The short train and bunched drapery rustled with every step, sounding like the autumns she remembered in Kansas. She didn't want to sit lest she spoil the knife pleats that edged the skirt. And she was far too restless for the inactivity.

Where was he? Delicious scents wafted out from the kitchen where Chu had been concocting a master-piece since midday. The dining table was draped with starched white linens and agleam with crystal and silver. She was tempted to pop open the bottle of wine she'd garnered for the occasion. If there was to be an occasion.

It was 7:45. She could hear Chu cursing in Chinese as he tried to salvage his meal. Purposefully, she strode to the sideboard and let the cork out of the bottle. How she had looked forward to this evening with Sam Wade. Ridiculously so, it now would seem. She wanted time alone with him, to talk of Blessing, to talk of their pasts, to talk of anything of importance to either of them or of things of no importance. She just wanted to hear a man's voice fill the rooms of her lonely home. To share the companionable atmosphere of her table. She'd wanted to feel alive, attractive, female. And she'd wanted Sam Wade to make her feel that way. He may not have been the best choice among the men of Blessing but he was her choice. And now it would seem she'd chosen wrong.

Lucy poured herself a liberal glass of wine. She wanted to be angry—damned angry—at the marshal

168

for making her wait, for possibly forgetting their dinner. But the fury couldn't quite best the disappointment. She felt foolish standing in her fine parlor, dressed in feminine splendor, her heart beating with quick little surges of excitement and expectation. He wasn't coming. She gulped down the wine and poured another. Foolish and dismally alone. There was nothing left to do but thank Chu for his efforts. She had no desire to eat alone.

A rattling knock on the front door made her pulse jerk and begin a crazy scramble. She almost followed suit by running to the door. Instead, she forced herself to remember the things she'd learned from Oliver; composure, decorum, dignity—the elements of being a lady. She was the widow of Oliver Blessing, not an inexperienced girl awaiting her first court. Although, in truth she felt much more the latter.

She waited, taking slow, measured breaths to conquer her giddy anticipation. She could hear Li speaking softly and the low murmur of a reply. Sam. Her breathing altered radically. She followed the sound of his boot heels to the doorway until they came to a stop. Another deep breath to control the flutters that threatened to break out in a rash of trembling, she turned slowly to greet her guest.

He stood in the hall, hat tipped down to shade his eyes even where there was no sun. His face was shadowed with a day's growth of whiskers. His shirt was irregularly stuffed into his Levi's and askew enough to suggest he'd been brawling. Or had redressed in a hurry. The smell that reached her discriminating nostrils was less subtle. Whiskey. Now she knew exactly where he'd been. At Nightingale's. But with whom? The temper she'd held so judiciously flooded her face with hot color.

There he stood, nearly an hour late, disrespectfully

sporting his Stetson, reeking of liquor and he had the absolute nerve to smile at her.

"I'm here for dinner."

Chapter Twelve

"Do you own a watch, Marshal?"

"Yes, ma'am."

"Do you know how to read it?"

"I surely do."

"Dinner was at seven."

With that, she turned on her heel and strode into the dining room with a sharp crackle of taffeta. She heard him follow and wished he would just go away. It was too late to make amends. The evening was ruined and she was dismayed by how its loss upset her. She could feel the dampness of disappointment welling in her eyes and fought it down with pride. He could not know how he'd hurt her with his callous disregard.

"Something still smells mighty good. Are you sure there's nothing left? A shame for it to go to waste."

She was in no mood for his cajolery. "The only thing gone to waste was my time and I've no more to spend at your expense. Good evening, Marshal."

His honeyed tone was laced with vinegar. "And I suppose your late and sainted husband never kept you waiting."

Lucy whirled back to face him. Her expression was one of startled pain and he wished he'd said nothing. Her soft mouth trembled for an instant then firmed into a thin line. Dark eyes blazed. "No, he did not. He was always prompt. And well groomed and impeccably mannered. You, sir, show a sad comparison."

"You're mistaken there, ma'am."

She should have been warned by the steel beneath that low purring drawl. However, she'd been shaken off guard by his observation and in no position to anticipate his next move when it came. All she could manage was a small squeak of surprise when he yanked her up against the mountain-hard range of his chest. Her alarm-parted lips proved the perfect quarry for the downward swoop of his.

Lucy fought him, wildly, with a rejecting strength of outrage and distress. His merciless grip was meant to dominate and subdue her and that she would not allow. The ruthless pressure of his lips was hurtful but that was not what brought a rush of tears to her eyes. Sam Wade couldn't crush her will with his brute force but he could easily rend her heart. He held her captive with determined muscle when a touch of gentleness from him would have bound her forever. And she hated him for not understanding that. This was the kind of man he was, the man who lurked behind the half-veiled mocking eyes: a man of violence and cruelty. And she'd not only been foolish to invite him with her hopes, she'd been wrong to think there was more to him. There was nothing in him for her to admire, to long for, to desire. He was dangerous — a lethal dose of male for one lonely widow.

She managed to break away and squirm from his controlling embrace. She glared up at him, her feet planted, her body braced to hold against another attack. Her dark eyes were bright with fury and with the anguish that washed down her flushed cheeks. She hadn't the strength of body to resist him should he launch a second wave in his unforgivable assault but her defiant stare conveyed an unconquerable spirit. And her tears and sobbing breaths, a vulnerable pain.

It was what he'd intended. She hated him now. That was better, much better than the temptation of her regard. It would make what he planned to do so much simpler. He'd purposefully stayed late at the Nightingale, filling himself with whiskey as the appointed dinner hour passed and the minutes ticked away. He knew it would aggravate her but he hadn't expected it to hurt her. At the last minute, he'd ordered up his horse and had ridden, hard, far, intending to flee Blessing empty-handed just to escape the torment of confusion. It hadn't been the bank's money that lured him back. It was the bank's owner. No matter how hard he pushed himself and his mount, no matter how much distance separated them, the pull of want didn't lessen.

So he'd returned in the whiskey-laden cloud of raw desires. He'd nearly staggered into her fancy house, reeking with liquor, reeling with uncertainty to give them both what they wanted. He didn't want her to like it. Hell, he didn't want to like it himself. He depended upon her anger for salvation. If he pushed her hard enough, she would stand firm and deny him. It was too late for him to halt it but he trusted her not to fail him. Any decent woman would recoil from his crude demands. He expected Lucy Blessing to send him packing with the business end of her pistol-quick tongue. That's what he'd hoped.

But he hadn't counted on the tears.

The sight of them, of the evidence that he'd grieved her, shattered his resolve. What he'd feared, what he'd shied away from, what he'd tried to avert, happened. The fires of hate and the ice of disillusionment that had protected him for so long thawed and extinguished one another. A great sweet ache of emotion swelled to take its place. And it was terrifying in its power. And wonderful.

"Lucy."

She slapped him. Hard but not with enough force to shake him back to reality and from this disastrous, inevitable course. He fit his palm, not against his own fiery cheek but to hers. He could feel the wetness of her tears, the soft, heated texture of her skin, her resistance, the certainty of her surrender. He began to lean down, his mind screaming for him to stop, for her to run, for one of them to have the sense to halt the tumble of momentum.

And then he kissed her. All resistance fled. With the light, searching claim of his mouth upon hers, desire would not be denied. She made a tiny sound, a little moan of confused delight as his tongue dipped between her lips then teased along them. It was devastating bliss. Her hands came up to cradle his roughened face between them, encouraging his possession by coming up on her toes, by opening herself to him. He plunged within once, stunning them both with the raw potential of their passion, then withdrew. Their lips barely touched. Their breaths mingled.

"I'm sorry, Lucy," he moaned softly, helplessly. "I tried to keep that from happening. I'd better go. Sorry about dinner."

"No," she cried fretfully. Her palms compressed his cheeks between them. Her fingers hooked behind his strongly cut jaw. It was madness, she knew. She shouldn't have believed him. She should have held to her anger. But it didn't matter. He was here and she couldn't release him.

"Don't go, Sam. Please."

Gradually, he shifted back into a safe distance but not far enough to escape the melting power of her gaze. Inside, he burned. Not with the searing heat of vengeance but with a mellow glow of warmth.

174

"My mama would've had my hide for treating a lady so badly. Can we start over?"

Lucy nodded, left dazed and dreamy by his kiss.

"Fine. I'm sorry to keep you waiting. I had some things to straighten out. I'm powerful hungry." His lambent stare conveyed more than his words, speaking of a different appetite that wanted satisfying. And to both, she said huskily, "I'll see to it, Marshal."

Her hands reluctantly relinquished his face so that she could ring a small bell. Her eyes never left his. They were seeking, asking; giving more than he knew how to take and it was with relief that he turned to the silent Li. He gave her his Stetson then, after an instant of hesitation, he unbuckled his hardware and extended his gun belt. Lucy realized the compliment he paid her and silently savored it as his palms ran nervously up and down his bared hips.

"I feel undressed," he muttered, giving her a lop-sided smile.

"I'll see that you don't mind it so much," was Lucy's quiet promise.

His pattern of breathing faltered and his smile grew slightly strained.

A rattle of dinnerware distracted them from each other and Lucy led the way to the elaborately spread table where Chu was just finishing his fussing attentions. Sam saw her seated and allowed his hands the pleasure of moving up from carved chair back to the tempting curve of her shoulders. He let them linger there for a long second then he went to take his chair opposite.

It was a luxurious meal. They dined on salmon from California, on oysters from Baltimore along with area-grown vegetables simmered in a delicate sauce. But neither of them tasted or appreciated a single bite as tension rose to create a more delicious fare. Sam was staggered by the consequence of sitting at Lucy Blessing's table. The exquisite trappings, the rich food made him feel uncomfortable and out of place but the look in Lucy's eyes transcended the difference. And created a new discomfort. The silence simmered between them, growing thick and palpable with what stirred unsaid beneath the proper table etiquette. Finally, desperately, Sam launched into conversation, hoping to slow if not stem the compelling direction they were headed.

"You're poking in a hornet's nest with your reform ideas, Lucy."

She seized on the distraction just as eagerly. Talk was safe. The silence had become all too threatening. "Good. That was my intention." At his surprised look, she explained, "It will force them to think long and hard about the value and quality of life."

"The menfolk won't much like you meddling in their right to pleasures."

"Their right?" Her voice was deceivingly low but he hadn't missed the spark that came into the coallike darkness of her gaze. "Since when is it a protected right for a man to race into town each time he has enough silver to rub together to get drunk on badly cut whiskey, get cheated at cards and shanghaied by some kohl-eyed harlot? It seems it would make your job easier if there wasn't a band of wild-eyed cowboys hopped with Tangle Foot ready to shoot up the town every Saturday night."

"Long as they shoot straight up so only birds and angels get in the way."

"It doesn't bother you that Henry Knight skims the pockets of innocent family men, leaving them without the means to provide for their wives and children?"

"Or pay their mortgages on time? Is that what's got you so riled? Maybe some of those men need a means to cut loose after a hard day. Maybe one of those painted pretties is the closest thing to home and womankind they've seen in months. Maybe they consider the money well spent. Ever think of that, Miz Blessing?"

This wasn't the kind of conversation she'd hoped they'd have over the supper table. Lucy had planned on genteel topics meant to lure some of Sam's past to the surface. All she was learning of him was that he was opinionated and single-mindedly male. He sounded almost as callous as Knight, himself, about the fate of the unfortunate who entered the doors of the Nightingale. She could not abide a man without compassion and Sam Wade seemed closed to the subject.

"Then you see no harm in holding women as no better than slaves to sin?"

"Some would see it as a sight better place to be than where they came from."

Lucy fell silent. Her features took on a strange glaze of reflection that poorly concealed the way his remark worked upon her memory. Was he right? Would she see them cast back to what they were, into the hands of those who would defile them more cruelly because they were the ones who should have protected them from harm? But then, she wasn't thinking to judge the women of the line for making the only choice they could. She wanted to give them something better to look forward to, something that wouldn't make them believe they deserved the miserable treatment they settled for. Sam couldn't understand that. For one thing, he was a man, not subject to the control of another, as was a woman. Nor was he limited to what he could do to support himself. She was lucky. Wyoming was a liberal territory. Opportunity existed to give women independence. Even so, when they married, traditional ideas prevailed and she was expected to care exclusively

177

for her own — her husband's — home. Jobs were limited and women were still by and large considered best as objects of a man's pleasure, whether in his home or in his place of entertainment. And Lucy rebelled against the unfairness of it. And against the terror of her own experience.

"I could never take pleasure from someone else's suppression, whether it be in spirit or in body."

The quiet of her claim whispered like a chill wind of warning. Sam prided himself upon his sixth sense. That disturbing intuition had kept him out of danger's hands on many an occasion. And he felt it now, an uneasy tension flowing from Lucy Blessing. What wasn't she telling him? Something that would add tremendous significance to her words. It was bothersome not to be able to read her thoughts. Unlike most women, she kept them hidden: out of intelligence and reserve he'd supposed at first but now he suspected it was from something closer akin to fear. An odd yet powerful want to protect her rose within him, a want to strike down whatever threatened the serenity of her life. At whatever drove her with such determined desperation to rescue others from their fate. That quality had annoyed him. He'd thought it was because she wanted to control the people of Blessing, to make them beholden to her, not because she cared for them. However, he'd seen her tears over Newt Redman and knew them to be genuine. Just as the deep currents of emotion shifting through her now were genuine. What made her need to be the salvation of the town of Blessing? He'd asked once and had been curtly rebuffed. Would she tell him now? No. She didn't yet trust him. She desired him. He could sense that from her in strong sensual waves. But, rightly, she didn't believe in him. In the lie he presented. And he chafed at the loss.

"What is it you want me to do, Lu?"

She heard the sincerity in his offer and leaned forward, expression warming with hope. "Help me, Sam."

"How? I carry a gun, not a Bible. The law tends to favor Henry Knight as long as he stays within it."

She pushed away from the table in frustration and moved into the parlor where she could stare down upon the streets of Blessing. She knew he'd followed. She could feel him behind her, his strength of masculine presence, and she longed to lean back, to be surrounded by it. It was an impulse she fought. He had yet to offer that support.

"There's no law against selling watered whiskey, in running rigged games, in extorting slavery of the flesh? Or in murder?"

"Can you prove any of those claims?" he asked softly. His hands had come up to rest lightly upon her trim waist, not making any attempt to pull her to him, just settling there with an ease of familiarity that seemed very right.

"Others have tried." That settled ominously like the darkness on the streets below. "Help me, Sam. Look what you did for Newt. You gave him his self-respect, a future. I want to do that for all those who need it."

Sam stiffened at her reference to Newt. It hadn't been any noble intention that prompted the appointment of Newt Redman as deputy. It had been plain, simple and cunning self-interest. There wasn't a charitable bone in his body. No room to care for others when self-preservation consumed him. That and the need for restitution. He had no time for acts of kindness, no gentleness of heart to prompt them. And Lucy Blessing couldn't restore that in him. Those ashes were cold. As cold as the remains of a farm in Clay County. A body had to help himself first. He couldn't be beholden to another. That was survival. And her want to make him feel all those tortures of caring again made

179

him unreasonably angry and short in his response.

"They aren't your children, Lucy. You can't keep them from making their own mistakes. You can control their coin but you can't be their conscience. Maybe what you need is a child of your own to take your mind off the town."

She whirled toward him, her features pinched with anger, with frustration. "That's a man's answer for everything. Keep her happy and quiet with a passel of babies. Keep her downtrodden and at home and out of a man's business and his pleasures. Maybe you've forgotten, but I don't have a husband to give me children."

"You don't need a husband for that, Lucy."

The unexpected sultriness of his tone stunned her, then turned up the heat like a generous wick through inflammable kerosene. His thumb sketched the curve of her cheek and lightly followed the contour of her parted lips. Thoughts scattered from her head, leaving only stark and frightening sensation. She trembled at the promise of his roughened hand. Such tenderness undid her emotions. Once, just once, she yearned to experience the excitement of a virile man's embrace. And she found no man as potently stirring as Marshal Sam Wade.

"Let the town take care of its own troubles, Lucy. At least for tonight" was his quiet suggestion. That was what he spoke aloud. So much more was extended to her in the trace of his fingertips, in the cool gray dawn of his gaze — so inviting, so filled with tantalizing mystery. Just once, she wanted to taste danger, to flirt with excitement, to unleash the woman long denied within her. Sam Wade could satisfy all those wants. If she was brave enough. If she was selfish enough to think only of the moment and what it could give her.

Lucy saw his surprise and the edge of disappointment when she stepped away from him. But he made

180

no move to stop her or to argue further. She went from room to room extinguishing the lights until only the beacon at the top of the stairs glowed in welcome. For a moment, she hesitated at the bottom of the patterned runner, drawing a deep breath for the courage to take that first irreversible step. It was what she wanted. For the first time, what *she* wanted. Then, Lucy began to climb.

She was halfway up, well beyond the point of no return, when she heard the quiet tread of his boots upon the stair. An urgent, quicksilver rush of emotion wrought a fierce trembling along her limbs. She forced herself to continue the climb on less than steady legs. Nothing was certain now. All was in a taut, delirious whirl of expectation and alarm. A thousand doubts and encouragements raced through her brain as Lucy lingered on the landing within the circle of lamplight. Its warm brightness cast her gown into molten brilliance, as hot and liquid as the feelings flowing within. Was she mad? This man was a stranger to her. What was she thinking? The scandal. The risk. The threat to her emotional solvency. Did she really want a man like Sam Wade inside the guarded vault of her sensibilities? She remembered her first impression — don't trust him, he had the look of a cunning thief. Would he slip inside her affections and steal away with her heart? She couldn't allow that. This was for the moment. No contracts. Nothing binding. And for that, for a brief flirtation with passion, he was the perfect man.

Lucy gave a start as his hands settled with unseemly heat upon her shoulders. This was wrong, her staid conscience cried. It was against every tenet of her beliefs. They'd been violated before out of necessity but this was different. This was by choice. How could she crusade for moral decency then undercut her message within her own home? It was a mistake. She would make him see that. She could explain . . .

Then Sam turned her to face him and she gave up her protests. He was everything she needed. Strong. Ruggedly, aggressively male. His intensity overwhelmed her. Her own passions made all else fade into insignificance. This was right. For now, it was right. She let her will be molded by the blissful prospect of his kiss, her body by the compelling, powerful curl of his arms about her. It wasn't like either of the kisses he'd given her before; not ruthless, not sweet. Rather it engulfed her with heated promise. His mouth was hungry, demanding to be fed by all the vibrancy in her soul. Nothing less would sate him. His tongue invaded with confidence, letting her absorb the intoxicating taste of whiskey and wine and desire. It was meet the challenge of his ravenous appetite or be devoured. And she had no want to miss such an exquisite feast.

"Which way?" he asked huskily against her passion-pouted lips. He glanced in the direction she nodded, a front room where, undoubtedly, she could look down upon the town of Blessing. Without further word, almost effortlessly, he lifted her into his arms, cumbersome bustle and all, and carried her to that appointed room. He didn't bear her immediately to the high bedstead where a turned-back quilt beckoned. Instead, he settled her in the center of the room and proceeded to slowly, deliberately disrobe her before the lacy curtain that hid the lights of Blessing from their view.

Lucy shivered as his large fingers worked with surprising confidence down the tiny row of buttons that held her bodice together. It was a modest instinct, one of uncertainty, of trepidation, more befitting a bride than a widow. The reaction embarrassed her and she'd hoped he didn't notice. Then was glad he had when he murmured, "Don't be afraid, Lu. I won't let anything happen that you don't like." His words reassured because they spoke of his care for her, of his concern. If it meant no more to him than a quick press of the sheets, he wouldn't have bothered to quiet her doubts. That trace of heedfulness went far toward soothing her fears and opening her heart. Suddenly, she felt the need to be soul-baringly honest with him.

"You're the only man I've done this with other than my husband."

He stared at her, his expression maddeningly impervious to her imploring search. Was he disappointed? Relieved? Amused? She couldn't tell and it was important for her to know.

"Does that bother you?"

A slow, one-sided smile shaped his lips, adding a sensual curve to their fine line. "Hell-fire, you're the first quality lady I've been with so we're both pilgrims here."

She responded shyly to his smile and his gentle banter. It made things easier, that momentary relief from the building tension. It made it possible for her to laugh at his confounded curiosity over her undergarments. He was positively bemused by the steel contraption attached to her rump by a series of belts and hooks.

"How in tarnation do I rid you of this critter?"

Lucy made a game of it, teasing the elastic ribbons off her shoulders and detaching them from buttons sewn on her skirt. He followed each motion with his eyes, thoroughly intrigued then weighed the spiral wires in his hands.

"I'm surprised you don't have fluttering birds in this thing, too." He gave it a toss and concentrated on the more familiar-looking terrain of chemise and petticoat and stockings. He allowed his palms a leisurely summation of her gentle curves until they met with cold metal. "What the—?"

Petticoats were rucked up and he pursed his lips at the sight of the sidearm sported upon one shapely hip.

"You think you were going to have call to use that over dinner, did you? And here I let you unman me. Woman, you're something, you know that?"

These buckles and straps he was acquainted with and it took no time for the gun belt to follow the bustle to the floor.

"Any other surprises?" he asked with a rueful smile. "A Spies .38 strapped to your corset bones? A Barns .50 boot pistol tucked in your stockings? A palm piece fitted to your bracelet? You're one lethal little lady. I'd better pat you down for my own peace."

An intriguing thought. One that made her shiver.

His large hands roved over bare skin and fine linen but it provided no ease of mind. It incited all sorts of notions. Hot, exciting notions. Then, his fingertips edged beneath the lace-edged chemise and pushed upward. Lucy's breath sucked in and held. She knew a moment of discomfiture. She was so small compared to the bounteous Ruby Gale and even Billie McCafferty. His palms cupped and claimed her less than generous breasts and she waited, anxiously, to read of his disappointment. When he took note of her stiff features, he questioned her with his gaze.

Lucy blushed deep. "I'm afraid there's not much to explore."

Sam chuckled, that low, gurgle of sound that romanced her so sweetly. "Darlin', there's more gold in foothills than in mountains." With that, he shucked off her undergarment to assess them for himself. His voice had thickened noticeably. "And the view is just as breathtaking."

She let her suspended breath out in a shaky sigh as his rough face lowered to nuzzle and rub against her softly rounded flesh. It became a gasp of startled delight as his mouth closed about each aroused crest in turn to tease and torment with his tongue and the hard pull of his lips. Her hands became meshed in his hair, holding him to her, encouraging him with the arch of her slim body. Eddies of sensation coursed like a fast-moving stream, undercutting the last of her reserve as she moaned aloud.

When he straightened, she went right to the business end of pleasure. Her fingers moved impatiently to undo shirt buttons and those of the long underwear he wore underneath. Then, there was just the smooth temptation of his chest, as hot and hard-packed as the desert floor. The trek across it was as magnificent as she'd imagined on the night she dressed his wound. The tape still binding his ribs was a reminder and she touched it in concern.

"Still hurt?"

"Not tonight, sweetheart," he vowed with a husky rumble. Then he quickly finished what she'd started until he stood jaybird naked in the soft glow of lamplight.

Her insides began a fierce trembling, heating and liquefying into a ready flame. In scant glimpses of a forearm, of the vee of his chest, she'd found his body tantalizing. Completely exposed to her view, he was awesome, almost frighteningly male. His build was hard and spare, formed to cruel contour with corded muscle and the taut stretch of flesh. There was no softness to him, no hint of accessibility, like the mountains that soared in harsh majesty across the windswept plains. It was her first sight of an unclothed man; Oliver never undressed completely even during their gentle lovemaking. Nor had he ever consumed her with his gaze the way Sam Wade did at that moment. Her body responded with a tremor of expectation, her mind with an almost numbing shock.

Witnessing her shift of mood, Sam cupped her chin in his hand and drew her up for a soul-searing kiss. His lips caressed, his tongue plunged; all the things he planned to continue with hands and body the moment she relaxed to allow it. He felt the instant her fears ebbed. Her hands slipped up to touch him, cautiously at first, then with increasing aggression. That was all the answer he needed.

The bed sank beneath their joined weight and embraced them in comfort. Kisses led to urgent caresses. Emboldened exploration. It was like nothing Lucy had ever experienced. Or dreamed of. She burned wherever he touched her, sensations waking and quivering frantically beneath the impatient stroke of his hand. She said his name, once, a soft plea of uncertainty when his caresses centered between her tightly clenched thighs. He worked the shy resistance from them, building instead an almost fearsome bind of pleasures. She fought them at first, those sharp, quivering feelings, frightened of the intensity, alarmed by the control he had over her emotions. Then, when he whispered hoarsely against her panting lips, "Let go, Lu," she shattered into shuddering surrender.

Even before the tremors eased, Sam was above her, kissing her fiercely, nudging her knees apart to accommodate him. She clutched at him, urging him not to delay with breathless little cries that begged fulfillment. He sank inside her, filling her with heat, with strength, with incredible completion. Until she wondered in dazed rapture how anything could measure to this moment of perfect joy. And then he began to move within her.

And Lucy found she'd just begun to discover pleasure.

Chapter Thirteen

The lacy curtains billowed out on the gentle breeze blowing up from Blessing. Occasionally, it carried the tinny strains of a saloon piano and pistol shots from a hurrawing cowboy. To Lucy, they were vague and no more real than the town below her; not as real as the man who held her in his arms and rocked her upon his chest with each breath.

She forbade herself to think or feel beyond the moment. Their lives would intrude soon enough. She wanted to savor each spectacular second, whether it be one of searing passion or of quiet, like now. She wanted to make Sam Wade her everything, for him to fill her thoughts and heart the way he had so magnificently filled her woman's form. While in his embrace, nothing existed beyond them. It was a wonderful, peaceful paradise for however long it lasted.

She felt deliciously languid, as if every fiber of her being had been tempted and tested and toned into exquisite focus then allowed a rewarding laziness. There was an infinite contentment found in his enveloping presence, a wantonness in stretching out beside him bereft of clothing; Oliver had always allowed her the modesty of a sleep dress. The nudity didn't embarrass her and that implied a trust in the man beside her that

187

she had yet to understand. She only knew how spectacular he'd made her feel and how good it was not to be alone in her big-bed. She shifted, tightening the slender loop of her arms about his middle and breathing deep of the scent of man. He responded by resuming the caresses that had driven her to such exquisite madness.

"Was your husband good to you, Lucy?"

She stiffened, taken off guard by the question and her own resistance to the topic. She didn't want either past or future to intrude on this perfect moment. "Yes, he was. He gave me everything I could want."

His fingers toyed gently with her left breast, creating a tingling tension in its rosy tip. "Not everything, else you wouldn't have been so surprised a minute ago. Hasn't a man ever pleasured you before?"

She wanted to squirm under the intimacy of the conversation and beneath the tantalizing things he was doing with his fingers. The truth was, no, she'd had no idea what could occur between a man and a woman until he'd gifted her with that wonderful knowledge. She still felt its golden aftershocks and was stunned by her greedy want to experience that personal delight all over again. How could she ask him to show her more without appearing shamelessly lustful? Or what was worse, naive. How could she allow him to leave her bed without bringing her once more to that glorious height of fulfillment. She'd been lawfully and consummately wed and yet so ignorant of the ways of life. How could she make him understand her circumstance without telling him all? And that, she couldn't do. That part of her was buried in silence if not yet forgotten in spirit.

"Oliver was a good man, Sam. But ours wasn't a marriage of passion."

"Then you were cheated, Lu."

She moved away from him then, denying herself the thrill of his touch and the truth of his words. With the sheet wound about her, she perched at the bottom of the bed, staring out the curtained window as if she could see below. "That's not true. A relationship doesn't have to be a physical rut in order to give pleasure. I needed other things from him."

"Like his money?"

She winced at the cut of his question. Her dark eyes were shadowed with hurt when they turned upon him. "No," she stated softly. "That was just as unimportant." She looked at him for a moment, seeing the figure of a man full of the independence of his gender, confident, in control of his own destiny. What would he know of helplessness, of compromise, of desperate fear? A bitterness settled inside her. How dare he judge her choices? What did he know of survival? "You wouldn't understand," she concluded brittly.

"There you go again," Sam complained in exasperation as he hoisted himself up on his elbows. "Lucy Blessing, you are the most contrary female I've ever known. One minute you're purring like a little cat and the next, you're as cold-jawed as a bronc." Her features reddened at the comparison but he wouldn't let her interrupt. "Damn if I can understand you. How'd you expect me to when you won't tell me anything? You're more tightfisted with your feelings than with your bank's loan money. And I'm here to tell you, it's not an attractive trait in a female."

"No?" she challenged coldly.

"Don't get your back up at me. I'm telling it like it is. You can rule this town and its people with an iron hand and keep them at arm's length. I don't care 'bout that. But this ain't your bank or your council meeting. You're in bed with me and I'll be damned if you'll get all starchy and bustled up. All I see from here is a darned pretty woman. Can't you act like one instead of a high-rolling wheeler-dealer while we're together?"

"I think you'd better go, Marshal."

"The hell I will. You invited me up for the evening and I've a mind to enjoy every minute of it. Providing you'll let me." He paused. He was on dangerous footing, both with her and with himself, and he knew it. He had no business pushing into her private affairs. Once entangled, he could end up caught and pulled under, just like a maverick steer in a mud bog. Mired by emotion, it was best to stay still, not thrash around to become more fatally enmeshed. He should have left it alone. He should have left, period. But something about Lucy Blessing held him just as sure and fast as that strength-sapping slough. Be it foolish, be it downright perilous to his intentions, he couldn't extract himself. He didn't want to.

"What's made you so hard, Lucy? What's made you hide all the softness in you?"

Lucy sat rigid. Her heart was pounding. She could feel its frightened beat crowding her throat, choking off her defensive objections. She didn't owe him an answer. What they'd had between them was simple and carnal. She hadn't given him the right to attach more to it. The right to question her, to make assumptions and draw unflattering conclusions. She didn't have to listen. She didn't have to suffer the awful truth he spoke. She'd invited him up to share his body, not his opinions. How harsh and cold that sounded, like something conceived in the mind of the woman he thought she was. Ugly. Calculated. Was that what she'd become? Had her determination stripped her of the ability to hold to basic feelings? That notion scared her. Because she feared it was true. Sam Wade had given her more this evening than a lesson in sensuality. He forced her to face her own fading humanity. And she was fighting against both with a frantic, feeble terror. She'd kept her emotions clamped inside too long to let them loose. She was petrified of their intensity, of the horrible rememberings. She'd never wanted to relive them. Ever.

"Damn you," she whispered in a voice so raw and filled with pain that he was moved to comfort her. As he came up, she turned away, hiding her grief-twisted features and closing eyes that mirrored her anguished fear. She tensed when his big hands rested on her shoulders, wanting to shake them off but lost to the incredible security she'd discovered in their strength. His fingers kneaded, unknotting the coiled resistance beneath them. His palms slid down her bare arms until their fingers could mesh together and hold. She clung to him, squeezing tight, using the power in his large, roughened hands to fend off the terrors rising up from the ugliness of her past.

Sam felt her tremble, felt her agony as sure as a Green River knife to the belly. Her pain tore through him, opening up his own wounds, bringing the spill of memory like his body's own vital fluid. He hurt for her, with her, because of her. It was an exquisite, self-inflicted torture. But it was too late to go back.

"Oh, darlin', I'm sorry. I never meant to cause you the miseries." His words thickened as they stemmed from aching heart rather than the cooler recesses of mind. "I care for you. Surely, you know that."

Lucy drew a deep breath, clutching his hands, clinging to her resolve. She managed the strength to plead, "Then help me, Sam. Please. Help me set things right in Blessing."

"That damned town," he growled, fiercely jealous of her devotion. It was an odd feeling, one that coiled tight and hot within him. "It can go hang."

"Sam, please. I've made promises I have to keep. I

191

have to do these things. I can't tell you why."

"Then I can't help you."

His sudden remoteness was more than she could stand. She'd been alone for so long, struggling so heroically to see her vows honored. Suffering the cost without complaint. She hadn't planned to let him get so close. She hadn't anticipated how important his presence would become to sustain her strength. She'd endured all manner of humiliations, all sorts of pain. It all came down to this one minor defection, the culmination of her woes, of her spirit-breaking grief, the final act that shattered her will.

Sam felt the sobs shake through her. He was surprised at first, then aghast at their intensity. A floodgate had opened, releasing a torrent of emotion on the wash of those tears. Her slender body quaked, having lost the resilience to stem that battering flow. Only the solid support of his arms kept her from sagging weakly to the mattress. She was turned toward him and collapsed limply upon his chest to wet his shoulder with her weeping.

"I'm here, Lucy. I'm here for you, darlin'. Let me help you. Let me in. You can't carry the whole town. It's not your responsibility."

"It is. Yes, it is," she argued despairingly.

"Why? What promise could be more important than your happiness?"

He reacted quickly to her defensive stiffening, tightening his arms, crushing out her protests by sheer force. He wouldn't let her pull away. He had to know, even if it was dangerous folly to pursue it, to discover what demons drove Lucy Blessing so mercilessly.

"Sam — " she began. His name came out with a hitching sob.

"Why would you risk the safety of the town to help a bunch of whores who don't want it?"

4 FREE BOOKS

TO GET YOUR 4 FREE BOOKS WORTH $18.00 — MAIL IN THE FREE BOOK CERTIFICATE T O D A Y

Fill in the Free Book Certificate below, and we'll send your FREE BOOKS to you as soon as we receive it.

If the certificate is missing below, write to: Zebra Home Subscription Service, Inc., P.O. Box 5214, 120 Brighton Road, Clifton, New Jersey 07015-5214.

FREE BOOK CERTIFICATE

4 FREE BOOKS

ZEBRA HOME SUBSCRIPTION SERVICE, INC.

YES! Please start my subscription to Zebra Historical Romances and send me my first 4 books absolutely FREE. I understand that each month I may preview four new Zebra Historical Romances free for 10 days. If I'm not satisfied with them, I may return the four books within 10 days and owe nothing. Otherwise, I will pay the low preferred subscriber's price of just $3.75 each; a total of $15.00, *a savings off the publisher's price of $3.00.* I may return any shipment and I may cancel this subscription at any time. There is no obligation to buy any shipment and there are no shipping, handling or other hidden charges. Regardless of what I decide, the four free books are mine to keep.

NAME

ADDRESS _____ APT _____

CITY _____ STATE _____ ZIP _____

TELEPHONE ( )

SIGNATURE _____

(If under 18, parent or guardian must sign)

Terms, offer and prices subject to change without notice. Subscription subject to acceptance by Zebra Books. Zebra Books reserves the right to reject any order or cancel any subscription. 069102

"You don't—"

"Then explain it! Tell me, Lu. Why does it all have to fall on your shoulders?"

Sam made it easy to confide in him. He was strong, he was supportive. His gliding caresses soothed a spirit rubbed raw and a heart swollen near to breaking. He was the law. He had the means to see her oath reality. He was a man, possessed of the power she lacked. And he was now her lover, which, like it or not, made him a part of her.

"I'm from Cincinnati." She chose a relatively painless beginning, a time when things were yet joyful that she could look back upon with fond remembering. Unfortunately, those times were scant and fragile. "My father was a Methodist preacher. He worked in a big congregation there. My mother came from a wealthy family. She was their only child and they didn't want her to marry a man more sworn to poverty than power. They made it—difficult, so when I was a child, we moved to Kansas. The church was sending its ministers west to inveigh against the spread of slavery. My father saw souls bleeding there and thought he could be of use." She sniffed loudly and rubbed her damp cheek against the hot sleekness of his skin as the memories darkened. Her hands had come up to seek purchase on his corded upper arms, her fingers spasmodically opening and closing as her anxiety grew. It was hard, hard to dredge up the past. Hard to face the reasons behind her convictions. But if she wanted his help, she had to. If she wanted him to understand her, she must.

"It was the church's stand to speak out on the abolitionist persuasion. It was a stand my father believed in with all his heart—his big, generous heart. Instead of settling us in an established town where we could have a home, he chose to work the circuit. My mother wouldn't hear of being apart from him so we all traveled from town to town, squeezing in three sermons and fifty miles every Sabbath." A bleakness edged her voice when she spoke of the loneliness that settled into her life, the endless wanderings, the constant pillar-to-post existence, living off the kindness of strangers, having nothing, wanting nothing. As a child, she'd struggled with her feelings of resentment and respect. She knew the good her father did. Yet, she could not help but long for a cozy house in any of the towns they passed through, for playmates her own age instead of only the stories of the Bible to keep her company. She learned of solitude, of restless emptiness upon that dusty trail. She learned to bear the shame of her conflicting feelings; of the love and hate she felt for the devout figure who was more preacher than father.

"He loved to set up spiritual camp meetings in a grove outside of town. The worship, baptisms and socializing would go on for a week. At first, they were uplifting times, then a shadow of hatred began to follow us. Father's words offended the proslavery groups. It started with murmurings, then angry words. Father wasn't intimidated by their threats but he begged Mother to take me to the North. She wouldn't hear of it. The nights were full of fear. We'd hide in our wagon and pray while they'd circle it, shooting off their pistols. Once, they even set fire to it over our very heads. Still, Father wouldn't temper his sermons against the evil of human bondage.

"It was in Atchison that they kidnapped him from a group baptism. He was tarred and feathered and returned to us with a letter 'R' for Rogue painted on his forehead. When he stepped forward to preach the next morning, they took him again. Only this time, they didn't bring him back. We found him two days later where he'd been beaten and left to die."

It wasn't the whole story but it was enough to satisfy him and to explain a lot about Lucy Blessing. He held her, not asking any more from her. He guessed she'd already wrung her soul dry. What he didn't anticipate was the consequence of listening to her confession. Not until she lifted her glassy eyes, still so fresh with hurt, to meet his. His chest seized up, clenched in a fist of emotion. Twisting until he couldn't draw a decent steady breath. Lord, how her misery made him want to beg for mercy. For them both. Looking into her plaintive gaze was like staring into a mirror of his own wretched soul. So dark, so sad, so lost. He was taken by the need to heal her, as if in doing so, he would ease some of his own anguish.

Lucy didn't resist as his palm fit to her cheek, cradling, caressing its damp softness. She was drawn into the slated cloudiness that overcast his gaze. His compassion acted strangely upon her, taking up some of the heaviness that pressed her heart. Could it be he understood?

"Oh, darlin', I'm sorry. I know all about that kind of hurting, the kind that gnaws at your innards and haunts your nights. Don't let it ruin your life. It will, if you don't bury it with them." How well he knew. That truth shone evident in his sorrowful eyes. It was too late to alter the course of his future but hers—if he could save her from the same devastation, perhaps his existence would come to some good.

"I have no life until I see to my promises, Sam." Sincerity tugged at her words. She meant them.

"Then I'll help you, Lucy." He had no other choice.

Her smile was tremulous, moved by an uncertain hope. "You will?"

In another bout of irreversible insanity, he murmured huskily, "My word on it."

195

"You'll help me break Henry Knight's hold on sin in Blessing?"

"If that's what it takes." His answer was an aching whisper.

A reviving tenderness swept through her as Lucy looked for and found his sentiments to be as sterling as the color of his unswerving gaze. He would help her. Emotion, pure and poignant, swelled up until she could not contain it. Her hand fit itself over the back of his and pressed. He felt solid and warm to her, those same qualities she sought in truth and trust. And she did trust him, this rough-edged gunman who walked with danger rather than honor. She trusted him because he'd seen to the passionate instruction of her body and offered to meet her heart's desire. She placed willingly in his hands that which she'd never bestowed upon another: her faith and future. And something more. Something even now half realized but too complicated to explore. Something all tangled in the unexpected beauty of the moment. In the unsuspected depth of Sam Wade.

She stretched up to unashamedly kiss him. For an instant, his mouth was thin and unresponsive in surprise. Then his lips eased and gentled beneath hers, accepting what she would share, encouraging it to become more. She was no longer the innocent who'd had her eyes opened to passion beneath his thorough tutelage. She aggressively courted it and found the return most profitable. Her hand went to his strong throat then curved behind his neck so her fingers could weave through the sunbaked hair that brushed his nape, holding his mouth pressed to hers as she tempted and welcomed the hot invasion of his tongue. Her moan was of sheer female surrender, not of submission, rather coaxing him to follow where she would lead. And he pursued, urgently, with a compelling fierceness. His fingers crushed in the loose tendrils of her hair, jerking her into fiery contact with his hard body.

"Lucy," he groaned, as if desperate to receive her encouragement. His eyes closed, his breathing grew fractured as her fingertips charted the angles of his face, riding the ridge of his cheekbones, sliding down the lean valleys to his stubbled jaw. He lay back and she came down with him, straddling his hips, languishing upon his chest while hungrily tasting his cheeks, his chin, his throat, his shoulder. It was more than a red-blooded man was meant to bear. With a great rumble vibrating through his chest, he seized her shoulders and rolled so he was atop her.

Her eyes were open wide and dark with desire. "Sam." When she said his name, it touched him like a physical force. He was trembling—with the restraint it took not to bury himself at once within her—with a sudden, inexplicable barrage of emotion. His mouth dropped down on hers, seeking compliance, finding an ardor that matched his own. He was panting when he lifted up. "Woman, you scare the be-jesus out of me."

She smiled then and it was the most tantalizing, seductive sight he'd ever seen. And not a man to hold strong against temptation, he took her wicked lips, savaging them, savoring them. He moved on to treat her breasts, her belly, her tender thighs to those same scorching kisses, scraping the sensitive flesh with his rough face, catapulting Lucy into the first throes of ecstasy. She clutched at him, crying out his name as she reached for new heights of splendor, not caring if her exuberant shouts rang clear down the streets of Blessing.

And when his mouth returned to possess hers, Lucy was impatient to know his claim completely. She exchanged kisses with panting urgency while tugging at him, expressing her desires with the arch of slender hips and the guiding pressure of her knees. She took in his manhood with a greedy delight. Her hot body closed about him, clasping tight as if to hold him forever captive. But she could not contain the unbridled need she'd created in him with her sweet, sultry enticement. Sam plunged and planted himself firmly, masterfully again and again and again until Lucy writhed in her search for satisfaction and surged up against him. He rode her slim taut body the way he would a maverick. Controlling, gentling while savoring the spirit. It was a breathless gallop that broke a lather, driving on wildly even to the point of exhaustion. And when her slender bucking hips clenched tight about him and a wail of deliverance tore from her throat, Sam finished with one final thrust so they could ride to paradise as one.

Dazed by the powerful explosions racking her body, Lucy received them in wonder, holding to Sam even after the tremors ceased. Other senses were slow to return to her; the quiet brush of the evening breeze along the satiny expanse of bared legs, the weight of him crushing her breasts, the sawing hoarseness of his breath as it rushed against her neck. Beautiful sensations, filling her with contentment and a dreamy pleasure. Her palms moved leisurely over the slicked contours of his back and shoulders. Her cheek rubbed against his damp hair. And when he would rise up, her embrace locked in protest.

"No," she whispered into his ear. "Stay a moment longer."

As he relaxed, Lucy reveled in the feel of him: the heat, the strength, the mighty maleness that gradually ebbed within her. Nothing could compare. How was she to endure the emptiness once he was gone from her? Desperate, resisting feelings grew, urging her to hold him, to never let him leave her. He completed her, not only physically but emotionally as well. Was she crazy to long for such things? To open her future, her very heart to a restless gunslinger who could be lured by wanderlust or lead to leave her in the lurch without warning? She prided herself on being a sensible woman but this had nothing to do with logic. It was instinct, pure and passionate. And Sam Wade, no matter how unworthy, stirred all the right things inside her.

"Sam," she began softly, before reason could catch up to the tendrils of romance curling through her soul. She stroked his hair, letting her fingers sink into its shaggy length, letting her desires sink in to color caution. "Oh, Sam, I—"

A sudden commotion below stairs fractured her heartfelt confession. A loud, desperate pounding upon Lucy's front door. Before she could think to stop him, Sam was up, reaching for his hastily discarded long underwear. Even before the sound of hurried footsteps on the stairs reached them, he was pulling on his Levi's and searching for his shirt.

There was a discreet tap on the chamber door.

"Marshal Wade, a lady downstairs to see you," Li murmured quietly. "She say it emergency."

Lord! Not only was she losing his company for the night, the whole town would know he'd been wrested from her bed. Lucy scrambled up and fumbled for a dressing gown. It was too late to think of modesty or reputation. She was consumed with fear by the steely determination that ruled his expression. He was rushing toward danger. And enjoying it.

Sam was already in the foyer talking to a breathless Billie McCafferty when Lucy raced down the steps on bare feet. Her robe billowed out behind her like a matador's cape, her unfettered hair a silken swirl above it. As she watched, clutching at the banister, Sam stalked into the parlor then out again.

"Where the hell are my shooting irons?"

His roar brought Li on the run with his brace of deadly pistols gingerly extended. He strapped them on with brisk, controlled movements, a warrior arming for battle.

"Sam?"

His gaze lifted. There was an impatience in his eyes that wounded. Lucy swallowed her hurt and murmured, "What is it?"

Sam's jawed squared. Muscles jumped along its strong line as he searched for the right words. Finally, he chose bluntness over diplomacy.

"Luke Redman. They found him at his shack."

"Hanged?" The word was a small whisper.

Sam nodded then added tersely, "And shot. Six times. Through the heart."

The significance sunk in slowly. By then, Sam had already strode out onto the porch where a half-dozen citizens milled about, muttering like agitated sheep. Without a thought to appearance, Lucy ran after him, halting only as the torchlight illuminated her disheveled form. Talk ceased immediately as eyes turned upon her. She drew the robe more closely about her in defense against those stares and called out clear and steady, "Sam, you be careful."

He drew up and looked to her again. The glaring light cast her cascading hair in molten bronze where it spun about her shoulders and etched the concern in her face into lines of sharp contrast. He saw fear in her eyes, a fear she would not speak. He was still buttoning his hastily donned shirt when he took the porch steps in one long stride and Lucy Blessing with a searing kiss.

200

"I will," he whispered as he pulled back just far enough to appreciate the lovely curve of her lips and the sweep of inky lashes as they fluttered against her cheeks. "Sorry to end our evening like this."

Not as sorry as she, Lucy mourned as he walked away, leaving her weak of knees and heart, clinging to her porch post.

Chapter Fourteen

"Six bullets placed in a pattern no bigger than my fist without a trace of powder burns? That was some kind of shooting. Professional-like."

Having planted the seeds of suspicion, Henry Knight leaned back against his bar and watched the faces before him. He could see his manipulating words shaping simple minds to the desired conclusion. And he refrained from smiling.

"Only one gun like that in Blessing," someone muttered.

It was enough of a spark to create a slow smolder. In the way of prairie fires, time would bring it to flame. Then the burning would be fierce and spread quickly out of control. And that was what Henry Knight hoped for.

"Now why would anyone want to kill old Luke?" another wondered. "He owed everyone in town a living. Sure, he was a mean cuss but he never done nobody no harm."

"Excepting his boy."

There was a nodding of consensus there. It took no time to connect the marshal's friendship with Newt Redman and his threats toward the boy's abusive father to a slaying done by a gunslick. They were all thinking it, but saying it . . . that was something else again. They'd seen Sam Wade draw on the Jarret boy. There'd been heat lightning in his speed. They had a healthy respect for that kind of talent and a healthy want to go on breathing. None were sure a ne'er-do-well like Luke Redman was worth riling their new marshal over.

It would take a little more kindling, the saloon owner realized. But eventually, Sam Wade would roast in the heat of his own reputation.

His attention was distracted by one of his girls passing by in street clothes. Too many had been slipping away of late and this one he refused to let go.

"Billie, honey," he called out pleasantly. He saw her freeze in panic then turn slowly to face him. "Come on over here a minute."

Reluctance plain in every step, she went to join her boss at the bar. Her head hung, her hands wrung nervously before her.

"Why aren't you dressed? You're supposed to be out there mingling. The fellas have a hankering to share a drink with a pretty thing like you."

Billie was able to muster speech on her second try but it was woefully weak. "Didn't Miss Ruby tell you? I don't work here no more."

"That right?" He managed to sound both politely surprised and menacing all at once. His smile never faltered but his eyes grew as flat and black as a sand rattler's. "Now, Billie, you know you're one of our best girls. Why Ruby was just telling me the other day the big plans she had for taking you on next door. You'll have more money and trinkets than you ever dreamed of."

"I don't want to work for Miss Ruby, Mister Knight. I got me a job at the millinery."

"Sticking feathers in hats?" He made no attempt to

203

conceal his sneer of disdain. "Now, that's got to be a well-paying position for a clever little thing like you. More than enough to tend you. It must be for you to go leaving our little family after we took you in off the street and took care of you."

"I'll get by, Mister Knight." She refused to look up though he could see the color of confusion rising in her cheeks.

"Is that the kind of gratitude you plan on showing us? Sneaking off when we need you?"

Her eyes came up then, all round and desperate. "Oh, no, sir. I'm real sorry about that and grateful to you, I really am. It's just that Miz Blessing got me this here job, a right proper job and I—I—"

"Miz Blessing." He spoke the name with venom dripping. "I should have guessed. She go filling your silly head with how turning your back on your true friends and getting an uptown job is going to make you into a real lady? Why, Billie, honey, you're good for nothing but slinging drinks and whoring. You and I both know that. Why you want to put yourself through the embarrassment and trouble? Those fancy ladies aren't going to buy a hat from no whore. How long you think you'll keep that job? Then how you going to take care of yourself?"

Billie's face was pinched with agitation. She knew a real terror of being destitute. It was nothing she wanted to feel again. But then there was another hope she held to in the warmth of her heart and she spoke up with surprising confidence.

"Maybe I won't have to work much longer at all."

"Plan on getting hitched? What kind of fool marries a harlot?"

"I'm no harlot and Newt isn't—"

"Newt Redman? Why, Billie, honey, Newt has all the problems he can handle right now what with his

204

daddy gone to glory and all. You'd be nothing but trouble to him. And you wouldn't want anything to happen to him, now would you?"

His meaning sunk its poison deep and the girl paled and began to tremble. Slowly, she shook her head.

"I knew you were a smart girl." A smooth, dangerous smile curved his lips. "Now you go get into your spangles and get to work. Tonight you're starting over at Ruby's. That all right with you, honey?"

Again, the puppetlike nod.

"Good. I'll make sure Miz Blessing gets proper thanks for offering you a job. But you won't need one. You got yourself a good job."

It was a dismal day for a burying. The clouds hung low in the late afternoon sky, slated and swollen with the promise of a deluge to come, casting a pall over the mourners gathered to see Luke Redman into the ground. Only a handful had come to stand beside Newt. The glum-faced group included Marshal Wade, Lucy Blessing, Mayor Mayhew who considered it his duty to offer a last farewell to any citizen, Jeff, the bartender from the Nightingale, a few drinking associates who'd miss Luke's crude humor and the dapper figure of Henry Knight.

The words spoken were brief. There was little to say about a man who'd led such a hell-bent life. Only Lucy came close to showing any sign of emotion, for son rather than father. Funerals were never pleasant occasions. She'd stood at far too many gravesides. She had hoped that she'd put away her black bombazine for good. Though she felt saddened for the loss of his only parent, she was enough of a realist to know Newt Redman's future could only be better for the lack of him. There would be no more beatings by a drunken bully. Someone had finally put an end to Newt's shadowed existence.

Someone.

Deep down inside, she was very afraid Sam Wade had killed the loathsome Luke Redman before coming to her door. And if he had, what would that mean to her and what she'd begun to feel toward the man? There was no getting around the fact that it was murder. Redman had been bound hand and foot. Hardly a sporting target. She'd heard the horrible anger shake through Sam's words. *I'm going to kill the son of a bitch.* Perhaps he'd decided to do just that. She could see how much Newt had come to mean to him, much more than just as a deputy. He'd taken to the lame young man the same way he tolerated the lazy rawboned hound: with grumbling, guarded affection. They were both strays who'd attached themselves to the marshal's side and, like it or not, they were very much a part of him.

Although she could incur no regret at Redman's passing, regardless of the means, she hated to think the same hands tenderly soothing her fears and coaxing her to exquisite ecstasy had hours prior, brutally, cold-bloodedly ended another man's life.

And if Sam Wade was that merciless killer? Could she blame him? Could she afford to condone what he'd done? Could she live with herself after making either decision? Which was more important, what was right or what was moral? Hadn't he asked her that same question? She was afraid to reach inside herself to seek the answer.

Lucy put a hand on Newt's arm as the circuit preacher intoned words meant to comfort the bereaved. Newt seemed not to notice either. His stare was glassy. Bruising on his face—a legacy from his father—had faded to a yellowish gray, giving him a jaundiced appearance to features that looked stunned but not remorseful.

Lucy was aware of the large, browned hand resting on the boy's shoulder just above her own. It was Sam Wade whom Newt leaned upon. She could see the marshal in profile. He was wearing the fine dark coat. The silver Stetson was in his other hand though its impression still remained to flatten his hair above his somberly set expression. His eyes were the same color as the threatening sky. Just looking at him woke a tangle of confused emotion that went far and beyond the solemnness of the occasion. It was a struggle to maintain an indifferent front when memories burned so hotly. When fears churned so upsettingly, Sam made it easier for her to hold to her composure. He hadn't favored her with a glance since his brief nod of acknowledgment. Granted, it wasn't the time to indulge in meaningful glances but she was plainly puzzled by his distant attitude. Perhaps he was thinking of her reputation. Or was his mind filled with other worries?

No tears quickened as the first shovelful of dirt landed heavily atop the plain coffin. Slowly, the small party of grievers who felt no real grief filed through the wrought-iron gates of the cemetery and headed back toward Blessing.

"You must be mighty relieved, Newt. It was no secret how that man treated you."

Newt looked dully at Henry Knight as if he couldn't comprehend the words.

"I hardly think that kind of talk is appropriate today," Lucy snapped as she stepped up beside the boy to offer a hand upon his shoulder as a silent bolster. Her dark eyes fixed upon the elegant gentleman with a glimmer of distaste.

"You might have the decency to wait until the man is cold," Sam agreed. He'd taken a stand on the other side of the shuffling deputy.

The sound of his soft drawl acted upon Lucy like the most intimate of caresses. Sensation rippled through her, raising shivers of longing so inappropriate for this place. Surges of life where there was meant to be only death. The unbidden response possessed her mind with frightening truth. She'd been waiting to hear him speak, yearning to hang on any attention from him like a moonstruck girl bedazzled by her first love. Love? With unfortunate, stunning clarity, her last words to him returned.

"Sam, I—"

What? What had she meant to say? What sentiments had moved her in the concluding moments of ecstasy? She was paralyzed with the sudden knowledge. Good God! She'd meant to confess that she loved him!

She stopped dead in the street, staring at Sam Wade. She couldn't have looked more horrified had he held one of his polished pistols to her head. It wasn't true. It could not be true. A ridiculous notion conceived in a moment of passion. That was all. Dear Lord, that had to be the answer.

Only Henry Knight's next words and their ugly insinuation had the power to draw her back from the abyss of panic to the realities of the present.

"Odd sentiments coming from you, Marshal," Knight stated silkily. "Considering the talk and all."

"What talk?"

"Oh, how the most likely suspect in Luke Redman's killing was you. 'Course I don't believe it."

Their group had come to a stop at the head of Blessing's main street. Fat drops of rain began to fall, spitting up tiny geysers of dust where they struck the road.

"What's this?" Mayhew insisted. He had yet to hear

the carefully spread gossip. That angered him. He hated being uninformed. Knight was pleased to enlighten him.

"Just that some folks were thinking since the marshal and poor Luke had some pretty harsh words the night he died and it would take a professional gun to dispatch the late gentleman in such a precise manner, that Marshal Wade might well have taken the law into his own hands. And here I thought we hired him to stop that kind of thing. Wasn't that your understanding, too, Mister Mayor?"

Sam started forward but checked the move. He issued a slow, thin smile toward his accuser in recognition of the challenge. "Seems we got some mighty active imaginations here in Blessing," he drawled easily.

"Is that what you'd call the livery man's claim that you ordered up your horse?"

"Marshal?" Mayhew turned to him for an explanation and quickly, unthinkingly, Lucy provided it.

"He came to see me," she stated flatly. She avoided the objecting gaze Sam shot at her and continued. "He thought if he took his horse no one would question where he was going. He tethered it behind my house. The marshal was there all evening. You can ask Billie McCafferty and a half-dozen townspeople who'll verify that's where they found him when Redman's death was discovered." There. She'd done it. She'd torn away every carefully garnered scrape of respect she commanded. Without regret. She'd backed Sam Wade with her lie and silently accepted the fact he might well be the killer. She stared at Henry Knight, daring him to refute her words, knowing he could not.

"All the same," the mayor blustered, "I'll expect a full investigation, Marshal. I want this kind of talk

209

stopped. We can't have the townsfolk doubting the man they trust to tend the law."

"I intend to, Mister Mayor." A cold glare of promise accompanied Sam's words. Knight responded with an impervious smile that made the reptilian glitter of his eyes all the more apparent.

The claim satisfied Mayhew. He was more than pleased with Blessing's new marshal, even after the unfortunate dealings with his daughter. Wade had handled the matter tactfully, if a bit unconventionally. He was more than willing to let Sam Wade investigate the murder of Luke Redman and would accept his findings—or the lack of them, to keep peace in Blessing. And if Lucy Blessing gave Wade an alibi and him the most tantalizing piece of gossip ever to be spread through the citizens of Blessing, he was not about to protest. When the rain became more aggressive, he nodded to the company and hurried beneath the nearest porch to keep unsightly botches from his Sunday best. And continued directly to Ned Pomeroy's Barber Parlor where he would supply the day's topic of converse. The others stayed put, oblivious to the increasing dampness.

"And Newt," the saloonkeeper added. "Miss Billie asked me to relay her regards. She couldn't come herself, seeing as how she's working at Ruby's. A herd of cattle just came into town and all those cowboys are needful of a little entertaining. And, Miz Lucy, she asked me to thank you for the job offer but she won't be needing it after all."

Lucy took the news like a cruel slap. She reeled then sought instantly to recover. "What did you do to her?"

Henry Knight's smile broadened in noxious amusement. "Do? Why, Miz Lucy, I didn't have to do anything. It was her choice." He tipped his low-crowned hat in a cordial gesture and they heard him chuckle as he walked away.

Lucy felt a hot, choking rage. Of all the girls she wanted to reach, Billie had come to mean the most to her. She'd seen in the petite bar girl a genuine sweetness and a sincerity in her pursuit of the Bible's teachings. She'd even asked if she could help with Sunday school. Not the actions of a young woman uncertain of what she wanted out of life. Lucy was sure she'd chosen a pure path over that of Miss Ruby's parlor. If she'd changed her mind, it was because it had been changed for her. Something had happened to dissuade her. Billie McCafferty may have been easy prey for Henry Knight's intimidation but she wouldn't be.

"Sam, do something," she demanded fiercely. She looked up at the marshal, seeing him as the law rather than as her lover of the night before. She'd forced the complexities from her mind. There'd be time to consider consequences and this was not it.

"Lucy, I'm afraid there's nothing I can do. The girl's of age. I can't keep her from doing something of her own free will, long as it's legal."

"But it's not of her own free will. Can't you see that?" she cried in frustration.

"No, I can't unless you can prove otherwise."

His comment was final. She stared at him in wordless, unfocused anger. He'd given her his promise that he would help her. He'd sworn it to her even as they entwined in passionate pursuit upon her bed. Had she been so naive, so hungry for his caresses that she'd been gulled into believing a lie? Had he made those vows only to promote her agreeability? Had he come to her, said whatever needed to be said, just to obtain an alibi for the time of Luke Redman's murder? And she'd given it to him.

Suddenly, Lucy found it hard to breathe. Uncer-

211

tainty clogged her throat. Dreadful knowledge made it ache unbearably. Slowly, miserably, she strangled on the truth not fifteen feet away from where Lute Johnson had met his terrible demise.

Sam Wade was a cold-blooded killer. His heart was as sympathetic as the lead strapped to his hips. He'd ridden out to Luke Redman's and had callously shot and strung up Newt's father. Then, with the vengeful violence of the deed still singing in his veins, he'd come to her door. And she'd let him in — into her home, into her bed, into her heart. And he'd misused all three. She'd sacrificed all . . . for nothing.

The pain, the incredible hurt brought a dizzying chill. And then, a cold objection.

"Thank you, Marshal," she said expressionlessly. "I appreciate knowing exactly where you stand."

Lucy saw him blink, quickly, with surprise and confusion. But she would have none of it. She would not be fooled again. There was no law in Blessing. It was time she took care of things herself.

Sam looked after her retreating figure. What had he seen flickering in her steady gaze? Anger? That much he'd expected. Hurt? She must feel he'd let her down but there was nothing he could do to reassure her now. It was something else, something deeper, darker, something he'd just missed catching hold of as it slid fleetingly behind her impassive stare. What? It made him uncomfortable not knowing. Suspicious and alarmed. She was going to do something crazy and dangerous. He could feel it.

He was distracted from his thoughts of Lucy when Newt began a purposeful limp toward Nightingale's. He caught up with the boy and slowed him with a staying hand.

"Don't try to stop me, Marshal. I aim to fetch her."

"Not now, boy. Not when your head is full of pain

and poison. They'll expect that. You got to face them with cool thinking. It's the only chance you'll have. Knight's no fool. He knows you'll come crashing in there. And he'll be waiting. Newt, let me handle it. Trust me."

Newt's eyes flickered between the Nightingale and his mentor. Indecision etched his features.

"Newt, trust me," Sam restated. "Can you do that? I'm asking a lot, I know. But it's the only way we can win this thing. My way."

The boy's mobile mouth trembled. Slowly, he nodded his great, shaggy head.

"Good. You go on back to the office and you stay there." Sam looked up toward Lucy Blessing's house, unable to shake the intuitive trickle of uneasiness. "I'll take care of things."

"All right," Newt mumbled.

Sam turned to him, the thought coming all at once. "Newt? I didn't kill your father."

Newt gave a small, grim smile. "It would bother me none if you had."

Newt sat in the marshal's chair. He was restless and unhappy but he'd given Sam his promise to remain. He did trust Sam but that didn't ease his shame at taking no part in Billie's rescue. He cared for her. He wanted to protect her. And here he was, hiding in the jail house, failing her by his very inactivity. Hadn't he failed at everything? Wasn't that what his father held most against him? That and his mother's desertion.

Pride chafing, he sought something to distract him. He picked up the newest stack of dodgers and flipped through the territory's most wanted. A group of hard cases who'd be smart not to tangle with Blessing's marshal.

213

He was about to toss one atop the others when his attention was arrested. It wasn't much of a likeness. It drew a much harsher image. But there was no mistaking the cut of high cheekbones, the narrowed eyes and mouth. His startled gaze flew to the description, devouring the words though they curdled inside him like spoiled fare.

Wanted—Dead or Alive for murder and bank robbery in the State of Missouri. Sam Zachary. $500 Reward.

Chapter Fifteen

The slatted doors swung open onto the scene of wanton revelry. None gathered in the dim, smoke-wreathed saloon seemed to care that a man had been murdered. None of them seemed to pay the slightest mind to the fact that the spangle-hipped ladies cooing and coaxing at their sides might be there against their will. Their vision was narrowed by selfish greed and lust, by the available charms of the moment. And they didn't want their eyes opened. Many had ridden hard to squander coin at the tables and in Miss Ruby's parlor. None wanted their enjoyment tarnished by the truth. They were happy to accept the skewed reality Henry Knight offered, not caring that the games held about as much opportunity for riches as the Wyoming hills, unmindful that the ladies purring for their attention were victims of necessity, happily oblivious to the fact that their whiskey was about as pure as their host's wide white smile. They came to the Nightingale to have the burden of conscience and care lifted from them and resisted having it forced upon them while about their entertainments.

Sam scanned the room with narrowed eyes. He was quick to spot the dapper figure of Henry Knight lounging at the chuck-a-luck table. There was a flash of bared teeth in the semblance of a smile when the two exchanged glances. Sam's gaze moved on. No sign of either Billie McCafferty or Lucy. Maybe he'd been wrong. Just the usual scene of indolent indulgence.

He moved up to the bar, accepting a beer from Jeff with a nod of thanks. Maybe he had been mistaken. He let the shiny brass foot rail lever between heel and toe of his boot as he adopted an easy pose. But he wasn't easy. His intuition was tingling, warning him of trouble to come. And he knew the source. Even though she hadn't put in an appearance, he felt far from relaxed. He knew Lucy Blessing well enough to know her as a proud and reckless female. A dangerous female when crossed. At the moment, he and Henry Knight were in her rampaging path, so he sipped his beer and waited for the charge.

Presently, the commotion came. However, instead of heralded by a bustled-up Lucy Blessing, it was foretold by a cowpoke in the process of pulling up his long underwear as he ran.

"Marshal," cried the distraught figure comically clad in boots, six-shooter and half-donned drawers. "You'd best come quick. Some het-up female is next door at Ruby's with a gun and a grudge."

Sam needed no further explanation to seize on the scene. From across the room, he saw one of Knight's men tugging for attention. As the saloonkeeper's face darkened in displeasure, Sam made for the door that linked the two sister buildings in sin.

It wasn't the first time she'd stepped into Ruby Gale's establishment but Lucy was assaulted anew by the opulent trappings. Every aspect of the decor was in exquisite style and obviously expensive, from woven tapestry rugs to prisms dripping light from the many chandeliers. For all its elegance, the scene purposefully evoked an atmosphere of dusky sensuality. A fortune spent in furnishings couldn't cleanse the air of heavy perfume and husky laughter. The most tasteful pastoral paintings couldn't ease the sight of a half-dozen females lounging about in various states of dishabille. A cheery tune tapped out on the piano couldn't disguise the fact that the only entertainment was found upstairs. Those things stung Lucy's sensibilities like a sniff of pure vinegar and made her want to back away from the offending source. But she could not. Not until she had what she'd come for.

Her presence caused immediate clamor among the girls. They knew her from her attempts to lead them to a less objectionable life but neither she nor any of her stalwart crusaders had ever ventured in during prime business hours. Several local shop owners turned as crimson as the damask draperies and effected a hasty retreat with money still in pockets. That would not do. Lucy Blessing would have to go.

As Miss Ruby was in her private quarters doing some entertaining of her own, the burly parlor bouncer known erroneously as Sweet thought to deal with the problem himself. Miss Ruby liked initiative and he decided it was time to show some. It was apparent in a few short seconds that he'd picked the wrong time to be assertive.

"Where's Billie McCafferty?"

"Working, ma'am," the behemoth rumbled. "Come back—"

He never got the rest of it out. The indignant lady gave him a shove. It was like trying to undercut a mountainside with a teaspoon. Undaunted, she

217

started to go around him. It was then he reached for her, thinking to exert a little less polite persuasion in evicting the determined female. And he found himself confronted with the business end of her Remington over and under. He stared at the pretty lady and her deadly argument, wanting no part of either.

"Just get out of my way," Lucy snapped. "I'll find her myself." With that, she took to the stairs, leaving the dazed Sweet gawking after her switching bustle.

It was a matter of trial and error. Lucy went down the dim corridor, opening each door she came to. She didn't stop to appreciate any of the novel sights presented, not even that of the corpulent Mayor Mayhew entwined with two nubile young Chinese girls. She was too angry. Inside she seethed at the thought of Sam Wade's betrayal. She clung to her fury because it would serve her better than the hurt. That would come later. The searing rage held fear and caution at bay, provoking her into the rash march down the hall, kicking in the portals of lustful pleasure and discouraging all objections with the wave of her two-shot pistol. If there was no decency left in Blessing, no honorable man to take up the cause, she would damn well see to things herself.

"Miz Lucy!"

Billie came up in the rumpled bed with a sheet held to her bare bosom. The gent who was fixing to remove the final leg of his long underwear to join her swiveled around with a menacing glower only to be cowed by the unblushing Remington.

"Get out," Lucy stated. When the fellow started to reach for the coins he'd left in good faith upon the nightstand, her words were punctuated with the cold click of the hammer. "Now." He decided quick that it would be more prudent to seek his pants. Long underwear flapping and arms bundled with discarded clothes and expectations, he slunk past the woman in the doorway to dart down the hall.

"Get dressed, Billie," Lucy continued in a softer tone. "You're leaving."

The girl hesitated. Her cheeks flamed with shame and her eyes were round with terror. "But Miz Lucy, I—"

"Do you want to stay here and earn your living like that?"

Billie winced at her cold summation. Hope began to eke back into her spirit. "No, ma'am," she said with a trifle more conviction.

"Then come on. We don't want to overstay our welcome."

Tactfully, Lucy averted herself while the young woman scurried about for her necessities. Instead, she kept a watchful eye on the hall. A few brave souls peeped out of their rooms but ducked back quickly when faced with her pistol.

"All ready, Miz Lucy," came a meek voice from behind her. As she turned, Billie offered a small smile. "And thanks for coming for me."

Lucy slipped an arm about her scantily clad shoulders and steered her toward the stairs. Halfway down, she could see the mammoth bouncer was still unmoved. But the discomposed figure of Ruby Gale had joined him. Lucy challenged the woman with a piercing glare of contempt and urged Billie forcibly to continue downward.

"Miz Blessing, to what do we owe this honor?" Ruby's polite veneer fooled no one. Her features were drawn up as tight as the drought-plagued Basin floor.

"It wasn't a social call. If you'll be kind enough to get out of my way."

Ruby and Sweet didn't budge.

"I believe you have something that belongs to me." The black eyes glittered dangerously.

"I don't think so." Lucy nudged her pistol higher, measuring the bore on the lengthy cleft between breasts wedged into shiny black satin. Ruby never flinched, perhaps thinking herself safe as there was no threat to wounding a heart that did not exist.

"Get back upstairs, you ungrateful tart!"

Billie jumped at the harsh command and quivered beneath Lucy's arm like a frightened jackrabbit. There was no doubt she would have leapt to comply had Lucy released her hold for an instant. But Lucy held firm.

"Miss McCafferty is retiring. You can find her at the milliner's. It looks as though you could use her services."

Ruby boiled beneath the other woman's insulting inspection of her plumed bonnet. Everything about Lucy Blessing set her teeth to aching, from her meddlesome crusade to her impeccable style. Henry Knight hadn't been as attentive since the pretty banker became a widow. And now the marshal seemed inclined in the same direction. It was too much for a woman of her incredible vanity to accept. Any chance to take the highfalutin Mrs. Blessing down a noticeable peg was one she couldn't miss.

"Miz Blessing, this is a business establishment. Lessen you're looking to return to your old profession, I suggest you leave now. Just you. Billie stays."

Ruby couldn't have chosen a truer means to Lucy's temper. Her skin went dead white, her narrowed lips paling to a slightly brighter shade. "Get out of my way before I blast a hole through you big enough to walk through!"

Something in the deadly purr of her voice was

220

convincing. Or perhaps it was the sight of two of her men creeping down the stairs behind the gun-toting woman. Ruby took several steps back and motioned for Sweet to do the same. Lured by the opportunity to escape, Lucy urged Billie forward then gave a gasp as her elbows were seized from behind. Her arms were jerked up, wrenching her shoulders cruelly. The pistol was pried from her hand. When she tried to struggle, she was lifted up off the patterned carpet in that awkward grip until the agony stabbing through her arms nearly had her swooning.

"Miz Blessing was just leaving," Ruby Gale announced coldly.

"That's right. She is," intruded another voice. "Now let her go."

The torturous pull on her shoulders released, Lucy stumbled and would have fallen had Sam Wade not caught her firmly about the waist to lift her down the last few steps. She was too shaken to resist his embrace or the fact that he kept her clasped against his side. She was too consumed with clutching to his coat.

"Miz Billie, you come on down, too." Seeing her uncertainty as she paused upon the stair like a frightened she-deer, Sam's voice lowered into a coaxing cadence. "Come on now, darlin'. Nobody's going to give you any trouble."

Billie's round-eyed terror provoked Lucy into action. Ignoring the discomfort it caused her strained muscles, she wiggled out of the curve of Sam's arm to offer her hand up to the girl. "Come on, Billie. You're coming with me. You can stay at my house as my guest. No one's going to hurt you. I won't let them. That's right," she urged as the girl began to descend. When she was close enough, Lucy enfolded her in a sheltering embrace then looked to

Sam for direction. The marshal was covering Ruby's men with his .45, his attention fully absorbed, so Lucy was startled when he spoke to someone behind them.

"Knight, don't give us any trouble back there lessen you want to pick lead out of these here boys and your good-looking partner."

The saloonkeeper relaxed his offensive stance and eased his hand away from the pearl-handled piece he carried beneath the underarm of his tailored coat. He didn't think Sam Wade had eyes in the back of his head but he didn't want to take any chances.

The presence of another player in their tense tableau was announced with a cool, "I got your back, Marshal," and the no-nonsense click on the hammer of Newt's double-barreled equalizer.

"Things are getting a mite crowded here," Sam drawled. "Time we took to leaving. 'Evening, Miz Ruby. Sorry for the inconvenience." He started to back toward the exit, carefully keeping the two ladies behind him and out of the line of his pistol.

As they edged by Henry Knight, he tipped his low-crowned hat to Lucy and offered a sneeringly sweet, "There's nothing worse than a reformed whore with religion. Especially one who's sharing the sheets with the town law."

The bead of Sam's gun never wavered as his left hand flashed out with a vengeance. The hard ridge of his knuckles delivered a stunning crack, raising a nasty split across Knight's cheekbone. Lucy caught his arm to stay a second blow.

"No, Sam," she said quietly.

"Not until I make that son eat his words." His voice was low, taut with fury. The bunched muscles of his forearm quivered beneath her hand.

"It won't make them any less true." She followed

that surprising revelation with a firm tug. "Sam, please. Let's just go. I got what I came for."

There was a pleading quality in her words that caused him to back down against his will. He continued to sidle toward the door until he reached the threshold where Newt stood with his shotgun at the ready.

It had been humiliating business. Knight couldn't resist taking the parting thrust. Fingertips pressed to the oozing welt marring his handsome features, he said, "You ever get to missing your old profession, you always got a place here, Miz Lucy. You could prove a real money-maker."

The sound of Sam's gun exploding in the narrow hallway was deafening. Smoke from the report didn't quite conceal the horrified surprise on Henry Knight's face as the bullet sang between his legs to chew up the panel behind him. Bits of wood splinters stung his thighs and buttocks to let him know how close he'd come to losing his virility to the marshal's unerring marksmanship.

The night was deceivingly peaceful. A gentle rainfall created quiet music upon parched earth and tapped on the shingles of Lucy Blessing's porch in a soothing rhythm. Lucy paused in her doorway before joining the shadowed figure standing at the rail. Her heart was an ache of confusion and shame. What was he thinking? What was he feeling? Her own head spun with conflicting messages. He'd come for her at Ruby's. He'd rescued Billie. He hadn't let her down. Had she been wrong, then, to believe him guilty of betrayal? It had been easy to doubt, harder to restore faith. Was it worth the reward to try? It could lead to another, more painful failing in the future. But would it be worth it to savor the satisfaction of Sam Wade's embrace?

"She all settled in?" Sam asked without turning.

"She and Newt are sharing a glass of composer in the parlor. I thought it best to give them a moment alone."

The silver Stetson dipped in agreement.

Lucy hesitated. He didn't look at her or offer any encouragement. She could feel the questions weighing on his mind and she wasn't sure how to approach them or him. Finally, he spoke.

"You should have let me kill him for saying those things."

She sighed. "You can't kill a man for recalling the past."

"Yes, I can."

The silence settled between them with only the quiet pulse of the rain to accompany their solemn musings.

"It's true then."

His statement sounded so grim, so angry, Lucy flinched. However, her answer was strong. "Some. Does it matter?"

"Could be it does."

Her soul twisted with anguish at that soft honest reply. She felt a bitter dampness prick behind her eyes. If only she could deny it. If only she could cleanse his mind of ugly suspicion with a single disavowal. But she couldn't. One lie wouldn't alter what she was or what she'd done. The truth was too easily found from men like Henry Knight, men who had no respect for her late husband's reputation and were not intimidated by her power. Influence couldn't alter fact, it could only suppress it, and Lucy's secret had surfaced. How a man like Sam Wade would accept it after he'd tipped his hat to and bedded a lie, she was afraid to imagine.

She was shamed by all the times she'd lorded her superiority over him, belittling him for his slovenly dress and crude manner. Such humbling irony for him to discover she was no better, perhaps much less than he whom she had sneered down upon. If he despised her, he had every right. She couldn't demand his respect. She wasn't the pristine Mrs. Blessing who could command it. She could offer no excuse, nor would she insult him with one. All she could do was explain and hope—pray—he had the compassion to understand and perhaps even allow for the mistakes of her youth.

"When my father was killed, my mother and I were left destitute. I was thirteen, too young to support us. We went to live with my mother's sister in Omaha. Mama had been sick for a long time, tuberculosis, but had been hiding it from my father so he wouldn't insist she leave him to seek treatment. It was too late for any by the time we got to Aunt May's. She was a kind woman and all too ready to take us in. Her husband, my Uncle Richard, wasn't as obliging. He thought the burden of two extra mouths to feed required restitution."

Her voice broke then. She couldn't help it. Memories crowded close, returning the chill of helpless terror, the vulnerability she vowed to never suffer from again. She braced against it as she hadn't been able to then and was able to continue at Sam's soft, "Go on."

Her uncle called himself an entertainment broker. It was a fancy name for pimp. The modest home he supplied for them was paid for by the unfortunate females who toiled in his filthy cribs. Lucy was young but she was a promising beauty. Richard's eyes gleamed with speculation the moment she'd come into his home. The daughter of a preacher, a sweet, unsullied child. It was a situation ripe for exploitation. She was family, May had argued, and her aunt stood firm in her objection to his adding the young girl to his stable of whores. Richard was clever enough to find a way to use her without compromising her virtue — indeed by profiting from it.

"The Union Pacific was spreading toward the Wyoming Territory. Uncle Richard kept his greedy eyes open and conceived of a way to capitalize on his business. Tent towns followed the railroad. "Hell on Wheels," they called them, and they weren't far from wrong. They'd set up at the end of the tracks to service the needs of the workers. Richard saw a gold mine. And he wasn't a man to pass on opportunity." Her voice grew hard, bitter, as if even as she spoke, she was evolving from fresh-faced innocent to tough survivor. She'd had no choice. It was comply with her uncle's plan or be left to care for her mother without a short bit to her name. By then, Lila Todd required almost constant care which her Aunt May was willing to provide and expensive treatments — useless treatments — that her aunt and uncle could afford. Unable to bear the thought of her beloved mother wasting away on some shadowed street corner when she could linger in dignity and relative comfort in her family's home, Lucy did the only thing she could. She packed her meager belongings and followed Richard's entourage to Benton at the head of the railroad in the Wyoming Territory.

UP camp followers were fast-dollar types: gamblers, saloonkeepers, con-men, pimps and whores who thrived beneath the billowing tents set up every sixty miles. Not a blade of grass or growing thing was in sight but twenty-three saloons and five dance halls spread around the "Big Tent," the forty by one hundred-foot frame structure covered with canvas and floored for dancing and gambling that was a bastion for slaking thirsts and lusts. Whiskey was cheaper than water in that lawless tent city where the population swelled from black-tailed prairie dogs to several thousand rowdy patrons of vice practically overnight. Under the canvas shelters were bars, fancy gambling equipment and brothels. Day and night the streets thronged with a motley assortment of peddlers, miners, bullwhackers, muleskinners, Mexicans, Chinese rail workers, Indians, capitalists and prospectors, all hungry to be entertained. Richard Graham's tent was just one of many but it held a novelty that drew men from miles around. For his canvas housed an angel, as pretty and pure as a man's dreams, with a hymn-trained voice that stirred the soul to weeping.

Women were a rarity, but a good-looking female was uncommon enough to draw a crowd of admirers. In her thin white gowns cut to be both prudent and provocative, when Lucy took the stage to sing she quickened a particular beast within a man; a want to protect and possess. Avid eyes gleamed up at her with a light burning hotter and brighter than the smelly lanterns. These were not men with souls to save, rather those eager to cast their lot with damnation. And Lucy had been terrified. Each night she was displayed before them and made to perform. The only way she could survive the shame was to distance herself spiritually from the surroundings. What the greedy, howling men saw before them was a pretty, empty shell. The heart and soul of Lucy Todd was safely encased in an emotional vacuum.

Lucy described how she was bartered at the end of each song to the man willing to offer up the most. That gent would have the pleasure of her company for dancing, conversation and as much groping as he could get away with beneath Richard's often inattentive eye. Though her virtue was uncompromised, her spirit was raped each evening. Sam listened with a sick horror to the dead tone of her voice. He didn't turn to her. He couldn't. He was afraid she would see the terrible emotion twisting his expression as his insides knotted in angry despair. As a young girl of fourteen, Lucy had been stunned by the blunt assault of her surroundings. Recounting them now, even with a maturity of years and the safety of her own home behind her, the old familiar horrors made her skin grow cold. The flaring gambling tents, the dance houses, the eternal strumming banjos, miserable women who danced all night with the forced energy of a prisoner in a treadmill. Games of faro, three-card monte, roulette, black and white, the mingling cries of "all down, all set, make your game — seven of diamonds and the red wins." The harsh din of quarrels and cussing, the intemperate drinking, the flash and bang of pistols. Shameless pimps, shameless women, broken gamblers, thieves of every manner. Depravity flaunted like a banner in broad daylight for all to see. A nightmare that made her hard as nails on the outside and a quiver of fright within.

"I remember the first time I saw Oliver." Her voice softened with relief as if even now he provided a salvation from the terror. "There was a fine alkali dust six inches deep in the streets and an incessant wind. An Eastern dandy stepped off the train in a black broadcloth suit and in a pair of seconds looked as if he'd crawled out of a flour barrel." A smile touched her lips, poignant, fond, amused. "He'd come in on Cornelius Bushnell's private train. Bushnell was one of the UP directors, a banker out of New Haven,

Connecticut. He brought family and friends for an inspection of the completed portions of the railroad hoping to encourage support of the Credit Mobilier. Oliver was one of those he thought to lure into financial backing.

"The next time I saw Oliver, he was watching me sing. I'll never forget the look on his face." It was a memory too personal to describe to Sam Wade. It was one she would hold in her heart to eternity, that revering, respectful gaze that brought a stirring of life back into her bleak existence. "He bought my company for the evening. And for the next. All he wanted was to talk: of himself, of his plans to build a town. They were wonderful, exciting plans. He gave me a beautiful dress and took me with him to a dinner inside the private rail car. He introduced me as his guest, as Miss Lucille Todd of the Kansas Todds and sat me down at their table as if I was fit to be among them, to sit at their fine table with all the mirrors and polished brass lamps and bright silver." She had to stop, for emotion ceased her voice. For several seconds, she struggled to swallow that clog of feeling.

"And?" Sam prompted quietly. He still hadn't turned. He stood tall and rigid, facing Blessing.

"He asked me to marry him. He wanted to share his dream and it was a dream I believed in with all my heart." She purposefully skipped over the humiliation of Oliver Blessing buying her from the greedy Richard Graham. "We were wed in Benton. I sent for my mother but she—she had already passed on. My uncle had known of it for better than a month but hadn't told me. He hadn't wanted to lose his gold mine."

Richard Graham. Sam filed away the name as a man worth killing. "And so you lived happily ever after as the wealthy Missus Oliver Blessing."

His voice was odd. Lucy couldn't decipher the emotion threading through it. He sounded angry. At her deceit? Because she pretended a prestigious past to cover the ugly truth? She had never lied to him. She never told him she was other than she was. She had never told him anything. A lie of omission.

"Yes," she answered with an equal quiet. She allowed no trace of apology to creep into her words. She wasn't ashamed. She hadn't taken advantage of a lonely old man. Theirs had been a unique arrangement, of sharing strengths, of respect and support. In a way, she had loved Oliver Blessing. For his goodness, for his undaunted vision, for rescuing her from death by humiliating degrees. And he had cherished her as companion and helpmate. Together, they built their dream and called it Blessing.

"I owe him, Sam. Perhaps in ways you could never understand. He saved my life. He saved my soul from a daily hell. I owe him the continuation of his dream. At any cost to me. And I owe it to myself to see that no woman suffers, helplessly, the horrors of a man like Richard Graham."

Sam looked to her then. His expression was shuttered behind narrowed eyes and close-gripped mouth. She waited, anxious, hopeful, fearing for him to speak of what went on behind that impassive false front. Had he offered the slightest hint of welcome, she would have rushed to feel the stabilizing strength of his arms about her. She might have gone so far as to confess the truth she'd admitted to herself just moments before when considering her relationship with her husband. She admired and respected Oliver Blessing. She loved Sam Wade.

But he extended no show of support or forgiveness. Sam held tight to his own churning emotions, forbidding them escape or expression. What could he offer while yet bound by his own secrets? She'd bared her past and the scars upon her soul. To go to her now, as he wished to with all his heart, with less than honesty between them would be reprehensible. Her sins were of circumstance. His were of choice. He knew she was looking for a sign from him. He could feel her reaching out to him, asking him for more than he could give. It would have been the perfect time to gain her confidence, to lull suspicions that would interfere with his own plans. All it would take was the offer of his hand. So simple.

He couldn't do it.

Sam looked deep into the well of hurt long stored in her wet gaze and saw a courage and determination there that overset the misery. She'd suffered, not unlike himself, but she'd chosen honor over ease, sacrifice over self-serving vengeance. What he saw made him feel sorely ashamed. Lucy Blessing was a damned fine woman and he no better than a common criminal.

"She's finally sleeping," Newt announced as he stepped out onto the porch. Preoccupied, he missed the meaningful undercurrents stirring out in the rain-drenched evening. "I thank you kindly for taking her in."

Lucy nodded absently. Her heart was heavy with despair. Sam had chosen to say nothing when he'd had the chance. He was either totally disgusted or just too much a gentleman to injure her feelings further by unburdening the contempt he felt. Which, didn't matter. He couldn't accept and he couldn't forgive. That much was plain. To find a man she could love then to lose him. It was a fate too cruel but justified. She still had Blessing and she would cling to that like a zealous mother protecting her brood.

"I trust I can continue to count on your help, Marshal?" How coldly formal she sounded, not at all like a woman who had just unburdened the blackness of her soul.

Sam responded in kind, heartbreakingly aloof, crushingly polite. "I gave you my word, Miz Blessing. And now I'll wish you good evening."

The silver Stetson was gallantly tipped, the way it would be toward a lady. Then Marshal Wade and his deputy hunched their shoulders against the mist of rain and headed down toward the lights of Blessing.

Chapter Sixteen

Henry Knight looked up from his glass of rye into the fires of hell. He recognized them when he saw them, blazing hot with the promise of an agonizing eternity. It was a sight meant to bring fear and fate to a quick maturity. All that glittered in the sharp-honed steel of Sam Wade's stare.

"Let's make some talk, barkeep." It was a soft suggestion, politely uttered, yet there was no mistaking the gentle buzz of warning before a deadly rattler strike. Without shifting the stab of his gaze for an instant to either side, Sam showed his awareness of the saloon owner's hired men easing up behind him. "Tell them to shy out of it." His right hand hung negligently at his side, palm turned toward the grip of his Peacemaker to punctuate the request.

Knight's golden head tipped slightly in a predetermined signal. The assailants sidled back and blended into the crowd filling the Nightingale. "My office, Marshal?" He gestured toward the dark recesses of the room.

Sam's teeth flashed white in a lazy smile. There was something latent, deadly and dangerous about him. Only a fool wouldn't notice. And Henry

Knight wasn't a fool. "Thank you for the invite but here's fine." In front of witnesses, his attitude concluded.

Knight shrugged in feigned indifference. "What can I do for you, Marshal?"

"Lessen you want me to adjust my aim some, you'll oblige me by leaving Billie McCafferty alone."

Knight spread his hands wide in an innocent appeal. "I've no want to tangle with you. I mistook the situation, is all. The girl's trouble. Good riddance, I say."

"See you keep to that same thought. And another thing."

"Yes?" That was a hiss drawn between tightly clenched teeth.

Sam leaned closer until scant inches separated them. "You fuss with Lucy Blessing and you're going have me to answer to. I'll gut you out and skin you till your own mama wouldn't recognize the leavings. Hear me?"

Henry Knight stood frozen as the marshal turned and strode from the bar. Then, he casually straightened his tie and glanced about to see who might have taken note of their exchange. Several attentive stares proved promising.

"That had the sound of a threat," he murmured as if surprised. "I wouldn't expect as much from a lawman."

"More gunman than lawman, I'd say," one of them muttered and Knight hid his grin of satisfaction. "More than likely on Miz Blessing'd payroll to shut you down and rid decent folk of our pleasures."

"An' I know how she'd pay him."

"Now that's mighty strong, friend," the saloon-keeper protested for effect. But the grumbling grew more pronounced.

"Ole Luke Redman turns up kilt and hung up like a side of beef and now the law's pandering to prostitutes over proper citizens," another chimed in. From there, the mood smoldered. Lucy Blessing's crusade had garnered a heap of resentment from the male populace of the town. They considered her influence a threat to the peace in their homes. One uppity female and pretty soon they'd be accountable for their every cent and second.

Henry Knight turned his cold black gaze toward the batwing doors. The muttering soothed his aggrieved pride but he had another ace up his sleeve to deal out against the meddlesome marshal. And against the pretty banker. The ace of spades.

"Belly up, boys," he called congenially. "Drinks are on the house."

"What's eatin' you, boy?"

Newt flushed and quickly shook his head. "Nuthin', Marshal," he mumbled, but Sam knew lying and the boy was offering up a whopper. Something was on his young deputy's mind elsewise he wouldn't be staring at him with the uneasy curiosity due a two-headed calf.

Sam had experienced better mornings. Even Newt's varnish-stripping coffee couldn't cut through the thickness of his thoughts. It was Lucy. He'd tossed the night in restless dreams, haunted by visions of Lucy Blessing in pure white spangles suspended in a canary cage over Nightingale's bar while Henry Knight sold tickets for a look see. What the hell was he going to do? Contrary to Lucy's belief, knowing the truth about her only increased his admiration and inflamed the attraction.

He'd been able to think of nothing but the feel of her satin-smooth skin. He'd been unable to shake the images of betrayal and torment in her eyes. Hadn't the woman suffered enough? How in God's good name would she survive what he had planned?

Newt was staring at him again with that round-eyed look of agitation. What was he so nervous about? It wasn't as though the boy could see into the quandary of his mind. In the boy's eyes, he was a hero. He'd been worthy of that awe at one time, during the war when he'd ridden for a cause. No. Not even then. Even when he rode for the Confederacy, he was riding for himself, to assuage the rage that burned within. His cause had been revenge and the end of the war hadn't ended his need. He was no hero but that's the way they made him feel in Blessing. His fingertips caressed the smooth stock of his prize Winchester. And it was scary how much he'd grown to like the feel of their trust.

Had he believed in such things, he would swear they'd cast a spell over him, the town and Lucy Blessing. He just hadn't been prepared for them. He hadn't expected their enveloping troubles to affect him quite so much. The moment they'd pinned on their star of tin, he'd begun to feel as though he was their marshal. Responsible. Protective. Of a bunch of folks he planned to rob? Ridiculous! No, terrifying. He hadn't wanted to belong but they made him feel he did. Newt with his worshipping eyes, Lucy with her sweet kiss, even the damned dog had saved his life and earned a place within his jaded heart. The place was cursed. Or was it just his plan that was ill-fated?

"If you're fixing to do nothing but sit and eyeball me all morning, boy, I suggest you go on over to Miz Lucy's to check on that pretty little gal of yours."

Newt colored at the linking reference but looked grateful for the excuse to escape the office. He reached for his hat and his shotgun. "You want me to tell Miz Lucy anything?"

"Meaning what?" Sam growled.

"I don't know. Jus' asking."

"Well, don't ask," he concluded with a snap only slightly softer than the steel jaws of a bear trap.

Newt stared at him, his jaw working as if there was something inside he was dying to speak on. His blue eyes were shadowed and worrisome. That was enough to give Sam notice.

"Newt?" he queried. "Something on your mind, boy? You been as jumpy as a frog on a hot skillet this morning."

Newt hesitated. He could feel the paper folded in his breast pocket. The damning words it held seemed to scorch him. This man, Sam Wade, the man who'd taken him in, given him a chance at respect, treated him better than his own paw had ever seen fit to, was a lie. His name was Zachary and he was a wanted hard case, not a man of the law. The badge on his chest demanded he do something about it. But his fondness for the man he knew, regardless of the name he went by, kept him silent and uncertain. It was a hell of a fix.

"It's nuthin', Marshal," he mumbled, lowering his eyes before Sam could read the confusion in them. He shuffled out with Cornelius loping at his heels.

Sam forgot the young man's strangeness as he brooded over his own situation. A hell of a fix. He looked unhappily about the tidy office. Home. That was the problem. Blessing felt like home. He'd been restless, leading a tumbleweed existence for so long. He'd been bone weary when he rode down the broad main street for the first time. And Blessing had eased his spirit. He'd grown to like the role he played. He gotten to like the people who looked up to him. He'd begun to care—too damned much about the banker he thought to rob. It was supposed to have been easy, a fat, ripe plum for the picking. Only trouble was, he'd gotten caught up in tending the precious fruit and couldn't bring himself to yank it from the tree.

Reflexively, he began to clean the Winchester. A beautiful piece. A token of the town's respect. He'd about busted his buttons with pride upon receiving it. Damn, what had these people done to his head? They had him believing he had to live up to their admiration. And he wanted to. It felt good to belong, to be needed, to be responsible. And when he thought of Lucy Blessing, his heart and mind got to churning something fierce, making him consider the impossible. She was the kind of woman who could make a man think. She was the kind of female a man wanted to come home to at the end of a day. Smart, pretty, hard when she had to be, soft when she wanted to be. Everything he could want. Just like Blessing.

And if he chose to stay, if he made Blessing his home, Lucy his woman, became Marshal Wade, what would happen when his past arrived? Each day he stayed worsened the consequences. Would the town still embrace him as a thief and killer? Would Lucy offer him her trust and open arms if she knew he was the same kind of man who murdered her husband? Would she ever believe he could change?

No.

He knew the answers, he just didn't want to hear them. There was no home for him here in Blessing, no future in Lucy's kisses. He would do what he came for and put them behind him. If he could. One thing he knew at that moment was that he could never march into the Blessing Savings Association and strip the town of its life's blood. He couldn't — wouldn't steal from those who trusted him. He could live with being a fool but not with being a man who'd betray those who believed in him. The payroll was a different matter. No strings were attached there. That would be satisfaction enough. Blessing would get over its shock in time at having taken a viper to its bosom. He just couldn't bring himself to inflict them with a more vicious sting. When the old men got to hard-wintering talk around the stove at Davis's, they would have a juicy topic for debate. And when Lucy Blessing got over her initial hurt, she'd thank him for not stealing more than the army's payroll.

The two voices mingling behind her were soft and poignant with strains of evolving affection. Lucy listened to the sweet tone rather than the individual words. It was music to the soul, a soul rubbed raw and stripped of hope. She listened with the bittersweet knowledge that such intimacy would never be hers. She didn't begrudge Billie and Newt their budding love affair. They were two lonely victims seeking solace and significance. They would grew strong with the nurturing warmth each had to offer. And Lucy was glad for them.

Lucy moved out onto her veranda and inhaled the delicate scent of lilacs that struggled so valiantly to overcome the thick, blackstrap odor of prairie sage. Such were her hopes, a faint transplanted dream trying to survive against the natural order of things. Though she was tempted to sink once again into the blue mood which had stretched her night out into interminable minutes, she fought the urge. Self-pity served no purpose. She had no right to feel discontent. She had everything. She was the most envied female in Blessing. She had a thriving business, a lovely home, a solid reputation, independence that others of her sex would never know. She had all those things accompanied by admirable goals for the betterment of her town. Her hours were absorbed with worthwhile pursuits but it wasn't until Sam Wade appeared that she realized how long the nights could be.

Damn him.

Lucy drew her shawl closer about her shoulders. She had every right to feel proud of the things she'd achieved. Tremendous adversities had been overcome. She'd survived horrors that still woke her to cold sweats. She'd gone from singer to councilwoman, determinedly burying her past and building upon fresh ground. Only there were those who would never let her forget that ground was tainted, that no matter how high she built, the foundation would still be rotten. Mostly, she ignored their snide remarks, or tried to. She let their references bounce off the tough veneer cloaking her more vulnerable emotion. Except, she wasn't as tough as she pretended. The slurs hurt. The memories yet burned with insatiable shame. There were days she looked in the mirror and couldn't find the affluent Mrs. Oliver Blessing. A frightened girl who cost four bits a dance was there instead. That haunted shadow would ever linger behind her stylish manners and cool poise. It would not be denied. Just as her feelings for Sam Wade would not be denied.

Oliver Blessing had been a singular man. He'd

had the generosity of heart to bestow unconditional forgiveness. Never once had he made Lucy feel the stigma of shame. He couldn't have treated her with more respect had she been born of a Boston blue blood. He'd drawn her gently, patiently into his life, demanding little, giving much. Her life had been perfect, filled with contentment and satisfaction. How unseemly to ask for more. How greedy to expect it. Gratitude alone should have sufficed. And it had. Until Sam Wade moved her through the steps of a country reel. Until he goaded her with his lazy smile and angered her with his staunch ideals. Until he flooded her senses with fiery passion atop her husband's bed. A bed in which she'd been treated like a treasured queen but never like a woman. Sam Wade had made her greedy, had made her discontent. And now she suffered for her grasping desires. She could pull herself up from depravity. She could become an enviable lady. She could run a business and control a town but she couldn't demand respect from the one from whom it meant the most. God help her, she couldn't force Sam to forgive what she had been.

Lucy sighed and tried to dislodge the congested emotion from her throat. Why his desertion should wound so was a mystery. He was no paragon of virtue, yet his stone of blame cut the deepest. He'd said it all by saying nothing. What more could she do to make him understand? What had she done but survive? Was that an unforgivable crime? One for which she should suffer daily? One for which she should be denied any happiness? Oh, the things she had, the comforts she shared, they were eases for the body and the mind. But she had nothing for the soul. She had no one with which to share the beauty of what she was inside. And all of Oliver

Blessing's precious gifts could not amend that lack. None of her riches and successes could measure up to the joy she'd found one evening in the company of the rough-edged town marshal. And that joy she could neither buy nor barter.

She looked down upon Blessing. It was no longer everything to her. It was buildings, folks who led their own lives. She was an outsider, a manipulator who could pull the strings but not join in the simple play. It wasn't enough. It would never be enough now that Sam had shown her what it was like to live. And to love. And to be alone.

The streets were busy below. It was closing on noon and she still hadn't gone to the bank. Cecil could handle things, she knew, but it was a rarity for her not to be there. She wasn't avoiding the town gossip. She wasn't afraid of Henry Knight's anger. She was hiding from the expressionless eyes of Sam Wade. His indifference was more than she could endure after the hopes she'd spun into a golden future. The truth raveled that dream, leaving threads and tatters. And she could not assemble her pride nor conceal her devastation. His rejection broke her heart. She had no more want to continue pushing through the emptiness of her days. So she would . . . what? What exactly was she to do? Close herself within her sanctuary and pretend such disappointments did not exist?

Lucy frowned. A prisoner in her own home? A prisoner of her own heart? Was that what she wanted to be? It wasn't her way to surrender to circumstance. She fought against greater odds and triumphed. She carried her dignity like a shield, wielded her pride like a sword. Would she now cower before a disapproving glance? Would she give Sam Wade the power to make her writhe in shame for a past she couldn't control? Would she allow him an uncontested victory or fight for his respect? For his love? The enormity of the challenge frightened her. But the rewards—oh, the rewards should she succeed!

The sound of gladsome laughter from within the rooms behind provoked Lucy into action. Would she prefer those rooms empty of all but memory or ringing with that cheerful noise? She began to walk, determinedly, down the puddled street. Her head was held high but a vulnerable heart raced with uncertainty within her breast. What was investment without risk? Only this time, she risked more than coin.

Sam watched her march down the street from where he stood at the jail house window. He smiled as he examined her brisk stride. Looked like she was off to tame the world. There was something in the way she moved that made him go all funny inside. There was a haughty confidence in her carriage, an arrogance which defied the soft femininity of her stylish flounces and fringe. She was a cold, clear mountain stream gathering speed as it swept downward over anything in its path. A man got refreshed just looking at the glittering plays of surface beauty. Sam was drawn to her as if he'd thirsted long and agonizingly. He'd tasted her sweetness, he'd been bathed in her splendor. Now there was no satisfaction to be found in anything less.

Against his better judgment, against every decision he'd just made, Sam stepped out onto the sidewalk and moved to the rail where he lounged with a carelessness that was all effect. The closer she came, the less easy he felt. As the distance decreased, a coil of emotion compressed until it was held, quivering and dangerous, by the mere thread of his resolve. She drew up, breaking stride when she saw him. For a brief second, he thought he saw fear in her lovely features. But no. It must have been a trick of sunlight, a reflection, for she continued toward him with a small, fixed smile. His hand rose to the brim of his Stetson, dipping it forward before pushing it back so no shadow fell over his keen gaze.

" 'Morning, Miz Lucy," he drawled.

"Good morning, Marshal."

"You're running a mite late. Got so a body could set his timepiece by you. Is everything all right up at the house?"

He was concerned about Billie, that was all. Lucy refused to be encouraged by his inquiry. "Fine. Everything's fine." What a magnificent whopper that was. She didn't care if he knew it. Let him wonder. She hoped it was guilt or regret that caused his gaze to cant down ever so slightly. She came to a stop on the narrow board walkway, so close she could have reached out to place a hand upon the bent knee he leaned upon. Close enough to count the creases that fanned out from the corners of his steel-gray eyes. One side of his smile dropped away, leaving only that half bend that could both mock and beguile.

"You're not fixing for any trouble today, are you, ma'am? I think the town could use a rest from the excitement. I know I could."

"I certainly wouldn't want to overtax your energies, Marshal."

He responded to her jibe with a suggestively crooned "No?"

Lucy sucked a quick breath and felt hot color suffuse in her cheeks. Jiggly sensations darted through her like a school of wiggly minnows. His single word conjured up all sorts of enticing images. Just as he intended. He was toying with her. To what end? Sam Wade was harder to read than the territorial guidelines. One silky insinuation did not make for an apology or an overture. She scowled at him, angry because he didn't offer more.

"Isn't there something you should be doing to earn your keep?"

"I was just waiting for you. Seems trouble follows on your heels so I thought to let you bring it to me."

"How very conservative of you. I'm sure the tax-payers would approve of the economy of your methods."

She started to pass, flicking her skirt impatiently away from the dusty toe of his boot. She shouldn't have expected miracles. He was acting as if nothing had happened between them, as if the terrible truth wasn't a wedge. Maybe—

"Lucy?"

His strong, browned fingers closed about her forearm in a gentle yet restraining grip. The contact was unexpected. Jolts of startled pleasure, like heat lightning dancing over still water, snapped through her. Her gaze flew up, filled with anxious hope, with uncertain dreams.

And Sam found he couldn't speak. Everything a man could want glimmered in her stare, nuggets of gold there for the taking. All he had to do was reach out and claim the wealth. Her parted lips asked it of him. The sudden softening of her stance beckoned the curve of his arms. And he was itching to comply.

His usually finely honed senses were focused on Lucy Blessing, dulling them to any other stimuli. That is, until he felt the cold, unmistakable chill of steel touch to the nape of his neck in a deadly circle. Followed by the equally inevitable click of Mister Colt's mechanics.

Chapter Seventeen

Lucy's gasp of warning came an instant too late as a low voice drawled, "You fixing to back your play or you wearin' those fancy pieces to hold up your britches?"

As she watched in horror, Lucy saw Sam's hands relax imperceptibly where they had dropped instinctively near the butts of his fast-draw pistols. Slowly, he turned until the big bore of the Dragoon rested atop the bridge of his nose. There wasn't the slightest flicker of fear in his razor stare but Lucy's heart was churning hard enough to rival the fastest UP locomotive.

"Lose lead or leather it. I got no desire to sniff your powder, friend."

Amazingly, Sam's harsh words brought a wide smile to the face of his assailant and the big gun began to lower. The second the muzzle ceased to be a threat, Sam drove his fist upward. The other man was lifted onto his toes by the power of the punch and reeled backward with arms flailing as he tried to keep his balance. Lucy expect the marshal to go for his hardware then but instead he reached out to keep the smaller cowboy from falling.

"You great lunk-headed fool. I could have killed

you," Sam growled as he righted his attacker.

"You ain't never been that fast, Zach. Hell of a greeting for your favorite brother-in-law."

"My only one."

The two men came together with a hardy round of dust-rising backslapping while Lucy struggled to control the wobbling of her knees. She forced her fingers to release the grip of her concealed pocket pistol. There was no threat. The two men were not only acquainted, they were related. She didn't know whether to swoon from the excitement or to knock their reckless heads together for giving her such a scare. Only her curiosity over the name Sam was called kept her from doing either.

"Sorry if our horseplay gave you cause for fear, ma'am," the newcomer announced prettily as his attention turned to her. He was smiling, a polite gesture to match his apology. He was smaller than Sam by a head and as stocky as a mustang with barrel chest and short, sturdy limbs. She must have mistaken the menace she'd felt in him. Now, his expression was so unassuming as to be cherubic with his mild blue eyes beneath unruly brown hair. The soft accent mirrored Sam's in origin. She found it easy to return his smile and accept his humbly offered sentiments.

" 'Twould take more than your lamebrained shenanigans to turn that trick," Sam asserted. "Lucy, this here ugly-looking cuss had the good sense to ask my sister to marry him and she had the bad sense to accept. Clay Bonner, Miz Lucy Blessing."

"A right apt name, ma'am," Bonner murmured sweetly as he bent over her hand. His fingertips moved caressingly within her palm as he kept hers captive just a mite beyond the proper. Perhaps he was just being charming, Lucy rationalized as she fought the urge to jerk away in annoyance. She glanced at Sam to see if he noticed anything but he was grinning with ear-to-ear delight and oblivious to all.

Lucy reclaimed her hand and again found herself wondering if she'd maligned the amiable Bonner. He seemed a small, good-natured man with a quick, easy grin. Not at all the type to wear the tied-down rig he sported all shaped to fit his piece and molded to expose the trigger guard. All the men of the West went heeled so a gun on the hip was nothing out of the ordinary. Of the two, Sam looked to be the more dangerous and gun-handy. Clay Bonner was the type you let marry your sister.

The code of frontier etiquette prevented Lucy from posing a direct question so she phrased herself with proper vagueness.

"You're a long way from home, Mr. Bonner."

"I'm a well-traveled man, Miz Blessing."

Seeing as how kin didn't require courtesy, Sam asked him point-blank, "What are you doing so far north? Last I heard you were still a resident along the Border." There was a meaning there that escaped Lucy.

"Got the wandering urge last year. Heard you was up this away and thought I'd stir you up. Like the old days."

Sam returned his brother-in-law's smile but with decidedly less enthusiasm.

"Happen, I'm here to tend some business and I saw your tall bay in the civic pound. Recognize that mean piece of gristle on the hoof anywheres. You hiring out?"

"Got me a job here. Just call me *Marshal* Sam Wade."

Slowly, Sam stroked back his coat so the morning

sun glinted off the star he wore. Clay stared at it then let out a great cough of laughter.

"Hell, Zach, you're a one. You surely are. Full of surprises."

"Let's make some talk, Clay."

When Sam gestured toward the jail house, Lucy knew herself dismissed. Zach? Her curiosity twisted becoming almost as acute as her annoyance at being interrupted by the untimely appearance of Clay Bonner. She would never know what had moved Sam to call to her with such urgent tenderness.

"I have to be going. The townsfolk get nervous when they think I'm not minding their money."

"Ma'am?" Bonner inquired with polite confusion.

"I run the Savings Association," she explained with a smile. "Perhaps we can do some business while you're in Blessing."

"Why, ma'am, there's every possibility of that." He grinned and sketched a courtly bow as she continued on her way.

Lucy wondered as she walked how a rough-cut like Sam Wade could have such a gentlemanly relation. Then, she paused upon the sidewalk in brief puzzlement. Hadn't Tolliver's letter of recommendation stated his deputy had no kin? Curious. She moved on toward the bank hoping that would be answered when she received her reply from Cheyenne.

"A tin star! Lordy, that's rich," Clay Bonner hooted as he dropped into Sam's office chair. "I don't believe in a horse changing color so tell me, Zach, what sweet deal you got cooking?"

"I thought you were in prison, Clay." Sam settled on the edge of his desk. His initial cheer in seeing his childhood neighbor was fast dimming as wariness set in. It was an instinct honed from long years of mistrusting everyone and he hated himself for attaching any suspicion on his oldest and truest friend. They went back farther than he wanted to remember, to a bond stronger than just an in-law relationship. Rather an outside-the-law one. Seeing Clay woke all sorts of tight, confusing little quirks of emotion. Part of him wanted to embrace the other with long-lost affection. Part of him wanted to hurry Bonner to the edge of town. Before he brought the past to present.

"Didn't like prison much. No ladies there." He smiled as he observed the taut edge of Sam Zachary's expression. "Sarah sends her love." That softened him, as he suspected it would. "It was she what told me you was up here. I owe you my thanks for seeing her well tended whilst I was locked up."

Sam nodded curtly, with a gruff avoidance of his gratitude. Did he expect him to treat his own sister any differently?

Clay sighed and put his boot heels up. "Yessir, got to missing Sarah and little George something fierce."

"Then why aren't you taking care of them?" Sam drawled out.

Clay quirked a quick smile at him. "I'm a man on the run, Sammy. That's no life for a woman and child."

"You could settle hereabouts and start over."

"That what you've done?" His bland blue eyes took on a cutting gleam. "You starting over, Sam? You put the past behind you? Forgot all about Georgie swinging in the breeze? About your paw and maw and mine?" He shook his head sadly. "Never would have thought it of you, Sam."

"I've forgotten nothing." It was a rumbling snarl, torn from festering memory. When he confronted

251

Clay with his fierce glare, the other smiled his pleasure. "There's an army payroll coming in in two days' time. Interested?"

"Count me in. Jus' like the old days. And the bank?"

"No." That was said firm and absolute. Clay raised a questioning brow.

"She's mighty purty. Can see how she'd turn a man's head all softlike."

"Shut up, Clay. Just the payroll, you hear? Then I'm done. I've had enough. I mean to go home and fetch Mary and the kids, start someplace new. How 'bout you? There'll be enough money in that delivery to set you and Sarah up in style. I know you've had a hankering to see the East. Why not?"

Bonner looked up at Sam Zachary, seeing not the worshipping boy who followed him and his own brother George on youthful escapades, into battle and then on to less innocent pursuits. This was no easily led kid spurred by a hot, reckless temper. There was a sharp, wolf-cautious look about him that hadn't been there when they parted company in Russellville, Kentucky. He'd gone to prison. Idly, he wondered what had happened to the impetuous kid to turn him out in such a deadly fashion. This man was no one's fool but he could still be courted by the fondness that held his heart.

"Why not," Clay reflected with a grin. "How 'bout you come, too? Family should be together. Time's is changing. Maybe it's time to settle down and be a family man."

"Sarah would like that. She's had it hard these last years."

"Fine woman, Sarah."

Sam nodded his agreement. He felt better. One last job. His family would be together, ready to heal.

Clay and Sarah. He would see to Mary. It could be good for them again. The war was long over. There seemed no focus for his hate. His heart wasn't hardened to the task of vengeance any longer. One last jab at Grant Tolliver. Yes, it would do. It would do nicely. Then, they'd go home, he and Clay. Just the prod he needed to move on, away from where temptation would never lessen, where dreams could never be.

Like old times.

Henry Knight approached the stranger with a doubtful eye. He'd expected someone — bigger. This man looked to be a kid's runt pony compared to the cool maverick he'd ordered up on reputation. Then, the man's gaze lifted to regard him with a stare so cold it could freeze coffee in the pot as it perked. This *was* the man he wanted.

"Do something for you, mister?"

"Depends. I'm Henry Knight. You the one I sent for?"

"Could be I am. Sit yourself. Make some talk."

Knight brushed back the tails of his coat and settled on the opposite chair. True to his profession, the gunman had chosen a seat that backed up against the wall. He liked a cautious man. No longer was he fooled by the small size. He'd seen death in those chill blue eyes.

"I believe we discussed three hundred dollars," he began.

"Who?" Right to the point. Strictly business; a deadly business.

"The town marshal." He saw the killer's eyes widen slightly and added, "You got a problem with that?"

Clay Bonner shook his head and gave the saloon-keeper an amiable smile. "No problem, only it's going to cost you five hundred dollars."

"That and more if you'll do it my way. I've got a little extra business I want you to take care of, profitable business."

"I'm listening."

It was the last place he should be but he couldn't seem to help himself. It was an uphill climb but he couldn't garner any resistance. It was foolish, he told himself. It would do no good for either of them. It would make things harder . . . considering. But those arguments fell away the moment he saw her standing on the porch, cooling herself in the night breeze. Her hair was down and she wore a satin wrapper tied about her slender figure. Obviously, she'd not been expecting company at the late hour. Nor did she seem to object to it.

" 'Evening, Marshal."

It was cool but the hot eddies in her voice stirred a fire inside him. Intuition should have warned him then but it stayed traitorously quiet and let him walk blindly to his own destruction.

"Howdy, Lucy."

"I didn't realize your rounds took you up this way. I'll sleep better at night knowing that." Liar, Lucy told herself. She wouldn't sleep at all tormented by thoughts of him near her door.

"Just thought I'd check on your guest." That sounded reasonable, didn't it? Not like he'd come mindlessly to her door like some moonstruck calf.

"She moved back into town this afternoon. The milliner's putting her up over the store." Lucy was surprised he hadn't already known that. Or had he?

Her heart began to beat faster. "I thought you'd be tending your own visitor." How handsome he looked standing on her walkway with the lights of Blessing behind him. Tempting, taunting her with a future she yearned for. Sam Wade and Blessing.

"He was more for cards than company," Sam explained. He was fast running out of things to say to her. He couldn't come right out and invite himself in. He couldn't just blurt out that he'd been hungering for her kiss since that morning. He knew she was angry with him. He also knew he had hurt her purposefully and would again if the madness of the moment continued. She was no whore to dally with without a trace of conscience. She was the woman he could have sworn undying loyalty to, had the circumstances been different. But there was no changing them and there was no place for Lucy Blessing in his future.

"I'll just be saying good night, ma'am."

As he started away, he heard her breathless call. "Sam?"

He turned back, knowing what to expect and wanting it despite every scrap of reason.

"I could use your company if you've a mind to share it."

Lucy waited and watched his face. There was little she could read there in the darkness. She was trembling. He would say yes or no and she would have to accept either as the direction of fate. And she was terrified. Everything depended upon his answer—her chance for happiness, for fulfillment, for love. She felt helpless and the tension increased as the silence of the moment stretched out between them.

He never gave her an answer. He never spoke at all. He came slowly toward her, climbing the stairs with strong, determined steps. He paused before her, letting her luxuriate in the dark passion of his gaze. And then she came up against him, her arms twining about his neck, fingers knocking back his Stetson to dangle by its tie strings as she sought the raw silk of his hair. There was nothing coy or hesitant about the kiss they shared. It was hot, urgent. Between two people who knew exactly what they wanted. Each other.

Lucy stepped away, panting, shivering with need. Her fingers hooked in the front of his vest to impel him to follow. He didn't need coaxing.

It was as beautiful between them as it had been that first night. The mood was intense, expectant, demanding. Gentle overtures were forgotten as desire seized control. It was skin upon skin; hot, sliding friction. It was mouth upon mouth; sizzling, seeking, devouring. Movements were ones of purpose and pleasure. Boundaries were reached and extended as discoveries became delicious explorations. They didn't talk. Words would have intruded. Instead, low sounds of passion spoke, from rippling murmurs to great rushing roars of satisfaction, then to deep whispers of quiet.

And because no time had ever seemed more perfect, Lucy told him, "I love you, Sam Wade." Then she waited, breath suspended, heart laid bare, for his response.

Sam lifted up so he could see her face, so he could study each flushed curve and appreciate every gentle contour. His thumbs followed the path his gaze had taken, skimming lightly over her heated skin to form a tactile image upon his memory. She was like the white prairie evening primrose, with the strength to take root and survive in a savage land and still retain the fragile blush of luminescent beauty. Her words twined around all that was decent in his soul and burst into poignant bloom.

Softly, because the mood was still, he said, "A man couldn't ask for more." And he kissed her, letting his bittersweet longing prolong the moment, sustaining the sweet agony. Her love twisted tight about his heart, piercing it cruelly because he was not the Sam Wade she would care for. His name was Zachary and what he was would soon choke out all the delicate beauty she offered.

Lucy felt his strength gather as he prepared to rise. Her arms clutched in an outward sign of possession.

"No. Stay the night with me, Sam," she pleaded, letting her lips trail along the sharp cut of his jaw. The caress slowed but did not stay him.

"I can't, Lucy. There'd be talk."

"Let them talk. I don't care."

"Yes, you do," he chided gently. "And so do I. I respect what you are too much to see you hurt by this."

No other argument he could have offered would have touched so tenderly upon her emotion. Unshed tears created crystal prisms in her gaze, nearly spilling as she nodded. She watched him dress, savoring each easy movement of his taut, sinewy frame. She'd never seen anything quite so fascinating as the play of muscle beneath his smooth browned skin. Knowing she couldn't maintain her impatience until their next meeting, she thought to alleviate her suspense.

"Will you come to dinner tomorrow night? You and your brother-in-law. I should like to get to know him better." And Sam better through him.

"I can't vouch for Clay's plans but I'm always ready for a home-cooked meal."

"At seven then. And Sam—"

He paused in the buckling of his gun belt. "Umm?"

257

They arrived on time, spit polished and groomed to dine in flattering silence on Chu's excellent fare. Then, in the parlor over her late husband's aged brandy, the trio relaxed into conversation. Actually, Lucy and Clay did most of the talking and Sam was mostly silent, sipping and watching them through half-shuttered eyes. Clay was a good-natured talker. He spun windies about the youth he shared with Sam until Lucy's sides ached from laughter. His stories were clever and harmlessly playful. He didn't speak of anything beyond the time of adolescence, the time when they would have been called to war. Lucy didn't push. She knew Sam was from Missouri. He would have fought as her enemy. Clay was being polite not to make it an issue between them.

As he rambled on, she began to notice Clay never said much of anything that could be classified as factual or specific. When he spoke of himself, he was charmingly vague. Polite or evasive? Lucy started to wonder and she watched him as he spoke. His smiles were frequent, his nettling of Sam, in good fun but she sensed no hilarity in Clay Bonner. Just a razor edge of tension. And that puzzled her, for he was making every effort to appear jovial. For her amusement? Or for his own?

"Where'd you latch onto a Chinee who could whip up grub thata way?" Clay asked as he patted his sturdy stomach in appreciation.

"The Chinese who laid tracks brought their own cooks with them to prepare their traditional meals. Chu and his wife, Li, came into my service when the workers moved on." She said that smoothly enough. The truth was too harsh for parlor amusements. Li had been on her uncle's string of fancy females. He'd found the affection between her and a lowly Chinese cook quite entertaining. Lucy had found it touching in a place where emotion was sold cheap. She'd insisted Oliver employ them. It was one of the few requests she'd ever made of him. The couple had seen loyally to her comfort ever since and, in turn, had shared the freedom to wed and find lasting happiness. Lucy couldn't keep her gaze from slipping to Sam to see what he made of the information. His return stare was impassive and she wasn't sure whether to be heartened or disturbed.

"Must be something having folks to jump at your every word," Clay mused. He was smiling but there was a twist to his lips and to his words.

"They're not my slaves, Mister Bonner," Lucy clarified rather crisply.

"No, ma'am. Didn't suggest they were. You good people here in the North put an end to that sort of thing right permanent. Reckon them two feel mighty important to know so many folks died over whether they'd be called slaves or servants."

He was still smiling but in that instant Lucy saw behind the mild effacing mask to the man Clay Bonner was. And she shivered. He was cold, soullessly cold. His smile was as deceptively pleasant as the first whisper of a deadly blue norther that could blast out of nowhere and mercilessly destroy. Clay Bonner was like that. She didn't have to know it. She felt it.

Did Sam know? Was he aware of what kind of man his brother-in-law had become? She found it difficult to believe he could hold an affection for the ruthless individual who sat mockingly in her parlor. Perhaps Sam held to kinder memories and couldn't recognize the change. Perhaps he only saw the childhood neighbor whose smile was genuine and humor at no one's expense. What Lucy saw was a stone killer and Clay Bonner grinned at her when he realized he'd been found out.

From that instant on, the evening was a charade of polite laughter stretched taut over terror. Lucy had seen Bonner's cut before. Upon the faces of the men who gunned down her husband. She vowed to speak to Sam alone the moment the opportunity presented itself but had no chance that evening. She wished them both a calm good evening and endured the cool press of Bonner's lips upon the back of her hand. What had brought such a monster into her town? What evil mischief was he about and would Sam be able to prevent it?

She was still pondering those questions when she opened the bank for business. While she carried her steeping cup of tea to her desk, she saw Sam ride out of town hell-bent for leather and sighed. Their conversation would have to wait, it would seem. As she readied to study the ledgers Cecil brought her from the opened vault, a boy came into the bank and directly to her desk.

"Telegram for you, Miz Blessing. Jus' came over the wire."

"Thank you, Sherman." She exchanged a shiny coin for the sheet of paper and settled back to read it. The description came with no name attached. She knew who it concerned. As she read, her brows began to knit and furrow and by the time she'd finished, she was thoroughly confused.

Born in Boston. Served in the U.S. cavalry during the war under Sheridan. No living relatives. Five foot ten. Black hair. Brown eyes.

That was Deputy *Jeremiah* Wade, a Northerner who had no brother-in-law named Clay Bonner.

So who was the marshal of Blessing? The man she loved?

" 'Morning, Miz Blessing. Right fine day."

Lucy looked up with a start to find Bonner standing before her desk wearing a grin and his Dragoon pistol. The message she held crumpled convulsively in her fist as that big gun was leisurely withdrawn from its molded holster.

"Would it be too much trouble for you to provide me with all the money in your bank?"

Chapter Eighteen

It was close to noon and hotter than a July in Hades when Sam rode back into Blessing. The ride had been a long one and, it proved, a fruitless one. He'd received an urgent message that morning directing him out to the Culpepper homestead. After riding hard for nearly an hour, he found no emergency, just a weary annoyance at whoever played him such a time-consuming trick.

He'd made the return trip leisurely, not only to give his mount a chance to blow but himself the opportunity to think. He'd been caught up in a lot of feelings lately but hadn't done a lot of thinking. The army payroll was coming in that afternoon. It would be his last in Blessing. His last with Lucy. If he rode with Clay, he would be riding back to what he was, not ahead to what he could be. When she found out how she'd been deceived, Lucy would hate him. Even Newt, trusting Newt, would despise the day he'd ridden into town. But he would have money and his revenge. And he had Clay's promise that they would return to Missouri to pick up their shattered lives.

Clay's return had stirred a hornet's nest of hatred inside him. Toward the citizens of the North, toward Tolliver and his brand of law, toward the banks and with them, Lucy Blessing. Each had taken a turn at tearing the stability from his life. He'd been a boy when it started, younger than Newt and in a way, even more naive. Newt had learned of life early from the back of his pa's hand. Sam discovered it in flames and blood along the Missouri-Kansas border. It had changed him from the man he might have been, the one who could have wed a woman like Lucy and been a respected lawman. There was no return to innocence, no way to cleanse his hands of the crimes they had committed.

When he saw the outline of Blessing rising up off the flat horizon, shimmering like a heat mirage, he had the strange sensation of coming home. He wasn't, of course. It just kind of felt that way and he allowed himself to enjoy the feel. Time enough to ruminate later on the long ride back to Missouri. It might as well have been a mirage for all the good his hopes did him. Fantasy. Folly. No fitting end for the likes of Sam Zachary. No place for dreams in a bitter world driven by demons of retribution. He'd given up the right to hold them on a frozen street in Liberty, Missouri.

Even as his big bay ambled toward the main street, Sam knew something was wrong. The town was full of activity. Not the purposeful kind of daily business but a frantic, fearful scurrying. Townsfolk flitted along the sidewalks like fleeting shadows, expressions dazed as if they'd been hit by a tornado. He drew up at the livery but no one was there to greet him. He curbed his curiosity long enough to loosen the girth of his saddle and rub the blanket back and forth to encourage the blood flow in the stallion's back. Then, he started for his office. Halfway there, he was met by the lanky yellow hound. Even Cornelius was skittery, weaving and whining about his legs

263

as he walked. Sam quickened his stride to match the accelerated beat of his heart. What the hell had hit Blessing in his absence?

Then he saw the first sheet-covered body and he knew.

Clay Bonner had hit Blessing.

Newt was sitting at his desk. His left forearm was bound to his chest with a clean white sling. A winding about his upper arm seeped an ominous red. His usually friendly blue eyes looked old and hard when they cut up from the two dodgers set out before him. The papers were significant; one on the escaped killer, Clay Bonner, and the other, for Sam Zachary. For the moment, Sam chose to ignore them.

"What the hell happened here?"

"You don't know?" Bitterness laced his words like sour cream through coffee.

Guilt stabbed through Sam. Of course, he knew. He'd been well aware of the viper coiled in the midst of Blessing. He just hadn't expected it to strike without his knowledge. His features tensed to contain his impatience with Newt, his anger at himself. "I been out of town all morning. You know that, boy. What's gone on?"

Newt leaned back in the chair and sighed. His stare never left Sam's. The fingers of his good hand never strayed far from the butt of his American Arms. "Your old pard, Clay Bonner, hit the bank. He and his men kilt Jed from the livery and Roy Walker. Shot poor ole Cecil and me."

He was leaving something out, something vital, something terrible. Sam felt his insides tense and tremble. He forced the word through suddenly parched lips.

"Lucy?"

"They took her with them."

264

It took Sam a long second to digest this, then with a low, throbbing oath, he turned toward the door. To be halted by the man-stopping sound of a hammer click on a double-barrel shotgun. He looked back at the somber-faced boy with hard-won control.

"If you're fixing to pepper me, do it quick 'cause I've got some miles to make up and I aim to do it even if I'm toting nine .32-caliber buckshot balls."

Newt hesitated. Then his finger stabbed down at the wanted poster. "This you?"

"Was me."

That calm claim threw the boy off stride. He'd expected Sam to deny it, to make excuses, to even go for leather. But he stood, hands spread away from his forward facing gun butts, his manner direct and honest.

"I can't just do nothing about it," Newt said thickly. Confusion and pain clouded his thoughts and a loyal affection, his heart.

"You do what you have to do, boy," Sam told him softly. "But be doing it after I get back. I'm going for Miz Lucy and the money and I mean to fetch both back with me."

"He has better than a dozen men."

"Wouldn't matter if he had a hundred. He knows that. It's personal, Newt. I can't expect you to understand."

"But I do." The hammer eased down harmlessly. "You take care, hear?"

"I aim to, Deputy."

Sam pushed open the office door and the crowd scattered like cowhands avoiding a fresh-branded steer. After a moment's hesitation, they swarmed behind him as he strode determinedly toward his near-winded mount.

"You gathering a posse, Marshal?"

"Nope."

That caused a ripple to race through the crowd.

"They're killers, Marshal."

"I know what they are and I'll do better going after them alone." His bay gave an unfriendly snort when he yanked the cinch tight.

"They got Miz Blessing."

Cold steel glittered as his gaze touched on the anxious faces. "I aim to bring her back with me." And not a one of them doubted the man whose stare cut like a honed Green River knife. They parted as he vaulted up afork his big horse and it was then Sam saw Henry Knight standing on the sidewalk, gawking at him as though he'd seen a ghost. He had no time to ponder on that look as he set the bay surging forward. He knew where to find Clay Bonner. He just didn't know if he'd be in time.

He was too late for those guarding the army payroll. Uniformed bodies littered the trail. He guided his mount around them. They were beyond any help he could give them. He had no time to pause for burying and that troubled him no little bit. Then his gaze lit on the scars left by wagon wheels. They cut deep for they bore a heavy cargo. Fresh horse droppings told he wasn't far behind.

Sam's heels thudded into the wet ribs of his bay and continued the pursuit. Clay Bonner had reached under his nose and stole something precious to him. The payroll wasn't important to him, nor was the bank money. He would have let Bonner have either without another thought. But Lucy, that was another matter. And Clay must have known that when he took her. They'd be expecting him and he didn't want to keep them waiting.

* * *

The buckboard bounced along the rutted trail dealing pain to Lucy's rigid spine like forceful blows from a hammer. She wouldn't betray her discomfort any more than she would display her fear, though both were nearly crippling. If she had to endure the horror, she would do so with dignity. No matter what the cost. And it cost her. Her insides were knotted with shock and terror and still shuddering from the events both in and outside of the bank in Blessing.

They'd swooped down with the precision of a military attack, paralyzing the town before anyone could think to react. While Clay Bonner held his big Dragoon pistol on her, Cecil cleaned out the vault at his command. Then Bonner shot him. It was a cruel, senseless thing and that, more than the sight of blood blossoming on her clerk's shirtfront, stunned Lucy into dazed compliance. He jerked her out into the street that now held the milling horses of his companions. They were shooting and hollering, sending the frightened citizens dashing for cover. Outside Davis's Goods Emporium, Roy Walker was loading the last of his supplies into his family's wagon. One of the robbers hopped into the seat and Walker was promptly killed for his protest. Lucy was dragged up onto the seat and left to cling for balance when the team was whipped up and sent bolting.

As she stared behind her, Lucy witnessed the gang's departure through desperate eyes. She saw Newt hobble from the jail house with his shotgun at the ready, only to be cut down in the street. She saw Ned from the livery come out to see what caused the commotion, felled by a pattern of buckshot. Then, Bonner with his satchel of bank money and the rest of his killers headed their horses out of town.

That would have been enough to thoroughly petrify her but it was not enough for the deadly crew. There was a purpose in their direction, as she was soon to learn. With the wagon hidden behind an outcropping of rock and Lucy safely trussed and gagged, the murderers slunk low and waited until a detachment of cavalry rode into their midst in escort of the payroll wagon. She was spared the sight of butchery but the screams echoed through her like slashes of a knife.

When their killing work was done, the rag was taken from jaws that ached with silent screams but Lucy's hands remained tied. It was a struggle to retain her balance once the band took to the trail but she managed. The difficulty helped take her mind off her perilous situation. She hadn't had time to consider why Bonner would want her along, but now those suspected reasons crowded close and smothering. The cold feel of her pocket pistol was some comfort. She could never take on the bulk of them. But if Clay Bonner meant to do what she feared, there would be time to send him to hell and spare herself the company of his companions. That secret knowledge gave her a thin edge of superiority and surprise. She clutched to that with grim satisfaction and kept a covert eye on the trail behind them. When Marshal Sam Wade discovered how his friend had betrayed him —

"Whatcha watching for, gal?"

Lucy turned her gaze straight ahead on the rumps of the mismatched team. She refused to acknowledge Clay Bonner's presence as he lounged in the saddle beside her.

"You looking for the marshal?"

She clenched her muscles, stilling them against reaction. She would take a savage pleasure in seeing Bonner hanging, be it from a gallows or a porch beam.

"Don't you worry none. He'll be along. To collect his share of the loot."

He gave a great barking laugh as Lucy's gaze flew to his in hate-filled disbelief. She said the worst thing she could think of. "Liar!" The jovial features clenched tight and for a moment, she feared he would strike her. However, his mood passed from fury to mocking humor.

"We'll see, missy. We'll see who the liar is."

He kicked his black gelding into a showy canter, leaving her to choke on dust and suspicion in his wake. It was then she remembered the reply that came back from Marshal Tolliver. The man in town was not named Wade, nor, it would seem, the law. Most likely, he was a part of Bonner's batch of thieves and had been sent ahead to scout out the town of Blessing. And she and the citizens had been very obliging with their trust and information.

Part of her wanted to scream a denial, to declare a defense of the nameless man she'd let into her home and heart. But reason murmured otherwise, a cold, weary reason that said he had used her from the start. Even as he whirled her through the steps of a dance. Even as he acquainted her with passion. Even as he heard her speak her words of love. She and the town of Blessing had meant no more to him than a nice fat payday.

She would not cry. Lucy bit her lower lip fiercely to still its trembling. She swallowed hard to shove down the scalding tears of hurt and betrayal that swelled within her throat. Never—never!—would let these vermin see how she suffered the truth. Her breaths came low and hard, like an engine drawing to come to full steam. Each fanned her fury, stoking her resentment with the strength she would need to go on. Anger and hate would help her now, not anguish and bitter weeping. There would be time for weeping . . . later. Now, she had to concentrate on how she was going to escape and recover the bank's money. The enormity and probable impossibility of the task didn't touch upon her narrowed scope of thinking. Weighing failure wouldn't help her either. She needed something positive to cling to, a reason to hope. And restoring the wealth to Blessing was the impetus she sought. That, and thoughts of using one of her double barrels to put a very final end to the man she knew as Sam Wade.

The day finished in a red and gritty dusk. Lucy could see the harsh jut of the Wind River range and wondered if they were planning to lose themselves amid the rocky foothills. However, the group gathered around the small glow of the night fire seemed in no hurry. Nor did they look to be worried about pursuit. She studied them in the flickering play of light, the Devil's denizen leaning in close to enjoy the heat and prosperity of his flames. Hard cases, all. She recognized the type. Trigger specialists with gleaming references strapped to their hips. Their laughter was coarse, their smiles as cruel as the land. This was no pack of casual bandits. They were experienced killers and seasoned professionals. And they enjoyed what they did, to a man.

Her presence at their campfire caused no little comment. Lucy was uncomfortably aware of their hard, speculative stares. The look of hungry men feeling the primitive urge to sate their needs. She'd endured those ravenous looks before but this time there was no Uncle Richard to discourage them from evolving from thought to deed. She shivered where she sat in a pool of crumpled satin and forced her aching spine to straighten. They could not know she was afraid. Animals could scent fear and it would send them into a merciless frenzy. Let them feel the cold bite of her contempt. Perhaps that would keep them at bay a bit longer.

But not forever.

In her situation, the prospect of taking a bullet from her own gun was less frightening than participating in what this group of hard, heartless men had planned. For the moment, Clay Bonner was keeping them in line, cuffing them should their gazes stray overlong or their comments get overly descriptive. But he wouldn't keep the tight leash on forever. Not on them or on himself. He'd towed her along for a reason unknown to all but him and when she'd served her purpose, she'd be used as indifferently as one of their guns or horses: to perpetuate their mood of violence. And she would rather be dead than be so abused. They would kill her anyway, in the end. She couldn't imagine them dragging her with them for any distance. If she was going to survive, she had to keep her wits about her and watch for any chance to escape.

Clay sauntered over to where she was trussed and helpless. He carried a plate of beans and a tin of strong-smelling coffee.

" 'Evening, Miz Lucy. Sorry I couldn't have brung along your Chinee help to tend you," he taunted as he hunkered down in front of her. He smiled. How had she ever believed him to be mild-tempered? He was cold and evil clear through. "You'll just have to settle for me. Your meal, ma'am."

Her hands may have been tied but not so her feet.

271

Her booted toe lashed out, catching the plate on the underside to flip it in a spiral of soupy beans directly upon his shirtfront. "I'd as soon settle for a rattler," she spat in the face of his surprise.

Slowly, but she wasn't fooled by the leisure in his movements, he drew out a handkerchief and wiped at the spill of her supper. A quick glance toward the fire quieted the chuckles of his men. When he was done, his gaze rose to pierce her and she recoiled from the gleam of menace in it. His voice was soft.

"Now that weren't very polite. We may not look like much but we do insist our guests be polite at dinner."

His hand shot out and twisted cruelly in her hair, jerking her head at a harsh angle.

"Maybe I'll forget your lapse of manner would you apologize real pretty."

There was another crude snicker from the fireside and Lucy stiffened, when Clay encouraged it with his grin. She let every ounce of her hatred and disgust glare out as she met his pale eyes. He smiled again, recognizing her rebellion, even admiring it.

"No? Too high and mighty to offer up an 'excuse me' to the likes of us, eh? No matter. You must be hungry by now. A shame for your dinner to go all to waste. Help yourself."

With that amused drawl, he impelled her forward, crushing her face against the smear of beans upon his vest and rubbing hard until satisfied with her muffled cries of protest. He jerked her back, expecting to find her humbled or at least showing a goodly amount of fear. She was neither. Though her cheeks were reddened and stained, there was no change in the cut of her stare.

"Pig," she hissed at him. The scent of him was strong within her nostrils; the repellent smell of dirt and sweat and tobacco. Fiercely, she wiped her face on the sleeve of her dress, hoping to scrub away the traces of him that lingered.

He laughed, echoing the hilarity of his men. But the sound he made held no humor. "Proud little thing, ain'tcha. Had me a little mare like you once upon a time. Wouldn't take to a saddle nor to me. I broke that little filly, rode her right into the ground. 'Course she weren't no good to me after that but she didn't sass me no more either." He grinned, a wide, promising grin. "I'm looking forward to breaking you, gal. I mean to ride you hard."

Lucy couldn't control the shudder of sheer revulsion that rolled through her. She could well imagine his touch, his possession; a mockery of what she'd shared in her husband's bed, with Oliver and with Sam. It wouldn't be lovemaking. Pleasure had nothing to do with what he planned for her. Terror seized her in its cold grasp and she fought to contain it. Her jaw clamped tight to prevent any sound of submission from escaping. If he thought her weak, he might pursue his intentions regardless of his words and she couldn't afford to invite his groping. If his roving hands came across the pistol she wore strapped beneath her skirt, her only chance to save herself would be gone. She had to knock him back on his heels. Hate him, her mind cried out. Hate him. That was her only weapon. That loathing spewed from her stare, was clear in the curl of her soft lips.

Her defiance didn't please him. He liked his women pliant. His big hand caught her face in its vee and his fingers squeezed tight as a vise, bruising her skin, hurting her purposefully.

"I'd mount you right here and now weren't it for Zach being on his way. After you carry me in the

273

saddle for a while, we'll see how proud you are. When Zach gets here, things'll change."

There was the sound of a soft footfall, just a whisper upon the buffalo grass not five feet behind.

"I'm here."

A clatter of hardware came from the fire as men caught unaware went for their guns but Clay calmed them with an easy laugh. "Leather 'em, boys. Howdy, Zach. Been saving a plate for you."

"Hope you mean to serve it to me in a neater fashion."

In two steps, he was within the frail circle of light. Lucy almost forgot herself to cry out his name. Then she was grateful the crush of Bonner's fingers kept her from that folly. The lean man from Missouri was not here to rescue her. He'd come to collect his cut.

A thorough glimpse told Sam Lucy was all right. She was mussed, dirty and frightened but as yet unharmed. Her eyes were bright and focused upon him. He'd seen them softened with relief and just as quickly chill. She knew. And she hated him. He'd expected it but still it struck him low, like the fat blade of a James Black bowie knife reaching for his vitals. Reflexively, he covered his distress with an air of lazy nonchalance.

"You changed plans without telling me," he complained mildly.

"Thought it for the best, boy. Weren't quite sure of you." Clay's cruel fingers stroked along Lucy's cheek. She saw it then, the reason she'd been taken. As insurance should Sam who-ever-he-was decide not to partake. Luckily for Bonner and his brood, Sam had no such difficulty.

"That was clever work, getting me out of town like that."

Clay chuckled, enjoying the praise. He released

Lucy with a slight shove that almost sent her sprawling and he stood. "More clever than you know. I collected me five hundred dollars I would have had to make good on were you to be on hand. Be glad my want to keep you around bested the saloon man's want to be rid of you. Guess I earned the money. You're gone."

Clay laughed at the twist of fate and Sam joined in a bit tightly. He wasn't at all surprised that Knight had put a bounty on his head and wondered idly if Bonner would have seen his deal through had he been in Blessing that morning. It wouldn't do to ruminate too long on that as he'd never know the answer.

"Thought we agreed to leave the bank, Clay."

"You know me, Zach. I'm a greedy son. Looky here, I even brung you a little something extra to make up for the dirty trick I played you." He gestured to where Lucy sat seething on the ground. " 'Course if you don't want her, the boys'd be mighty happy to take her offen your hands."

Sam ignored that. With a courtly graciousness, he swept off his Stetson and bowed formally to their bound guest. "I don't reckon we've ever been correctly introduced, ma' am. The name's Zachary. Sam Zachary of the Missouri Zacharys, or what's left of them."

Lucy caught the clip of bitterness in his tone and responded to it with a haughty tip of her chin. "The pleasure is all mine, I'm sure," she said in a molasses-laced-with-strychnine voice.

"I'm sure it has been, too, ma'am," he countered with drawling insolence. "And I mean to see it is again, real soon."

It was more than she could tolerate, his smug mockery punctuated by the crass chuckles of his

275

friends. Lucy struggled up in the twist of her skirts to gain her feet and face him squarely. She knotted her fingers together and with every ounce of strength she could muster swung her bound fists at him. He took the two-handed blow to the tip of his chin and it rocked him. He stumbled back a step and laughed as he rubbed his abused jaw. Before she could react, he reached out, catching her forearms and jerking her up to the hard chest that no longer sported the badge of Blessing's marshal. Ignoring her mewling growl of objection, he took her lips with a savage mastery, using his grinding mouth to humble her in a manner no amount of words could manage. His hand lowered to rest familiarly upon her hip, stroking, rucking up the ruined drape of satin in a suggestive manner.

And then his palm fit over the pistol and Lucy froze in horror.

Her fear that he would strip her of her only means of safety made Lucy yield in terror to his embrace. She allowed his tongue to part her lips and plunder within for a long, impassioned moment. Even knowing who he was and what he was didn't diminish the sudden jolt of pure desire that paralyzed her senses. She might hate him but she hadn't enough experience to hide the love that still defied control.

He felt that instant of surrender and fought the want to enjoy it to the fullest. Instead, he pulled back to find her dazed eyes upon him and he took a chance by whispering one short sentiment for her hearing alone. She didn't betray him. Her features were quick to lose their confusion and hardened into hatred. When he released her, she stumbled and fell upon her bustled rump. Sam shared in Clay's laughter and together they went to join the others at the fire.

Lucy sat panting in the darkness. She didn't dwell on her own shameless response to the man who stole her pride and betrayed her trust although her heart was yet churning. She sat for long, silent minutes wondering over what he'd said to her and what he might mean by it. She didn't dare hold to any hope. He was the last one among the thieves gathered at the fire who she could ever believe in, for he'd already proved himself a skilled deceiver. Even knowing that, she still considered his words and they instilled an unconscious calm within her spirit.

"Hold to your piece and don't do anything crazy, like shooting me, until I tell you."

Chapter Nineteen

They started out early while the cool still settled over the short prairie grasses and treeless landscape. Having cited the exhaustion of his horse, Sam was at the reins of the stolen homesteader wagon with his big bay tethered behind. Lucy sat stiff and stoic beside him on the seat while Clay seemed to take great amusement in the situation when he rode on up ahead.

Though Sam didn't try to draw her into any kind of conversation, Lucy was painfully aware of him. Ironically, even though she didn't trust him, his presence beside her was a source of comfort. She knew she had nothing to fear from him. Bonner and his men were ruthless, amoral creatures but she knew that wasn't true of Sam Wade—no, Sam Zachary. He was a man of conscience and conviction, be it somewhat subjective. She'd seen him jeopardize his plans to help a farmer and his family, people who were strangers to him. He'd taken a bullet and again had risked all to protect a cowboy against a silly female's pride. He'd nurtured Newt Redman's confidence and had given Billie McCafferty a chance at respect. Why would such a man, a man with honor, with compassion for his fellow man, ride with the likes of Bonner? She

278

mulled that question in stony silence as the wagon seat rocked and tipped, threatening to spill her against him. She clung to the edge of the seat, refusing to suffer the indignity of holding to him for balance.

Lucy recalled Clay Bonner's boastings at the fire. As in her own parlor, Bonner talked and Sam stayed silent, not agreeing or objecting to anything the other said. She listened with mute disbelief to the tales she knew were more than windies meant to impress the other men. There was an ugly ring of truth to them and they filled in the background of a man warped from goodness by circumstance beyond his reckoning. He told of how he and Sam's older brother George had ridden with Quantrill in the burning of Lawrence, Kansas. He spoke with pride of how Sam had taken his brother's place beside him as they raided the Border States with Bill Anderson. And of how they had graduated from the war to plunder with the likes of Frank and Jesse James and Cole Younger.

"Yessir," he'd reminisced fondly as the glow of the fire warmed his smiling features into an incarnation of evil. "When we rode into Lawrence after that free-stater coward, Jim Lane, we sent him jumping out of bed buck-naked with the house afire over him, I heard tell he had to borrow clothes from a friend to escape us. That must have been some sight, him in pants so short they showed his bony ankles and in shoes that fit so poorly he could hardly run away from the fires of hell we set for him.

"I recall well the day we raided Centralia, Missouri, in sixty-four under ole Bloody Bill. Stuck up a Union train and took three thousand dollars from the express car, gunning down twenty-five of them blue bellies in the process. And that same day, remember, Sam, we rode against the two hundred they sent after us. We charged up a grassy ridge and slaughtered 'em nary to a man. 'Twas young Jesse what shot down their commander. He was seventeen, a couple years older than you were, boy. Them were the days." He said that with a wistful sigh, as if looking back upon the happiest days of his life, days filled with violence and killing and greed. Sam had no comment but the shadows in his eyes said he well remembered.

"Yessir, took up with Frank James and his pal, Arch Clement. Shame ole Arch cashed hisself in at the raid on the bank in Lexington. Never met another of his cut till Cole joined us to take Russellville in Kentucky. Got away with fourteen thousand dollars and would have had a grand time spending it happen George Shephard hadn't got loose with his lips and yelled out at that bystander the way he did. 'You needn't be particular about seeing my face so well you'd remember it again.' Hell, he remembered all right and led that detective, D.G. Bligh, right to the door and earned me ten years in jail."

Sam would have been all of fifteen when sucked into the brutality of war. So young. Unwittingly, her sympathies softened as she pictured him in boyhood. She'd heard it said that the army was a breeding place of lawlessness in that fierce struggle between North and South, surpassed only by penal institutions in its hardening of men. Many of its veterans went from camp to cell. Crime soared when hostilities ceased. War was a demoralizer of virtue and the movement of its soldiers led to a restless life of trampery and discontent. It unleashed upon the citizens of a raw and wounded country thousands of mentally scarred who retained their sidearms and deadly manner.

What better place to cull criminals? Quantrill and Anderson's guerrillas were country boys familiar with horses and guns, used to relentless drills in riding and marksmanship. The methods they used to execute raids were well suited to bandits on horseback—hitting targets by surprise with lightning swiftness then scattering into the surrounding countryside to become virtually invisible. How easy to slip into a life of lawlessness. But Lucy considered it no excuse. She wrenched her thinking from its compassionate bent almost angrily. Thousands returned from war without using their guns against their neighbors. She could not condone savagery as a byproduct of war. Nor could she justify the way Sam Zachary chose to lead his life. Killing for one's country and personal beliefs was not the same as murdering for profit.

As she gripped the warped plank seat, Lucy compared the two men joined by guilt and family. Clay and Sam both had the same hard edge about them, that same mocking contempt through which they viewed the world. She'd seen both draw with the intent to end life and therein lay the difference. When Sam threw down on a man, it was a matter of kill or be killed. It was a grim business, one that benefited from a cool head and clear eye and he went about it in that coldly professional manner. Clay pulled a gun because he enjoyed the rush of power. She'd seen it in his eyes—that unholy sadistic gleam. She compared them to two prairie predators, the coyote and the timber wolf. Both resembled each other and shared the same cunning. Either could kill but one was a coward at heart while the other was courageous. Sam Zachary was that fearless tawny wolf. Clay Bonner was the coyote, sneaky, craven, a skulking, conniving creature of the shadows. But neither could change the kind of animal he was, the type that preyed upon the weak and took what he wanted. Both carrying bounties and living solitary on the run.

She canted a glance at the man beside her and found she was admiring the clean cut of his profile.

The same ruthlessly handsome features that had intrigued her from the first. Looking at him still made her helplessly weak inside. And in the head, she amended fiercely. He was not at all what he seemed. But, she was surprised to find, that was not true. He'd never pretended to be a kind or a gentle man. He'd taken on another man's name, something not uncommon in the West, but had made no attempt to alter his character. Too liberal for a lawman but in the selfsame manner, too conservative for a killer. He fit no mold. Was that why he wandered? She remembered him telling her once that he wished things could be different. Was this what he'd meant? Had she meant something to him or was she fooling herself, trying to ease her tattered pride by making him somehow more palatable than Clay Bonner. After all, she'd lain with him, she'd admitted him into her heart. The thought of such intimacy with a man like Bonner was too repulsive to entertain.

Suddenly, she had to know. The female in her warned that she should gird her pride in silence but her rational mind sought answers.

"Why?" she demanded.

Sam glanced toward her in brief surprise then he adopted a lazy smile. "Why what, darlin'?"

His choice of endearment made her bristle and brought a crisp cadence to her voice. "Why would you choose this way when you could have made a decent life for yourself in Blessing?"

How to explain such complex reasoning when he wasn't sure he understood it himself. Sam looked at the woman who sat captive beside him and was tormented by what he saw. She was there against her will, hating him, and in no mood to really listen to his motives. Her mind would be closed just as her heart was now closed. No use trying to batter down a wall. He chose instead to ply an evasive defense, one that would keep the barriers up between them. Better that way. He'd made himself responsible for her safety but not her education.

"Decent? Happen that's your point of view. Sure, I could have gone on skimming profits off Knight, could have continued to have my hands tied while vigilantes worked their own kind of justice, could have sat by and watched you and Knight lock horns over who could bully the most folks into seeing things their way. Yep, a nice, decent little town, Blessing. Full of honorable folks trying to cheat one another."

"What do you know about honest people?" she shot back at him, aiming her words to kill. She was annoyed when he deflected her jibe with an easy smile.

"A lot, seeing as how I'm not one myself." He jingled the harnesses and when the buckboard jerked forward, Lucy was rocked against his side. His arm was instantly about her waist. "Easy there, darlin'."

Lucy pushed away with her elbow and sidled to the far side of the seat. "Don't call me that. I'm not your darling."

Sam shrugged with an indolent indifference. He might well have torn the heart from her chest with that careless gesture. She should have had the sense to leave it at that, to nurse her wounds and rally her pride. But she hurt, she hurt something fierce and she wanted him to know it. Suddenly, she didn't care if he mocked her pain. She wanted to give his conscience something to chew on for a long piece.

"It was all a lie, wasn't it?" she stated with cold disgust. "You played the town and me from the very first." She glared ahead at the back of his compatriot in crime. "I'll bet you and Clay had a good old laugh over how much we trusted you. Is that why he dragged me along? The ending for your cruel little joke?"

Sam said nothing. His eyes stared straight. A muscle jumped along the ridge of his jaw but that brief spasm could have been caused by anything from guilt to gloating.

"When do you plan to let me go? When you've humiliated me a little more? Believe me, you've done a complete job of it already." She tried and failed to keep the jerk of emotion from her words as the shame and twist of anguish delivered a double-barreled load. "Or is it because you have 'genuine feelings' for me? Just say so and I'll believe you. After all, when a man cares for a woman, he wants to drag her reputation through the streets, to hold her up to ridicule, to toy with her feelings for his amusement. You must care a lot to force me to suffer the disgrace of your company. Or was it all a part of the lie, Marsh—Mister Zachary?"

"All a lie, Miz Blessing. Every bit of it from the git go. That's what you want to hear, wasn't it?"

Lucy was too upset to note the thread of anger that laced his words with bitterness. She was too crushed by the merciless way he destroyed her hope and pride, shedding both without remorse. She'd been mistaken. He was every bit as insensitive as Clay Bonner.

"And what of the real Deputy Wade? I suppose you killed him to make good your scheme."

She wielded her words with all the skill of a Union broadsword, slashing, hacking, paring right down to bare the bone. And Sam determined she'd never know how fatally accurate they were. His reply was uttered in an exaggerated drawl so each syllable rolled out coated with sugary cynicism.

"Happen he was already heaven-bound when I came across him. 'Course, I don't expect you to buy into that. You got it all figured out, don't you?

284

Shucks, ma'am, it's not in my nature to argue with a lady."

Her hot gaze fell to the forward facing butt of his Colt peacemaker where it rested so temptingly at his side. Five shots added to her two. With a hurtful fury clogging more rational cautions, she edged her fingers toward it.

"Wouldn't try, were I you, Miz Lucy," Sam said casually. "Being there are fellows along that'd not think twice about drawing down on a female."

Her hands pulled back to settle in tight fists upon her lap. "I suppose you'd have me believe that you're not one of them," she sneered.

"Believe what you're inclined to," he answered mildly. "Happen you mean to anyway. You want to think I loose lead on women, kids and pets, go right on ahead and suit yourself. I don't aim to tangle with any mule-headed freethinker."

"I hate you!"

She said that low and virulently, without thought behind it. It was pride not true feeling that made her say it. She saw him wince and should have been savagely pleased. Instead, his reaction served to intensify her empty pain.

"I'm right glad you do, ma'am," he concluded coldly. "Now, grip your jaws and give a man some peace."

The horses sensed it first. As the sun reached its highest point in a blistering haze of heat, the animals grew restless and harder to control. The riders looked ahead for relief from the melancholy plains where dead creatures were passed so regularly it seemed they were laid out to serve as milestones on the dreary journey. The wagons tossed like ships at sea, making their crossing even less enjoyable.

They reached the Big Sandy toward the end of the afternoon. As there were hours left of daylight, Clay decided to push on into a second twenty-five miles to get ahead of their next day's travel. The Sandy was a clear shallow stream running in a soft bed and easily fordable. It shouldn't have caused the horses to be as ornery as they were. The wagons were driven across and the fidgety animals quieted as the caravan of thieves rode onward.

Toward dusk, the wind began to blow from the east. Clouds gathered heavily and soon shut down over the heavens like the drawing of a heavy drape to leave not the slightest gleam of light in the sky though it was hardly sunset. Just as the riders began to cast nervous glances at the unfriendly turn of nature, rain pelted down thick and fast in their upturned faces. Thunder growled behind and around them and the frequent flash of lightning spooked the horses.

"Might as well ride as try to sleep in it," Clay shouted to Sam as he cantered by, passing the word that they'd forge on. Sam tipped his Stetson to funnel off the rain and fought to keep the team steady. Had the road not been straight and even, he never could have kept on it. He kept his doubts about Clay's wisdom to himself.

Beside him, Lucy began to shiver as the temperature plunged downward. Her satin gown was no match for the beating chill of rain. Soon it clung to her, intensifying her misery in a wrap of cold and cloying fabric. Then she felt the unexpected drape of Sam's coat about her shoulders. Pride should have demanded she shrug it off but blued fingers clung gratefully to its lapels as she huddled within its warm, dry folds. She moved a futile hand across her face, stroking back wet tendrils of hair and trying to clear her vision. There was nothing to see. The road had vanished from sight. The dim outline of the hills blended into sky and was soon indistinguishable.

Still, they pushed onward, moving stubborn and blind through the darkness. Rain lashed down upon them as the play of lightning around the horizon provided teasing glimpses of the trail. It was miserable but not yet dangerous. Until the storm broke in all its terror directly overhead.

Light shivered crazily like a lantern in the hands of a drunk. A terrific rage of hail came down in chips the size of hens' eggs. Sam wrestled a buffalo robe from under the seat and yanked it over their heads for protection. Lucy had no compunction about hunching against him. While he struggled to hold to their ineffective canopy, the rattling shower of ice threw a fright into the already panicked horses and they veered off at a frantic gallop through the bushes. Lucy heard Sam's startled oath but it was impossible for him to check the runaway team when all his effort went to maintaining his seat.

It was a wild, careening ride. Lucy was choked with silent screams of terror as they plunged through the murky blackness, expecting at any minute to be thrown to her death in some ravine. She clung to Sam and the madly pitching wagon seat and prayed, possibly aloud, she wasn't sure, for their safety. She included Sam unthinkingly in those desperate pleas as the fearsome dance continued for what was at least two miles.

Then, the hail ceased. Though the rain continued in torrents, the horses were blown enough to be brought under control. The lightning was vivid all around them but gave no clue to which way was east, west or south. They continued on through the soft, sucking clay in search of the path only to become hopelessly lost in minutes and afraid each step would lead them farther astray.

Sam uttered another oath then let loose a piercing whistle. The answer was silence and the drumming of the rain. As he slipped his Colt out of its holster, it came to Lucy all at once. The two of them were alone. Clay Bonner and his band were who knows where and Sam was about to fire a shot off to give away their direction. And she would never get another chance as good as this one.

"No," she cried out as he began to lift the pistol. She brought her bound hands down atop his forearm with all her strength. Startled by the attack, Sam's finger jerked, sending a screaming bullet right between the nervous horses. That was all it took to restart the panic. The animals lunged ahead, toppling both passengers into the wagon bed. After several undirected yards, their luck gave out. The right wheels of the wagon spun out into empty space and the conveyance rolled.

The mud cushioned Lucy's fall but the breath was slapped from her. It took several minutes for her to gain a sufficient draw. She was all over wet and dark with cold earth. A flash through the cruel heavens delineated the overturned wagon, its wheels spinning skyward. The tongue had snapped. The horses were gone as was Sam's big stallion. Sam . . .

Lucy staggered to her feet, thrusting sodden hair from her face as she gazed around in fright.

"Sam?" she called out. There was no reply. "Sam? Dear God." It was a whimper. In the matching blackness of her mind she could picture him sprawled and broken. An eerie feeling crept over her as all kinds of monstrous shapes seemed to crowd close in the gloom. The rain falling in the bushes sounded like running footsteps — Bonner's men? Indians? She was suddenly afraid to move or make another sound. Sam. She made herself thrust away the terrible vision. This was her chance to escape in the confusion. To where? She could wander in circles all night and still not find a path. Or end up smack dab in Bonner's camp.

A low groan sounded from nearby and thoughts of escape fled. Quickly, she began to search about her, feeling blindly until her foot snagged an immobile shape. She went down in a tangle of wet skirts, driving an "oof" from the figure beneath her.

"If my ribs weren't already broken, I think your knees just finished 'em," Sam moaned.

"Oh, Sam," she nearly sobbed out, feeling along the hard line of his arm. "You're all right. I was afraid —" She broke off in confusion. She should have been hoping he'd broken his neck in the fall. Lucy scrambled back on her heels and crouched in the sea of mud while Sam eased up into a sitting position.

"Just knocked a little silly for a minute there. How 'bout you, gal?"

"I'm fine."

Sam noted the frigid cut of her tone and smiled wryly in the darkness. Yes, she obviously was at that. He hauled himself to his feet and wobbled to the wagon. Every muscle he owned seemed bruised and eager to shout about it. With the horses gone, there was no alternative but to hunker down for the night and weather out the storm. He put a shoulder to the wagon and heaved mightily. Both groaned in complaint but the wagon finally surrendered and bounced over. He rubbed his back and gave thanks that the buckboard was constructed light for short hauls. When he felt able, he scrounged around through the scattered supplies, coming up with a blanket and the damp buffalo robe. The first he spread on the soggy ground beneath the comparatively dry shelter of the buckboard.

"Come on over here, Lucy, and get out of the rain."

She eyed him mulishly and growled, "I'd rather drown."

Sam tucked the edges of the robe about himself and muttered, "Suit yourself," in an agreeable manner. He unstopped the bottle he'd also managed to salvage and took a long drink, listening to the relentless pound of the rain overhead and waiting for the stubborn creature sitting out in it to come to her senses. It took awhile but finally he saw her shadow pass beneath the rim of the wagon. Still, she would not come close, preferring to shiver with pride intact. Temptingly, he lifted the robe.

"Scoot on over. No sense in you freezing. You can hate me just as much from here as you can from there and you'll be a sight warmer in doing it."

Again, there was a long hesitation from the danged haughty female. Then, wordlessly, she slid atop the blanket and reluctantly beneath the awning his arm created. He hooked it about her, pulling her quick and tight up to his chest. She engaged in a moment of angry struggle before surrendering to his superior strength and determination to keep her there. And when the heat of him seeped through to thaw her trembling form, she cast off pride and snuggled closer. The darkness hid his smile.

"Might as well try to grab some sleep. Not much else we can do till morning. Consider shedding them wet things elsewise our blankets will be just as chilled."

Lucy's teeth set in belligerent objection. Until they began to chatter anew. He was right. Damn him. She'd never be warm unless she stripped off the wet garments that clung to her skin. She felt a tug at her wrists as he cut through the lacing to free her hands. Angrily, she pushed away and struggled to peel off the heavy weight of satin flounces. Beneath her dress, her undergarments were damp but not disagreeable enough to warrant removal. She heard him stirring at the same time and assumed he was likewise disrobing. She didn't suspect he'd taken the task right down to the skin until he coaxed her back beneath the drape of his arm. Then, it was too late. His arm held her fast and his heat sapped her resistance. As tense minutes passed, her arms crept about his middle and her weary head sought the comforting contour of his shoulder. What did it matter, she reasoned. It wasn't the first time she'd felt the smooth, naked strength of him. She was only doing what she needed to survive. She had to stay warm, to fight the chill. What she should have done was concentrate on fighting down the emotions even now curling within her.

Sam's palms were rubbing up and down her arms and spine, restoring warmth beneath their rough friction. Exactly when that purpose altered, she wasn't certain. All she knew was suddenly the heat was all from inside her as his hands began to focus on specific areas. Her chilled breasts provided hard points of reference, encouraging the attention of first his palms, then his teasing fingers and, finally, exquisitely, the taunting tug of his mouth. Thoughts of protest never registered. Desire swept denial away as easily as the rains undercut soft clay. She made a single sound, not of objection. Of impatience with the fabric that was between her and blissful freedom. She delayed the purpose of his caress only long enough to rid herself of remaining garb and guilt.

Then, she was pulling at him with equal need, her fingers tangling in the wetness of his hair to hurry his kisses. They were deep and drugging. His tongue dragged over her parted lips to plunge again and again between them. He lowered her down upon the yielding ground and continued to share his ravenous kisses while he made her burn beneath his touch. The battering of the rain echoed the thunderous surge of sensation and her low cries rolled like passionate thunder. At that moment, she didn't care who or what he was. All that mattered was what she wanted and what he so freely gave.

He took her in the mud, beneath a buckboard wagon, but no soft mattress, no cozy room could have brought a finer point to her satisfaction. He swelled within her like the storm without, driving, pounding in rhythmic fury until that tempo beat clear through her. She clung to him but she might as well have been clutching at the winds. There was no security in their world of buffeting passion. No longer did she seek it. Instead, she gave herself up to the swirl and frenzy, letting it shake her, letting it roar through her with unchecked power. His name burst from her lips on a revering sob only to be swallowed up as the maelstrom centered and broke within her upon his answering cry.

Then, there was only the sound of rain, gentle now, soothing. Against her neck, Sam murmured in breathless wonder, "Darlin'. Oh, darlin', what you do to me." Then there was the patter of rain and the quiet rush of his breathing. Then, just the rain.

Chapter Twenty

Lucy woke to find the moon shining through white scudding clouds. The rain had passed leaving behind a damp residue of cool air. She shivered slightly and began to draw the robe more closely about her, thinking it the cause of her comfort. Finding it wasn't shocked her into full wakefulness. The warmth spread from Sam Zachary where he was stretched out beside her, his limbs entwined with hers.

Without passion to color her judgment, Lucy felt the full brunt of what she'd done. She'd lain with him, willingly, enthusiastically, after he'd betrayed and stolen everything she cherished. He'd tricked her again, twisting her feelings of fear until she grasped at those of deeper-seeded need. And after he'd taken his fill of pleasure, he would carry her back to the pack of coyotes he ran with. Then what would become of her? She had to go. She had to get away now, while there was a chance. Even afoot. Even miles from nowhere. It was better than here. It was better than waiting for the worst.

Lucy began to ease out from under the slack weight of Sam's possessing arm and at the same time turned her hips so his leg slid over and off of hers. It was light enough for her to see his fancy rig. One pistol nestled safe. The other had been thrown from his hand when the wagon overturned. She stretched out an eager hand, moving, slipping out from under him. The staghorn grip felt smooth beneath her questing fingertips. Just a little farther. Just a little . . .

A shrill cry escaped her as his fingers closed about her wrist. She followed it up with a desperate wail and flung out her other hand. It, too, was caught and held helpless. She fought him wildly then, thrashing with all her strength, flailing elbows and knees with vicious determination. He gave several heartfelt grunts as they connected before pinning her effectively with the full press of his body.

"What's got into you, Lu? You figuring to squeeze off a few whilst I was sleeping? Or were you going to wait until I came after you?"

The confusion of hurt in his voice failed to reach her. All she knew was she had failed to get away. Her chest heaved with the force of her fear and her words burst out in an anguish of dread.

"You won't take me back there. I won't go. You'll have to kill me first."

"What on God's green earth are you rambling about, woman?"

"I'll die before one of them puts a dirty hand on me. If you won't end it for me, I'll see to it with my own hands. I won't be passed about for your filthy entertainment. It's bad enough to bear the shame of whoring beneath you."

"Whoring?" He sounded incredulous. "Lucy, what the hell are you talking about?" Then, he gave a startled yelp of pain as her teeth sank into the fleshy part of his thumb. The instant his grip loosened, she was clamoring for his gun once again.

"Stop it, Lucy."

She felt a surge of victory as her fingers curled about the wicked-looking gun but before she could turn it toward any meaningful target, Sam dealt her a chopping blow to the forearm. Numbed fingers opened and he quickly knocked the pistol away.

"No," she wailed in desolation. "Let me use it!"

Scared half to death and trembling, Sam jerked her tight into his arms. His heart was chugging like a runaway train when he thought what might have happened had he been a second slower. It wouldn't have mattered who the bullet struck. He would have died either way.

"Stop it, Lu. Easy now, darlin'."

She was no longer fighting. If she couldn't best him, she would have to play upon whatever decency might linger in his jaded soul. Tears fell freely, wetting her face and his sleek bare shoulder. "Sam, please. Don't give me back to them. Don't let them have me."

He understood then and it came like a wild lightning bolt down to sear clear through him. The terror in her voice unbridled a proprietary panic. The thought that any man might lay a mean hand upon her quickened fury, red-hot and wild, to seethe through him. In a thick, impassioned tone, he vowed, "No one will hurt you, Lucy."

That fantastic understatement returned her edge of fury. "Who was going to do it, Sam? You? Who planned to pull the trigger when you were done with me?"

"Lucy . . ."

"Or were you going to let that animal do your dirty work? He'd have no trouble killing a woman."

"Clay? What are you saying? Clay wasn't going to kill you."

"No?" she shrilled a bit hysterically. "I suppose you both meant to take me politely back to town. Fool! What do you think he had planned? He's not going to let me go. He's going to kill me, Sam. How could you not know that? How could you not care?"

She continued to sob and clutch him with anxious fingers. The combination ripped at his heart. "Sam, please. Let me go. If you have any feeling for me at all, don't turn me over to them. I'll die if you do. I can't bear the pawing and the grinning. I can't. Sam, you have to let me go."

In that second, everything was settled in his mind. His words were low and soothing when he told her, "I can't, Lu."

"Why?" she wailed. "Can you hate me so much?"

The incredible anguish trembling in her voice caused his breath to alter and his arms to squeeze to the point of rib bruising. "I can't let you go, darlin', because I'm taking you back to Blessing myself."

She was still, as still as the land after enduring the devastation of a storm. He felt her shiver then stiffen. "Why should I believe you?" she asked softly.

"Because I love you, Lu."

Slowly, Lucy pulled back until she affixed him with blank eyes. "You love me," she repeated, as if trying to make sense of the words. Then, abruptly, her features congealed with fury. Her voice hissed. "You *love* me." Her hand dashed across her cheeks, knocking the tears aside in a damp shower. "How dare you! Just how gullible do you think I am? Love me! Please! You flimflam my town, you plot to make fools of us all, you have an animal like Bonner come in to rob and murder us, you let him abduct me, you let me make myself ridiculous moaning in your arms and now you insult me with this—the final lie. You love me. You incredible liar!"

Sam's slate-colored gaze half shuttered. There was a slow, mocking drawl to his words. "If I'd known how sweet and sentimental you were going to go on me, I'da kept my big mouth shut."

She launched her fist at him then sobbed in frustration when he deflected it easily over his shoulder and caught her to his chest. She knew what he was going to do. And she could raise only a meager struggle.

His kiss was heaven and hell. The more she resisted, the more it contrarily gentled until she was drugged by the melting tenderness of his mouth. His big hands cradled her face between them, palms rubbing with a delicious roughness against her soft, tear-dampened skin. For Lucy, it was exquisite torture. She could believe in his passion, in his desire for her but that wasn't love, not the kind of love that twisted her soul in sweet misery. What would a man like Sam Zachary, a man who killed and stole for his livelihood, know of love? He made it his business to deceive and destroy, not to nurture devotion. If it was true—But she knew better and that irony was bitter.

She might have submitted to their desire for one another. It burned hot, consuming them both with equal longing. She had no objection to that fierce attraction between them. But he ruined it by again murmuring the unforgivable.

"God, Lucy, I do love you."

He felt her stiffen as if disbelief poured a fast-cooling steel through her veins. He tried to sway her with another kiss, but this time her lips were thin and resistant to the persuasion of his own. He sighed in frustration and elected to simply hold her for a time, ignoring her rigid denial in favor of the man-pleasing, heart-stopping feel of her in his arms.

"And when we get back to Blessing?" she asked in a brittle little voice. "What then?"

He nuzzled his face into the spill of her glorious auburn hair and whispered, "I'm going to do the best thing I can for you by riding the hell out of your life."

Great shivers of emotion took her. His arms tightened, trying to suppress what could not be warmed, what could not be stilled. A horrible emptiness settled inside her.

"Am I to thank you for that, Mister Zachary? For telling me you love me then riding off? And you expect me to believe that you hold feelings for me?"

He gave a low moan. It rippled with anguish. "It's not what I want. It's what has to be."

"Why? Why does it have to be?"

His words were harsh, raw. "You wouldn't understand. There's a lot of me that you'd get to hating and I couldn't stand seeing it. Lucy, I want you so bad, I'm . . . I can't hurt you. It wouldn't work out."

Lucy sat back and looked up at him. The pain etched into his taut features slammed into her with an unexpected power. She hadn't known such suffering was possible. It set her back, frightening her. What horrors did this man carry in his soul? And suddenly, all she could think to do was quiet them, to give him peace. Her hand rose to fit against the sharp curve of his jaw. She felt the spasmodic jerk of muscles play beneath her palm.

"Sam, there's nothing you've done that can't be forgiven."

His eyes misted over, becoming dark shadowy wells of remembered agony. His answer was hoarse, naked. "There's things I've done that I can't forgive me for."

Her touch grew caressing, coaxing and, for a moment he pressed his cheek into her hand. The dampness she felt upon it made her heart seize up in dismay. "Sam, tell me," she encouraged gently.

He shook his head, unable to form the words at first. Then, they spilled out in a ragged rush. "I can't, Lu."

She came to him, trailing her lips along his temple, stroking the rain-softened shaggy hair, easing him down until his head rested upon her shoulder. Comforting him like she would a nightmare-troubled child. When she felt the awful memories shudder through him, she begged softly, "Tell me, Sam. Let me help. I'm tough enough to take it."

For an instant, she thought he would. His strong, lean body sagged upon her, relying on the circle of her arms. But only for an instant.

He pushed away, rocking back on his heels. Even in the dimness of near dawn, she could see the cold edge of control settle over his expression, a control that didn't quite overcome the haunted cloudiness of his gaze. Until he blinked hard and his eyes grew impassive.

"You can't help, Lucy. What's done's done. Talking won't change things."

"But it will help me, Sam. Share yourself with me. You've listened to my demons. Could yours be worse?"

The look flickering over his face said yes. Its intensity gave her a jolt of sheer terror and made her wish to beg him to say nothing, to leave her ignorant of his past. Perhaps she wasn't strong enough to hear it. But she couldn't back down now.

"If you love me as you say you do, you would trust me with the truth."

"Dammit, Lucy, that's not fair," he growled.

"No, but then precious little is." She followed that harsh fact with the featherlike stroke of her fingertips along his taut cheek. "Please, Sam."

He shook off her hand, wildly angry and afraid. She vowed she could take it but that was one hell of a risk. He could scarcely contain his own disgust at what he'd been, at what he'd done. She'd trapped him good, called him on his own words and it was show or fold. She wanted the truth—He'd give it to her with both barrels.

"In sixty-one, Jim Lane followed General Price into Missouri looking for evens and when he couldn't find him, he and his killers settled for seconds. They looted and murdered nine men at Osceola. My pa was shot down cold where he sat in our wagon. He wasn't even armed."

Lucy flinched at the easy way he spoke of that atrocity. His tone may have been misleading for its mildness but a spark had come into his eyes, filling them with a flicker of hate that grew with each word.

"Mama sold our farm in Osceola and moved us north to Clay County where her sister's husband's family, the Bonners, let us buy up some of their land right reasonable. Mama tried to keep us out of the trouble brewing but when the call came to grab up arms, my brother George and our cousin, Clay, were the first to enlist. George, he was a good-hearted feller, gentle as a pet pup, but he believed in the grievances of the South and was willing to go to battle for them. Clay, hell, he was a hot-head spoiling for some excitement."

Lucy could see the admiration in his eyes. She could bet he'd hated to see them ride off, leaving him behind. He'd have been too young, maybe twelve or thirteen, to understand the political calling but the right age to feel an impatient fervor to be a part of it.

"George married his sweetheart afore he went in and by the time she'd birthed them their first girl, he was home with a ball through his leg. Lamed him up too much to ride. I think he was glad to be shed of it. He wanted to be a simple farmer, like my pa. He wasn't the same after Lawrence, like he'd lost something he valued. I didn't understand then." Sam looked out toward the paintbox of pastels spilling over the distant hills but he saw Missouri and that gaze was wistful with the wisdom of hindsight.

"George's saddle was scarcely cold when I threw myself up in it. With him at home to tend the women, I was hell-bent to ride with Clay. Mama jerked me down and beat me black and blue but all the time she had such a scared look in her eye. I don't recall her looking that way when George lit out. Maybe it was because I was a wild one, like cousin Clay and didn't have the sense of a seam squirrel. But I loved my mama and I wouldn't have broke her heart for nothing. Turned out, I didn't have to. General Ewing's troop took care of it.

"The Union commander wanted to flush out guerrillas from the border region. He issued his notorious Order Number Eleven in sixty-three, in evens for Lawrence. It gave known Confederate sympathizers in four border counties fifteen days to quit the region. Mama dug in like an old mule. Said she'd left one good home and wasn't about to be driven from another. The pro-Union guerrillas and some of Ewing's troops swept in from Kansas like a plague of hungry locusts. They stripped the land bare with their looting, burning and killing. Homes were razed, crops burned for no good reason. When they came to our place, a little group of about nine or ten, Clay was over visiting my sister, Sarah, who he was sweet on. The three of us, Clay, George and I met 'em with rifles."

His voice grew inflectionless as he spoke of a home in flames behind them, of the screams of the stock trapped in the blazing barn. The women had scrambled from the burning house in terror but at the last minute his mother had tripped and fallen just shy of the doorway. And before any of them could act, she was engulfed in the fires of hatred that spread throughout the land.

"There was nothing to keep me home. George stayed back with Mary and Sarah while Clay and I took off to join up with Bill Anderson. I was thirteen but they took me on 'cause I could ride and shoot and cuss as good as any of 'em and because I was too young and stupid to be afraid. I didn't care nothing for the Confederate Cause. I wanted paybacks for my folks. Every raid I rode on, I was looking to settle that score. But it was never enough. It never made the hurt and the rage go away. That jus' kept feeding and growing. And I didn't know how to stop it when they said the war was over. I couldn't give up that hate, that anger. It was all I had and I couldn't go back to nothing.

"There wasn't no amnesty for the Missouri guerrillas like they gave to the regular soldiers. They hadn't gotten over the hate either. We couldn't go home and forget. They made us outlaws and a lot of us got to thinking that maybe we should make the best of it. Our farms had been raped by troops from both sides. We needed money to rebuild. The bankers were close-fisted with their loans, charging rates no one could afford to pay back and we got to hating them as much as the Union for the suffering of our families. I was a scared, angry kid. I didn't care much about right and wrong. I felt wronged and it

302

seemed right to strike out at the bank when Clay got to talking about it. George, he was all against it but he had another baby on the way and no money to meet mortgages or buy supplies. Clay and Sarah had just married up and needed a grubstake to start out on. The Clay County Savings Association had turned him down cold a week before so we rode into Liberty like we was on some righteous work."

He sketched out the next year with brutal frankness, detailing his participation in Liberty as a lookout and the unnecessary death of a young man named George Wymore with a philosophical shrug. Even the wealth gained from that first strike didn't satisfy. Revenge and greed drove them on to Lexington and Savannah, spurred on by a war-weary citizenry who heralded their raids as heroic and justified. That was all that was needed to close a boy's eyes to criminal intent, that and Clay Bonner's encouragement. At fourteen, Sam Zachary was a veteran of battle and a victim of bitterness when he rode into Richmond, Missouri, as one of six who would hold the town under siege while six others robbed the Hughes and Wasson Bank. The town's mayor ran toward them with his revolver waving and was shot down by horsemen. They rode to the jail and freed former guerrillas who advocated continuing the pursuit of Confederate secession. The jailer's son hid behind a large elm tree in the courthouse yard next to the jail and managed to get off a few shots before he found himself caught in the horsemen's deadly crossfire. Seeing his fatal fall, the jailer ran toward him and died sprawled across his son's body, some of those bullets riddling his heroic form from Sam Zachary's hot pistols. Townspeople began shooting from windows, chasing the bandits from their streets. Sam was hit in the shoulder and barely

303

managed to cling to his horse long enough to evade the heavily armed posses and collapse in his brother's kitchen.

The event was far from over. Pinkerton detectives were brought in, their leader, the legendary Union war hero, Captain Grant Tolliver. Under his direction, friends, neighbors and relatives of the James, Youngers, Clay Bonner and Sam Zachary were harassed and threatened. When none of the robbers were captured, public outcry caused the Pinkertons to escalate their measures from menace to murder.

"They came to our door after supper," Sam recalled with an ominous quiet. "George sent Mary, the children and I to the root cellar while he went out to greet them. We could hear their voices raise from where we were crouched down in the dark. Mary was big with their fourth child and I was still weak from my wound. I wanted no more to do with killing. I kept seeing that John Law throwing himself down over his boy in the street every time I tried to sleep. When things started to sound ugly, I wanted to go up and turn myself in but Mary wouldn't hear of it. She said they'd hang us both for sure, that them not being able to prove anything would kept George safe. They were lawmen, after all.

"Happen it got real quiet and after a time Mary crept up to see if they'd gone. They were gone all right and they'd left my brother swinging from a limb on the oak tree in the front yard."

Lucy's hand went out instinctively to cover his but he jerked away, too caught up in the past to accept her sympathy. She wanted to ask him to stop. She'd heard more than enough to create a throbbing ache in her heart and she sensed from the guarded look upon his face that the worst was yet in coming.

"I guess I went a little crazy after that. I dogged

Tolliver's men, goading them onto the gunfighter's sidewalk in the center of the street to shoot them down. I'd rob anything I heard they were watchdogging. Clay cut loose from me then. I was dangerous, reckless and without fear. He thought I had a death wish. Maybe I did. By seventeen, I'd killed a dozen men in more or less fair fights and Tolliver wanted me almost as bad as Frank and Jesse. Clay got himself caught with George Shephard about then and sentenced to ten years. My being in Missouri was a danger to Mary and my sister, so I wandered and sent them money to keep up the farms between them. They didn't ask where I got it and I didn't offer to tell 'em. I kept edging north and west until I got word there was a spread hiring stock inspectors." He laughed harshly. "A fancy name for paid killers but that was pretty much all I was good for. It was my only salable skill. And then I came across the unfortunate Deputy Wade and the letter he was carrying from Tolliver. I thought I'd found the perfect way to discredit the man who dragged my family through hell and kept me from going straight."

"And your vengeance was Blessing," Lucy finished for him in a strangled little voice. And she died a bit inside when he answered with a grim, "Yes."

Sam fell silent then, staring out at the dawn that was still several hours away. Lucy was stunned to silence as well. She felt raw inside from the intensity of what he'd suffered as she sat, trying to transpose what she'd just discovered atop the man she already knew. Layer upon layer, she added the aspects of his character into a complex prism of qualities. The marshal who was dependable, determined and devoted to the town of Blessing. The hard case killer driven by revenge and relentless demons who'd come to see it destroyed. The man who claimed to love her.

It was a confusing whole, one that frightened and intrigued her. While she could feel exquisitely for his pain, she couldn't condone his methods. He'd stolen from the people who trusted him. He gave no indication that he would ever change. Or that he ever wanted to. Sam Zachary's was a restless, tormented soul and she'd be a fool to hold to him with any degree of hope.

As if he'd sensed the quandary of her thoughts, Sam stated, "Now you can see how impossible it all is."

This time, she answered with the expressionless monotone.

"Yes."

Sam looked to her. His features showed the wear of emotion and a weariness so deep, Lucy wanted to weep for him. He was seeing the violent, necessarily abrupt end to his own future compared to the lingering enjoyment he could have shared with Lucy Blessing. Had there been a way. His hand reached out toward her, his knuckles grazing her soft cheek. There was no future but there was the moment.

"Lucy, I do love you, gal."

She trembled at the truth of his soft words. Her first attempt to answer ended in a painful rasp of sound and spill of tears. Then she managed a hoarse, "I'm sorry, Sam."

"Me, too, darlin'. Me, too."

His fingers eased around to the nape of her neck and slowly drew her to him, until her head rested over his unhappy heart. She felt the frustration in his lingering caresses, the poignant regret in his kisses when they finally came. He could give her nothing beyond the splendor of the moment and vowed to make it memorable. He bore her down to the chill blanket where he told her with his lips, his words, his touch, his body how much she meant to him, how much he needed her. And she gave in return, kiss for kiss, endearment for endearment, caress for caress then welcomed him within for the most intimate sharing of all.

Sam had meant to luxuriate over every nuance of lovemaking. He meant to shower her with all the beauty and goodness he'd managed to cling to through the rest. He wanted to prolong their pleasure so Lucy would remember him always with a wistful smile and chafe of longing. Too soon, she was panting and arching beneath him, begging him for a glorious release. Thoughts of leisurely indulgence were scorched by the twining of her supple limbs, by the coaxing of her husky moans, "Sam, oh, Sam."

Anxious to supply her need, he drove deep and clung to the breathless sounds of her delight. He savaged her damp, hungry mouth with all the impatience of the past weeks, with all the desperation of an empty future. And when he felt her completion build into a series of gripping tremors, he found himself lost within her, as engulfed by the act of love as he was in loving her. Stunning, explosive sensation wrack him, leaving him drained and weaker than he should have ever allowed himself to become. Yet it felt safe to be vulnerable in her embrace and all too easy to sleep.

Sam slept hard, with a deep concentration he never succumbed to while on the trail. Of course, he'd never been on the trail with a partner like Lucy Blessing. He was smiling over that fact when he drifted toward wakefulness. Through slitted eyes, he could see Lucy moving about the wagon. At first, only the drag of her ruined skirt then as she stepped farther away, he enjoyed the whole picture. A female had no call to look so beautiful when so obviously bedraggled. She'd detached the useless bustle from her gown, leaving the hem to trail in the soft mud. Its demure satin neckline was devastating with several of the small jet buttons left undone. Her chestnut tresses were simply braided and left to swing along her shoulders. Damn, she looked fine and that was enough reason for him to start scooting out from beneath the buckboard.

And the businesslike way she swiveled his Colt peacemaker to greet him was enough to stop him cold.

"Get your clothes on, Sam. We're going after Clay Bonner."

Chapter Twenty-one

Sam was unmoving for a moment, then he stretched in a luxury of male nakedness inch by sinewy inch, until sufficiently limbered. He regarded her with a quizzical half-smile.

" 'Morning, darlin'. Coffee ready?"

"I'm not funning, Sam. Get up. I've no intention of waiting here for them to find us."

"Now, why would they want to bother? What have we got that they want?"

Lucy's features tensed as she recalled Clay Bonner's hungry gaze. That might be enough of a reason. Sheer meanness was another.

Sam frowned at the harsh conclusions he read. "Lucy, you got Clay wrong. Sure, he's headstrong and hell-bent but he's not a real bad actor. We were planning to head home to Missouri. My sister's waiting there with his son and daughter. That's all he could talk about was being a family man again."

She looked at him long and hard, seeing his readiness to believe that about his favored cousin and brother-in-law. But she also knew there wasn't a chance Clay Bonner planned to return to farming and the arms of one woman. She didn't have to know him to *know* him. He was a restless rover bound by no ties of affection. His thoughts were of his own pleasure, not of obligation. A man like that felt no loyalties. She knew Clay Bonner and his type very well.

"I never figured you for a stupid man, Sam," she said quietly.

His lips thinned into an unpleasant line when he took her meaning. "He never would have hurt you," he stated brusquely.

"Sure, and horses can fly."

Nettled by her unreasonable dislike of his best friend, Sam got to the business of dressing, tugging on his long underwear, shirt and as-yet-damp Levi's. Before his boots, he reached for his fast-draw rig and grimaced at finding it empty. Because he would have felt buck naked otherwise, he buckled it on about his lean hips then completed his wardrobing.

Lucy took a cautious step back when he stood, unwinding to his full height and impressive stature. She was angry at herself. She'd been all too affected by the strong display of manliness as he'd donned his clothes after resolving that she wouldn't. That made her testy. Sam Zachary was a lethal, cunning man and she couldn't drop her guard for an instant.

"Why the gun, Lucy?" he drawled with a nice touch of injury to his voice.

"Because I trust you about as far as I can throw your horse."

He followed the jerk of her head and grinned. There, placidly grazing on buffalo grass, trailing reins, was his big bay stallion. Sam ignored the defensive posture of the pistol and walked to the animal, murmuring soft words as he quickly checked each hock and hoof until satisfied the mount was sound.

"We'll have to double on him," Lucy was saying.

310

"Is he fit for the task?"

Sam gave her a haughty look as if she'd insulted his manhood. "This here horse could carry you, me and that there wagon if he was of a mind to."

"Just the two of us will be sufficient. See what you can put together from the supplies. Anything we might be needing to go after Bonner."

"I don't see no prayer books or shovels. We might just as soon put that gun to both our heads, shoot and then bury ourselves."

"If there's any burying to do, we'll be doing it."

Sam lost all vestiges of humor. His jaw squared mulishly and his eyes took on that glint of flinty toughness. "Never happen," was his low promise.

"I mean to see it does. Now, see to those supplies lest I start by burying you."

With a look as much curious as sullen, Sam saw to her order. As he picked through the tumble of goods, Lucy felt herself trembling and took a firm breath to still it. She wasn't fooling either of them. She couldn't place a fatal hole in Sam Zachary. They both knew that. She kept the gun more to show him of her seriousness and he was intrigued enough to allow her to have it. If he wanted it otherwise, he could disarm her in an instant. Knowing that didn't make her any more confident.

Lucy had spent long hours watching the man beside her sleep, loving him, searching frantically for a way to keep him. Plans were conceived and discarded as folly. He was an outlaw. She was a banker. Not exactly a comfortable mix. She looked ahead at her own grim future: a female banker who'd lost the town's money through ill-fated lusting. She saw the struggle for respect renewed by day and the long hours of empty yearning stretching out by night. She had nothing to look forward to, nothing to lose. And Sam, what of him? Riding to the end of a rope beside Clay Bonner? Letting his obsession with Grant Tolliver rush him to ruin? There had to be a means of straightening both pictures and it had its roots in returning the money to Blessing.

"This is crazy, you know," Sam offered up somberly.

"Maybe."

"Your pride could lead you right into a corpse and cartridge affair."

"I know that."

Her quiet determination struck him hard, with fear, with frustration. "Then, you danged fool female, why are you doing it? For money that's not even yours? Let them have it. Go back to Blessing while you still can. Start over."

"With what? Bonner took everything and he won't get away with it. When I go back to Blessing, it will be with every cent he stole."

"With your shield or on it." The classical reference of Sam's searing drawl surprised her. But then she knew he was an intelligent man. And the description was apt.

"Yes." She moved quickly then, closing the distance between them, letting the gun drop heavily to her side as she wielded a weapon with far more stopping power. Her hand touched his stubbled cheek, stroking gently, stoking fires of longing in his cold gray eyes. "Sam, you promised you'd help me."

It almost worked. She could see a brief thaw then his gaze hardened. He struck at her hand and stalked several stiff strides away. With his back to her, the only proof of his agitation was in the rapid clenching of his fists where they hung impotently next to the empty holsters.

"Not in this, Lu. I won't fight Clay over your damned bank money. It's not reason enough to kill a friend."

"Wasn't it reason enough to kill countless other innocent people?" she flung at him in angry thoughtlessness. He winced. Lucy instantly regretted the words but there was no calling them back. She gave up. "I'm going after them, Sam. I'll need the horse. You can wait here. I'll come back for you."

"The hell you will," he growled, snatching up the reins of his bay. He swung up into the saddle with a quick, fluid grace and for a moment Lucy was absolutely petrified that he meant to leave her.

Then, he put down his hand, his features set in narrow lines. When she placed hers inside it and took the stirrup he vacated, he brought her up easily behind him. His heels lashed back, setting them off with a jerk. Her arms flung about his middle for balance with the barrel of his Colt lying in a deadly bead on his heart. He redirected it with a wary hand so an errant piece of tumbling sage would catch any accidental discharge rather than his own flesh. She didn't correct the aim and they rode in silent pursuit.

The weather stayed dry and agreeably cool. The countryside they covered was mostly level changing into long, low, undulating hills by noon. They rested by a small well near Dry Sandy, then moved on toward Pacific Springs. There, they saw lush patches of green among the hills. Lucy insisted they continue hard and fast though Sam's big bay grew winded under the double weight it carried. As sundown approached, they rode through a valley of long grasses and willow bushes but she overruled Sam's suggestion that they camp. Her eyes were on higher ground, following the path Clay Bonner and his band had taken.

The evening was stunning in its beauty. The west looked stormy over the grand old hills. Sunset streamed in long ribbons through its misty crags. The lofty range ahead where splintered summits were flecked with snow and bathed in dusky solitude led the way to South Pass City and accommodation for the fast gaining night.

It was a deserted village at best, still as a church on a weekday morning. Two streets formed the letter "T" snugged in the shelter of two hills. Of the near fifty dwellings, most were either forsaken or never used. The majority of the main street stores, their proud false fronts fading, stood empty. The population of South Pass City inhabited a scatter of meager log or rubble stone dwellings which dotted the back of the hills. It was a desolate sight with a few green spots wedged in wild rock and ragged brush crowned with timber. Of the thousand men drawn in to make the big strike, 999 were disappointed. Little was left save forgotten hopes and the few who yet prospected in hopes of uncovering the Hidden Hand of rich float rock.

Lucy stiffened when Sam pulled up his blown mount outside the slatted doors of the saloon. She was tired and bone-sore and eager for a meal and a bed. Feeling her resistance, Sam swung his leg over the pummel and slipped down, offering his arms up to her. When she hesitated and cast a disapproving eye toward the batwing doors, he sighed in exasperation.

"We need another animal. The bay can't carry us both up into the high hills. Lessen you've got a

314

stockpile of gold someplace I haven't seen, I mean to earn us enough to buy a sturdy horse."

She couldn't challenge his logic. Resignedly, she set her hands upon his broad frame of shoulders and allowed him to lift her down. "What have you got to stake into a game?"

Sam chewed on that a minute then reached out to finger the butt of his Winchester. It was a reluctance in that gesture.

"No," Lucy put in quickly to save him from the sacrifice. "You'll be needing all your hardware. Here." She reached behind her neck and undid the clasp of a bit of jewelry she'd worn tucked inside her bodice. Sam had noticed it before, a flashy circle of winking stones her husband could afford to give her. When he scowled and refused to take it, she pressed the necklace into his palm. "It won't do me as much good as a horse. Here. Take it."

His fingers clenched about the pendant and he nodded. "You go on over there and get yourself a room and a nice hot bath in that hotel. I'll see to our finances."

"No."

The terse tone and the tense manner in which she gripped his arm had Sam gazing at Lucy in surprise. Until she explained.

"I'm going in with you."

"In there?" He glanced over the doors and frowned at her. "Darlin', that ain't no place for the likes of you."

Her chin squared belligerently. "It won't be the first time, Sam."

His eyes narrowed into suspicious slits. "You thinking I mean to sneak out the back, that it?"

"Don't be ridiculous," she snapped at him but she gave no other reason for staying at his side. He wouldn't have understood it. The nature of the town, crude, masculine and rough, quickened a nervous terror in Lucy. She didn't want to be alone for a minute. Stalking boldly into the interior of the saloon on his arm was not half as frightening to her as lying alone on a strange bed leaping at every sound with remembered panic.

His jaw clamped angrily and after he saw she meant what she said, he shoved open the door and held it. "After you, Miz Blessing. We can't have you worry about your money, now can we?"

The sight of a pretty woman had a galvanizing effect on the hard cases gathered around simple tables of chance. They stared to a man and Lucy sidled close to the protection of Sam's side. Without a thought, she slipped his Colt into its custom-formed holster so his hand could dangle near it with meaningful menace.

"Looking for a game, mister?" called out one rather dandified gent.

"That and a whiskey. I already got the willing woman and what more could a man want?"

There was a ripple of ribald laughter and Lucy endured it stoically, knowing he'd mouthed the provoking words to establish her place at his elbow. No man would challenge his outright claim or the casual way he stroked the butt of his .45.

A chair was kicked back to accommodate him and a whiskey poured. Lucy stood behind him, her fingertips resting atop his shoulders. It wasn't a coquettish ploy as it might have looked to the other hard-bitten men. She needed to feel Sam Zachary's strength to bolster her own.

Cards were flipped expertly onto the tabletop after the necklace was accepted as due tender. Sam was a fair hand at poker, his expression unreadable, his wagers shrewd. In the matter of an hour, he'd amassed a tolerable amount of the other players' coin. With a hand-rolled cigarette clenched between his teeth and his Stetson tilted low, he continued to increase his winnings until he had enough to inquire, "Does anyone know of a man willing to part with a good horse and a reliable pistol for what I've got in front of me?"

"Could be I do," one of them avowed and slowly amended, "but 'twill take a bit more than you have."

"What would it take, pard?"

"Could be your lady friend has the talent to make up the difference."

Lucy's fingers bit into the cording of Sam's shoulders. Suddenly, she felt very vulnerable. How easy it would be for him to trade her off to these lonely, female-starved men and ride away the richer for it. She forced herself to remain still, forced her panic to subside long enough to gauge his reaction.

Sam sat the chair with the relaxed grace of a cougar on a limb. His features were wreathed in a cloud of tobacco fumes. But none could mistake the gun-ready grit of his voice when he murmured low, "You'd best be explaining yourself, mister."

The man opposite gave a jump of alarm. "I didn't mean nuthin' by it. Honest. I jus' thought maybe she could oblige us with a little bit of a song or a dance. We ain't seed nuthin' close to entertainment for a lotta months and I'm sure all the boys would be willing to put in should she be agreeable."

Sam's hand quit its hovering over the staghorn handle of his Colt and rose to cover Lucy's curled fingers. His rubbed gently. He looked up and back at her rigidly set features and said, "Lucy, darlin', it's up to you. I can keep playing."

He saw the terrible indecision in her face, the tear of memories that haunted her eyes and he couldn't allow her to suffer them again.

"Sorry, boys. The lady ain't of a mind."

Lucy's breath expelled with a quiver and with it went her fear. She could see the exhaustion lining Sam's features and knew, to gain the kind of money they were talking, it would take him near to sunup. That would put them either late on the trail or Sam too sluggish to be of any use to her. Then she shifted her tentative gaze to the miners gathered at the table. They were grizzled and gamy but she sensed no meanness in them. They regarded her with hopeful expressions, not with ones of lust or disrespect.

"It's all right, Sam. I can sing a few songs if there's someone to accompany me on the piano."

A fellow leaped up with a grin and scrambled to the yellowed keyboard. Sam's fingers tightened to stay her a moment. His gaze questioned and her smile reassured. Then she stepped up to the bar and let one of the miners boast her up atop it.

"Sorry if I don't look like much in the way of a fancy entertainer," she said with a regretful brush at her mud-stained skirt. There was a quick chorus of "it don't matter" and "you looks jus' fine" as the men settled back in their chairs sporting expectant grins.

Sam slouched in his chair and waited as Lucy spoke to the piano player. Even in her soiled, shapeless dress, mud-spattered and tousled, she looked every inch a lady to him. He started to sip his whiskey when she began the first bar of a sentimental Civil War tune. It took him a whole minute to swallow and by then his mouth felt raw. The soaring splendor of the range about them couldn't match the airy beauty of her voice. It rang pure and sweet with a passionate strength beneath it. A shiver crept over his skin as it tugged at his emotions. An appropriate choice, "Just Before the Battle, Mother." What man could think on lustful thoughts when a woman was toting his mother in song?

Sam found himself listening to the powerful, tear-twisting lyrics. He found himself remembering Emma Zachary as she stood ready to brace the whole Union army if they stepped across her door. She'd had more fight than a silver-tipped grizzly and more heart than a blue tick hound. What would she think of the way he'd chosen to avenge her? How would she have seen George's sacrifice to save his younger brother from his sins? She had held against killing but had seen the inevitability of it when they'd gone to war. But what about now? Would she understand about the number of souls he carried to his credit? Or would she roll beneath the rich Missouri ground if she knew what he'd made of the life she'd given him? Most likely she'd grab up his pa's Sharp's rifle and shoot him down like a rabid animal with no trace of remorse.

Lucy sang three songs, all of them soft and aimed toward swelling the breast with tender remembrance. When she finished, the rough-sawn miners brushed away their tears and passed Sam's Stetson among them, returning it heavy with gold. Then, they bid her a quiet good evening and filed out to head toward home, having lost the urge for further gambling. The final man vowed to bring around his mare and a good shooting piece in the morning before bowing politely to the songstress and shuffling into the night.

Without counting the coins, Sam dumped them into his bandana and knotted it tight. His chair

319

scraped as he pushed back. Lucy puzzled over his withdrawn mood.

"Let's get ourselves a couple of rooms and a few hours of sleep," he suggested.

"One room," she amended quickly, still unwilling to brave the night alone. Sam shrugged and ambled across the street with her in rapid tow.

It was a big if somewhat neglected room, boasting more of dust than comfort. Sam didn't bother with the lamp. Instead he threw back the spread and sheet and sat down to pull off his boots. He hadn't spoken to her and Lucy was uncertain of his mood. He could still be angry over her decision to pursue Clay Bonner. That was probably it. She watched as he stripped off his coat, vest and Levi's and pulled his long underwear to his waist. Water sloshed in the small basin as he washed then restored the underwear in place before settling on the clean sheets. Without saying a word, he'd stated a mouthful. They might be sharing a room but he wasn't for sharing anything else.

Silently, she discarded her gown and kept on her chemise. She refilled the basin and enjoyed the feel of the tepid water upon her skin. The want for a bath and hair washing would have to wait. This night was for sleeping. Tomorrow they'd be back on the trail.

Far from refreshed but passably clean, she turned back to the single bed. She saw Sam's pistol belt hung up on the bedpost so the staghorn butt was a split second away from his palm. She had no plan to reclaim it. She had her own two-shot strapped to her leg and vowed to wear it while she slept no matter what the discomfort. This wasn't Blessing and Sam Zachary was no docile companion. She rounded the bedstead and sank down on the yielding feathers. A groan of pleasure escaped her. How much better it felt than the hard ground of the last two nights. She could hear the light, fast sound of Sam's breathing and knew him not to be asleep. However, when he made no move closer and no offer of a good night, she shut her eyes and accepted her solitary position in his bed. Her weariness was quick to overtake her and of such depth that she never felt him collect her into his arms. Nor did she realize that he held her in that embrace even as slumber claimed him.

Lucy shivered at the cool touch of mountain air and pulled the covers up to her chin. She snuggled deep within them for several long, languishing minutes until all thoughts of rest were dashed by sudden knowledge.

She was sleeping alone. Sam Zachary was gone.

Lucy bolted upright in alarm. Her eyes leapt to the door. It was closed. The floor was clear of the scattering of his clothes. Then, a moment before panic had its way, she caught sight of his heavy Colt revolver nestled on the pillow beside her.

She had no time to relish her relief. There was a timid tap at the door and a female voice asked for entrance. Drawing up the sheet, Lucy bade her come in. The woman was middle-aged and tolerably good looking although her figure was not a model of symmetry. She carried a bundle of clothing with a tray atop it.

" 'Morning, Miz Zachary. Your man bid me come up with some clean duds and breakfast. Sorry we don't have no private baths. Mainly we just use the creek until she freezes over."

More would freeze over before Lucy considered a public bath in such a place. As politely as she could manage, she murmured, "Thank you. I think I'll just freshen up here."

"Suit yourself," the woman muttered as if she thought Lucy odd indeed.

"And where might I find Mr. Zachary?"

If her tension was noticeable, the woman paid no mind. "He's down in the saloon jawing with the menfolk. Said you'd best be shaking a leg."

"Did he now?"

The woman lifted a brow at the untidy female's imperious tone but had nothing more to say and so sauntered from the room. Discovering herself to be ravenous, Lucy launched herself upon the breakfast tray as she pondered the clothes Sam sent up for her. A red union suit, a checked shirt, brown denim breeches and a low crown black hat. She supposed there was no ready-made dress shop to be found in South Pass City and that these "duds" were far more practical, but she felt no hurry to try them on. Finally, with her meal complete and washing done, she slipped into the odd garb. The long underwear felt cozy against the chill of the higher altitude and the pants were plenty roomy and long enough to require a cowboy-type cuff above her fashionable half boots. She regarded the shirt with some dismay, for it fit her with a glovelike familiarity. Though she couldn't boast of much in the way of feminine curve, the checked shirt made the most of them with its torso-hugging cling.

With the flat hat set squarely atop her braided hair and Sam's pistol weighing down the waistband of her Levi's, Lucy strode across the street in the mannish clothes and pushed into the saloon. No one within took her for a man or half-growed boy.

Sam had been sipping beer at the bar when he heard the eddy of murmurs in the room. He turned and likewise stared in unabashed appreciation. Remembering himself and that he was not alone in the gawking, he shrugged off his coat and motioned Lucy to join him. Quickly, he slipped his vest over the eye-popping checked shirt and fastened it with less than steady fingers. It was loose enough to quiet the rush of rapid breathing that had overtaken all the men present. Then, impatiently, he donned his coat and tossed back the last of his drink.

"A bunch of riders passed through late yesterday afternoon. We're not more than a couple hours behind them if they likewise stopped for the night. Hauling a heavy wagon, can't see they had much choice," he told her curtly.

"Let's go then."

He followed her to the slotted doors then caught her arm in an urgent grip. She looked up in question.

"Lucy, you damned certain you want to be doing this?"

She eased his fingers from her arm and replied with equal sincerity, "Yes, I am."

"No use arguing then."

They'd come to the roughly peeled hitching rail where Sam's bay stood beside a surefooted paint mare. Lucy paused a moment to drop Sam's Colt into his holster, noting the other side offered the working end of a plain-handled Navy revolver, making him looked deadly and well-heeled. She fit her foot into a stirrup and as she hoisted up, had Sam's large hand cupping her trouser-clad bottom for a bit of an extra boost. She didn't know whether to grin or slap him so she did neither. Instead, she gathered up the reins and gave him an impatient look.

"I'da preferred handling the front of that there shirt but seeing as how I'd have to fight off half the

323

town who'd want to do likewise, I figured I'd best settle for second best."

He was looking up at her with the most impertinent male grin on his face. She finally gave way to a reluctant smile that in no way reflected the way her pulse accelerated into a gallop then nudged the mare on Clay Bonner's trail.

Chapter Twenty-two

There was no time to admire the surroundings. They ascended the higher hills and were allowed a magnificent view of the rolling mountain lands which stretched toward the Wind River Valley some thirty miles distant, but Lucy was only interested in the ruts of the army payroll wagon scoring the ground beneath them. Pointed black slate rock lined the edge of the gradual incline and were, in turn, shadowed by a line of high limestone cliffs. Far overhead, they could hear the rip and roar of the wind but it calmed as they passed into a dense wood screen to become a soft singing through the pine boughs. The air was pungent and pure and so fresh it was a luxury to breathe. Abruptly, they broke into a field of fallen trees, all neatly chopped off at the roots. The great pines were not cut by woodsmen but by nature's fellers, the beaver. Marks of their razor-sharp teeth were plain on the fresh stumps.

For a moment, Lucy was distracted by the perfect serenity of the scene. Overhead two hawks wheeled and swooped, riding the thermals of air against a clear blue sky. All at once, she was taken by the desire to lie down with Sam Zachary in the quiet sunshine, to roll in his embrace beneath the pines and rest in sated splendor beside him, looking up through the vista of green branches toward the calm heaven above. She looked to him, savoring the sight of him astride his bay, his head thrown back as if to test and taste the beauty of the day, his hands resting as easy on the reins as they would upon her bare shoulders. Then those thoughts scattered as the pathway took them along the back of a high bald ridge which looked down into an irregular valley. There, on the rocky floor next to a silver, threading river, was a caravan of riders escorting a wagon.

Lucy's heels stabbed back into the mare's flanks. The paint jumped forward and would have charged down the slope had Sam not been quick enough to catch the reins. He hauled the horse up so abruptly, she nearly lost her seat.

"What are you doing? Can't you see them down there?" she hurled at him, unaware of how her voice echoed out and rolled down the valley.

"Shut up," he hissed and jerked her horse around, leading it away from the ridge. "Sure, I saw them. Was it your plan to just ride on down and demand they return the money? Or to make so much noise they'd be lying in wait for us?"

Shamefaced, Lucy said nothing and allowed him to draw the mare up in a small shelter of pines. He kicked out of the stirrups, slid to the ground and was trotting toward the crest. Quickly, choking down her embarrassment, she followed. She dropped to her belly beside him on the hard ground and watched, as he did, the slow-moving column of men.

"They have no idea we're following them," she said smugly.

Sam shot her a look. "Why would they suspect a fool thing like that? Don't imagine they're losing sleep over the notion of one man and a crazy woman sneaking up on 'em."

Lucy squinted and counted ten men on horseback and one handling the wagon. Sam's guns carried ten rounds, his Winchester seventeen. Her own piece, two. If they placed their shots . . .

Sam stood and stalked toward the horses. She scrambled up to go after him. "What are you planning, Sam? Do we wait until dark to hit them?"

"Makes sense to me. We'll mosey on into their camp and over coffee ask real politelike for them to surrender to our superior force."

She bit back her reply. Suddenly, she could see the tension in his face. Was he worried about the odds? Or about Clay Bonner being among those below? Would he balk now that he was faced with the unpleasant task of riding on a friend? Or would he turn on her regardless of his vow to see her safe? She had no illusions of what her future would contain should she fall again into Bonner's hands. It was up to Sam. She couldn't do it alone with her two-shot pistol. She needed his deadly calm and professional draw. She needed a killer and that was exactly what Sam Zachary was. But this killer was not without a heart and she could see she was tearing it with indecision.

"Sam?"

He glanced at her fleetingly then away. Muscles jerked along his jaw and his fingers limbered beside his mismatched guns. "This was what you wanted, Lucy. Once we commit to action, there's no going back. You sure that pride and greed for gold are reason enough to risk lead?"

She caught his arm, needing desperately for him

327

to understand. "It's not the money, Sam," she explained passionately. "It's the dreams of the people of Blessing. Don't you see? If Bonner gets away with it, our town will be marked for failure. Every cent in my bank represents hope and a future. You're asking me to give up on that, on them. I can't, Sam. My promises are no less binding than yours. And even if I die trying, I mean to try. I owe it to my father and to Oliver and to every man, woman and child who placed a grain of trust in me."

Sam stood silent. She could see him mulling her words, resisting them and what they stood for. Then, without a word, he drew his guns one at a time and checked their chambers. It was a smooth, cold move of experience and determination. She didn't know whether to cheer or recant. She could well be sending them both to their deaths and she had no right to demand that of him.

"Sam—"

"I don't suppose you'd stay here if I told you to."

He made a harsh face when she shook her head, leaving her words unvoiced.

"Mount up then and do exactly like I tell you. Surprise and sheer insanity are about all we've got in our favor."

Clay Bonner looked in surprise as a lone rider approached from the mouth of the valley. Using his hat to shade his eyes, he waved off the line of rifles instantly aimed on that single figure from around the ring of their campsite.

"Damn," he muttered to himself, feeling both pleased and cautious. Then, louder, he called out, "Zach, that you, boy? Come on in. Hell, I didn't expect to see you. We couldn't find a trace of you and your lady friend. Where is she?"

A man who'd survived long on his wits, Clay's eyes quickly swept the ridge of rock rising above them and was relieved to see no movement. Sam continued to advance on the camp and still said nothing. Clay peered at him, trying to fathom his stony expression.

"Hey, now, hold hard. You don't think we left you apurpose, do you? I saved your share."

When Sam spoke at last, his voice was soft but rang with unquestionable strength.

"I didn't come for my share, Clay. I came for all of it."

Clay gave him a quirky smile. "What say, boy? You're funning me." He saw the glint of metal pinned upon his young friend's jacket and that smile died. His hand began to edge down toward his Dragoon.

Sam kept riding forward. His announcement startled a panic among the bandits. "You're surrounded, fellers. As marshal of Blessing, Territory of Wyoming, I demand you surrender your arms to me."

In answer, Clay grabbed for his gun. A crack from a shooter above made him hesitate just long enough to keep Sam from feeling the bite of his lead. Then he lunged aside to avoid getting trampled.

The moment Clay went for a draw, Sam kicked his bay from walk to full gallop. He charged down on the camp of startled thieves, flames blasting from either pistol. Even at a dead-out run from horseback, most of his shots were true. By the time he rode through once, the number of opponents dropped from eleven to five.

Sam drove his horse up into the outcroppings of rock and flung himself behind their protection. It only took the milling badmen only a moment to figure that the thunderous echoes rolling down the valley came from one rifle and that they faced two shooters instead of a posse. Emboldened by that knowledge, they stood their ground and returned fire instead of surrendering up like the cowards they were had there been a mightier force.

Lucy held her breath suspended until Sam was tucked safe behind the rocks. Then she began the serious business of finding a target below. She nestled the Winchester into the hollow of her shoulder and eyed down the long barrel. Eventually, one of the robbers popped up to get a shot off at Sam and she sent him staggering back, cashed by a slug in the chest. She didn't take time to think about the consequence of her act, that she'd just ended a life, but was quickly searching out another at the end of the rifle's sight. Grit exploded in her face, cutting her forehead in a wide, dull pattern of pain. Immediately after, she heard the flat slap of another close-passing bullet.

Crouched behind the rocks on the valley floor, Sam picked carefully and was rewarded when one of the men went down in the boned-appearing way of a man shot dead. That left two and Clay Bonner. He had repeated opportunities to drive lead into his brother-in-law but let them pass, concentrating on the pair he didn't know. And didn't care if they lived or died. A dark Stetson poked up from behind cover and the Colt rocked back in his palm. Two left.

Above, Lucy wiped the dripping blood away with the back of her hand. Her head ached something fierce but she ignored it. Slowly, she eased up to peer down below. Mostly, she saw the sprawl of fresh-killed men. Clay was hunched down and well hidden, which she found she regretted. Sinking lead into him would have been a savage pleasure. Instead, her bead was drawn by a furtive flicker of movement as the other bandit thought to dash toward the horses. She played out the long barrel of the gun and sighted slow before squeezing the trigger. He dropped on the spot. And that left Clay Bonner.

"Dammit, Clay, I don't want to kill you," Sam shouted out. "Throw out your piece and I'll let you walk away whole."

There was a long silence then, cautiously, Bonner rose to pitch his Dragoon out onto the blood-soaked ground. Lucy surged up pulling down a line on him.

"No," Sam hollered up at her. "Don't shoot."

Something in the wild panic of his voice stopped her and she let the barrel tip downward. Of all of them, she'd wanted Bonner the most. Perhaps because his attack was the most personal. Perhaps because he held a dangerous influence over Sam. Whichever, she wasn't anxious to leave the two men alone long enough to enjoy a conversation. She clamored up on the paint, glad for the freedom of her britches, and nudged it down to the valley floor where Sam was slowly approaching his friend and his sister's husband with a look of infinite regret.

Clay was doing what he did best, playing out every angle to find his best advantage. He grinned at Sam with a friendly welcome, as if he hadn't done his best to put a bullet in him minutes before.

"Glad to see you're all right, boy. That was some fine shooting. Yessir. Ole Bloody Bill would have been right proud. Look around. It's just you and

331

me and nothing stopping us from heading south for home."

"I'll stop you," came a rumbling promise as Lucy reined in the paint. Sam glanced at her and she didn't like what she saw in his expression. A protectiveness toward the vermin she meant to see exterminated. Rifle at the ready, she advanced to stand at Sam's side. Her glare cut across at the stocky Bonner and in a brief exchange each recognized the threat of the other.

Clay swung his persuasive charm on his younger comrade from childhood, war and robbery. "Sam, you going to let her make talk like that? Tell her we go way back, that we're blood and kin. Let's go, Zach, boy. We got some hard riding ahead of us."

"If you were heading home, you were either lost or taking one long way around," Sam observed softly.

"The boys was meeting up with Charlie Waters tomorrow and we was making the split. I was planning to head out then. I was hoping you'd be joining me."

"The only place you're going is back to Blessing to stand before a circuit judge," Lucy interjected. Her worried gaze darted between the two men. She had no means to stop Sam should he decide to ride out with Bonner. He had no reason not to.

"Hell," Clay said expansively. "If all she's fretting about is her bank's money, let her have it. We got enough from the payroll to pay us back. They owe it to us, Sam, them that killed your folks and Georgie."

Memories and hate dangled like poisoned bait. Sensing she could well lose him to the manipulative Bonner, Lucy put a hand to his arm. "Sam, it all goes back to Blessing. That's the only way." The

332

muscles were bunched tight as steel beneath her palm. "Bonner, too."

Clay swallowed hard and tried to read the other man's closed expression. It spoke no good for him that Sam was taking this long to decide. He needed prodding. "You going to listen to that? Zach, you going to take me in and put me behind bars again? You going to write Sarah and tell her you helped get me hanged? No, you won't be able to, 'cause that gal means to see you dangling right beside me. You think you're just going to walk away from this smelling pretty? Boy, you're in it every bit as deep as I am! She's going to see us both dancing at the end of a length of Manilla."

"You're not going to hang, Clay. I'm fixing to let you loose."

"What?" Lucy was stunned by the soft words and even more by the set determination in Sam's features. She glared at the stone-cold killer then back at the man beside her. "Sam, you can't."

Harsh gray eyes cut down to her. "I can, and I will. I got you back your gold. That's what you wanted. Now, I'm doing what I want. I ain't taking him back to hang. I told you that much. Be satisfied with that."

She drew a breath to argue then saw the futility in it. With a helpless sigh, she nodded. Abruptly, his expression clouded and his fingertips touched at the gash on her forehead. She took quick advantage of the tenderness she saw. Her fingers covered his.

"Sam, come back to Blessing with me. Don't ride out of here with him. Please. I love you."

Bonner gave a savage cough of laughter. "A woman? Is that what this is about? Zach, you're letting this here female step between all that we are to each other? She's a banker, for pity's sake, a

333

Northern banker, one of them what got your family torn apart."

"No." Sam turned to him and slowly shook his head. "No. The war did that. I did that."

Bonner's voice gentled into a soothing croon. "No. She's got you thinking all crazy. You know inside you did what was right, what had to be done. Don't let her and her kind twist you up. She's just a female, Zach. Hell, a good horse is worth more than a woman. There'll be plenty to be had where we're going. One ain't no better than another and this one here, she's trouble."

"And what about Sarah? You thinking of trading her for a good horse, Clay?"

Clay smiled slickly to ease the venom in his brother-in-law's voice. "Sarah's my wife. She's family. This here gal's, she's just something to press the sheets with."

Lucy stepped forward in thoughtless rage, meaning to slap the smug-faced Bonner to stop his filthy spew of lies. Too late, she recognized the danger. His big hand darted out the moment she was in reach, snatching for the Winchester. With a scream of surprise, she reeled back and Sam had both guns cocked at the ready.

"Shoot him!" she cried out. "Sam, shoot him. Kill him!" She stumbled and caught her balance, panting with fear and hate. Clay Bonner unarmed was more dangerous to her than anything she could imagine. As long as he lived, Sam would never be safe. He would never be hers.

The guns grew unsteady in Sam's hands and slowly the hammers eased down on empty chambers. A noxious, gloating smile began to spread across Bonner's face and was quickly erased by a stunning strike from the back of Sam's hand. Clay staggered, touching the blood on his lip with blank startlement.

The change was immediate and apparent to all. Sam moved to where the Dragoon had fallen and expertly emptied the remaining chambers. Clay stared at him in stark disbelief, Lucy, with a wash of weak relief.

"Lucy, think you can handle that army wagon?" he called quietly.

"I'll manage," she answered, trying to still the trembling of her limbs. She didn't attempt to fool herself. She'd won by an uncomfortably narrow margin.

Clay caught the emptied Dragoon. His face had hardened into lines of cold fury.

"I gave you my word, Clay, and I'm seeing to it. This settles things between us. You come into Blessing and I can't promise you nothing."

"I'm not leaving without the gold, Zach," came the low, hissing promise.

"You'll not have it."

"Who's going to stop me when I ride in with Charlie Waters's boys? You? You going to kill us all? For that sly slut?"

Sam looked at him long, with a stare every bit as deadly as the bore of his Colt. "If you weren't family, I'd kill you where you stand."

"Do it, Sam!" Lucy whispered harshly but he didn't spare her a look. Clay did, long and hard as if making himself a mental promise. Then he turned back to the resistant figure he'd led since childhood.

"And I should have finished what that fancy saloon man paid me to do. You're making a mistake, boy."

"I've made 'em before. But this time, I don't

think so." He caught the horn of his saddle and swung up onto the big bay. "You'd best commence with the burying then start your walking."

"Walking? You mean to leave me aground?"

"Can't be watching my back, Clay, and I know you too well. Cool a spell and get your thinking straight."

"A man afoot ain't no man atall. You can't set me down!"

Sam motioned to Lucy and she urged the wagon forward, out of the draw. As he nudged his bay to follow, Clay Bonner's words echoed and rolled with vengeful thunder along the high walls around him.

"I won't be forgetting this, boy. You watch your back, you hear? Watch it good 'cause I'll be coming, for you and your fancy lady. And I mean to pull that town down around you."

It was a long, silent ride back to Blessing. The moon was full, flooding the hills with enough silvery light for them to push right on through until morning. Though Lucy was swaying with weariness, she made no request to stop. One look at Sam's taut features and she knew he was pushing for a reason. He wanted to get far and fast away from Bonner and he was in no fitting mood for conversation. She let him ride with his own troubling demons, hoping he'd sort through them by the time they returned to town. There, she'd do everything in her power to help him overcome them. He'd taken the first step on his own and, regardless of his straight-as-a-lodge-pole-pine position in the saddle, she knew he was wobbling inside. But he'd be all right. She meant to see he never had room to regret the decision he'd made.

No sight was ever sweeter to her than that of Blessing rising up from the sage prairie. She suffered a moment of panic when Sam lagged behind her, but then he drew alongside to escort her right down the main street. With his Stetson angled down to shade his eyes, she couldn't guess at what he was feeling.

The townspeople rushed out to meet them. The arrival of Lucy Blessing in bullwhacker britches toting the stolen gold was enough to fan the fires of talk for winters to come. Then their looks settled on the man riding with her. And there was no doubt from those expressions that they were seeing not their Marshal Wade but a killer named Zachary.

Lucy hauled the reins in at the livery and sagged in the seat. She felt beaten over every inch and dirtier than a hog in its favorite wallow. A clog of sudden emotion lodged in her throat when a broad-shouldered fellow came out of the livery. Not father but capable son.

"Cal, see that the contents of the wagon gets transferred into the bank. I'm going to soak in a tub until I'm as wrinkled as the Widow McDonald."

As she crawled down out of the wagon seat, her weary eyes lit with joy. "Cecil," she whispered in disbelief as she saw the small, wiry little clerk approaching. He was none too steady on his feet and sporting a sling but he was grinning from ear to bespectacled ear. With a care for his injury, she wrapped him in a hug of sheer delight, streaking her dusty face with rivulets of tears. "Thank God. I thought he'd killed you."

"No, ma'am. I won't dare up and die and leave the bank unattended whilst you was gone."

She managed a hoarse-sounding laugh. "Think you can escort our funds back where they belong?"

337

"Be my pleasure, Miz Lucy."

Sam slid out of his saddle and held out the reins of his blown mount to the livery boy. "Treat him good. He's done earned his keep."

Silence hung as the boy made no move to take the reins. His stare held a blank dislike for the tall Missouri man. "See to him yourself, Zachary," he growled at last.

Sam stiffened and Lucy surprised him by lighting in like a dog on a bothersome tick. "Cal, you take the marshal's horse for him and you see to it proper or I'll settle on you so hard you'll think a grizzly bear had at your backside."

The boy blinked then sullenly snatched the reins. Sam didn't worry over his bay. He could see the boy had too much respect for horseflesh to abuse it regardless of the hate he might hold for its owner.

"Sam?" Lucy watched the eddies of controlled emotion play about his face. She started to reach out to him, to show her support but he moved a step back and out of range with a nervous sort of wariness.

"Cecil, you see to things for Miz Blessing," he said flatly.

"Yessir, Marshal Wa—" He broke off, looking embarrassed and confused.

Sam wheeled about and stalked to the jail house, aware of each hostile stare as if they held a crippling caliber. Newt had been napping in his chair and was instantly on his feet, favoring his arm. He regarded Sam with astonishment as the other collapsed upon the corner bed. Sam let all his weariness and tension flow out on a whooshing breath and let his head drop back against the wall as his eyes slid shut. Still, he could feel the boy's eyes on him.

"You got something to say?"

"Good to have you back, Marshal. I didn't have no doubts atall."

A pitifully weak one-sided smile sketched across Sam's grimy face. "Glad to hear it."

"Put your feet up for a spell, Marshal. I'll tend things for you."

"Reckon I will."

But before he could indulge in the luxury of rest, he heard the click of boot heels pause at the door and smelled the identifying odor of bay rum and good cigars. He cracked his heavy eyes open to glower at Henry Knight as he lingered at the jail house door.

"Surprised to see you come crawling in," Knight stated mildly and drew on his fat cigar.

"Reckon you would be since you paid to have it otherwise."

The cool drawl set the dapper saloonkeeper back a step but before he could speak words to deny it, Sam cut him off impatiently.

"I got no time to fool with the likes of you, Knight. I'd crush you under my heel but I don't have the energy. My mind's on more important things."

"Like keeping your neck out of a noose? Found a right interesting wire on Miz Blessing's desk at the bank. Description of our supposed Marshal Wade. It surely weren't you. Did a little checking, Mister Zachary, and you're one high-priced outlaw."

"You meaning to collect the reward to recover what you paid Bonner? Try it. I may look as low as a snake in a wagon rut, but if I got called, I could muster the stuff to blow a hole through you. Were I you, I'd be busy boarding up my windows. Bonner's aiming to come back for the gold. Lessen you're

339

figuring to go out and ask him to give your money back."

Knight chewed on that information as well as the stump of his cigar. "That puts you in one hell of a fix, don't it, Marshal? Got murdering outlaws on one side and a hangman on the other. No one in this town's going to stand with you. You must be fretting something awful about which way to run."

Sam leveled a double-barreled glare. "I ain't planning to run anywhere. But you might consider it."

Knight grinned, all compelling golden charm mixed with a potent dose of evil. "You know, I'm not worried at all." He turned as if to continue on to the Nightingale then paused to impart one final fact. "See, I wired the U.S. Marshal's office and he's coming to collect you, personal. Think you know him. His name's Tolliver."

Chapter Twenty-three

"I sorry. Miss Blessing no receive any visitors now. She go to bed. You come back tomorrow."

As the door began to close before the impassive Chinese face, a voice called out from the stairs beyond.

"It's all right, Li. Show the marshal in."

With features schooled to betray none of her misgivings, the small Chinese woman opened the door and bowed to Sam Zachary as she shuffled back to let him pass.

With his Stetson turning in his hands, Sam stepped into the foyer and looked up to where Lucy stood on the landing above. His heart bobbed up into his throat, forcing him to swallow hard to dislodge it. She wasn't making it any easier for him with her fresh-washed hair all tumbled loose about her shoulders and her slender figure enfolded in the shiny silk of her wrapper. He was having a hard enough time keeping his thoughts straight without that kind of distraction. And, Lordy, she was distracting. When she spoke, her voice rippled in a sensuous whisper. It was the way his hands would sound rubbing over the glossy robe. The felt brim of his hat came close to being mangled in his twisting grasp.

" 'Evening, Sam. I was hoping you'd stop by to see me."

"Looks like you were fixing to entertain company," he remarked. The words came out almost as dry as the inside of his mouth felt.

Her soft laugh stirred a chill of gooseflesh along his forearms. He tried to pull his gaze away as she came gliding down the steps to greet him. Finally, he was able to break the fascination and jerked his stare toward the parlor.

"I wanted to talk to you a mite before I rode out." He cringed at how clumsily that tumbled out but at least he'd said it. He heard the quiet tread become a rapid flurry on the carpeted stairs. He could hear the quick pant of her panicked breathing as she came up beside him.

"Sam? You're leaving? Now?"

He took a long, steadying draw of air and expelled it hard. He couldn't look at her. "I reckon I'd better. Tolliver's on his way and I don't guess I have to tell you what that means."

"No," she whispered in a strange little voice. "I guess you don't."

"If I stay, he'll hang me. He's been itching to do it for a long while. His men being here will keep Clay from causing mischief. You understand, don't you?"

"Oh, yes. I understand. I understand everything."

The hush of her words caught at him, causing him to slip a glance her way. It was damned unfair for her to be looking so still and composed while he was shaking and close to sobbing like a babe. "Lucy . . ." He choked on her name and looked down to study his crumpled hat brim with a fearsome concentration. "There's a lot I want to say to you, if I can get the words out right."

"Tell me in the morning."

That low, throbbing command jerked his head up. He looked at her, all scared and shiny-eyed, and saw every desire a man might ever own up to offered in her melting gaze. His breath faltered and failed then restarted with a noisy gasp. "No." He peddled back, shaking his head. He should have lit out without stopping for a word with her and run like a rabbit. But he hadn't. He'd had to see her one last time. And now she was turning up the fires of his private hell.

"Sam . . ."

"No, Lucy. Wouldn't do neither us no good."

She pulled the worried Stetson from his hands and gave it a toss into the parlor, causing the little birds to set up a chorus of nervous song from within their gilded cage. He followed its floating path until it settled on the sofa then whipped his tormented eyes back toward temptation.

"Don't . . ." It was a moan. His eyes slipped shut to squeeze tight in agony as her fingertips brushed over his lips and bristled cheek. His breath was puffing like an engine trying to conquer a particularly steep hill.

"In the morning, Sam," she said again and he could feel his will tremble.

"Be better if I headed out now," came his weakening protest. He found himself leaning toward the fingers that raked restlessly through his sandy-colored hair. "You're making things worse."

"I mean to. Much worse."

Something in that husky promise should have alerted him but he stood, dulled by desire, and watched through glassy eyes as she eased the robe from her shoulders. Beneath it she wore linen and lace. White. Filmy. *Familiar*. The night dress from the catalog, he remembered with sluggish surprise.

Need exploded inside him. Hands she'd counted on him not being able to control rose to sample her small waist when she swayed up against him. His face was warm and rough between her palms. Her thumbs touched lightly at the sun-creased corners of his eyes to dab away the dampness gathered there. And she kissed him. Softly. Sweetly.

Lucy came down from her toes with a smile. Over her shoulder, she called, "Li, use the rest of that hot water to pour the marshal a bath and fetch one of Mister Oliver's dressing robes and his shaving gear."

There was a brief mutter of Chinese but Lucy never took her eyes off the man before her.

"See to it, Li. Mister Oliver would be happy that I put his things to use again." Her fingers stroked over Sam's cheeks and she smiled again before stepping away. "I'll wait for you upstairs, Sam. Don't be too long."

Sam stayed rooted to the floor, watching the wisps of linen twitch about her hips as she climbed the stairs. Then he headed blindly into the parlor to pour a hefty glass of Oliver Blessing's bourbon. The decanter clattered on the glass and the smooth liquor shivered all the way down. It was crazy for him to stay. He knew it as sure as he knew Lucy would be pacing the floor overhead. She'd done it on purpose and he should have been mad as hell.

What he was, was anxious to get the bath over with so he could fall right in with the rest of her plans.

Lucy was pacing, pacing and fretting. His announcement that he was leaving had delivered a stunning blow. Fortunately, it hadn't dulled her wits. The seduction had been unplanned but it had

344

worked. Each second had been a nightmare in which she feared she would do the unforgivable and cling or cry until, at last, she realized she had him. For at least one more night.

Then, how was she going to let him go?

He was a wanted man. He didn't have to paint a more explicit picture when he told her Tolliver was on his way. Sam would hang and her hopes for any future would strangle with him. She could run with him but knew, even without asking, that he wouldn't buy into it. He wouldn't make her a party to the aimless, rootless life he led.

"Oh, Sam, what are we going to do?" she moaned softly to the night and the soft lights of Blessing. With all her wealth, with all her influence, she was still helpless.

She hadn't heard his approach on bare feet and gave a start when his hands settled big and warm upon her shoulders. Quickly, because she would not have him know she'd been close to crying, she forced a smile and turned toward him. She needn't have worried. She didn't think he ever saw her face. His eyes were in the process of closing, his head lowering. She sighed into the searching tenderness of his kiss, willing to let go of the worries. At least while in his arms.

The night sounds made soft music to the accompaniment of Sam's slow heartbeat. It was a melody Lucy could listen to for the rest of her life without ever growing tired of its repetitious beat.

"Where will you go?"

His big hand paused for a moment then continued along the gentle wave of her hair.

"I don't know. To Missouri, maybe. I haven't seen

my family for a spell."

"Won't they think to look for you there?"

"It doesn't matter."

The heavy acceptance in his words made her blink hard. She'd been fighting back tears ever since the last eddy of pleasure left her. The sweetness of his loving only made the words come harder.

"It matters to me, Sam." Her voice gave a little catch and the arm he'd wound casually about her waist seized up in response.

"Don't you go a-crying now, you hear," he warned in a less than unaffected tone. His lips pressed hard against the top of her bowed head. "I wish I could give you all the happiness you deserve but wishin' won't make it so. I gotta be leaving in the morning and no amount of wishin' will change that, either. It ain't going to be much of a life without you in it, darlin', so it don't much matter what happens once I leave."

"Then don't leave."

A simple solution. An impractical one.

"Lucy . . ." he began patiently but she cut him off with an excited fervor.

"Don't go, Sam. You've got a home here in Blessing. You've got a good job. You've got people who respect you for the man you are."

"You mean for the man they thought I was."

"You are that man. Give them time to come around. They'll see you're the best man they could possibly have to protect them."

"A killer?"

"Who better than a badman to fend against his own kind? You've proven yourself to these people. When they get over the fact that they were deceived, they'll take you at face value. I did, after all."

"I worked at getting you to change your mind, if

346

you'll recall. You were more than ready to shoot off anything vital when we first met up. You got a tolerable mean temper on you, gal."

Lucy smiled into his shoulder. Her fingers traced the puckered seam along his ribs that the doctor had sewed into a fairly neat line. "You're what Blessing needs. You're what I need, Sam. If you keep running, you'll end up just like Clay Bonner. Is that what you want?"

He said nothing and she craned to see into his face. His expression was lean and hard and it troubled her. She stroked his jaw, hoping to soften it beneath her fingers but he rolled his head to one side.

"Lucy, I came to Blessing to rob you!"

"But you couldn't." There it was. "You couldn't do it, could you? It was Clay's idea to take the bank, wasn't it? You were telling the truth about that. You couldn't take the money because you care about this town. You can't leave tomorrow because you care about me."

"Dammit, woman!" He heaved onto his side, putting his broad back to her, but the barrier didn't deter her. His breathing was a harsh hiss that sucked in sharp the moment her arms went about him. "Think and say all the pretty things you want, Lu, but that ain't going to stop Grant Tolliver from coming and Clay right behind him. Whatcha going to do then? Whatcha going to do when some time down the road when we got us a houseful of kids and ole Cornelius under foot and some gun-slick ambles in with my dodger and shoots me dead in the yard right in front of you? Won't it be simpler if I just go now?"

"No," she argued doggedly. "I want that houseful of kids and you for as long as I can have you!" She pressed her wet face to his nape and did what she promised she wouldn't. She cried. "Sam, I love you

347

so. Give me a day, two days, six, a month, a year. Anything. I'll take it. I won't complain. We'll make a home. We'll be happy."

"And we'll forget I have a noose hanging over my head. Lucy, gal, think straight. You'll be jumping at shadows. I'll be sleeping beside you with a brace of Colts under the pillow. It's no good."

"Fine!" She shoved away and rolled to the far side of the bed. "You go. You run. You live like some scared animal being hunted for its pelt. Just don't you expect me to come to see them hang you." For a time, she gave way to her frantic weeping. Then she felt the mattress dip and rise as Sam stood on the other side. In a flash, her tears were dashed away and she was up with her arms around him. She hugged him hard, breathing in the clean soap smell of his skin, kneading the dampness of his hair. Loving him with a fierceness that was an agony to endure.

"You gave me until morning. You promised me that long. Don't you dare try leaving before then, Sam. Don't you dare cheat me out of those hours or I'll hate you until I die."

With a gentle hand, he lifted her tear-washed face and kissed each glistening drop away. There were no more words said. And Sam Zachary kept his promise. He didn't leave until dawn.

It was cool and clear, the makings of a beautiful day. But Sam had no eye for sunrises. He was tormented by the vision he'd left curled trustingly beside the hollow he'd made in the sheets. He'd been careful not to wake her. Coward that he was, he couldn't face another confrontation. The moment he'd opened the door to the bedroom, the inscrutable Li had been there with his cleaned clothes draped over her arm. She gave him a flat, black-eyed stare and silently slipped away while he dressed in the upper hall.

Still buckling on his gun belt, Sam started toward town. He'd made a vow to himself that he wouldn't look back. Had he, he might have seen the lacy curtains pushed aside at the upstairs window. He might have caught a glimpse of the tear-stained face hovering there as he strode away. Better he not look back.

Sam tried not to wake Newt upon slipping into the jail but the long yellow hound set up a loud thump of welcome with his bony tail, causing him to stir. The young man didn't venture any questions about where he'd spent the night but Cornelius had plenty, sniffing and snuffling and circling around him.

"Marshal," Newt offered tentatively. His features grew grim as he watched Sam stuff his war bag with cigarette makings and extra cartridges. "You heading out?"

"Yep." He didn't look up. This was another goodbye he'd hoped to avoid.

"Good luck to you then."

The solid generosity of the boy's offer brought Sam's stare to the outstretched hand. As a mighty lump of feeling began to swell in his throat, he took it and was surprised by the firm grasp.

"I know you don't got no time for drawn-out gab but I'd like you to take Cornelius with you. He's grown mighty fond of the way you tries to ignore him and he'll be good company for you on the trail."

With tremendous effort, Sam managed a smile that didn't waver. He wasn't quite so successful in keeping the thickness from his voice. "That's right kind of you, boy, but I travel best alone."

The shaggy head nodded and the toes of his worn

sodbuster boots scuffed the clean-swept floor. "It's been a real pleasure knowing you, Sam."

"Likewise."

Newt hesitated then came out straight with what was on his mind. "If you was of a mind to turn yourself over to the law, a good lawyer could finagle around the gallows. There's plenty of folk here in Blessing who'd speak up proud in your behalf. Why, Miz Blessing, she'd even bend the ear of the territorial governor. And with you bringing in that army payroll, you might be talking only a couple of years. Folks here wouldn't forget you."

Sam's first attempt at speech resulted in a raspy rattle. After clearing his throat, he muttered, "I'm going to have a heck of time finding someone who makes coffee as good as you do. You take care of that little gal of yours and keep watch over Miz Lucy."

"Happen I know she'd rather you do it."

"I know but that just ain't possible. And here. Here's something else I think you're man enough to handle."

Sam began to reach for the badge pinned to his vest when the office door opened, halting his movement. Ruby Gale was someone he'd never expected to see in a jail unless she was there on visiting days. She was tricked out in glossy silk, black sequins and fringe, managing to appear flamboyant even in the somber color. She glanced out toward the street then shut the door in a conspiratorial manner.

" 'Morning, Marshal Wa—Marshal," she oozed.

"Miz Gale." Sam's reply was a mite chilly, seeing as how well he remembered their last meeting.

Realizing she wasn't going to warm him with her obvious charms, Ruby cut right to the purpose of her visit. "Marshal, I've always fancied myself as a businesswoman, a gal who looks out for her own interests, if you know what I mean."

"I think I have a fair notion, ma'am," Sam drawled. He chafed at the delay her visit caused but his upbringing held him at polite, if impatient, attention.

"As you know, Henry Knight and I are engaged in an equal partnership but lately things are getting a bit more equal on his side."

"This is all fascinating, Miz Ruby, but—"

She sliced off his restless evasion with a cold glare. "Hear me out, Marshal. You might find what I have to say more interesting than you realize." She took a minute to compose her ruffled feathers then continued in her leisurely style. "As I was saying, Henry's been getting a mite greedy as of late. He hasn't been quite honest in regards to profits and such. I get the feeling he'd prefer to handle everything on his own. Being a wise woman, I prefer to guard my investments. I believe in loyalty but it does have its limits."

Sam found himself listening, hanging on the suspense she was crafting in her roundabout tale. "Oh, I do agree, ma'am," he supplied with an encouraging smile that didn't quite touch an answering warmth within his gaze.

"You see, when Henry decided to dissolve his partnership with my dear, late husband, he had it done in a rather messy and final fashion."

"You're saying he had your husband killed."

"No, Marshal. I'm saying I saw Henry do it." She brushed at the back of her spangled gloves and added casually, "Now if you were to provide me with immunity, I could help you build quite an interesting case against Mister Knight. You might say I know where all his skeletons are buried and who they belonged to."

"Amnesty would be no problem, Marshal," Newt slipped in quietly.

"Tell me more, Miz Ruby." Sam settled on the corner of his desk, forgetting his appointment with the road in favor of a previous debt. One owed the man who'd put a price upon his head.

"I can link Henry to just about all the vigilante killings, including your deputy's father. I know for a fact that he arranged the robbery that took Miz Blessing's husband to glory and that his murder was no accident. Henry doesn't much care for folks who inconvenience him. He also hired that gun-slick, Bonner, to rob the bank and make off with the lady. Only she wasn't supposed to come back. And I guess you know he paid to have your chips cashed as well."

"You've got some mighty intriguing bits of hearsay, ma'am," Newt interjected. "Happen you have any proof?"

She leveled him with a curious then attentive glance as if Newt Redman was some species she'd never seen before. "Happen I have Henry's ledger which pens out rather concisely who he paid to have what done. What do you mean to do about it, Marshal?"

Marshal.

Damn.

Sam looked from the expectant Ruby Gale to his ready packed bedroll. Blessing's problems weren't his problems. The U.S. Marshal would be through in several days' time. He would be better equipped to handle things.

Except, oh, how he'd like to be the one to bring the wily Henry Knight to justice.

It would fulfill his promise to Lucy.

It would keep him in Blessing a little longer.

But did he have the time to spare?

Just then, a boy he recognized as one of the Thompsons burst into the office.

"Marshal, there's a passel of hard-eyed, gun-hung men gathering aways outside of town. My pa recognized one of them as the one what robbed Miz Blessing's bank. He sent me in to tell you."

Too late.

Sam was quick to take action. After thanking the boy and sending him off with an eagle in his pocket, he said with inarguable authority, "Newt, you take Miz Ruby here over to Lucy's and you see they stay put. Then I want you to warn all the shopkeepers to batten down for one hell of a storm. How many do you think I can count on to back me?"

Newt fixed his stare on the floorboards, flushing with an uncomfortable rage. "You got me, Marshal."

"I see." Sam couldn't let on how disheartened he was. The two of them against a vengeful Clay Bonner and Charlie Waters's gang of cutthroats. "Go on now, boy. You do like I tell you while I get ready to greet our guests."

While Newt hurried Ruby Gale up the hill toward Lucy's, Sam opened the gun rack on the wall and began to break and feed the shotguns. He had at most an hour. Maybe less. Then all hell was going to ride into Blessing and the Devil was looking for him by name.

Chapter Twenty-four

When Sam stepped out onto the street, the first thing he saw was Lucy Blessing. While he watched, she went door to door, from business to business along the main street. Danged if he knew why he should feel surprised. He'd never known her to do the safe or sensible thing. If she knew he was there, she paid him no mind, bustling along the dusty walk intent upon her mission. He allowed himself a moment to appreciate the dance of tassels along her flounced skirt and permitted a single-sided smile. Leave it to Lucy to stir up a whirlwind of motion in the middle of a desert calm.

Which was exactly what Lucy was trying to do. She was very aware of Sam Zachary as he slouched against the hitching rail across the street. However, she feared if she acknowledged him, he would be moved to send her packing back to her safe house without doing what she could to help him. Which, unfortunately, didn't appear to be much. By the time she burst into Davis's Goods Emporium, she was out of breath and out of patience with the good citizens of Blessing.

Having seen her approach, the gaggle of men who'd been crowding the window quickly assumed their usual seats around the cracker barrel but their silence was far from typical. At the dry goods counter, Mayor Mayhew stopped in midsentence as both he and Jeremiah Davis looked at the virago that swept in off the street.

From the way the men canted down their glances, Lucy assumed they were well aware of her purpose. Their cowardly stances nudged her temper toward a dangerous level but she forced a calm and strode to the counter.

"Mister Davis, I'd like to purchase that Starr Double Action Army .44 you've been polishing the wood off of and a box of cartridges."

Edgar Mayhew regarded her with obtuse surprise. "Miz Blessing, what call you got to be packing a piece like that?"

"It's self-cocking so that's one less thing I have to remember to do when I'm helping the marshal defend my bank. And your money." That got the desired result of hanging heads but failed to muster the courageous response she needed.

"It's Zachary what's the problem, Miz Blessing," one of the men muttered, ignoring a prod to the ribs to continue boldly. "He's drawing those hard cases right into our town. Let them take him, I say. Save us from having to do something about him."

She saw it clear then. The bunch of them, cowardly cringing old hens that they were, were terrified of the deadly gunfighter planted in their midst. Though well aware of who he was, none had the spine-stiffening gumption to do anything beyond mutter. Sam Zachary's presence held them hostage by their fear and they thought of Clay Bonner as salvation. Fools!

"What is the matter with all of you?" She turned to include them in her angry stare. "That man out there is ready to die for you and you shiver and whine in here like a bunch of runt pups. Those killers coming in mean to steal back your money, money the marshal and I went through hell to return to you. Do you think they plan to be neat and polite about it then obligingly dispose of your little problem? Think again! Clay Bonner is a ruthless murderer. He killed two of our friends and wounded two others. And he wasn't even mad, then. Oh, I'm sure he'll kill Sam Zachary for you but I seriously doubt he means to stop there. Why not just open the door of the bank up wide and line up along the street to provide them with a little shooting-gallery entertainment. Because that's what they're going to make of this town."

Lucy halted her speech and looked from man to man as she recovered her panting breath. None would meet her eyes. "At this moment," she told them passionately, "I have never been so ashamed of anything as I am of being part of this town."

"You want us to stand up for the likes of him? The man's a killer, himself." The others were quick to nod agreement with the portly Davis.

"Yes, he is. He's been and done terrible things but so have I and you don't shun me on the street. Or is that because I support all of you with my wealth? Is that the price of overlooking the past? Sam Zachary is a wanted man. He's been a criminal and worse but he's also been the best damned marshal Blessing has ever had. He brought back your savings and the army's payroll. Mayor, have you forgotten how he risked his life and was wounded in the process rescuing your daughter? He's been brave enough to take on the evil that corrupts this town and you're all willing to just turn your backs on him. Damn you!"

"Lucy, that's enough."

All turned toward the quiet-voiced speaker. Sam strode in and was quick to take a weeping Lucy into his arms. He spared no interest in the others cowering beneath his expected wrath. All his attention went to the precious woman he held close to the thunder of his heart.

"Lucy, gal, don't. Stop your crying now, you hear?" Contrary to his roughened words, his hand began a gentle massage upon her shaking shoulders.

"Sam, I can't just let them ride in and kill you."

"Well, I don't aim to just let them either. But I can't do my job here when I'm a-worrying over what craziness you're doing. Go home, Lucy, and stay there. Take your piece and shoot any son that comes up on your porch until I get there. I'll be in time for dinner. And don't you go carrying no grudge against these here folks. This town needs you, Lucy. If half the men in it had a grain of your grit, no ornery cusses like Clay Bonner would dare show their faces."

He lifted her chin and wiped her cheeks dry with calloused fingers. Her breath was jerking fiercely.

"Sam . . ."

"Hush now, darlin'. You go do what I tole you."

The awful fear in her face was slowly replaced by a seeping, steadying pride. Her voice was uneven but strengthened by steel threads of love. "You take care, Sam Zachary. I'll expect you at my table on time."

"Yes, ma'am."

He gave her a heart-melting smile and leaned down to brush her lips with his own. Then he gave her bustle a hearty swat. "Now, git gone so I can settle up accounts."

She rose up on her toes to impress a hard kiss upon his mouth then announced proudly, "I love you, Marshal Zachary," before sweeping through the mercantile with a haughty, dismissing tip of her head.

The men in the room froze solid as Sam stabbed the cold gun metal of his gaze at each and every one of them. His look had all the deadly promise of a stick-teased rattler in its coil. They would have expected a man with Zachary's reputation to have at it with his ready pistols. Instead, he let loose a frigid blast of words to strike them in the heart of conscience.

"This town don't deserve the likes of Lucy Blessing."

With that, he walked away sporting the attitude that they were all something unpleasant to be wiped from boot heels at the door.

The street was quiet. No horses stood at the hitching rails. No laughter or music floated from the slatted doors of the saloons. He was all alone.

With a casual ease that defied the alert cut of his eyes, Sam started along the sidewalk toward the bank. His jacket was pushed back displaying his butt-forward pistols and shiny star. He wore both with confidence.

His flickering gaze caught movement and he watched Henry Knight stroll out in front of the Nightingale to observe his passing from across the broad main street. Knight was wearing a Smith & Wesson .44 in his belt to spoil the elegance of his attire. Slowly, he selected a cigar from his inner coat pocket and struck a match on the porch post. As blue smoke wreathed the hard, handsome lines of his face, he tipped the low crowned hat he wore in a mock salute. Sam continued walking. He imitated a slow-motion draw with an empty hand, lining his forefinger to sight on Henry Knight's ruffled shirt bosom and launched his promise with a thin-lipped smile. The saloonkeeper frowned and flickered the fresh cigar to the street before slipping back inside the batwing doors.

Newt met up with Sam outside the bank. The young deputy carried a shotgun under each arm and was looking grimly competent.

"Got the word out, Marshal. Sorry about Miz Lucille. She sorta got away from me."

"Don't worry on it, boy." He had no intention of letting Lucy Blessing get away from him and planned to tell her as much when he'd finished his business in town.

From behind them, the bank's door opened and a pasty-face Cecil peered out. Not so timid was the appearance of his carbine.

"Newt, you get on inside with Cecil here and don't let anyone through that door." He'd spotted a growing dust cloud at the end of the street and began to limber his long fingers. "I'll just extend a howdy to our visitors."

With every indication of ease, Sam mosied to the board edge of the walk and waited. His folded arms kept his hands close to the handles of his mismatched guns. As the first riders came into sight, he heard the unmistakable sound of a rifle brought to full cock. Then several more. He let his gaze shift along the street. From window, from doorways, from balconies protruded a bristling of business-minded barrels wielded by the citizens of Blessing. A slow, half-smile touched his lips as he looked back to the street where hired guns gathered in number for a kill, like the lowest kind of turkey buzzards. Each man held an air of truculence, a group of all-fired hard cases, cross-grained and mean as hell. They wore their guns in the fashion of men who knew how to use them. And Sam was sure they did.

In their midst sat Clay Bonner, as pleasant-faced and harmless-looking as a choir boy on Sunday. One who didn't know him might not see beyond the amiable smile to the death-hard eyes above.

"Howdy, Clay. State your business."

"Zach. We come to make a little withdrawal."

There was a ripple of gritty laughter, then silence.

"You got an account with this here bank?" Sam drawled, making no noticeable move toward defense.

"You might say that."

There was a stab of downward movement off to Sam's right. Sam's hands crossed in a sight-defying flicker, flashing toward his guns. Three fingers curled around each butt, thumbs hooking over hammers and starting to draw back. Forefingers slid into trigger-guards as soon as the blued barrels slid clear of leather, slanting away from his body and glinting dully as they lined. The move was smooth, effortless-looking, dangerously professional and if any of the men who rode with Clay Bonner had doubts about their leaders warning about the gun-handy potential of Sam Zachary, they were put to rest at that instant. His guns boomed and the target he made on the sidewalk was momentarily hidden as black powder smoke whirred eddies around him. Two of the riders fell dead as stone and Sam Zachary was no longer an easy mark.

Horses wheeled and scattered. Rifle fire and the crack of handguns exploded as men fell dead and dying from the unexpected crossfire to the hoof-churned dirt of the street. It was over as quick as a final Sunday prayer and an eerie silence settled as quietly as the dust.

Sam straightened from his gunfighter's crouch. Smoke dribbled up from the barrels of his emptied guns. As he plucked cartridges from his belt to effect a quick reloading, the people of Blessing crept forward onto the street to survey the carnage. Seeing the threat at an end, they began to mill and congratulate one another on their consolidated bravery and more than a few cast ashamed glances toward their marshal. But Sam paid them no mind. He was counting bodies.

Clay Bonner's was not among them.

Uttering a low curse, Sam moved down the street, ignoring those who would approach him. The people of Blessing backed away to give him room. For as he walked, fast and purposefully, each step brought eager hands brushing against the butts of his guns. It was the hard, dangerous walk of a killer on the prod and none wanted to interfere.

Sam took the porch steps in a single leap. The scent of lilac teased with that of gunpowder and the sweat of fear. The etched glass door stood ajar, bringing home his suspicions like a fist slammed to the gut. He toed it open cautiously, fighting down the hard hammering of his heart that would send him charging in with a reckless fury. The hall was dark. His mood was darker.

There, at the foot of the stairs slumped the figure of a woman. A dark, unidentifiable stain spread outward from beneath her still shoulders. But Sam didn't have to see the color to know it was red.

With a thick, disbelieving sound tearing up from his throat, Sam advanced two quick steps into the hall. By the time he'd controlled the raw ache of grief enough to realize the dead woman was Ruby Gale, he'd placed himself in a vulnerable spot before the opening to the parlor.

"Sam?"

The sound of Lucy's voice quavered like fragile crystal. Relief ran loosely through Sam's taut muscles to settle, trembling, in his belly. Slowly, he turned toward the room, knowing he was going to pay for his moment of mistaken identity.

"Come on in and join us, Zach. Party's just starting."

He moved with a light, wary tread into the shadowed room. Lucy was seated on the roll-armed sofa. Her dark eyes were huge and fixed on him with pleading terror and regret. Though she was pale and mussed, she looked to be unharmed. Once that was settled in his anxious mind, he scanned the room with a cold glare.

Clay Bonner lounged at the bourbon decanter, a glass in one hand, his Dragoon in the other. Its yawning barrel was lined up on Sam's star. Lucy's new pistol lay useless next to the liquor.

"Now, ain't this a cozy reunion," Bonner drawled in a friendly manner. "The three of us together. Like old times."

"He killed Ruby, Sam," Lucy whispered in a strained tone. And with her, their hopes of convicting Henry Knight.

"Now that was a mistake," Clay explained as though the needless death concerned him. It didn't, of course. "I didn't know your lady friend was entertaining. She came acreeping down the stairs. Took me by surprise, she did. Thought perhaps it was you trying to get the drop on me."

"What now, Clay? You meaning to make the two of us just as dead?"

"Why, Sam-boy, how can you suggest such a thing, after all we been to each other? And the little lady, why she ain't no good to me lessen she's kicking, if you get my meaning."

Lucy did. And her pallor increased. Slowly she felt along her skirts to the reassuring firmness of her pocket pistol. If anything happened to Sam, there'd be one for Clay Bonner. And if she missed, one for herself. That knowledge gave her the gumption to greet Bonner's wolf-savage grin with the remote indifference of one who knew it would never come to pass and set him back enough to purse his lips pensively.

"She worth it, Zach? She worth all the trouble? You and me could have made big names for ourselves. We could have been respected men."

"Like the Jameses and the Youngers? Like Hickok? That ain't respect. That's fear and a healthy dash of dislike. I got respect here. And Lucy." His hard gaze dropped to hers and softened imperceptibly. "Yeh, she's worth it. You got a good woman at home, so you should know that."

"Sarah? I had enough of being leg-shackled to a whiny female. Scratch in the dirt? No, sir. Not me."

A slow understanding came over Sam's expression. Lucy could see him adding piece upon piece with the reluctance of someone putting together a fearsome puzzle. She could see his desperate want to believe there was some scrap of decency left in Clay Bonner. She couldn't claim none had ever existed, for she didn't know the kind of man he'd been before the war. Perhaps he'd been as carefree and jovial as his expression pretended. Perhaps he'd always been a dark-hearted, charming sham who lured a young, impressionable Sam Zachary down the path of wrongdoing with malicious intent. But she knew, crystal clear, no matter what fond memory Sam might have of that companion, before her stood a man with a shriveled soul and no thread of conscience.

However, a shared past did cloud Sam's perception but the mists were rapidly clearing. "You had no intention of returning to Sarah, did you?"

"That weren't never a part of my plans. No slur intended upon your sister."

"And just what are your plans?" Sam's tone cut like a viciously honed James Black bowie knife and Clay's smile faltered.

"The money, of course. I'm going to use the lady here to clear my way to the bank then she, the money and I are going to ride out without a fuss."

Sam shook his head slowly. "Never happen."

"Feared you be of that mind. And it's real sorry I am."

Never had Sam actually believed his childhood friend would fire upon him with a killing intent. Until he saw him begin to pull back on the four-pound, one-ounce, thumb-busting 1847 Model Colt Dragoon. Lucy could see the surprise and recognition of death flicker in his eyes but that fine, split second of hesitation could not be overcome by even the fastest draw. Guns leaped from leather with the speed of desperation and skill but it wasn't enough. Driven by the full force of forty grains of prime du Pont black powder, the soft round ball struck with a shocking force unequaled by any new model handgun. Bonner aimed for the mid-body where the stopping power would be the greatest but he hadn't anticipated the position of his opponent's lightning quick hands. The ball smashed through one of the small bones in Sam's right forearm and cogged in the mechanics of his left-draw Navy Colt.

The punch of impact was enough to hurl Sam backward into the hall. He fell hard, guns dropping, all the while staring at Clay with a dumbfounded look of hurt amazement. He could hear Lucy screaming his name and the pounding of his own blood roaring through his head. Somehow, he managed to hang on to consciousness, peering up through red mists of agony at the man who calmly stalked him. He flung out his shattered arm, teeth grinding as numbed fingers yet twitching from shock groped the carpet for his Colt. A casual kick sent the Peacemaker spinning into the next room. Sam's low groan was one of futility and pain.

Clay sighed regretfully as he squatted down on his heels. "Didn't mean to cause you such considerable pain, boy," he clucked softly. His palm rested briefly with what might have been affection against Sam's taut, sweat-slicked cheek. "You were like a brother to me, Zach, and it's going to grieve me to kill you. But, I can't leave you here and be looking over my shoulder for the rest of my life. One day, you'd be there."

"Damn right," Sam hissed between gulps for air. He jerked his head to one side, away from Bonner's pretended care.

Clay smiled with a benevolent evil that chilled Sam right to the bone. When he straightened slowly and lined the Dragoon at his leisure, the fallen man had no remaining doubts that he would use it.

"I'll make it clean this time, Sam. My word on it."

"Go to hell," he spat out then called louder, "Send him, Lu."

Bonner had forgotten all about the woman at his back. A last, fatal mistake. He began to turn.

Seeing Sam shot had stunned Lucy into a moment's inaction. Horrible, bloody images flooded her mind, of Oliver, his arms pinwheeling as he fell already lifeless to the floor. The knowledge that Sam was dead was too much for her senses to contain and so they left a merciful blank of response. Then she saw his boots shift and had cried out as she was able to feel again.

As soon as she knew he still lived, she reached carefully for her hidden Remington. Slowly so no rustle of skirts would betray her, she stood, studying Clay Bonner's back with a cold deliberation. But she couldn't see the direction of his pistol and feared a careless bullet would discharge it into Sam. So she waited, scarcely daring to breathe less the shaky breaths draw notice. No one was going to snatch Sam Zachary away from her. Not as long as she lived and breathed. She would go at his attacker with a gun, with a knife, with fists and teeth if need be but she would not allow Bonner to snuff out the cherished life which had restored her own.

Sam's order caught her by surprise but she knew immediately what he was asking and did, for once, as she was told. She could have fired waist-high from instinct had her pistol provided the necessary man-killing accuracy. But with her little Remington, she took the extra fraction of a second to bring it shoulder high and take sight. Bonner looked at her with a smug challenge and she fired.

The bullet took outlaw high in the chest but didn't topple him. As his Dragoon began to lift with unerring purpose, she let the other barrel go in hasty panic. And missed. With a sob of horror, she flung the useless pistol at his head. On the floor behind him, she could see Sam struggling to gain his knees, trying to gather enough strength to launch a protective offense. And Lucy knew with a sickening sense of certainty that he wouldn't be able to in time.

Clay was grinning, a death's head smile, confirming he knew the wound he'd received was fatal. He continued to raise the heavy Colt, confident he would have the chance to discharge it one last time. He worked the hammer as Lucy stumbled and fell back in mute terror upon the sofa. His grin froze into a mask of incredulous pain as something struck him in the back and tore down toward his vitals.

Lucy let out a tremulous cry as Chu jerked the long blade of his kitchen knife free and Clay Bonner crumpled upon her floor, no longer a threat to anyone. She tottered on legs almost too shaky to hold her, making a wide circle around the fallen man so she could kneel beside Sam Zachary. She hugged him, heedless of the blood, mindless of her tears. And never had the circle of his arm felt so good about her.

"Help me up, darlin'."

"What? No, you stay where you are. I'm going for the doctor."

"I'll meet up with him in town when I'm through." He was wedging his feet under him, heaving, groaning until she supplied him with a shoulder and the boost needed to hoist him upright.

"Through? Through with what?"

"One more thing left to do. Bind this up, will you? I'm making a tolerable mess of everything." He glanced down dispassionately to the bright pattern splattering her carpet and his Levi's. Wordlessly, Li provided clean linen and set to tearing it in strips.

"You seem to be making a habit of bleeding all over my house, Mister Zachary," Lucy remarked lightly but her thoughts were far from levity as she rolled up Sam's sleeve. She bit her lip to keep in words of fear and when she could control her voice, said, "This needs doctoring now or you'll go from a two-handed gun to a one-armed gun."

"I'll let you nag me on it later, Lu. Just stop the dripping for now."

"But, Sam . . ."

"Do you want me as town marshal or not? If so, let me do my job."

Lucy swallowed hard. Yes, that was exactly what she wanted. As gently as she could, she began to wrap the linen. The bullet had passed through but not cleanly once it had broken the bone. She could only hope the doctor's skill was adequate. She heard Sam suck a harsh breath and begin to blow noisily but didn't look up, nor did she stop until she'd tied the strips neatly together. Her hands were damp, her knees were shaking but she'd done it for him. And he was not unaware of the effort it caused her.

Tenderly, he tipped up her chin with the fingers of his left hand. He was smiling. His eyes were a soft, dawnlike gray. "You'll make a fine lawman's wife, Lucy-gal."

For an instant, everything inside her quivered then she spoke up firm and confident. "Oh, I intend to, Marshal. I intend to."

Gingerly, Sam bent and searched Clay Bonner's pockets until satisfied. He straightened and paused a moment, waiting for the dizziness to recede. Between thumb and forefinger, he held five hundred dollars.

At Lucy's worried gaze, he gave a crooked smile and told her, "I'm heading down to the Nightingale to repay a debt."

Chapter Twenty-five

It was time to get the hell out of Blessing.

Henry Knight was hurriedly stuffing the contents of his safe into a leather valise. There would be more next door at Ruby's. That meddlesome female had absented herself at an advantageous time. When she returned, she'd find herself the sole owner of both her own place and Nightingale's but he didn't consider it a bad trade. The saloon for his life.

Sam Zachary was coming for him.

And that knowledge equalized everything.

He'd seen the collapse of all his plans out in the street. The citizens of Blessing had rallied behind their lawless paragon and now there'd be hell to pay. Zachary didn't look to be a man who'd take an attempt on his life lightly and the mood of the townspeople would likely swing in his favor. His methods of business wouldn't stand up to close scrutiny even if the gunman left him alive long enough to go to trial. Henry Knight was a man who liked risks only when they were stacked in his favor.

With his bag bulging, Knight thought regretfully of what he couldn't take. He'd spent eighty-five dollars in New York for a gross of advantage decks. He'd purchased three dozen pair of dice cubed from the best ivory at five dollars for a set of 9-3 high, 3 low and 3 square. There was the beautiful bar and the painting of Ruby. He wasn't much of a sentimentalist but that was a nice work of oil. Perhaps when the danger cooled, he could work a deal with his ex-partner for the return of his prize goods. No time to worry over it now.

A footfall sounded at his office door.

"You look in a powerful hurry, Mister Knight. Going somewheres?"

His shoulders sagged in relief as his fingers eased on the butt of his Smith & Wesson. Deputy, not marshal. Fixing his features into a smooth smile, he turned toward Newt Redman. The young man had a shotgun cradled in his elbow but had not assumed a menacing pose. As if Newt Redman could be considered menacing.

"Why, Deputy, you can't blame a man for getting nervous with all the gunplay going on outside. A man has to look out for his interests."

"That's what Miz Ruby was a-telling us," the young man drawled in a remarkable imitation of his mentor.

"Ruby? What are you talking about?"

"It's her what's been doing the talking. Let's you and me mosey on down the street. I think Marshal Sam has some things he wants to air with you." The shotgun moved from the crook of his arm to line on the expensive carpet. It would take one movement to bring it up and into deadly play. Henry Knight saw in that moment that he'd sadly misjudged the lame deputy. Just as he'd misjudged his employer. He took a gamble, knowing he'd have no room to bargain once inside Zachary's jail.

"This bag is full of a powerful lot of money, boy. Take a minute to consider what you and little Billie could do with a handsome sum." He dangled the offer, anticipating a greedy response from the boy who'd gone without his whole life.

"Keep your dirty money, Mister Knight. Billie and me are fixing to come by our dollars honestly."

"You're stupid, cripple. I'm giving you the chance of a lifetime!" Knight's black eyes flashed in a frustration of anger.

"No, sir. I got that chance when Sam Zachary rode in."

Knight's hand shifted downward and the shotgun sights aligned.

"Don't try it," Newt warned. His voice was far more steady than his hands. To this point, he'd been fueled by a righteous sense of purpose. He was doing his job and he was damned proud of it. And toting the crooked, death-bringing barman into jail would go far to righting all the injustices he'd suffered over the years of his young life. The marshal would be repaid for his confidence. Jailing Knight would reconcile the many kindnesses Miz Lucille had shown him. And Billie would be so proud and free at last.

He'd considered all those things and they made him puff up inside with strength and courage. But prodding a man along at the point of a gun and letting loose a blast from that weapon were miles apart in his thinking and his plans. Though he'd been prepared to, he hadn't happened to kill any of the bandits outside the bank. The few shots he'd gotten off had veered wide. But standing across the room, holding death at his fingertip, there was little chance of missing the mark. He would be killing his first man and even though he knew Henry Knight warranted killing, he wasn't sure he could be the one to do it.

"Everything all right here, Newt?"

He started to turn in relief, willing to give it all over to the experience of Sam Zachary. And then, he and Knight both saw the condition of the marshal. The wounded man looked ready to topple from the weight of the pistol dangling at his side. From out of the corner of his eye, Newt saw Knight's hand twist and snap down to claim his revolver. Without thinking, Newt stepped in front of Sam and brought his shotgun into play. Both barrels let go with a deafening roar, filling the room with acrid smoke. For a moment, Henry Knight just stared down at the front of his immaculate white shirt, watching in bewilderment as a wide pattern of crimson spread and seeped. Then slowly, almost reluctantly, he slid to the ground.

The young deputy was taken with a fit of trembling as he stared at the lifeless form. Dead. He'd shot a man dead. And in doing so, he'd saved the marshal's — his friend's — life. He steeled his jiggly limbs and quivery stomach. A fair exchange. Newt looked to Sam in question when the marshal tucked a wad of green money into his shirtfront. He didn't have to count it to know it was a tolerable fortune.

"Reward money," Sam told him. "For Sam Zachary, dead or alive. You just killed him."

Chapter Twenty-six

From the shade of Lucy's broad porch, they stood arm in arm watching the workmen below. The hammering was sweet music to Lucy's soul, a song she'd been waiting to hear all her life. It was beginning to take shape; the bell tower on the impressive building, the dreams she'd carried as a child, the hopes she'd held as a woman. All right here in Blessing. Just that morning, four boxes of fine leather-bound hymnals had arrived at Davis's. Soon, the music ringing up from Blessing's first church would be that of voices lifted in glorious song. By week's end, they would be fitting the brilliant stained-glass arches and on Sunday, even if they had to stand, Blessing would know its first service in a church. The church dedicated to her father.

It was the kind of building she'd longed for him to have when she was a child and they had traveled from town to town. She'd heard his resonant voice ring out in saloons, in schoolhouses, in parlors but never had thrilled to its powerful sound swelling to fill the soaring spaces of a real church building. He would have loved this one and she would see it was home to the words he lived by.

Lucy felt Sam's hand nudge at hers and happily

laced her fingers through his. His grip was damp and tight enough for her to cast a quick glance up at his fine profile. Worriedly, she wondered if his arm was hurting him again. Two weeks ago, she'd clung to this same left hand while the doctor prodded and pieced and stitched on the right, unable to offer any certainty if the limb could be saved at all. She and Li tended his fever and his pain round the clock, watching with dread for the signs of which Doc had warned. But Sam Zachary was tough and just plain ornery. Bone and flesh began to knit and it became a struggle to keep him in the bed for no other purpose than rest and healing. And last night, he'd convinced her that he had rested and healed enough. She'd found him up when she awoke, taking his coffee on the veranda while watching the building below. When he'd turned at the sound of her approach, her heart had melted like a spring thaw. Aside from an indoor pallor and the bulky white sling cradling his forearm, he looked fit and fine.

And distracted.

She'd noticed it after they'd made love and even moreso now. It was the way his eyes canted toward her then flickered away without engaging hers. And she knew it with an aching certainty.

He was thinking about leaving.

Lucy tried not to let the news affect her. But she'd hoped. Things had all seemed so perfect — she and Sam and Blessing. Perhaps that much happiness was not meant to be. At least for her. Her first reaction was to cling, to plead her case with tears and panicked words. Instead, she relied heavily on her pride for a source of strength and nestled into the warmth of his side in silence. She should have known. She should have suspected when Sam had called for Newt soon after the doc had left him. It was the deputy he'd asked to draft the letter to his sister that had accompanied Clay Bonner to Missouri. Did he hold her in some way responsible for Clay? Had his death at her hands in this house made it uncomfortable for him to stay? Had he even in the drafting of that letter been making plans to return south to his family? She could ask Newt but she knew she had to hear it from Sam. And she didn't want to.

He was still weak. Despite the fact that he was on his feet, it would be days before he could ride, maybe even weeks. She had him until then and she vowed she wouldn't spoil that time, not with weeping, not with recriminations. A man like Sam Zachary was a once in a lifetime thing and she would cherish the time they'd shared for the rest of her days and be glad for them. If she couldn't hold him, she'd hold the memory. All the memories she could make.

She turned his head with the light persuasion of her fingertips and stretched up to kiss him. His arm tightened behind her back, drawing her up close into the hard contours of his body. She put all her longing, all her passion into that kiss and when she stepped back from him, his eyes searched hers in question.

"Thank you, Sam," she said quietly.

"You're welcome, darlin'. For what?"

She stroked his rough cheek. He had yet to shave. His hand was steady enough to tend the chore himself now. His strength was returning rapidly, she was both pleased and dismayed to note. "For keeping all your promises."

Again, there was that flicker of uneasiness and Lucy feared she'd pressed too hard. The last thing she wanted was for him to leave her house and return to town. He'd been lying in her bed for two weeks though last night was the first time they'd shared it.

The folks in town seemed none too concerned about the arrangement, knowing how bad hurt he was and how much care was needed to aid in his recovery. They met her with questions about the state of his health not the state of their moral standing. So far. As soon as they saw him up and around, there'd be talk but Lucy vowed not to care. If she was to have him for just a short while longer, she wanted all of him she could get.

"Lucy . . ." he began in an oddly pitched voice.

No! Not now. Not yet, she thought in panic. She wasn't ready to hear his words. She wanted to handle his good-bye with dignity. She didn't want him to remember her as a weak and wailing female. And that's what she'd become if he continued.

"The building's going along remarkably well, don't you think?" she asked a bit frantically. She turned her attention down to the construction below so he couldn't see how shiny her gaze had become.

"Lucy," he persisted.

"I'm going to ask Reverend Longford to preach on Sunday. I know things won't be perfect yet but—"

Sam's fingers closed about her chin, forcing her to face him. She looked up with a stricken expression and blurted out, "Sam, please . . ."

"Hush, now." His fingertips touched to her quivering lips. "Hear me out. I been trying to come up with some way to say this and it always comes out all tumbled up and clumsy. Damn. I didn't think it would be this hard."

She swallowed the lump of remorse in her throat and faced him bravely. "Just say it straight out." Sam Zachary was a straight shooter and his words were aimed right for the heart. She braced for the impact.

"Lucy, I'm moving my things back down to town. It'll be better that way—for both of us."

She nodded, fighting back the dampness filling her eyes.

"Oh, hell," he grumbled. "Here."

He took up her left hand and jammed a circle of gold onto her finger. She stared it, mute and stunned. A woman's ring with chips of sparkling stone.

"I know it ain't much and you deserve a lot better but it was my mama's. I asked Sarah to send it up to me when I shipped Clay home for burying. It ain't worth much—not like ole Oliver could have gived you but—"

"Oh, Sam, shut up," she cried in delight and flung her arms about him. He reeled then recovered to hold her in a crushing embrace. She could feel his heart hammering as loud and quick as the carpenters' below, like he'd been scared to death. Of proposing.

"I just figured since your church was almost finished and it don't look right for the two of us to be wallowing around in wonderful sin," she could feel his grin against her hair, "that maybe on Sunday we could christen it with a wedding."

She jerked out of his embrace and cried, "Sam, that's four days!"

"Too long?" he drawled mildly.

Lucy laughed and hugged him hard. She didn't notice the figure jogging up from the street below until Sam gently pried her away.

" 'Morning, Bart," Sam called amiably with Lucy still very much in the curve of his arm. "You can be the first to congratulate us. We're getting hitched on Sunday."

The young telegraph clerk looked flustered, not at all the reaction they would expect to the news. He looked at his feet and fidgeted. "That's right nice to hear."

"What is it?" Sam demanded bluntly.

"Marshal," the boy choked out. "There's a man down in your office a-waiting to see you. Says his name is Tolliver."

Lucy's world came crashing in. She swayed and only Sam's support kept her from crumpling. She heard him reply in a soft voice that seemed to come from miles away.

"Tell him I'll be there direct."

"Yessir, Marshal."

"Li, fetch me out some of Mister Oliver's brandy," he hollered into the house then he addressed himself to her in a firm tone. "Lucy-gal, pull your wits about you, you hear? I can scarce hold myself up without having to tote you like a sack of grain."

The words and her concern for him had the combined effect he desired. Her knees steadied enough to hold her but her voice still trembled. "Oh, Sam, what are we going to do?" She wept in abject misery.

His palm moved over her glossy hair in a calming gesture. "We may have to postpone the wedding for a time. Can you wait?"

Her head came up. Her eyes were wild and wet. "We could ride out now. We could start over—"

He silenced her with a sad smile. "Darlin', I done all the riding I care to do. I want to marry up with you in that church. I want to sleep with you in that big bed upstairs. If you don't want to wait for me—"

She pulled him down and kissed him savagely, the strength of her fear lending a bruising force. Against his warm neck, she panted, "They won't hang you, will they? Sam, I couldn't bear it!"

"Newt tells me that's not like to happen but I can't promise. I can't run either. You going to help me face this square? I don't think I could make that long walk down alone." He was speaking of more than his body's weakness and she couldn't have loved him more at that moment.

Li supplied two glasses of brandy and they both drank as if they'd thirsted for weeks. Lucy was grateful for the heat of the smooth liquor, for inside she was cold as death.

"I'll walk with you, Sam," she told him quietly.

Arm in arm, they started down the hill. The citizens of Blessing were waiting in an oddly silent cluster. Lucy and Sam regarded their presence curiously as the townspeople parted to let them pass. The ranks closed in behind them and the somber procession followed to the jail house. There, on the front walk, stood Mayor Mayhew, Newt and a tall, rawboned man. Lucy felt Sam recoil in recognition and tightened her arm about his middle. It was then she realized he'd left his gun belt up at her house. That had been no chance omission, she knew, because he never went to the privy without it. He was going to meet Tolliver, the nemesis of his youth, with his arm in a sling and his hip naked.

"There he is now," Mayhew was saying. "He can fill you in on all the particulars about how our deputy here took down Zachary."

Lucy gave the mayor a perplexed look and he smiled confidently at her.

Sam's arm disengaged from about her as he reached out his left hand to grasp the U.S. Marshal's. His expression was inscrutable, betraying nothing of the turmoil within. Tolliver. The man who'd seen his brother hanged. He swallowed down the bile of bitterness and gritted his teeth against pain both physical and mental.

"Marshal Samuels," Tolliver said cautiously. His eyes narrowed. "You look tolerably familiar to me."

Mayhew stepped in with a hardy laugh. "Don't see how that's possible. He's my sister's boy. Brought him up myself from Witchita, Kansas, must be five years ago. He's been our other deputy. 'Twas my pleasure to pin the marshal's badge on him."

" 'Twas him what brought back the army payroll and our bank's money," the portly Davis spoke up. "And saved Miz Blessing from the likes of Bonner and Zachary. We owe him a lot, Marshal. A hell of a lot."

"Yessir," drawled Newt. "Couldn't ask to serve under no better lawman." He shifted the shotgun up so that its sights were resting in the cup of his palm. He was smiling but his eyes were as steely as the double-barrels.

Tolliver glanced around. The man before him wore no hardware but the rest of the town fairly bristled with a subtle show of firepower. Coats were casually flipped back to display old Army and Navy issue Colts. Carbines and rifles were easily shouldered. Smiles abounded and stares were cold as lead.

Lucy stepped forward in the spirit of the town. She extended her hand with the offer of a warm smile. "Marshal Tolliver, I'm Lucy Blessing. My husband spoke highly of you. I believed it was his generous contribution that helped you get elected." She shook his hand with a firm, dry grip. "I had the town council wire you for a marshal after Tom Bradshaw's death. What an odd twist of fate."

"Yes," Tolliver drawled. "The mayor and your deputy were just telling me how the outlaw Zachary managed to replace my man Wade in a plot to rob the bank."

"Had us all fooled, too," put in Ned Pomeroy, the barber. "All except Marshal Samuels and Deputy Redman. They knew something was funny with him.

380

Can't change a wolf into a sheep by covering him with wool, you know."

"Yes, I know." His stare pierced the cool gray gaze of the heroic Marshal Samuels.

"If it hadn't been for their devotion to duty," Lucy continued smoothly, "Blessing would have been picked clean at the loss of many of our fine citizens. And voters. I hear you might be running for Territorial Governor, Marshal Tolliver. If you'd care to join my fiancé and me for dinner, perhaps we can discuss a sizable donation to your campaign." Her arm linked through Sam's so there could be no mistake. Her gaze was as steady as the double bore of her pocket Remington. "If you've a mind to stay, we'd be honored to have you at our wedding this Sunday. We had to postpone it when the marshal was wounded bringing down that horrid Clay Bonner."

Grant Tolliver was a clever man and had the shrewd makings of a good politician. It had been a lot of years ago but he'd recognized Sam Zachary on first sight. Curiosity made him play along with whatever scheme the townsfolk were spinning. He wasn't sure he understood why but he knew they meant to protect the wanted gunman with their easy lies and ready weapons. And he was aware the name Blessing carried considerable clout.

Slowly, he took the measure of the man they called Marshal Samuels. The last time Tolliver had seen him, he'd been a wild, hell-bent for lead kid with a quick and vicious pair of .44s, riding in the shadow of Clay Bonner. Of the two, Bonner had been the true hard case. He had to allow Zachary'd had cause for some of his contempt of the law, especially after the regrettable doings at his family's farm. He looked long into the cool gray steel of the other's eyes, seeing an edge of unbending toughness, an unrepenting spirit but none of the seething fury he remembered in the boy. Age had mellowed Sam Zachary's mood. Or perhaps it was the woman who stood so staunchly at his side. But the honed look of a dangerous man was still there. Although he sported signs of a serious, maybe even crippling wound, he knew Zachary to be one of the true ambidextrous guns. He might be a tad slower with the left but that still notched him a far peg above average fast.

All that aside didn't explain why Zachary had come to meet him with no guns at his side, with a scrap of tin shining proudly on his vest. He'd run one heck of a risk. A brave man. A dangerous man, but possibly the makings of a darned good lawman. In a way, there was little difference.

"Thank you for the invite, Mrs. Blessing, but I won't be staying. I guess I owe you and your town a thanks for ridding me of Zachary. He was one hell of a hard customer and I for one won't miss him."

"Maybe he thought he had reason," Sam said softly.

Tolliver shrugged. "Maybe he did, at that." Distractedly, the lawman pulled out his heavy gold watch. "Well, now, if I hurry, I can make the return trip to Cheyenne. Marshal, a pleasure to meet up with you."

Sam took his hand, this time with his right, in a grip that was weak but sure. "Under the circumstances, I reckon so."

With a tip of his hat, he murmured dryly, "Mrs. Blessing, keep him out of trouble," to let them all know he hadn't been fooled but was willing to be tolerant. He allowed the talkative mayor to escort him back to the train and was able to leave Blessing assured that he'd seen the last of the Missouri outlaw.

With smug mutterings and quiet laughter, the

crowd dispersed until only Lucy, Sam, Newt and the old yellow hound stood on the walk in front of the jail. Sam looked after them, the people of his town, and allowed a slow, contented smile.

"A wedding Sunday, you say?" Newt was grinning like a well-fed possom.

"Got something presentable you can wear when you stand up next to me?"

Newt blinked and, impossibly, grinned even wider. "Don't reckon it'd hurt me none to have a new suit of clothes on hand. Never know when another wedding might come up."

"I'll mosey on over with you and maybe get something for myself. I don't know if you've heard this or not, but the bride, she's a mighty particular female when it comes to proper attire. Jus' might pick up a new pair of pearl-handled Colts while I'm a looking."

"For the honeymoon?" Newt wondered slyly.

Sam slid a glance at Lucy. "Might be needing 'em," he confided.

Lucy scowled. To the marshal with the lazy, one-sided smile and inviting eyes, she said, "Dinner at seven," and to his deputy, "See he gets there." Then she was satisfied to leave them to their manly camaraderie, knowing she would have the handsome marshal at her table that night, and every night from then on. Feeling Sam's gaze upon her as she started up the street, she put a little extra swing in her walk.

Just to make sure he wasn't late.

HEART STOPPING ROMANCE BY ZEBRA BOOKS

MIDNIGHT BRIDE (3265, $4.50)
by Kathleen Drymon

With her youth, beauty, and sizable dowry, Kellie McBride had her share of ardent suitors, but the headstrong miss was bewitched by the mysterious man called The Falcon, a dashing highwayman who risked life and limb for the American Colonies. Twice the Falcon had saved her from the hands of the British, then set her blood afire with a moonlit kiss.

No one knew the dangerous life The Falcon led—or of his secret identity as a British lord with a vengeful score to settle with the Crown. There was no way Kellie would discover his deception, so he would woo her by day as the foppish Lord Blakely Savage . . . and ravish her by night as The Falcon! But each kiss made him want more, until he vowed to make her his *Midnight Bride*.

SOUTHERN SEDUCTION (3266, $4.50)
by Thea Devine

Cassandra knew her husband's will required her to hire a man to run her Georgia plantation, but the beautiful redhead was determined to handle her own affairs. To satisfy her lawyers, she invented Trane Taggart, her imaginary step-son. But her plans go awry when a handsome adventurer shows up and claims to *be* Trane Taggart!

After twenty years of roaming free, Trane was ready to come home and face the father who always treated him with such contempt. Instead he found a black wreath and a bewitching, sharp-tongued temptress trying to cheat him out of his inheritance. But he had no qualms about kissing that silken body into languid submission to get what he wanted. But he never dreamed that *he* would be the one to succumb to *her* charms.

SWEET OBSESSION (3233, $4.50)
by Kathy Jones

From the moment rancher Jack Corbett kept her from capturing the wild white stallion, Kayley Ryan detested the man. That animal had almost killed her father, and since the accident Kayley had been in charge of the ranch. But with the tall, lean Corbett, it seemed she was *never* the boss. He made her blood run cold with rage one minute, and hot with desire the next.

Jack Corbett had only one thing on his mind: revenge against the man who had stolen his freedom, his ranch, and almost his very life. And what better way to get revenge than to ruin his mortal enemy's fiery red-haired daughter. He never expected to be captured by her charms, to long for her silken caresses and to thirst for her never-ending kisses.

Available wherever paperbacks are sold, or order direct from the Publisher. Send cover price plus 50¢ per copy for mailing and handling to Zebra Books, Dept. 3427, 475 Park Avenue South, New York, N.Y. 10016. Residents of New York, New Jersey and Pennsylvania must include sales tax. DO NOT SEND CASH.